Mike Faricy

Dog Gone

Published by Credit River Publishing 2015

Copyright Mike Faricy 2015

All characters in this book are fictitious, and any resemblance to actual persons, living or dead, is purely coincidental.

ISBN-13: 978-1535181716

10: 1535181710

Acknowledgments

I would like to thank the following people for their help & support:

Special thanks to Uncle Tony, Elizabeth, Julie, Mattie and Roy for their hard work, cheerful patience and positive feedback. I would like to thank family and friends for their encouragement and unqualified support. Special thanks to Maggie, Jed, Schatz, Pat, Av, Emily and Pat, for not rolling their eyes, at least when I was there. Most of all, to my wife Teresa, whose belief, support and inspiration has, from day one, never waned.

To Teresa

"Sometimes you can act so violent."
"Which is the reason I'm still alive."

Mike Faricy

Dog Gone

Chapter One

It was one of those intimate moments … sort of.

"Oh, Dev. Oh, Dev. Yes! Yes!" Maddie's voice ratcheted up with passionate excitement.

She was a beautiful, blue eyed, natural blonde, with a gorgeous figure, sexy southern drawl and a fascinating little lacy tattoo across the small of her back. At the moment her back was arched so just her heels and shoulders were touching the mattress on the four poster bed. Her head was hanging partially over the side and her eyes had that faraway look like she'd been transported to a very magical place. The three of us were making love, Maddie, me and apparently Morton.

Morton was her dog. A three year old Golden Retriever the color of a peanut butter cookie who, at the moment, was busily licking Maddie's face.

Even I found it impossible to maintain concentration and finally rolled over on my side next to Maddie. "I'm not sure I'm comfortable working with an audience," I said.

She laughed and Morton poked me in the back of the head with his cold nose.

"He's a people dog."

"A people dog?"

"Yeah, he likes people, in fact, he probably thinks he's a person and he wants to be involved."

"That might be okay if we were taking a walk, but this is…."

Her phone rang, it was just after midnight. Experience had taught me nothing good ever comes from a phone call at this hour.

Maddie rolled off the bed, gave Morton a pat on the head, picked her jeans up off the floor and dug the cell out of her back pocket.

"Oh, wow, it's my dad," she said sounding puzzled then answered. "Dad? Hey, is everything okay?"

I sat up and leaned against the carved wooden headboard.

"Oh? You're kidding, when? Where is she now?" Maddie said looking worried as she sat down on the edge of the bed.

She listened for a few moments, occasionally interjecting a one word response. "Yes. No. Yes. Possibly…." Eventually she said, "No, Dad I need to be there. I'll book a flight and be down in the morning. No, don't be silly it's not a problem. I need to be there. Yes, Midtown? On Peachtree? No, I'll grab a cab. No, now not another word. I'll see you in the morning, love you. Yes. Okay, bye, bye."

"Everything okay?" I said stupidly.

"Not really, that was my dad. Apparently my mom was in a bike accident and broke her hip. She's okay, they've got her in Emory University Hospital, but I need to get down to Atlanta. Dad's worthless at this sort of thing."

I knew for a fact that Maddie's dad had started with nothing and now ran a number of very successful firms doing business in Georgia, Alabama and Florida and I doubted he was worthless at this or anything else. I also knew enough not to offer that opinion. "Anything I can do to help?"

She walked over to her desk and turned on the computer then pulled a sexy little black silk robe from the back of her bedroom door and slipped it on. The robe had red piping along the edge and around the button holes, and barely fell to her thigh with slits along the side up to her hip bone. I liked it, a lot.

"I'm going to have to book a flight for tomorrow. I'll have to take Morton."

"Morton? You're kidding." At the sound of his name Morton's tail kicked into overdrive and he looked back and forth from Maddie to me panting with his tongue hanging out.

"Well, I can't very well leave him on his own. He doesn't like boarding in a kennel, like I said, he thinks he's a person, not a dog."

"Maddie, nothing against Morton, but he's going to present one more complication you don't need right now. Not to mention your folks."

"They like him, sort of, I think."

"I'm sure they do, but when your mom gets out of that hospital you're going to need to focus on her, and your dad. Morton's going to be in a strange environment. It's just not the best idea. What if he jumps on her? Or what if he tries to lick her or something and she falls?"

"I had him at the Bed and Biscuit for a weekend, but that didn't work out too well."

"Bed and Biscuit?"

"It's a place to board your dog, but he somehow got into the same kennel as this high-bred female Collie and well…."

"What did he do, bite the thing?"

"Not exactly, I guess she was in heat and he maybe sort of impregnated her."

"But that can't be his fault, he can't help it, he's a guy."

She rolled her eyes then said, "That argument doesn't really help. The kennel ended up having to pay damages and sort of nicely told me not to bring Morton back, ever again. I don't think he does very well in that sort of environment, anyway."

"I just think it's not the best idea, bringing him to your folks right now."

"Well, what else can I do?" She was online now, clicking keys, she pulled a billfold out of the purse at her feet and rifled through it to get a credit card.

"Don't you know someone? You must have a friend who could take him? You're only going on a short trip. What? A couple of days, tops?"

"Only a day or two, problem is just about everyone I can think of already has a dog or a couple of cats and Morton doesn't really like other dogs and he hates cats. His therapist said he just doesn't like to share the spotlight."

Therapist? "Well, there must be someone you can think of."

She was inputting her credit card number and understandably seemed focused on the computer screen at the moment. She clicked a few more keys and suddenly her printer fired up.

"There's my boarding pass. Nine o'clock flight tomorrow morning. Hey, I've got an idea," she said and stood up with a devilish grin on her face. As she turned to face me she undid the little silk robe and pulled it back placing her hands on her hips, completely exposing herself in the process. She was trimmed in the shape of a martini glass.

I felt my pulse ratchet up, but I think it was from the wave of panic spreading over me, "Oh no, no, that would be a bad idea. A really bad idea."

"What?" She said and slowly strutted around the end of the bed toward me with her hands still on her hips. She moved her shoulders from side to side with every step and my eyes began tracking her breasts as they bounced and swayed back and forth.

"I, I can't take him. I wouldn't know what to do. I don't know the first thing about taking care of a dog."

"He really likes you. Y'all are kind of alike in some ways, you know, immature, irresponsible, sort of lazy and in need of training and an awful lot of direction. Both of you tend to be bad boys," she said and then slipped the silk robe off her shoulders letting it fall to her waist.

"Maddie, this isn't fair."

"What? Is it my fault I suddenly can't seem to help myself? Can't seem to get enough of you?" she said and licked her lips suggestively. "You just seem to have that effect on me, Dev. God only knows what I'm liable to do. You know how I get when I really, really want something. I'm liable to do anything, absolutely anything." Her eyes suddenly seemed to project heat and she stuck her tongue out ever so slightly and moved it back and forth between her sensuous lips.

The silk robe suddenly dropped to the floor and she ran a hand down my foot to the ankle then slowly started to walk her fingers up my leg. "Guess - what - I - really - really - want - right - now?"

"Don't do this…."

Chapter Two

"So, I typed instructions up this morning while you were still asleep. This has everything you'll need," she said handing me a multi paged document that was stapled in the upper left corner. The cover sheet just said 'MORTON' and the second page was an index. It was a little before seven in the morning and the day already seemed to be headed down the drain. I had just pulled into the entrance to Terminal One at the Minneapolis/St. Paul airport. The taxi behind me leaned on his horn as I merged into the lane marked departures.

"I typed out his schedule, it's on page two. It's pretty simple, he just needs a little walk, twice a day, maybe just an hour or so in the morning and then again in the evening. On page three I've got his vet listed, and then a backup just in case. His therapist is over on Marshall Ave., Morton has his regular therapy appointment on Thursday, at two, don't be late. I better make a note to email you a reminder," she said typing with her thumbs as she input something on her cellphone.

"I've got his food schedule on page four, the green bag is for the evening, the tan one for the morning. One-and-a-quarter cups for both servings, please no additives or scraps, he's got a number of allergies. I find he does a lot better if I sit on the floor and have breakfast and dinner with him."

"Which dog food is your favorite?"

She ignored me. "Oh, and *do not feed him from the table*. It's bad for him in so many ways. While you were asleep I put his food and water dishes and his favorite chew toys on the floor of the back seat. I taped the prescription bottle with his heart worm pills to his morning food bag, that's when he gets the pill, every morning. You should grind up his heart worm pill and sprinkle it on his food, he won't eat the pill if you just put it in his dish. I try and feed him about ten minutes after seven in the morning, I find he does best if you keep him on that schedule. Don't forget. His blood pressure meds are taped to the evening food bag. Just half a pill, fifteen minutes before he eats, that's in my notes, too so don't worry. I put his bed in the trunk of your car. He'll probably be most comfortable sleeping in your bedroom, it's good Feng Shui if he's aligned with the window and the sun. Oh, and his favorite TV show is "The Voice.""

"TV show?" I said as I pulled in front of the main terminal.

"Yeah, "The Voice," you know the reality show with Tom Jones? He really likes the singers. Hey, I'm flying Delta and I already have my boarding pass. I've just got carryon so you can drop me off anywhere, all I have to do is clear security."

I pulled to the curb in front of the next entrance. "You just take care of your mom and don't worry about Morton, he'll be fine."

She turned round and knelt on the passenger seat then put on a sexy face.

My first thought was this probably isn't the best place for more kink, but….

"Oh, good-bye, Morton," she said in her high pitched, little-girl Morton voice. "Now you behave and take good care of Dev while I'm gone. I'll be back just as soon as I can. I'll call you everyday so we can talk." Then she wrinkled her nose and let Morton lick her all over her face. She leaned over and gave me a quick peck on the cheek rubbing a heavy dose of Morton drool along the side of my face in the process.

"Oh, I just know you two are going to have fun. Okay, see you later boys," she said from out on the sidewalk then she slammed the car door closed and headed into the terminal.

Chapter Three

When I edged away from the curb Morton immediately started whining. As I picked up speed he began barking and pacing back and forth looking out the rear window, his wagging tail kept hitting me in the back of my head.

"Okay, settle down back there, Morton. Settle down." At the sound of his name the tail began to wag even faster against the back of my head.

"Morton, damn it," I shouted and reached behind to shove him over. A horn blast from alongside got me to swerve back into my lane. The guy sped up, gave me the finger as he sailed past and took off down the road. The remainder of our drive home was uneventful.

I pulled into my driveway then opened the passenger door and grabbed Morton by the collar. I walked him up to the front door, opened it and let him inside, then walked back to the car and began unloading everything Maddie had packed up. I put Morton's bed in the kitchen, set the food bags in the pantry, tossed his chew toys on the kitchen floor and filled his water dish. I left the single spaced multi page instructions on the kitchen counter, closed the swinging door that led to the dining room and drove down to my office.

Maddie phoned about an hour later. "How's it going?"

"I'm doing fine, still in the recovery mode from our love session last…."

"I meant, Morton."

"Oh, great, not a problem."

"Really?" She sounded more than a little surprised.

"Yeah, he's just taking it easy," I said. I didn't want to let her know he was locked in the kitchen back at my place.

"Can I talk to him?"

"What?"

"Let me talk to him, just put the phone by his ear. We do it all the time."

"We?"

"Yeah, Morton and me. Come on, we're about to board and I'm going to have to turn this off in a few moments."

"Okay, hang on," I said then sat at my desk for a long moment listening.

"Hi Morton, hi Morton, miss me?" Maddie said in that screwy, high pitched, little girl Morton voice.

I panted into the phone. Just as I barked the office door opened and my office mate, Louie walked in.

"What the hell?"

I put a finger to my lips signaling Louie to be quiet then panted some more.

"Okay, bye Morton, bye, bye, bye," Maddie said.

"Wow, he really seems to know who's on the phone. He looks really happy," I said.

"I knew it. Thanks again, Dev. I really appreciate it."

"Not a problem," I lied. "Hey, best to your folks. I'll see you whenever you return."

"Thanks, I'm stepping onto the plane now so I'm going to ring off. Bye, bye, bye," she said sounding very happy.

"What the hell was that? You're seeing a woman with a dog fetish?"

"You wouldn't believe it."

"Try me," Louie said as he tossed his computer case onto his picnic table desk.

I told him the story about Maddie's late night phone call, her booking the flight and not having anyone to take care of Morton. I left out the part about her unique, payment in advance plan.

"I never figured you for being much of a pet sort of guy."

"I'm not, but it just seemed like she didn't have any other options. She was under pressure, and well I just thought it would be the right thing to do and help her out."

"Never figured you for the caring, sensitive type, either."

Chapter Four

I worked the rest of the day checking out references listed on a series of job applications for a position at an insurance company. It was boring drudgery, but it paid the bills, at least some of them. Occasionally, I scanned the apartment building across the street with my binoculars hoping the two girls on the third floor might be home early. They weren't.

"You give any thought to heading over to The Spot for just one?" Louie asked, it was getting close to five.

"I could use it, it's been a long day," I said, placing the binoculars back on the window sill and turning my computer off.

Louie looked up from his legal pad. "Oh, you're set to go right now? Let me just finish this section and I'll catch up, shouldn't be more than five or ten minutes."

Mike was tending bar and he'd just set my third beer down in front of me. I was drinking an Abel, a new micro-brewery in town when Louie finally showed up. "Sorry about that. Just got a call from a former client, his third DUI."

"Oh-oh, not good."

"Yeah, add to that the assault charge when he took a swing at the arresting officer and he's going away for awhile."

"Why did he call you if he's a former client?"

"He wasn't *former* when he called, I just fired him ten minutes ago. Guy's abusive, obnoxious, still under the influence plus he never paid me for the last time I represented him."

"Charming."

We chatted for awhile, Louie bought a round then I bought a round. My phone rang and I made the mistake of answering without checking the caller id. Some guy behind us was just in the process of loading up the juke box.

"Hi, Dev, let me talk to Morton."

"Hey, Maddie, how are things going?"

"Where are you?"

"Me? Oh, I'm just out running a quick errand. I wanted to pick up some of these rawhide chews for Morton, thought he might like them." Bob Seger fired up on the jukebox behind me. Mike was clearing away our empty glasses.

Louie looked at me and shook his head in disgust.

"Sounds like you're in a bar."

"No, just some kids driving by playing the radio too loud," I said slipping off my stool and heading out the side door.

"You're not leaving him alone are you? He needs his walk for starters, and then social interaction."

"We already went for his walk," I lied. "Really fun, and I'm just heading back home, should be there in about fifteen minutes."

"Okay, I'll call back, then," she said and hung up.

I went back inside, threw some cash on the bar for a tip then said, "I gotta run, man. I forgot all about this dog sitting gig. And she's going to be calling back in fifteen minutes."

Louie snorted and said, "Sounds like you're the one on the leash."

I was busy cleaning up the kitchen when Maddie called back. Morton had peed on the floor, more than once. He'd gotten into the pantry, dragged both dog food bags out and scattered the contents all over the kitchen floor. He'd chewed up one of the legs on a kitchen stool and pulled a loaf of bread off the kitchen counter and ate the entire thing.

Maddie called while I was down on my hands and knees attempting to separate the two different types of dog food spread all over the kitchen floor. Morton's tail started wagging as soon as my phone rang.

"Put him on," she said.

I thought about putting him on a plane down to Atlanta, but then held the phone up to Morton's ear. His tail wagged back and forth, and he barked a couple of times. I could hear her saying dopey things in that ridiculous voice she used with him. After a couple of minutes I put the phone back up to my ear as she continued. "Did you have a fun day, Morton? Are you on a little vacation?"

"There you go," I said trying not to sound too pissed off.

"Sorry if I was crabby before, I figured you were probably out in some sleazy bar. Does he like the rawhide chew?"

"I didn't want to give him one until after you called, you know, so he wouldn't be interrupted."

"Oh, that's so sweet."

"Yeah, that's me. How are your folks doing?"

"Pretty good, hopefully Mom will be discharged in a day or two. I'll hang on for about twenty-four

19

hours to get them sorted after that and then I should be able to come back home."

I looked around at my destroyed kitchen. Great, just two or three more days of coming home to this. "Okay, no rush, just keep us posted."

"Thanks, Dev. I know he's in good hands."

Yeah, I thought and those hands are about to be wrapped around his neck. "Talk to you later, Maddie."

"Okay, bye, bye, bye," she said and hung up sounding a lot happier.

I looked around at the mess. If I was honest it was at least partially my fault, I mean Maddie had the poor guy seeing a therapist for God's sake and I'd completely forgotten about him. He stood opposite me, staring and no doubt conjuring up his next stunt. I had a better idea.

"Come on, Morton, let's go for a walk."

Chapter Five

I grabbed his leash and tried to get him to calm down so I could click the thing onto his collar. He kept jumping around and his tail was banging like a base drum against the kitchen cabinets. I finally got him hooked up then crunched through all the dog food scattered across the kitchen floor as we headed out the door.

We walked about four blocks over to Summit Ave. It's one of the city's attractions and I think it's billed as the longest elegant Victorian street in the country, or maybe St. Paul just made that up for tourist purposes. Either way, it's a nice walk with wide sidewalks, elegant homes, lots of walkers, a fair amount of joggers and plenty of pretty girls to look at.

We passed a lot of people walking dogs. Morton ignored each and every one of them. In his mind he was a person, after all. We'd walked close to a mile and it was beginning to turn to dusk when we heard voices coming from a front porch.

The house was three stories of buff colored stone, topped off by a red tile roof. There was a brown and white camper parked in the driveway with a bumper sticker on the back that read "Uppity." The porch ran across the front of the house and was mostly hidden behind a large, untrimmed hedge. Despite the porch light it was impossible to see who was on the porch. Whoever it was, they didn't sound all that happy.

"You've absolutely no business being here, it's time for you to leave."

"And you better listen if you know what's good for you."

"I want you to leave, now."

"Not without the princess."

"Absolutely not, she remains with me."

We kept on walking, I probably picked up the pace just to get out of there, I really didn't need to get involved in someone else's domestic.

"I'm taking her, that was our deal, otherwise everything falls apart if she stays with you."

"Don't you…get your hands off of me. Let go, no, no, help, let go, let go."

The woman's cries suddenly turned substantially louder and we stopped and stood out there on the sidewalk for a brief moment, I was just hoping it would all go away.

"Help, help, I said let go of me," she screamed. It was beginning to sound pretty damn serious.

"Come on, Morton," I said and we cut across the small front yard and stood at the base of the steps leading up to the front porch.

"Everything okay up there?" I called.

"You take your hands off her right now, Tommy. Stop it, no, no. Help, help me please." I heard a sort of bang, then glass breaking.

"Let's go, Morton," I said and I took the steps two at a time up to the porch. Morton came up with his tail wagging and his tongue hanging out, ready to play.

There was a couple wrestling at the far end of the porch. They seemed to be tugging back and forth while standing amidst wicker furniture. One of the wicker armchairs was tipped over on its side with a broken wine glass next to it on the porch floor.

The guy looked about my size, with glasses, a goatee and slicked back dark hair. He wore what, in the dim light, looked like an expensive sport coat over an open collared red shirt. The woman he was struggling with looked like some sort of hippie throwback and appeared to be wearing cast off Chinese army fatigues. Her salt and pepper hair was pulled back in a tight ponytail that fell to the middle of her back.

The guy turned and pointed at me. "This is private, pal none of your damn business, so just get the hell out of here before you bite off more than you can chew."

At this point the woman half turned and kneed him squarely in the crotch.

He immediately let go of her and crumpled to the floor, coming to rest against a wicker coffee table on the way down. "Oh, God," he groaned.

She shook her head and folded her arms across her chest. "I think its time for you to leave, Tommy."

"God," he groaned and half rose to his feet.

"You heard her, probably best if you left," I said and indicated the steps with a nod of my head.

A wine bottle sat on the wicker coffee table and he picked it up by the neck, rose to his full height and seemed to take a deep breath. Then he pointed an accusing finger at me and I noticed the heavy gold chain wrapped around his right wrist.

Morton's tail started to wag and he gave an excited bark, like he expected the guy to throw the bottle and then Morton could fetch it.

"I've had just about enough of you, you're about to learn an important lesson, pal," he said then took a step toward me with the wine bottle.

I reached behind my back and pulled out a snub .38. "I wouldn't do that, real bad idea."

"Whoa, now you just hold on, there," he said wide eyed. He placed the bottle back down on the table.

"Just move off the porch and get the hell out of here," I said.

He raised his hands in a 'take it easy' sort of gesture, telegraphed some sort of message with a quick glance to the woman, then gave Morton and I a wide berth as he hurried off the porch.

Once he disappeared she sort of tugged at the edge of her fatigue shirt pretending to straighten it and said, "I don't believe that sort of response was necessary." She indicated the .38 I was still holding with a nod of her chin.

"You ever been hit in the head with a bottle?" I asked and stuffed the pistol back into the small of my back.

"I abhor violence of any sort," she said in a superior sort of manner.

"Yeah, me too, especially when it's directed at me."

She moved her eyes up to the left suggesting a "*whatever*" sort of response and gave a slight sigh. Then she returned the wicker chair to its upright position and picked up the pieces of broken wine glass.

For the first time Morton and I saw a dog peek around from behind the wicker couch, a French Poodle about Morton's size only snow white, with a powder blue collar and a matching silk cover over her back. The poodle's coat was perfectly groomed with a large ball of fur at the end of its tail and around its chest.

"Oh, forgive me, where are my manners? Please, allow me to introduce Princess Anastasia, she's a bit shy," the woman said.

Morton was checking *Madame Poodle* out and the speed of his wagging tail suggested some serious interest. It was the first dog he'd paid any attention to all evening. Nice timing, the princess belonged to some hippie who was hassling me because I had the temerity to stop a guy from beating her up.

"Did you know that guy?"

"Yes, Mr. Allesi, Tommy, just a slight difference of opinion, I'm afraid."

"He didn't appear to really be in the mood to discuss."

She ignored my comment and said, "May I interest you in a glass of wine? I have a lovely white Burgundy, an eighty-nine"

"Really," I said pretending to be interested.

"Quite impressive, actually. Five stars. I'll just be a moment. Princess Anastasia," she said and snapped her fingers.

The poodle followed her off the porch giving Morton a disdainful passing glance along the way. Morton's tail banged back and forth across the corner of the wicker chair and he strained at his leash in an effort to follow.

Chapter Six

Her name was Natasha Kominski. She was a St. Paul native although she hastened to add she couldn't wait to get out of town. When she talked, she clenched her teeth so tightly together that her lower jaw never seemed to move. Her pronunciation came across in a put on Ivy League accent.

She seemed rather vague about what she did for a living, other than her line about "*being extremely involved in a variety of important issues.*" Given her locale on one of the most expensive streets in town that led me to believe she was probably a trust fund baby, which allowed her to be *extremely involved* in whatever she wanted and not have to worry about any financial repercussions or responsibilities.

She'd undone the next two buttons on her wrinkled Chinese army shirt when she returned with the bottle of wine and no Princess Anastasia. Morton stopped wagging his tail, gave off a little moan then settled onto the porch floor and rested his head on his front paws. He glanced at me from time to time, but otherwise remained staring at the front door while Natasha droned on.

"Before Radcliffe I took a course at the *College de Sorbonne*, I was just fifteen."

"Is that the cooking school over on the east side?"

She flashed an unimpressed quick smile. "No, I'm afraid not, it's located in Paris." She raised her eyebrows. "The Fifth *Arrondissement*," she added like I'd know what that meant.

"Interesting," I said only because I didn't know what else to say then emptied my wine glass and wished for a beer.

"Yes, it was 1968, I arrived just in time to participate in the *Situationist International*. Quite an experience, let me tell you."

I was afraid she would tell me and figured I had the jist about Paris from all the New Orleans Mardi Gras video clips that I'd watched over the years.

"I'd better take Morton home, it's getting late and past his bedtime."

"You sure I can't tempt you, Mr. …I'm sorry, but I'm having a bit of a senior moment."

"Haskell, Dev Haskell," I said then reached into my pocket and pulled out a business card.

She tossed my card on the table without giving it so much as a passing glance, then refilled her wine glass. "Would you care to stay for another wine? Who knows where it might lead," she said and fumbled with another button on her uniform.

"I better not."

"Does my directness make you feel uncomfortable?"

"Directness?" I flashed back to Maddie last night and thought *I'll tell you about directness*.
"No, hardly, it's just been a busy day and I was up working very late last night."

She took a sip of her wine and finally glanced at my card. "Private Investigator. Really? Oh, interesting. So, that explains the gun."

"I'm just glad everything turned out alright. Thanks for the wine, Natasha, but we really should be on our way. Come on, Morton," I said and stood up. Morton hopped to his feet and headed toward the front door. "I guess he just wants to say good-bye to your dog," I laughed.

"Princess Anastasia," Natasha corrected.

"Yeah, that's the one."

"She's a champion, we'll be starting the show season in a little over a weeks time."

"The show season?" I said and headed toward the steps.

"Yes. Princess Anastasia has qualified once again, she'll be competing in the Blessington Kennel Club show," Natasha said raising her eyebrows to signify this was something big, very big, something everyone who was anyone would be aware of.

I didn't have the slightest idea what she was talking about. "That's nice. Well look, we better get moving if we want to make it home in time to watch a movie."

"One can only imagine. Thank you for stopping to lend assistance, although I had things in hand," she said

Yeah, that's why you were calling for help I thought. "Hopefully the next time we meet it will be under a more positive circumstance. Thank you for the wine, it was a pleasure meeting you."

She smiled like that made perfect sense and replied, "Au revoir."

Chapter Seven

Morton was lying on the floor next to the couch. I was on the couch with a bag of Bar-B-Que potato chips resting on my chest. We were watching some Netflix movie whose name I'd already forgotten. I occasionally passed a chip Morton's way. He seemed to like them and I had to believe they tasted a lot better than that healthy dog food Maddie had him eating.

The two women in the movie were in the process of robbing a bank. They were carrying very big guns while wearing very small bikini's. Morton gave me a look suggesting this was really stupid.

I held another chip out for him and said, "Yeah, I know, it's pretty bad. So you got a little jazzed for that French hottie in the blue outfit tonight, right Morton? Princess Anastasia."

At the mention of her name his tail started wagging.

"I don't know, man she looked like she could be an awful lot of work. We've got to get you socialized, get you meeting more of your own kind. That will help more than any dog therapist Maddie might have lined up for you." I chuckled then handed him another chip.

"Yeah, I thought so, Princess Anastasia," I said and watched his tail start wagging again as he sat up and anxiously looked at the door.

"Might be nice to see her again. We'll have to check her out on another walk. Which reminds me," I said and grabbed a pen and the notepad off the end table. I want to do some checking on that Tommy Allesi guy tomorrow, see what his deal is.

We watched the rest of the movie, or at least we were in front of the TV. When I woke up Morton was asleep on the floor. I got up and turned things off then shook Morton awake and brought him out to the kitchen.

"See you in the morning, pal." I said then turned out the light and went upstairs to bed. Everything was quiet for about five minutes before Morton started to bark. I pulled a pillow over my head. He just kept on going and didn't stop. I pictured him down there in his dog bed, barking, wondering how long I'd be able to last.

At about the twenty minute mark I got out of bed and went downstairs to the kitchen. I flicked on the light and said, "Morton, I need to sleep, so knock it off. Okay?"

He wagged his tail and I patted him on the head. That seemed to settle him down until I turned off the light and closed the door. His barking started about a nanosecond later. I sighed when I got to the stairs, turned round and went back to the kitchen.

"Hey, Morton, its bedtime, knock it off."

He looked like he was expecting me to say something else.

"Okay, I'll leave the light on," I said and closed the door.

I got about halfway to the stairs when the barking started up again so I turned round. This wasn't going to work. I opened the kitchen door and said, "Okay, come on Morton, but just tonight, only until you get used to the house."

He wagged his tail and followed me upstairs. "Don't even think about it, because you're not getting in my bed, Morton. So just lie down and go to sleep," I said then placed his bed on the floor next to the door.

I woke early the following morning. I felt cramped, my back was killing me and I hadn't slept all that well. Morton's back was up against me with his legs stretched out across the bed and he was snoring.

I crawled out of bed and made my way to the bathroom. My head was in that grey space between being fully awake and realizing I wasn't going to be able to go back to sleep. Morton was still snoring when I came back to the bedroom. I stumbled downstairs, turned on the coffee pot, then clicked on my laptop.

I answered emails, checked the local news and had a leisurely breakfast. About forty-five minutes later I heard Morton land on the floor upstairs in the bedroom and then groan as he stretched. I called his name from the kitchen and a few minutes later I could hear him coming down the stairs. I let him out the back door and got his breakfast ready while he did his business.

Morton came back in and gave a disparaging look at the health food breakfast I'd poured in the dish for him.

"Sorry, man. No Bar-B-Que chips for breakfast, we finished them up last night. Better eat that breakfast, pal we gotta get moving." I really couldn't blame him, but the healthy dog food was all I had on hand. I'd have to pick up more chips on the way home.

Chapter Eight

I tossed Morton's bed in the car and we headed for my office. I got him set up in front of the file cabinet then turned on my computer to do some research on my new friend, Tommy Allesi the gentleman who was going to hit me over the head with the wine bottle last night. The guy I pulled the .38 on.

Apparently, Tommy was quite a busy man. He seemed to be involved in a number of undertakings; black jack, roulette, high stakes poker, horse racing, dog racing, sports betting in general, golf in particular. To sum up, Tommy was a gambler, a high-stakes professional gambler, with quite the reputation. He once bet a thousand dollars a hole on a Sunday morning golf outing. "Just to keep it interesting," he'd been quoted as saying.

Over the years he'd attracted scrutiny from the authorities in Minnesota, Kentucky, Florida, Nevada, and New Jersey as well as the FBI and the SEC not to mention an ongoing list of rumors and allegations. Nothing illegal had ever been proven.

In an article in the Minnesota Times he was alleged to have ties to the mob.

"That's one of the dumbest, most ridiculous things I've ever heard," he said the following evening in a national interview.

Since 2000 there were at least four investigations into his dealings with local politicians. Allesi acknowledged contributing to political campaigns.

"It's not rocket science. If you're in business, community leaders are going to be your business partners. I followed the law in regard to contribution limits and I try to maintain a positive working relationship with people I have to deal with, whether that's someone on the city council or the guy who picks up my trash bin every week. That's just good business."

All four investigations ended up going nowhere.

All in all, Tommy Allesi had been charged on a variety of counts over the years; illegal gambling, money laundering, illegal bookmaking. In each and every case the charges were eventually dropped. Nothing ever stuck.

He was quoted as saying, "No industry is better monitored than the legal betting industry. If only Wall Street were regulated as well. I've been swindled each and every time I made a Wall Street investment. After the third or fourth time, even I start to catch on and realize I have a better chance of winning watching horses run or cards being dealt."

I had a tough time thinking a guy with Allesi's apparent contacts would wash up on Natasha Kominski's front porch in the hopes of a romantic interlude. I was trying to recall exactly what had been said between the two of them. Did Allesi just want her dog, Princess Anastasia? Or, did he want her dog off the porch so he could woo Natasha?

I was pondering the question when my office mate, Louie waltzed in the door. Morton attacked with a wagging tail and his slobbering tongue.

Louie bent down and rubbed Morton behind the ears as Morton licked the breakfast crumbs off Louie's suit coat. "Whoa, what's this? You went out and got yourself a dog? You gotta be kidding me, you're barely responsible enough to take care of yourself," he said.

"Not exactly, kind of a long story."

"Try me. I'm just back from pleading a DUI case on behalf of the client from hell and trying to get bail reduced for another idiot on a domestic. I'd love to hear how this happened," Louie said.

He gave Morton another rub behind the ears before he took his coat off and sat down behind his picnic table desk. Morton wandered back to his bed and settled in.

"I don't suppose there's any coffee left?" Louie asked.

"Let me fill your mug and I'll make a fresh pot."

"How long has that stuff been on?"

"Oh, I don't know, maybe fifteen to twenty hours."

"I'll wait while you make a fresh pot, meanwhile you can enlighten me on your friend, here."

"His name is Morton," I said. I could hear Morton's tail thumping on the floor as I poured the remnants of the coffee pot down the sink in the closet. The coffee steamed as it hit the cold, white porcelain sink and I was afraid it was so acidic that it might just melt the enamel on the sink.

"So, I was over at Maddie's place the other night."

"That the woman who threatened to file a restraining order? The same gal you panted and barked at on the phone yesterday?"

"Yeah, but that restraining threat was just a little misunderstanding, we sorted it out a while ago."

Louie didn't look too sure.

34

"Anyway, she gets this middle of the night phone call…." I went on to explain how Maddie's Mom had an accident. Maddie had to grab an early flight back to Atlanta, and my suggestion that bringing Morton along wouldn't be the most helpful idea. "And so, I got him for just a couple of days."

Louie nodded at a foot high stack of job applications I was supposed to have finished verifying for my insurance client. "And you thought he'd be able to help you verify employment records on that stack of applications you were supposed to have finished yesterday. I get it, makes sense to me," Louie said.

"More like I can't leave the guy at home because he'll destroy whatever room I put him in."

"Probably just needs some exercise."

"You mean like last night?" I said and proceeded to tell Louie about my introduction to Natasha Kominski and by extension, Tommy Allesi.

"God, compared to you I lead an incredibly dull life. This Tommy Allesi, is he the gambler?"

"You know him?"

"You better grab some coffee and let me fill you in."

Chapter Nine

I was on my second mug, listening to Louie give me the lowdown on Tommy Allesi.

"I've never seen a guy as focused as him. I think he spends every waking moment trying to figure an edge to whatever the odds are. They say he once studied roulette tables and determined that after a certain age they were more likely to land on the last four numbers more often than the others."

"As far as I know he's been banned by a number of places out in Vegas. He doesn't win each and every time, but he wins consistently and with the sums he bets, well it's not very good for a casino's bottom line."

"They can ban you from a casino because you win too often?"

"Sure, at the end of the day, they're just a private business."

"Everything I read online made it sound like he was still a player."

"I'm sure he is, but what he does now is he has someone go in and place bets for him."

"Won't they just ban that guy?"

"No, because there's a bunch of guys. He might have forty or fifty different people betting for him on everything from the World Series to some rinky-dink college basketball game. He had some system he came up with, I forget what it's called, but he uses computers to analyze odds and then he has all these characters go into joints and place bets for him. He could have five guys in the same place betting on different things, baseball, NASCAR, golf. He pays them a percentage. Rumor has it he can bet so much dough that he actually influences the odds."

"And you know this guy?"

"Know *of* him, really. He grew up in my neighborhood, but he must be about ten years older than me. Father died at a young age, I hear Tommy was a loner sort of kid who learned early on what he wanted to devote his life to. And, he's certainly been successful. He owns the Lady Slipper Country Club, a number of commercial properties, God knows what else. Last I heard he was getting into hedge funds and legit investments, guy's certainly got the head for it."

"I had no idea."

"And your way of an introduction was to pull a gun on him?"

"Only because he looked like he was going to come after me with a wine bottle and well, I couldn't have him spilling good wine."

"No, of course not, that would never do. To be honest, I haven't seen Tommy for years and probably couldn't pick him out of a crowd of two," Louie said.

"Well, if last night was any indication he likes expensive clothes, he's wears a heavy gold chain around his right wrist. Dark hair that's slicked back, a goatee. Ring a bell?" I said.

"That sort of sounds like the guy, the goatee is a new addition in the past decade," Louie said.

"I just wonder what he wanted with Natasha's dog?"

"You might want to ask her that question. The other thing is I'd maybe keep a sharp lookout. Like I told you he's never been convicted of anything I'm aware of, but he's always right on the edge. It wouldn't be a huge leap to imagine him making a phone call to some idiot who'd like to get on his good side by doing something unpleasant to you."

"Maybe we'll just have to stop by on our walk to-night and ask Miss Natasha Kominski what, exactly was going on?"

"Just be careful, dealing with an unknown quantity who is somehow tied in to Tommy Allesi is maybe not the best recommendation."

"Then I'll just have to study up on Natasha."

Which was exactly what I did for the better part of the next two hours. If Tommy Allesi always appeared to be just on the edge, yet ultimately never charged, Natasha Kominski was his polar opposite.

The earliest record and mug shot I came across was from 1969 in a newspaper article covering her protest and then arrest for supposedly pouring blood over records in the St. Paul Courthouse. She was a senior in high school and it wasn't actually blood, but rather strawberry Kool-Aid thickened with corn starch and enhanced with food coloring, none-the-less, against the law.

She and her accomplices, four individuals all tolled, had gained access to files and were protesting the military draft. Unfortunately, it seems they had taken a wrong turn in the court house and poured the mixture over building permits rather than draft records. They were labeled the 'Misdirected Four' in the newspaper. Even in her mug shot from almost fifty years ago she looked like intriguing.

In 1970 she was photographed in the early morning hours at the Lincoln Memorial in Washington DC listening as President Richard Nixon, with his butler in tow, addressed fellow student protestors.

She was back in St. Paul again in 1974, this time arrested and charged with indecent exposure in a 'burn the bra' protest. The accompanying arrest photo showed an outraged Natasha on an apparently cold day surrounded by a large number of smiling cops all vying for position to get a good look at the 'protestor'.

Things were quiet for a decade until the breaking and entering charges in January of 1985 when she made her way into the medical labs at the U of M and set free one hundred lab rats. Unfortunately, the rats were a special hairless variety used in a unique kind of blood research. They all froze within minutes when Natasha released them outside on a minus forty degree Minnesota night.

She was arrested twice more in Washington DC, once for protesting President George W. Bush's 1989 invasion of Panama and again in 1998 for protesting what became known as the Monica Lewinsky scandal. During a tour of the White House, where she was attired in a blue dress similar to the one Lewinsky wore, Natasha attempted to enter the First Family's private quarters and confront then President Bill Clinton about his behavior. He wasn't home at the time.

In 1999 in California and again in 2002 in Colorado, Natasha was arrested, charged and fined for operating a medical marijuana facility without the proper license. Actually, in both instances she had no license what-so-ever. She had simply opened a store front which the authorities promptly closed that same morning.

She was arrested for trespassing when she attempted to free the wolves in St. Paul's Como Park

Zoo in 2012, not the best idea in the middle of a seven county residential area. She had scaled two separate fences and entered the zoo's 'Wolf Woods', a natural habitat enclosure for grey wolves, only to learn the wolves weren't really interested in her political views or her attempt to free them. Natasha was rescued after having to climb a tree to save herself from the intended beneficiaries of her enlightened viewpoint.

Since then things appeared to have been quiet, which based on Natasha's history, gave one pause.

Chapter Ten

Morton ignored his health food and looked longingly at the cheeseburgers I'd just taken off the grill. We were in the kitchen and I had just placed two cheeseburgers on my plate, along with some lime flavored Dorito chips. I was in the process of opening a beer.

Morton sat next to my stool just beneath my plate. He kept staring back and forth with his big brown eyes looking first at my cheeseburgers and then at me. I was working to ignore him.

"Don't even think about it, buddy."

I don't know how he did it, but he somehow managed to look even sadder.

"No way, man, besides Maddie would kill me." As if on cue my phone rang.

"Hi, Maddie."

"How are things going?"

"We're just having dinner before we go on our walk. He's doing fine, we're getting along famously. How's your Mom?"

"She can come home tomorrow, but she's confined to bed. We've got a therapist coming in tomorrow afternoon to get her started back on the road to recovery. Can I talk to him?"

"Yeah hang on, he's right here." I placed the phone up to Morton's ear and he listened while Maddie said "Hi Morton" a half dozen times. Morton wagged his tail and stuck his tongue out. I got back on the phone after a minute, Maddie was still talking to him in her annoying little girl voice.

"I guess he's involved with dinner," I said.

"Is he eating okay?"

"Seems to be," I said and tossed a couple of lime flavored Dorito chips onto the floor for Morton.

"Well, okay just checking in. Don't forget he's got his therapist appointment tomorrow afternoon at two."

"Yeah, I was going over your instructions this morning and saw that. I check them out every morning, right before our hour long walk," I lied.

"I like to arrive at the appointment a few minutes early, just to let Morton become acclimated to the surroundings and give him a moment to clear his mind, maybe take a cleansing breath, sort of speak."

"I'll be sure to do that, Maddie it sounds like a really good idea."

"Okay, well I guess I'll talk to both of you tomorrow," she said.

"Talk then," I said and hung up. "You know, Morton nothing personal, but that kind of hovering would drive me nuts."

Morton remained in place, watching me eat my cheeseburger. I finished the first one and started in on the second. I tossed a couple more lime chips his way, he snatched one before it hit the floor then attacked the second one a moment later. I really didn't have the appetite for the second cheeseburger and Morton kept giving me the sad eyes so I set the plate down on the floor.

It was gone before I stood up. "We're pals now, Morton. Come on, let's go for that walk." His tail started to wag at the mention of a walk. "We'll stop and see if we can spend some quality time with Princess Anastasia," I said and Morton suddenly jumped and drooled at the sound of her name.

Chapter Eleven

It was our third time walking past the house before Natasha called out to us from the front porch. Morton had assumed his 'person' persona and ignored absolutely every dog we'd passed along the way.

"Well, if it isn't my hero's, hello you two. Might I interest you in a glass of Vino?" Natasha's voice called to us from somewhere behind the unkempt bushes hiding her front porch.

"We'd love to," I said.

I turned toward the sidewalk leading up to the porch and Morton took off, straining at the leash, nearly yanking my arm out of the socket in the process. I was able to more or less rein him in by the time we reached the steps. He was panting and drooling, no doubt thinking of Princess Anastasia. I had to admit, I knew the feeling.

"How very nice to see you again," Natasha said. She'd been sitting on the wicker couch and stood as we climbed the steps. She was barefoot, wearing a pair of baggy, worn, blue jean bib overalls, and a black T-shirt that had 'Proposition 501' stenciled in white letters across the front. The words were surrounded by a red circle with a line through it. She looked sexy in a casual sort of way, like she didn't care or was just unaware of the fact. I was afraid to ask what the proposition was about.

"How's everything tonight?"

"Everything is fine," she said. Princess Anastasia sat next to her on a wicker chair with a little navy-blue beret perched on her head. She gave Morton a brief, disdainful look.

Morton immediately drooled when she glanced his way.

"Would you have time to join me in a beverage?" she asked.

"Yes, I would, that would be nice, as long as we're not imposing."

Her wine glass was almost empty; the wine bottle on the wicker coffee table was empty. A large glass ashtray that looked to be cut crystal was on the coffee table and filled with ashes. Two small roach clips lay along the edge of the ashtray. Next to the ashtray was a small bottle of red nail polish and I noticed that her toe nails looked to have been recently done.

"You're not imposing at all. In fact, I was just about to open another bottle. Please have a seat," she said and indicated a corner of the wicker couch with her hand. "I'll be right back."

She gave some sort of hand signal to the princess who immediately leapt off her chair and pranced alongside Natasha into the house.

Morton strained at his leash and then whined when he couldn't follow. He seemed to focus on the princess's tail as they left.

Natasha popped her head back out of the door-way and said, "I do have some beer in the refrigerator, if you would prefer that."

"A beer would be perfect."

There were two table lamps turned on in the front room that faced out onto the porch. The room looked like a museum setting with a twelve foot high ceiling that could have come out of the Sistine Chapel. It was painted in a sun with clouds and a vivid blue sky sort of affair. The ceiling mural was reflected in the large gilt edged mirror hanging over the fireplace. The large, elaborate fireplace was centered on the exterior wall with a carved, white marble mantel. A window was on either side of the fireplace and the top half of both windows were stained glass. A large landscape painting framed in an exotic looking gilt frame hung over a couch on the wall directly opposite me. The large entry to the room could be closed off by massive sliding doors that disappeared back into the walls.

The entire room, doors, windows, ceiling and floors were trimmed in what looked like walnut or cherry. The floor was a light colored oak with a design pattern of inlaid walnut running around the entire room about eight inches from the wall. A thick, plush red and blue oriental carpet covered most of the floor. The two couches and four chairs that I could see were all carved the same and looked like a matching set that probably cost somewhere in the neighborhood of what my entire house was worth.

"I hope this will be to your liking," Natasha said as she set a round glass tray onto the wicker coffee table. The tray had an etched glass bottom with silver sides and two ornate silver handles, an empty pint glass and a silver ice bucket were positioned on the tray. The bucket was filled with ice and held a bottle of wine and three beers. Princess Anastasia was nowhere in sight.

"I'm sure this will be perfect."

"Would you do me the honor of opening the wine bottle? I can never seem to get that damned corkscrew to work properly." She sat down on the opposite end of the wicker couch and held out her wine glass expectantly.

I proceeded to open the bottle of wine. The corkscrew was the kind where you twist the top and the two arms on the side gradually rise. I pushed the arms down then pulled the cork out the final half inch. It made a loud popping sound as it left the bottle.

"May I pour you a glass?" I asked.

"Please do, it's one of my favorites, Portuguese, sparkling. I buy it by the case and absolutely adore this wine."

I smiled.

"Vinho verde," she continued. "Green wine, from the northwest corner of Portugal. Have you ever been there?"

"The northwest corner? Gee, no, I don't think I have."

"Quite a verdant area, cool, hilly. You really must make an effort to get there."

The wine bottle was clear glass and had a peacock on the white label. Right now I felt like hitting myself over the head with the thing, just to end the geography lesson. Instead, I filled her glass then used the end of the cork screw to pop the bottle cap off one of the beer bottles, a Stella Artois. The stemmed beer glass was emblazoned with the Stella logo and I wondered if she'd stolen it from a bar.

"Here's to you, both of you," she said raising her wine glass and giving Morton the nod. "I trust you enjoy French beer, it's really some of the best there is."

Got you, I thought. "It's a very nice beer. I guess I've always been sort of partial to German beer, and then all the local micro-breweries that are popping up around town."

"Yes," she nodded dismissively, "but the French, well, c'est la vie."

"You know, Stella is actually a Belgian product."

A blank look washed over her face.

"Yeah, brewed in the city of Leuven, I think since the late twenties. It's part of the Budweiser family now-a-days."

"Budweiser?"

"Yup, capitalism at it's best," I said and raised my glass in a toast. Natasha appeared too shocked to respond.

After a long, quiet moment she changed the subject. "I wanted to thank you for interrupting your walk yesterday evening."

"Not a problem."

"I fear I could have been just a little more gracious last night."

"No, no you were great. I'm just glad there wasn't a major incident in the end."

She smiled, took a sip and set her glass down on the table.

"So tell me about your business, a Private Investigator, it must be very exciting."

"Sorry to disappoint," I said. "Actually, it's quite boring. Just today I spent hours online and on the phone checking work experience references listed on a stack of resumes. The word dull doesn't even begin to cover it."

"But you must get involved in some exciting situations investigating crimes, gangsters, murders and that sort of thing."

"Actually, no. Most of that type of business would fall under the heading of *Police Work*. If there was some sort of crime committed I might be hired by

48

a defense attorney to get a second pair of eyes looking at something. If that's the case, nine times out of ten what I find usually corresponds to the official findings."

"Do you always carry a gun?"

"No, in fact I left it locked up at home tonight."

"How thoughtful," she said not sounding all that sincere. "Tell me, do you ever provide protection?"

"I have, on a few occasions. Most often it's in the form of an event rather than extended protection for a specific individual. Someone comes to town and they need a local guy to get them to and from a place. Maybe ensure they don't get hassled by reporters or fans, something like that."

"What is it you do in that case?"

"Oh, I don't know, just use common sense, make sure I try and keep a low profile, maybe take the occasional back way into some place."

"How long have you had your dog?" she asked glancing at Morton chewing the toe on my shoe.

"Oh, Morton He's not really mine. I'm just watching him while a friend is out of town for a couple of days."

"Just a couple of days?"

"Yeah, bit of a medical emergency in the family. She'll be back probably late tomorrow or the next day."

"Oh, a girlfriend? Partner? Sorry am I being too inquisitive?"

"No, no and no," I replied.

"Then we should talk," she said and took a large swallow of wine.

Chapter Twelve

"I've an inordinate amount of time and money invested in Princess Anastasia," she said. This was after she'd been going on at length about the dog's blood lines, the schools Princess Anastasia had attended, the past couple years worth of dog shows all across North America that they had competed in and won. Not to mention the reporters, potential advertisers, breeders and movie producers who were begging her for a contract and a piece of the princess action.

"Is that why Tommy Allesi was here last night, he wanted to make a movie about your dog?"

"I'm afraid not," she said using a dismissive Ivy League tone. "Through some sort of unfortunate circumstance, which I must admit I don't fully comprehend, Mr. Allesi has assumed a one-thirty-second percent share in Princess Anastasia. He was here in an attempt to persuade me to withdraw our entry in the Blessington Kennel Club show."

"And how did that work?" I asked setting my empty glass on the tray next to the three empty beer bottles.

"I believe the behavior you witnessed was the result of my rejecting his request. It would appear Mr. Allesi is an individual who is used to having his own way."

"You mean, just because you intend to compete in some dog show, he went off the deep end?"

"Precisely."

"Blessington Kennel Club, where's that?"

There was a long pause before she answered. "The show is here, in town, actually, it's held at the Xcel Center." She said that last bit in a tone that suggested everyone in town except me would automatically know this fact.

"No shit?"

"Yes, Mr. Haskell, *no shit*, as you so aptly put it," she said then flashed an insincere, broad smile for just the briefest moment.

"And you'd like me to do what, exactly?"

"I'd like you to make sure no one interferes while we work during this final week. The show begins in just six days and we'll have no further need of your services at that point. I fully intend to win best of show with Princess Anastasia."

At the sound of her name Morton's head bobbed up.

"I really don't know."

"Perhaps if you gave the matter some thought, Mr. Haskell. I don't need an answer this minute. Maybe sleep on it, unless, perhaps you'd care to remain here and see what develops?" she said raising an eyebrow and smiling.

"I'll sleep on it and give you an answer in the morning."

"Does my directness offend? Perhaps shock you, sir?"

"No, it's just that I...."

"I've always found the events leading up to a competition extremely stressful. This competition, the Blessington, is no exception. It has been my experience that the sexual act can serve as an extremely effective stress release. Does that offend you, Mr. Haskell? Perhaps make you uncomfortable?"

"No, not really,"

"A woman speaking of sex, Mr. Haskell, of intercourse, does that give you pause?"

"Hunh?"

"The act of coitus, Mr. Haskell. The physical union of male and female genitalia accompanied by rhythmic movements usually leading to ejaculation on your part and orgasmic pleasure on mine if you know what you're doing, does that bother you in some way, Mr. Haskell?"

"I guess I've never really felt bothered, at least that I can recall."

"No doubt," she said and flashed another one of her nanosecond smiles. "Very well, to all things there is a purpose. Thank God for batteries," she seemed to half say to herself then raised her glass and drained it. "I shall await your call tomorrow. Please consider my offer." She stood up and held out her hand to shake.

"Yeah, I'll think about it and call you in the morning. You know, about the protection thing."

"Excellent. I can offer you employment along with a rather unique benefit package, she winked. "Well, good night, Mr. Haskell."

"Please call me, Dev."

"Very well, Devlin, good night," she said then walked into her mansion, closed the door firmly behind her and then we heard the lock click. Morton and I stood there alone on the front porch. A moment later the overhead porch light went off, and then the lights in the fancy room that looked out onto the porch were turned off.

Morton and I stood there, alone in the dark with the empty bottles. For half a second I thought about stealing the silver tray, but the odds were I'd never get away with it so. Morton gave me a look that seemed to say, *'Don't be stupid,'* so we just started to head home.

Chapter Thirteen

It was a G class Mercedes, dark blue not black, sporting some kind of fancy chrome wheel rims. I think the car went for somewhere north of a hundred grand. It had driven past us three times now, circling a couple of blocks and passing again, slowing down ever so slightly to check us out. The windows were tinted so I couldn't see who was in there.

We turned the corner at Summit and Arundel to walk the four blocks down Arundel over to Selby and home. It was dark now, close to ten o'clock. Morton was at my side and behaving, for the moment.

I saw the Mercedes sitting about a block ahead under a street light that was out. It was parked on the same side of the street that we were walking on. Arundel dead ends at the parking lot we cut across to get home. It's not like it's a busy thoroughfare, it's more the kind of street you'd be on only if you had business there. I had a bad feeling we might be tonight's particular business for the guy in the Mercedes.

When we were about a half block away from the car I crossed the street so we'd be on the opposite side. I kept walking, thinking maybe I was being just a little too paranoid. That thought stopped the moment the doors opened up on the Mercedes and two guys climbed out.

They were large, way larger than me, either one probably came in at double my weight and looked like they hadn't missed too many meals. At the moment, the one coming out the passenger side looked to be eating a large submarine sandwich wrapped in paper. Neither one appeared to be in what I'd call tip-top physical shape.

"Excuse me, sir, I wonder if you might help us, we seem to be lost," the driver called, he wore one of the largest black T-shirts I'd ever seen. He appeared neckless, had thinning ginger colored hair with pork chop side burns. He looked an awful lot like the Fat Bastard character from the Austin Powers movies and after he spoke he reached into the back seat and pulled out a baseball bat which he proceeded to swing slowly from side to side. I had trouble believing he'd be able to run to first base, let alone make it all the way around to home plate.

"Sorry, but I'm not from around here," I said and picked up our pace.

Morton's head perked up as Fat Bastard cut between two parked cars. He continued to swing the baseball bat back and forth and wore an evil grin on his face. His pal behind him wore a Hawaiian print shirt roughly the size of a table cloth, powder blue with large red flowers the size of dinner plates. As he waddled across the street he took another large bite from his submarine sandwich and seemed to chuckle at my response.

Fat Bastard suddenly wobbled forward and swung the bat at me, wide, missing by a good six inches which to my way of thinking was still too close.

Morton looked up for the first time, noticed the sandwich in the other guys hand and leapt toward him. "Get the hell out of here," he shouted and kicked at Morton.

Morton jumped back, in the process wrapping his leash around Fat Bastard's massive legs. He swung the bat at Morton and missed, strike two. Morton jumped for the sandwich again this time knocking it out of the guy's hand.

As he jumped the leash pulled tight and Fat Bastard suddenly went down with a groan. His forehead bounced off the concrete sidewalk, I felt the ground shudder when he hit and then he just lay there, very still.

Morton immediately began to gobble up the sandwich on the curb. I grabbed the bat off the sidewalk and headed for the Hawaiian shirt backing up into the street.

"Now just hold on there a minute, buddy. We weren't gonna really hurt you or anything. I'm sure Denis was only kidding," he said glancing at the massive figure face down on the ground. He raised his hands up in an effort to plead his case, and apparently trying to calm me down at the same time. It wasn't working.

"You follow us for the past twenty minutes and then come after me with a damn baseball bat." I gave him a quick jab in his massive beer belly and backed him up a few feet.

"You try to kick my dog." I jabbed him again backing him up a couple more steps. He attempted to swat the bat away, but he was too slow and I poked him again, hard.

"I think we might have made a mistake, pal. I'm sorry, about that, really I am."

"Seems to me like you weren't being very friendly," I said then faked a jab to his beer belly, he flung his arm wide to the right, opening up. I swung the bat low and caught him across the kneecap.

He was suddenly down on his back in the middle of the street moaning and rolling from side to side. "Ahhh-hhhh, oh God, sweet Jesus," he groaned.

I walked over to the Mercedes and opened the driver's door. The keys were still in the ignition and the alarm gave off a classical music tone.

Morton was finished with the sandwich and wandered out into the street, dragging his leash. He stopped to sniff the guy holding his knee, rolling back and forth.

"Come on, Morton, come on up, boy." I called then indicated the open car door.

"Oh, no, no, you can't do that, come on. That's not really our car, we borrowed it from, from a friend," the guy in the street called then groaned some more through gritted teeth.

"Nice talking to you, enjoy your evening," I said then tossed the bat into the back seat, climbed behind the wheel and we took off.

Chapter Fourteen

I pulled the Mercedes into my garage then backed my car up the driveway and against the garage door. Once in the house I slipped the pistol into my belt, opened up a beer and some Bar-B-Que potato chips then flaked out on the couch in front of the flat screen. Morton took up his position on the floor next to the couch and gave me the sad eye routine.

"Okay, okay, I'll get you a bowl and you can have some of these as a reward for taking that guy out tonight." I went out to the kitchen and put some chips in a bowl for Morton then went back into the den. My beer bottle was on its side, empty. Morton had licked all the beer up off the floor and just sat there giving me an innocent look.

"Pals don't do that, Morton," I said, giving him the bowl of chips before I went back out to the kitchen for another beer.

I woke the following morning just before eight. After sleeping on the couch all night I felt like a bent piece of plumbing. I sat up and rolled my shoulders and neck, listening to my body snap and crackle. Morton remained asleep.

I picked up the empty chip bag, collected the beer bottles and headed out to the kitchen. I was halfway through my first mug of coffee before Morton showed up. He did a long stretch in the middle of the kitchen then headed for the back door. I filled a travel mug with coffee and grabbed the leash.

We didn't walk for Maddie's prescribed hour, it was more like ten minutes before we were back in the kitchen. Morton didn't look all that thrilled when I filled his bowl with healthy dog food instead of Bar-B-Que potato chips.

"Don't look at me like that. We got your shrink appointment this afternoon so we better get you back on good behavior. We might have to stop and see Princess Anastasia though, after your appointment," I said.

Morton moved his head from side to side in time to his wagging tail.

"Well, I'll give you this much, you've got good taste in girls, pal."

We finished breakfast and just on a whim, after our little incident last night, I brought my AR-15 out and placed it in the trunk of my car then drove down to the office. Morton was curled up in front of the file cabinet while I used the binoculars to check out the third floor apartment across the street. Based on the body language it looked like the two roommates weren't the best of friends this morning. There seemed to be words exchanged with heads wagging back and forth in an "*I told you so*" manner. When one of the girls turned around to get into the refrigerator her roommate stuck out her tongue and gave her the finger. Unfortunately, they were both dressed.

Louie suddenly came through the door and headed for the coffee pot.

"That's all you've accomplished this morning, window peeking?"

"It's a particular skill I've developed. Besides, I got a gig."

"You're kidding, doing what?"

"Don't sound so surprised, I'll be providing protection, for a full week as a matter of fact."

"Seriously? Hey, that's great, anyone I know?"

"Princess Anastasia," I said. At the sound of her name Morton raised his head and began to wag his tail, it sounded like a base drum beating against the file cabinet.

"Princess? Where the hell is she from? Sounds Eastern European."

"No, French, actually. I told you about the trouble the other night where I sort of stepped in. That basically got me the gig. In fact, she just made the offer last night. I'm gonna give her a call and let her know I'll do it."

"You didn't mention anything about royalty. French? Really, is she good looking?"

"I suppose you could say so."

"And this was on that front porch the other night? With Tommy Allesi?"

"It wasn't much, really. Which reminds me, I better make a phone call now that I think about it, I've got to check something out."

Louie shuffled back to his picnic table desk while I punched in numbers on my cellphone.

Chapter Fifteen

"Thank you for calling the Department of Motor Vehicles, how may I direct your call?"

"Donna at extension four-one-three, please."

"One moment and I'll connect you."

I waited two rings before she answered. "This is Donna, how may I help you?" She sounded fairly professional, maybe even cheery on a good day.

"Hi, Donna this is Dev Haskell."

Silence.

"Hello?"

"I thought you were finished with this sort of harassment," she hissed.

"I just need you to check the registration on a license for me."

"I've told you before, but this time I really mean it. This has got to be the final time, I think I've been more than patient and you have certainly gotten more than your pound of flesh from me."

"Maybe. Of course that hardly even begins to stack up when compared to all the action you got. I suppose we could check with the Governor's office, see how they feel about a state employee, now a supervisor no less, shacking up with a college intern. Course if the Governor was busy I suppose I could just call your husband."

"That's always your answer, isn't it?" she whispered.

"Then why do you even bother to ask?"

"Just give me the license number."

I gave her the license number of the Mercedes parked in my garage. "Do you want to just email me that information?"

"Oh please, the last thing I need is an audit trail leading to the likes of you. I'll have it up in just … here we go, all right, that's a dark blue G class Mercedes, 2015?"

"If you say so."

"God, it appears to be a corporate registration, Lady Slipper Enterprises, happy?" she hissed again.

"I will be once you give me an address and a phone number." Lady Slipper Enterprises, Tommy Allesi's country club, no surprise.

"I could lose my job," she whispered.

"You will for sure if I show them the photos of you leading that baby faced college intern astray."

She gave me the address and phone number then her voice suddenly went soft, and she said, "Mmmmmm, there must be something we could work out, here. Would you be interested in meeting for a drink, talking this whole thing over? Who knows, where it might lead, could be beneficial for both of us, not to mention just a hell of a lot of fun."

"Sounds good, of course I'd still want to call you for the occasional bit of information."

She hung up.

I dialed the phone number Donna gave me.

"Lady Slipper Enterprises," a pleasant voice answered on the third ring.

"Tommy Allesi, please."

"Who may I say is calling?"

"My name is Dev Haskell, it's regarding a vehicle."

I waited on the line for a good minute or two while some sort of elevator music played in the background. I picked up the binoculars and scanned the apartment across the street while I listened to classical music that sounded familiar although I could never tell you who had written it. The girls in the apartment appeared to have finished their arguments for the time being and the place looked dead.

"Thank you for waiting, Mr. Haskell, I'm sorry, but Mr. Allesi is in a meeting just now, may I take your number and have him call you."

I gave her my number, then I phoned Natasha and ended up leaving a message to call me. She was probably busy attending a protest somewhere.

Chapter Sixteen

My phone rang a little after the noon hour. "Mr. Haskell, Tommy Allesi returning your call."

I recognized the voice from the other night on Natasha's front porch and immediately conjured up an image of him holding that wine bottle by the neck and starting to come toward me.

"Thanks for calling me back. I believe I have something of yours."

"Something of mine? And just what might that be?"

"It's big and dark blue," I said then repeated the license number to him.

"Really? Now how did that ever wind up in your hands? I reported it stolen just last night? You didn't take it, did you?"

"Not in so many words, two bad guys had it and I figured you'd probably want it back. I'd like to return it to you."

"I think right here at the Lady Slipper would be the perfect place. Tell me, do you golf, Haskell?"

"Sorry to say I don't, I could swing by oh, say later this afternoon and return the car to its rightful owner."

"I'll look forward to that, could you make it about four if that's not too much trouble? I'm in a meeting mid afternoon."

"See you then," I said and hung up.

I drummed my fingers on the desk for a moment, then, against my better judgment I placed a call for some backup. He answered almost immediately.

"Yes," he almost seemed to sing the word.

"Hi Luscious, Dev Haskell how's it going?"

Luscious Dixon was a one time player in the NFL. I think he held the record for being cut by more teams in a single preseason than any other player, three teams to be exact. The new, tidier NFL really didn't have a need for Luscious and his anger management issues and the league very quickly decided they were looking at a public relations nightmare. That was fine with me, as long as I kept him supplied with doughnuts we seemed to get along just fine.

"I guess you could say things are going pretty well, Dev."

"You interested in taking a little drive this afternoon?"

"What you talking?"

"I'm just dropping a car off to a guy, need you to follow me in my car, then I'll give you a lift back home."

"That's it?"

"Yup, pay you in cash, maybe take an hour, how's a hundred bucks sound?"

"Sounds good to me, could you pick me up at the Lowry Medical Building?"

"Everything okay?"

"Yeah, just my therapist, I've got a two o'clock appointment."

Therapist, Morton's appointment, I suddenly remembered. "I'll pick you up a little after three, at the main door if that works."

"I'll be there," Luscious said and hung up.

After a late lunch I grabbed the leash and we headed out to Morton's therapist. The therapist office was located in a one story brick building with a fenced, quarter mile track attached to the back of the building. You had to press a buzzer on the gate at the rear of the building to gain access.

Morton was straining at the leash the moment I got him out of the car. He was all excited about whatever was going to happen next.

"Yes," a pleasant voice answered after I pressed the buzzer.

"Hi, I'm here for Maddie Swanson, I've brought her dog Morton for his therapy appointment."

"Very well, please complete once around the track before entering."

"Around the track?"

"Yes, at least once. You'll find a dispenser just inside with plastic bags."

"Plastic bags?"

"For the droppings, dogs need to pooh," the voice said then clicked the gate open.

Morton charged in and headed for the track. I pulled a blue plastic bag from a dispenser attached to the gate then yanked the leash to bring him back alongside of me. "Calm down, buddy you're giving a bad impression."

We walked around the track, Morton calmed down about a quarter of the way around, I checked my watch and we were still a few minutes early so I took him around a second time. I deposited the blue plastic bag with Morton's contribution in the trash bin by the gate and then we entered the office.

Chapter Seventeen

It was probably the only doctor's waiting room I'd ever been in that featured a concrete floor with a drain in the middle. The receptionist was wearing jeans and a T-shirt and looked like a college kid.

"You can just have a seat, Dr. Spenser is finishing up with a patient and will be out in a moment," she said. Morton's tail was wagging excitedly and she smiled then reached into a large bowl and tossed a dog biscuit to him. He caught it in mid-air and had it devoured in two snaps.

I adjourned to an orange plastic chair and waited. I noticed a garden hose curled up on the floor next to the receptionist counter, which, given the clientele probably made perfect sense.

A few minutes later a door opened and a smallish woman holding a furry, little brown dog walked out. Behind her was an attractive, dark haired woman with her hands in the pocket of a white lab coat.

"Thank you, Patrice, we'll see you next week. Remember, you're in charge," she said.

Patrice didn't look all that sure.

Morton was up with his tail wagging, banging it against my chair. I stood up as the doctor approached, Morton lurched forward and planted his nose between her legs.

"Well Morton, how are you today?" she said then gave him a good rub behind his ears. "Hi, I'm Chris Spenser, and you are?"

"I'm Dev Haskell, a friend of Maddie's. She's out of town on a family emergency for a few days and I'm watching Morton."

"Okay, well the way we work things is the three of us usually sit down and review our progress, see how Morton feels he's doing. How has he been for you?"

"Well, to tell you the truth I'm not much of a pet type of guy, but we're getting along pretty well." I didn't feel the need to mention his reaction to Princess Anastasia or tripping that fat guy on the walk home last night and knocking him out. The doc probably wouldn't approve of Morton eating a cheeseburger, Bar-B-Que potato chips or drinking a bottle of beer so I sort of let that go by the wayside as well.

"Well, I have to say you must be doing something right, just at a quick glance this is about the calmest I've seen him. I tell you what, why don't you take a chair and we'll just talk."

That sounded fine to me. I figured I could chat up the sexy looking doc and Maddie was going to pay for it. But, with that, she took the leash from me and said, "This won't take long, you might as well wait out here." Then she left me standing there in the middle of the lobby watching as she led Morton back to her office.

I walked back to the plastic chair with a shocked look on my face as the doc closed her office door. The college kid turned her back to me and busied herself at a counter. I think she was laughing.

I must have drifted off for a moment. When I opened my eyes Morton was just bounding out of the doctor's office.

"Well, we had a very nice chat. He seems to be doing fine. What are you doing that's different?"

"Not much, to tell you the truth. He's staying at my place. I take him to my office during the day, that's pretty quiet. We go for a walk at night."

"Well, he seems to be substantially calmer. Whatever it is you're doing, keep it up."

I took her assessment to mean Morton could stay with the cheeseburger, beer and chips.

"Can I ask you something, Doctor? What do you know about the Blessington Kennel Club Show?"

"What do I know about The Blessington? Well, highly competitive, it's the Super Bowl of dog competition in this region. People work for years to get there and once they do it's really the first step in the big competitive leagues. If you're thinking of Morton he may not be quite ready for it."

I glanced over at Morton, he was up on his hind legs staring at the bowl of dog biscuits sitting on the receptionist's counter and drooling. "Gee, too bad, I thought he might have had a chance."

"Actually, there is trainer right here in town with one of the better entries this year. Natasha Kominski, with…."

"Princess Anastasia." I finished. Morton turned at the sound of her name and his tail started wagging back and forth.

"Oh, you've heard of her?"

"Actually, I've met her, just recently. I was more interested in the event itself. You mentioned the Super Bowl, are there bets placed on the entrants, that sort of thing?"

"Mmm-hmmm, the seamier side of the competition world, I'm afraid. As I said, The Blessington is highly competitive and unfortunately with that, there is a certain undesirable element that's attracted."

"No offense, but attracted to a dog show?"

"Actually, it's a competition. Officially there's betting in the usual places, Las Vegas of course, locally probably Mystic Lake or the Grey Wolf casino up north. Unofficially, there are the occasional unsavory incidents that seem to exist in any competitive situation, always the potential of bribery, or perhaps a questionable breeding practice, that sort of situation. Just recently at Crufts, that's the biggest competition in the world, it's held in Birmingham…."

"Alabama?"

"No, the UK," she laughed. "Anyway, a dog named Jagger took second place in his class for best dog and the poor thing was poisoned two days later. So, unfortunately, even in our innocent little world *people* are more than capable of doing some awful things." She reached down and gave Morton a rub behind his ears.

"Please give my best to Maddie, I hope her family emergency isn't too serious and everything works out," she said and then extended her hand to shake.

"Nice to meet you," I said taking her hand and then we left Morton's therapist to go find Luscious Dixon at his therapist's office.

Chapter Eighteen

Luscious Dixon was waiting downtown, exactly where he said he would be waiting, outside the door of the Lowry Medical Arts Building eating the last of a submarine sandwich. He was leaning against the brick wall and looked large enough to serve as a building support.

I honked the horn as we pulled up then put the window down and said, "Luscious, take your time, but you better finish that sandwich before you climb in. I've got a dog in here who would just love to share that with you."

Luscious, did just that, took his time, savoring every bite like it was his last. When he finished his sandwich he pulled another one from out of nowhere and started in on it. When he eventually finished the second sandwich he examined the paper wrap for any crumbs he may have missed before depositing the wrap in a trash container. He carefully licked each of his fingers and then climbed into the front seat.

Luscious weighed in at somewhere north of three-hundred- and-fifty-pounds and the car tilted decidedly to the right as he settled into the passenger seat then pushed the seat back as far as it could go.

"Good to see you, Luscious. I appreciate you being able to help me out today."

"My pleasure, Mr. Dev who's this?" he asked just as Morton stuck his head into the front seat and began to lick any remnants of submarine sandwich from Luscious's face.

"This is Morton, I'm watching him for a friend. Morton, meet Luscious."

Luscious seemed to enjoy the licking. Once I pulled away from the curb Morton settled down on the back seat.

"Here's the deal, Luscious. I have to return a car to a fella, drop it off at the Lady Slipper Country Club. All you have to do is follow me over there, might as well come in with me once we get there, then I'll drop you off at home. Simple enough."

"I think I can do that. Might have to stop at McDonald's or somewhere after, but yeah, glad to help."

"You ever get your driver's license back."

"I think it's almost ready to happen, maybe, I hope."

Not surprising. I wasn't sure why his license had been pulled, again, but we were going just a short distance, staying in town, so hopefully there wouldn't be a problem.

"I've got the other car in my garage, it's only about a ten minute drive over to the Lady Slipper from my place. I'll have Morton ride with me."

My idea of a ten minute drive was based on someone normal driving. I'd forgotten for the moment that I was dealing with Luscious. He was setting the pace, behind me, burning up the road at a blistering eighteen miles per hour.

Marshall Avenue is a busy street with two lanes traveling in either direction. It runs parallel to the interstate which right now was backed up with bumper to bumper traffic. That meant a lot of folks had jumped onto Marshall as an alternative route. This, in turn, accounted for the long line of cars that had formed behind Luscious who was being extremely careful not to come close to approaching the speed limit nor raise any dust.

I had to slow down to keep Luscious close to me, which made it look like I was the guy holding up everyone else on the road. So, I became the recipient of all the colorful comments and folks of all ages flipping me off. More than one person shook their fist at me. Some guy riding a bike flipped me off as he shot past shouting curses. Thankfully, I couldn't hear the comments screamed in my direction as cars sped by, in large part because of all the horns honking in frustration behind us. Luscious appeared oblivious to it all.

We traveled the length of Marshall Avenue, almost to the Mississippi River and the Lake Street Bridge leading across the river into Minneapolis. I took a right just before the bridge and a block later a left brought us into the Lady Slipper parking lot. True to form, Luscious turned on his blinker for both turns once he'd already made them. We had arrived far enough after the lunch hour and before the happy hour crowd so there were plenty of parking places, in fact there was just one other car in the members lot. We pulled into two side by side spots just a few feet from the front door and strolled inside.

I held Morton on his leash and had to pull him forward so he didn't lift his leg on a potted shrub at the front door.

It was still too early for the golf season and far too cool outside for the pool to be open so the place was virtually empty. Soft, classical music seemed to drift through the building. Off to the left the wall papered dining room overlooked the Mississippi river valley and stood virtually empty with the exception of a lone woman setting tables for the dinner trade. We headed down the hall in the opposite direction toward the clubhouse bar which was just past the restrooms and a candy machine.

"Hey, Dev I gotta use the can, how 'bout I just wait for you out here," Luscious said eyeing the candy machine.

"That'd be fine, I shouldn't be more than a minute or two," I said and headed into the bar.

The clubhouse bar had the look of a place that in a previous era had most likely been the exclusive purview of 'gentlemen'. I've always believed the adage that behind every fortune, if you dig deep enough, you'll usually find a crime. It seemed a fair assumption that in its day the clubhouse bar was probably where more than a few crimes had been hatched and consummated by the city's elite.

I entered the bar by pushing through a set of oak double doors, each with a round porthole window of thick beveled glass. Both doors had an engraved brass sign just below the window that read "No Smoking." I pushed through and entered a spacious room, paneled floor to ceiling in dark oak. The light fixtures hanging from the ceiling were old enough to have originally been illuminated by gas.

The floor was covered with large, dark ceramic tiles. The oak bar was heavily carved, topped with a grayish marble that was worn in places by almost a hundred-and-fifty years of glasses sliding across it. The same classical music played in the background.

A guy in a bow tie, black vest and a gold nametag was pouring a five gallon pail of ice cubes into a sink just behind the bar. If he noticed me he gave no indication. Morton raised his head and appraised the place by sniffing the air.

One wall had a massive fireplace centered on it with a carved oak mantel that matched the bar. Over the mantle hung a gilt framed portrait of some grey haired, bald former governor from before the Second World War.

In a distant corner, the darkest corner in the place, Tommy Allesi sat at a round oak table watching us and sipping a cup of coffee behind a smoldering cigarette. Other than the bartender he was the only guy in the place and I had the feeling he would have been content to just sit and examine us for quite some time.

Chapter Nineteen

I tugged on Morton's leash and we headed toward the back of the room, winding our way through a maze of tables and chairs toward the corner where Tommy continued to stare at us through a plume of cigarette smoke. It looked like he was wearing a white golf shirt underneath his black V-neck sweater. The sweater was embroidered with a Lady Slipper flower and the words "Lady Slipper Country Club" beneath the flower.

I noticed a flat screen TV was mounted up high on the wall just a few feet from where he sat with a horse race playing, the sound on the TV was turned off and Tommy seemed to be listening to the classical music. He glanced at the flat screen once or twice, but otherwise remained focused on Morton and me as we wove our way toward the back of the room. There was a plastic sign screwed into the oak tabletop, white with black letters that read, "PRIVATE RESERVED".

Tommy took a long drag off his cigarette then blew a cloud of smoke up toward the flat screen. "No dogs allowed," he said with a deadpan expression once we finally made it to his table. He took another long drag from his cigarette, blew a cloud of smoke up toward the ceiling then set the cigarette back in the ashtray. Morton's tail began wagging and bouncing off a couple of the wooden chairs around us.

"It also said "No Smoking" on the doors into this place."

"Humpf," Tommy grunted. "You seem to be developing a knack for getting in my way."

"Believe me, it's not intentional, it just sort of worked out that way. Someone calling for help or an idiot coming at me with a baseball bat, it's not like I have a lot of options."

"Well, I hope you'll forgive my behavior the other night, I might have been a little anxious."

"On the porch at Natasha's? I guess it worked out okay. Have to tell you I wasn't all that wild about the two guys I met last night"

"Those the two who stole my car? I really wouldn't know anything about that, Haskell. Could be you just seem to have that kind of effect on people. You did bring it back, didn't you, my car? I mean that's why you're interrupting my afternoon's work, right?"

"Yeah, the car's out in the lot, right by the front door," I said and placed the keys for the Mercedes on the table.

"Please tell me you didn't put him in my car," he said and nodded at Morton.

"As a matter of fact, I did. Actually, he wanted to drive, but I didn't think that would be such a good idea."

Tommy didn't smile.

"Once I found out who the car belonged to I just wanted to get it back to you, the Mercedes. Small world isn't it? I run into you the night before and then some dumb shit steals your car and I sort of find it."

"Yeah, amazing. You said you don't golf?"

"Not really. I'm a good nineteenth hole guy, I'll always buy the first round, but I've never really had a lot of patience for the game itself."

"Too bad, I would have enjoyed taking your money."

"One of the many reasons I don't play, I don't like to lose."

"Sound advice. You know, Haskell, occasionally you can find yourself in a no win situation and it just might be advisable to fold your cards and simply move on. Don't you think?"

"Like you said, *occasionally*."

"I don't like to lose, either. So you know, hypothetically here, when someone agrees to do something for me and then pulls out at the last minute that tends to screw things up. I'm not a very happy camper when that sort of thing happens. In fact, it makes me mad, real mad, ruins my day," he said then glanced up at the flat screen as a set of racing odds flashed across the screen.

"Hmmm-mmm, better than I thought," he half said to himself. "Maybe you're bringing me good luck, Haskell. Can you do that? Bring good luck."

"Not that I'm aware of."

"Probably right, I appreciate you returning the car all the same."

"Yeah, shame about the two guys who stole it from you."

"I wouldn't know anything about that," he said then took a final drag and stubbed out his cigarette in the ashtray. "Funny thing, there always seems to be someone who thinks he's cute and doesn't take me seriously and then things have a habit of not turning out so well for that individual. I guess there are just bound to be folks who don't listen to reason."

"You mean like Natasha?"

"Maybe, among others."

That sounded like my traveling music. "If there's nothing else I guess we'll be on our way."

Tommy nodded and said, "I think that would be a good idea. If you'll excuse me I have to make a business call, safe trip home."

"Nice to see you again," I said then turned and headed toward the door.

As we made our way toward the doors I could hear Tommy on his cellphone giving betting instructions to whoever was on the other end.

I found Luscious near the rest room door leaning against the candy machine. I noticed a crumpled-up potato chip bag in his hand. He was currently in the process of devouring a large chocolate bar. He raised his eyebrows as I approached.

"Don't talk with your mouth full. Come on, let's get out of here," I said. We went out the front doors toward the parking lot. Morton stopped and sniffed the air then proceeded to lift his leg on the potted shrub just outside the front door, this time I didn't try and stop him.

I opened the back door to my car and Morton hopped in just as a black car roared across the lot, zipped in next to us and screeched to a stop. I closed the car door then looked over the roof of my car and stared at the jerk who had just pulled in. There were now four cars in the entire parking lot. This car, a flat black Chevy Camaro, was centered on the yellow line, so it actually took up two spaces.

The car rocked from side to side as a large figure climbed out from behind the wheel. "I suppose you think you're pretty damned cute," a voice roared. He was fat, unshaven with thinning ginger colored hair and pork chop side burns. This afternoon he wore an olive drab T-shirt that hung out over his large beer belly. He had accessorized his wardrobe with a large, gauze bandage across his forehead. Both eyes were black, and there was a gash across the bridge of his swollen nose making his already ugly face even less attractive. Fat Bastard.

"If you're looking for your baseball bat, I already gave it to some school kids who'll take better care of it."

Luscious casually strolled around the front of my car munching the last of his chocolate bar as he approached. I walked around the back of my car to come at Fat Bastard from a different angle.

He looked Luscious up and down, and appraised the situation. "I'll see you around, Haskell," he said then turned, and quickly waddled up the front steps and into the clubhouse. He glanced over his shoulder a couple of times to make sure we weren't coming after him.

"Want me to go get him, Dev?" Luscious said then tossed the final third of the chocolate bar into his mouth.

"No thanks, Luscious. Let's just get out of this high class environment and back to what we know."

Luscious groaned into the passenger seat and I climbed behind the wheel then backed out of the parking space. With Luscious in the passenger seat the car leaned hard to the right. I had to drive away with the steering wheel cranked over to the left to guide my car more or less down the lane.

Chapter Twenty

"So was he serious, those two guys really stole his car?" Louie asked.

It was just the three of us sitting at the bar in The Spot, Me, Louie, and Morton. I was feeding Morton from a bag of pork rinds, giving him one at a time.

"I'd say he was serious about everything except those two idiots. Like I said, the one guy pulled up just as we were leaving. I don't know where they ended up last night, not like I was going to wait around to find out. That's kind of beside the point. It was pretty obvious he was telling me to stay the hell away from Natasha and Princess Anastasia."

At the mention of her name Morton sort of wiggled around on his stool and drooled on the bar.

Mike the bartender came over, "You want a beer or something for him, I don't know, water maybe?"

It's a pretty rare occasion when someone just orders water at The Spot, even if it is for a dog sitting at the bar. "Yeah, if you could give him some water that would be great, Mike."

"You still going to take that job?" Louie asked.

"I called her this morning and left a message telling her I would take it. I called her again after I dropped Luscious off and left another message. Yeah, I plan on taking the job, if I can reach her or she ever decides to call me back."

Mike came back with a chili bowl full of water and placed it in front of Morton. Morton looked at my beer then gave me a sideways glance as if to suggest water wasn't going to cut it.

"Do you believe it? Look at him, the guy wants a beer. No Morton, you're on water rations for the time being," I said.

"That might be okay for him, but I'll have another," Louie said sliding his empty glass across the bar. "You up for one more?"

"Yeah, sounds good," I said just as my phone rang.

"Hello."

"Hi, Dev how's it going?"

"Great Maddie, had a nice appointment with Morton's therapist." I shot a look at Louie. "She said she'd never seen Morton so relaxed. We're just about to head out on our walk."

"Let me talk to him."

"Okay, hang on," I said then placed the phone up near Morton's ear. His tail began wagging as he listened. She was speaking loud enough that we could hear her using her Morton voice. Louie and Mike looked at one another and then just stared at me. Mike eventually shook his head, walked away and poured our beers.

I got back on the phone after a minute, Maddie was still talking nonsense, "Morton, Morton, Morton, are you being a good boy, Morton? It's mommy, Morton."

"So how's your mom doing?"

"Oh, you. We're making progress," she said returning to something close to normal sounding. "Her physical therapist is pleased, but it's just going to be a long, slow recovery. Fortunately, it's given me a chance to reconnect with some folks I haven't seen since high school. I was with a couple of them last night and a bunch of us are going to get together tonight. I'm really looking forward to that."

"Sounds like it could be fun." I was curious if it was just going to be girlfriends, but couldn't bring myself to ask the question.

"Yeah, it will be nice to get a break from the home front. Much as I love my folks a couple of hours off would be alright with me."

"Well, not to worry, everything's fine up here, like I said we're just about to head out on our walk." Mike returned and slid a fresh beer in front of me. He pointed to another bag of pork rinds and I nodded. Morton's tail started wagging furiously as Mike pulled the bag from the rack behind the bar.

"Good, thanks again for doing this Dev," she said, then hung up. I noticed she didn't add, "I'll make it up to you."

"Don't say a thing," I said to Mike and Louie as I put my phone away.

Mike just shook his head then looked at Morton. "After hearing that gibberish nonsense on the phone the poor guy could probably use a beer."

We stayed for a couple more, by the time we left it was dark outside. I drove past Natasha's, but the lights were all off and the place looked deserted so we continued home.

Chapter Twenty-One

I was asleep on the couch when the phone call woke me. Morton had crashed on the floor next to the couch. We'd been watching some B-grade movie on Netflix and based on the screen it looked to have been over for quite some time.

"Haskell Investigations," I said and then had to clear my throat.

"Natasha, returning your earlier call, Mr. Haskins." Her voice sounded heavy and the words were slurred.

I glanced at the digital read on my flat screen, it was 2:27AM. Morton stirred on the floor, sort of rolled his shoulders then gave a deep sigh before he settled in and went back to sleep.

"Oh, yeah, thanks for calling. I'd like to accept your job offer."

"For the entire week?"

"I think that's the length of time you mentioned."

"Splendid, I'll have the paperwork drawn up. Perhaps you might be interested in maybe coming over now to review things?"

"Actually, it's getting sort of late for me so I probably shouldn't. How about tomorrow?"

"Tomorrow?" She waited for a long pause. "Very well, don't make it too early, shall we say about ten-ish?"

"That would be fine. I'll be at your door tomorrow, at ten."

"Actually, I've a better idea. You can meet us out at the polo grounds. Do you know where they are?"

"You mean at Fort Snelling?"

"Precisely. Sure you wouldn't be interested in swinging by this evening?"

"I wish I could, but it's awfully late for me."

There was another long pause before she said, "See you tomorrow morning. What time did we say, again?"

"Ten, tenish to be precise."

"See that you are, precise that is. I've not a moment to spare what with Blessington on the horizon," she said and then hung up.

I shook my head thinking "What a piece of work," then got up off the couch, turned off the lights, left Morton asleep on the floor and went up to bed. I woke a little after eight that morning. My body felt knotted and I was all the way over on the edge of the bed almost hanging off the side. Morton was lying on his side with his back up against mine and his four legs stretched out across the bed. His head rested on the spare pillow and he sounded like he was lightly snoring.

I rolled off the bed and headed toward the shower. Morton was still asleep when I returned to the bedroom. I slammed a couple of drawers getting dressed, but it didn't seem to faze him. I went downstairs for coffee and some breakfast. I was on my second cup when he finally made an appearance.

"Oh, sorry was I making too much noise and woke you?"

He found a warm sunny spot on the kitchen floor where the sun was shining through a window and made a long throaty sound as he stretched.

"Yeah, I know, I'm sure you're absolutely exhausted after having to take all that space in the bed. Let me finish this coffee and we'll go for a walk."

At the mention of a walk his tail started wagging and he took up a position at the back door. I filled my travel mug and we headed out the door. We did a quick three blocks and were just walking back up the driveway about to have breakfast when my phone rang.

"Haskell Investigations."

"Oh hi, Dev let me speak to Morton," Maddie said. No "Can you talk?" No "How are things?" No "Am I interrupting?"

"Yeah, hang on a second." I placed the phone up to Morton's ear as she started in with her Morton voice.

After her normal enthusiastic greeting and what passed as baby talk she launched into a description of her evening. It was like some sort of psychological misstep where she was bursting at the seams and had to unload to someone and after all, who could keep a secret better than Morton? Only I was holding the phone and the sound of her dopey, childish, insane, grating, ridiculous, obnoxious, stupid voice carried.

"So we all got together, it was just one big giant class reunion. And guess who was there, Morton? Buster."

I could only hope Buster was someone's dog.

"Remember? We used to date in high school, but broke up when we went to different colleges. Oh, he's still *so* hot."

At this point I put the phone up to my ear. Morton gave me a look that suggested, "Thank you."

"We were all doing shots and laughing and talking and well one thing led to another. Buster has a beautiful house with a great big yard that you would just love. He's a very important partner in his law firm and we were up all night … umm, talking and then sort of catching up."

She paused after that last oops just long enough for me to get a word in. "We better ring off, here Maddie. We're in the middle of our walk and I want to keep going. How's your mom doing?"

"She's improving, but it looks like I might have to extend for a couple of days, if you don't mind."

"I guess that would be okay, I suppose." I waited for her to say something like, "I'll really make it up to you." But, apparently she was still in the recovery mode after spending the night *catching up* with that important lawyer, Buster.

"Okay, thanks," she said and just hung up.

Morton gave me an all knowing look.

"I know, I know, I should have seen it coming. Come on, let's go have breakfast. We gotta be out of here in an hour."

I made a double batch of French toast and left Morton's healthy breakfast food in the bag in the pantry just to pay Maddie back. We inhaled our breakfast, Morton had three pieces and I had two, then we set out for the polo grounds.

Chapter Twenty-Two

The polo grounds are located on the old military base of Fort Snelling. The original fort was the first white settlement in what was described as wilderness in 1823. From a small beginning the area expanded over the decades to the now vacant old cavalry barracks and a half dozen Victorian homes. I guessed the polo field had originally served as a parade ground, but I couldn't be sure.

I was sure of one thing, there was no one on the polo grounds. Anywhere. It's not like you had to search all that hard. The grass field was flat, lined with trees that were just beginning to bud. There was virtually nowhere to hide. I figured Natasha would be out here putting Princess Anastasia through her paces getting ready for the Blessington show. But if they were out here I sure couldn't see them.

A brown and white camper was parked at the far corner of the field and we drove over in that direction. The camper seemed to age the closer we got to it. There were patches of rust above all four wheels. The dash board appeared to be littered with papers and maps. The side view mirror on the passenger side held only half a mirror and the passenger door was dented.

The door into the camper was centered on the rear of the unit and had glass louvers that theoretically could be adjusted for air flow. The bottom louver was missing and the next two were held together with duct tape. There was a bumper sticker stuck crookedly on the back of the camper next to the door that simply read, "Uppity."

The bumper sticker rang a bell and I remembered seeing the camper parked in the driveway the first night I met Natasha. I pulled alongside and climbed out.

"Morton, watch the car for me while I go meet with our new clients," I said careful not to mention Princess Anastasia for fear Morton might attempt to jump through the window.

He seemed content to just lie in the back seat. He raised his head when I spoke, but then settled right back down when I closed the door. I'd have to re- member French toast as a calming breakfast for him.

I had to knock a few times on the door before Na- tasha finally called out.

"Who is it?"

"Dev Haskell, Natasha. We were going to meet at ten this morning."

"What time is it?"

I pulled my cellphone out and checked the time. "It's about ten after ten," I said.

"Already? Oh it can't be. All right, just give me a minute and I'll be with you."

I had the feeling I may have woken her up. It was more like twenty minutes before she appeared and when Natasha opened the door you had to wonder what she'd been doing for the better part of a half hour. Obviously make up and getting ones self look- ing presentable had never entered the picture.

She was dressed in grey sweatpants that looked like they hadn't seen a wash since this time last year. The knees were soiled as if she'd crawled across the polo field for a good fifty yards. The sweat shirt was grey, but a different shade of grey. It appeared to be soiled as well, but more from what looked like chunks of food, some sort of sauce splatter and one large red wine spill. The cuff on the right sleeve was torn and frayed.

She still had a semblance of bed head, hair standing up on one side and completely flat on the other. It was sort of tangled and knotty and looked like she just ran her fingers through her hair instead of using a brush.

The door squeaked loudly as she stepped out. She placed a foot on the bumper and sort of half jumped to the ground, landing with a groan and taking a couple of quick steps just to keep her balance.

"So, Haskell, we're meeting at ten?"

"Yeah, we spoke on the phone last night. Do you remember?"

"Of course," she said, but in such a way that I thought she probably had no recollection.

"We discussed me taking on the position and you said you were going to draw up some paperwork"

"Right, I think I've got it on the table, somewhere. Won't be but a minute," she said and climbed back into the camper. It was more like ten minutes before she climbed back out. She was wearing lipstick and eyeshadow now, sort of a nuclear pink lipstick and the eyeshadow, another shade of pink, only seemed to accentuate the bloodshot eyes. Her hair was still a mess and she clutched a two page document held together with a large paper clip.

"Here, read through this contract just to make sure it all makes sense."

I took the paper and began reading. The initial paragraph covered the top two-thirds of the first page and was simply a laundry list of Princess Anastasia's blood lines starting with the paring of Constable and Lady Zsa Zsa De Wallen over fifty years ago.

I read through the next six paragraphs, none of which consisted of more than a sentence or two. The second page of the contract had a large round stain in the lower right hand corner that looked suspiciously like red wine. Natasha had already signed and dated the document.

Basically, all I had to do was make sure she, Natasha, could work with Princess Anastasia, uninterrupted for eight hours per day until they went to the Blessington show. I was allowed a forty-five minute lunch break, but I was required to eat on location, wherever the location was on any specific day. I would be paid upon completion of my duties.

It seemed simple enough and I signed on the line.

"Let me just get this notarized," Natasha said then pulled a notary stamp out of the pocket of her sweat pants, stamped the document and then signed the signature block on the stamp.

"Here, you might as well keep this damn thing, I know what it says." She handed me the notarized, wine-stained document. I folded it in half, then half again and stuffed it into my back pocket.

Ten minutes later she was drilling Princess Anastasia out in the middle of the polo grounds over and over in a series of routines, from walking alongside her at a fairly brisk pace to leaping over obstacles using hand commands. Even as someone who isn't into dogs and training I have to say it was pretty impressive. If this was all I had to do for the next week it would be a cakewalk.

A little after two they took a break and walked back to the camper. I'd been sitting on the back bumper wishing the clock would tick a little faster. Still, getting paid for doing absolutely nothing was just fine with me.

"Well, Mr. Haskell, we'll be taking a short lunch break and then starting up again in forty-five minutes. You'll of course maintain your position," Natasha said.

"Not a problem. I have to tell you that was pretty impressive. Especially the hand commands."

"Yes, well thank you, consistency is the key. I may ask for your assistance this afternoon."

"My assistance?"

"Nothing much, I would like you to provide a slight distraction as we go through our moves, you see. It would simply consist of you clapping your hands and letting her become used to fools attempting to create a distraction." She was suddenly over em-phasizing her Ivy league accent and clenching her lower jaw again as she spoke

"I can be a good fool," I said.

"No doubt," Natasha said, but didn't comment further.

Chapter Twenty-Three

They worked until six that evening. I did my part and played the fool, clapping and calling the princess whenever I got the nod from Natasha. By the end of the afternoon I felt almost as well trained as Princess Anastasia.

"Thank you, Mr. Haskell, I'd invite you in, but we've got quite the journey this evening. I would like to meet at the same time tomorrow, ten o'clock."

"I'll be here," I said.

"I'm afraid that won't do."

"No?"

"No. Do you know Lake Phalen? The park over there?"

"Yeah, I think I know where you mean."

"That's where we'll be."

"Okay, so you're heading home now?"

"No, I'm working on the assumption that a moving target is more difficult to find. So we'll be staying in here," she nodded at the camper. "Until we are registered at the show at which point I'll be staying there."

"Have there been problems since the other night?"

"Let's just say I'm playing it safe and leave it at that, shall we?"

"Does this have anything to do with Tommy Allesi?"

"Among others."

"If you're worried about something or someone in particular, Tommy Allesi for example, it would be nice to know so I can keep an eye out."

"At this stage I'm worried about everyone. I'd appreciate it if you would be wary of everyone and anyone who might approach. There's a good deal of wagering that follows this competition, not to mention the potential cash cow once Princess Anastasia wins Best of Show and I make her available for breeding. And, we do intend to win, Mr. Haskell you can rest assured of that."

"So you're going to do what? Remain here over night?"

"No, we were here last night. I believe I explained the moving target concept just a moment ago. I intend to be somewhere else this evening, please don't take offense, but I think the fewer people who know where we'll be the better. Now, I'll plan to see you tomorrow at Lake Phelan, ten sharp. Questions?"

"No, I guess not."

"Of course. It might be wise if one were to arrive with a lunch tomorrow."

"I'll be sure to do that."

"I bid you adieu, Mr. Haskell," she said then opened the door to the camper for Princess Anastasia and followed her inside. I heard the dead bolt slide into place from where I stood.

As I approached my car it suddenly dawned on me that Morton had been locked in there for the better part of eight hours. I opened the driver's door and my first thought was where did all the leaves come from? Then I realized it was bits of foam. Lot's of foam. Morton had pretty much chewed up the passenger seat.

"You gotta be kidding me, Morton what the hell were you thinking? Did it even taste good? You idiot."

He refused to look me in the eye.

"Morton, damn it, look at me. You are one stupid son-of-a-bitch." I grabbed him by the snout and rubbed it into a pile of foam. "No, no, bad dog, bad dog," I said, but to tell the truth my heart wasn't in it. I was the one who'd left him to his own devices and now I paid the price.

Chapter Twenty-Four

Morton sat sheepishly in the back seat all the way home. My phone rang just as we were pulling into the driveway, Heidi's new ringtone, Blondie's "Call Me," *'Cover me with kisses....'* It had been about three weeks since we'd been together. I knew she'd started dating some hairdresser and three weeks was right about at the point when things suddenly seemed to always go sour in her new relationships.

"Heidi, long time, darling. How are things?"

"Do you really want to know?"

"That bad, hunh?"

"You wouldn't believe it. I've got a fund that's seriously under performing. My phone's ringing off the hook with investors who want to jump ship because of missed projections, I have to take my car into the shop tomorrow, the floor in my living room is being refinished and can't be walked on for twenty-four hours, and my love life crashed and burned this noon."

"That hairdresser guy? What was his name, Alphonse?"

"No, Alexi, and don't ever mention that worthless scum bag again."

"That bad?"

"He got me out of a meeting for an emergency phone call."

"He okay?"

"He just wanted to dump me," she said, then screamed, "On the fucking phone, can you believe it?"

"What in the hell is he thinking? God, I'm sorry to hear that, Heidi. Honest," I tried to sound sincere.

"Yeah, sure you are, not. And don't go telling me that you warned me he was a snake. Believe me, I'm well aware of it."

"Okay, I won't mention the fact that I warned you," I said and let that just hang out there.

There was a long pause and I thought I heard sniffles. Then Heidi said, "Dev, can I come over tonight? I can't sleep in my house with all the fumes from the floor being refinished. I'll wake up and be brain dead or something. I'm sorry, I guess maybe you had a point and I should have listened to you earlier." Huge admission from a person who never makes a mistake.

"Forget what I said, Heidi. Yeah, I suppose you could come over. I gotta warn you I'm not alone. I…."

"That didn't take long, a couple of days. You know what, forget it, it serves me right thinking I found Mr. Right who turned out to be a complete jerk off. I deserve all this shit and…."

"Will you calm down and just listen. Yes, I want you to come over. No, I'm not alone. I'm watching a friend's dog for a couple of days. So Morton is here."

"Morton, that's the dog's name?"

"Yeah."

"Oh, he sounds so cute," she said sniffling and then suddenly sounding all cheery.

"Cute? Really? Believe me he's anything but, as a matter of fact right now he's in the dog house with me, pardon the pun."

"Oh stop it you big crab. I'll pick up dinner and wine. See you about eight?"

"Eight works for me. I should tell you I'm working with a client and we have to be out of here by about 9:30 tomorrow morning."

"Not to worry, I'll be gone long before that. I'm back in the fray with an investor meeting first thing."

"Okay, see you whenever you get there."

"Bye, bye, bye, bye," she said and hung up.

I twisted round to look at Morton lying in the backseat. He turned his head away so he wouldn't have to look at me.

"You are on thin ice, pal. And by the way, you're back on that horseshit, healthy dog food that Maddie packed for you. Cheeseburgers, Bar-B-Que potato chips, pork rinds and beer are a thing of the past where you're concerned, buddy. And you can forget about Princess Anastasia, too."

Morton sat up and stared at me, his tail was slowly moving from side to side just waiting for the go ahead from me before he started wagging. "No. No way. No, Morton, no."

That got him looking dejected and he put his head back down on the seat and refused to look at me.

Chapter Twenty-Five

Vintage Heidi, she arrived about forty-five minutes late. She had three bottles of wine, enough Thai takeout to feed ten and a large soup bone for Morton.

I met her at the front door and took the bag of wine and the shopping bag full of takeout food. She had a new hair style, again, sky blue on the top before it morphed into a darker blue on the side, from there it changed to burgundy, then fire engine red, until the final quarter inch became pink along the very ends. It was parted on the left flowing across the top of her head and hung down to her right shoulder. Both sides and the back of her head were her natural brown hair color, I think. They'd been shaved to about an eighth of an inch long so it was tough to tell. I tried not to stare and focused on the two large bags with all the food and wine.

"Heidi, all this food, it's just you and me." At which point Morton walked into the front hallway and introduced himself by inserting his nose between her legs.

"Oh, this must be Morton, he's adorable. Did you teach him this move?" she said giving him a good rub behind the ears. Morton's tail banged excitedly off the door frame and walls.

"Yeah, right. He's still in deep weeds with me. He basically ate the entire passenger seat in my car today."

"You're kidding, how long did you leave him in there?"

"That's not the point. Don't you think after the first bite he'd catch on that it didn't taste that good?"

"So in other words you abandoned him, didn't you?"

"He was just in there for a little bit."

"Sure he was, I'm guessing hours. You're just lucky it wasn't hot out or he could have died in there. I could ask what in the hell you were thinking, but it's obvious you weren't. Sorry, but it's your own fault, Dev. Don't blame this poor guy," she said and gave him another series of hardcore rubs and scratches behind the ears.

"Hey, I could go for some of that action," I said.

"What you can *go* do is bring this food out to the kitchen, open a bottle of wine and pour me a glass while I bring my clothes in. I've got that early pain in the ass meeting tomorrow morning and I'm going to have to leave from here. There's something for Morton in the bag, too."

I had a glass of wine waiting when she returned. She had a conservative looking dress and blouse in a dry cleaning bag along with a suitcase on wheels and a makeup case. Just hanging there in the dry cleaning bag the conservative outfit seemed to clash with her bizarre hair style.

"You staying the week?" I asked and handed her the glass of wine.

"We'll have to see how you behave."

I didn't want to stare at her hair so I took the dry cleaning bag and her luggage and ran them upstairs to the bedroom. I quickly changed the sheets and tossed the old ones into the closet then went back down to join her in the kitchen.

Morton was in the far corner of the kitchen attacking his soup bone. Heidi was sitting at the kitchen counter and had this look on her face that said, *"Go ahead, get it over with and ask me about my hair."*

I chickened out and said, "So how's the wine?"

"If it wasn't good I wouldn't have brought it."

I'd been here uncountable times before and knew there was a battle on the horizon if I didn't nip it in the bud. "So you want to tell me about the breakup?"

At the word "breakup" she moved her eyes involuntarily toward the top of her head, took a big double gulp of wine and said, "Don't ever mention that scum bag to me ever again. I don't want to talk about it. *Ever*."

"Okay."

"Look at what he did to me. He's made me the laughing stock of the entire nation. Four hundred million people think I look ridiculous."

"That number might be a little high."

Her eyes flared at me and she drained her glass. I was afraid she was going to throw the empty at me, but instead she thrust it out and said, "I'll have another."

I quickly filled her glass and considered myself lucky.

"The bastard said he had this cutting edge, avant-garde style and I'd be the first woman with it. He failed to mention I'd also be the only woman stupid enough to trust him."

"That might be a little harsh."

"Not by half," she said and gulped more wine.

"I'm getting used to it, it's kind of cool, I like the way the color flows and it works well with your eyes." I didn't add especially when they look ready to kill, which at the moment they did.

"Really?"

"Yeah, I mean what was it before this, white blonde, right? And then, didn't you have that blue at the very end? This is a huge change. It will take some time, especially for you because you've always been so particular about looking your best. When did he do this to you?" I didn't mean to make it sound like an assault, but I think that's the way Heidi took it.

"Two days ago. I brought in a photo as a general idea. He wouldn't let me see it until he was finished, served me prosecco the entire time, it took about three hours. He had this assistant bitch named Adella helping him. Guess where he was last night?"

"The salon?"

"No, idiot, Adella's. I can only hope he had to wait in line before climbing on top of that fat slut," she said and thrust out her empty glass again. I refilled her glass and took the first sip from mine.

"Can I make a suggestion?"

"I'm not getting a wig. And, if it's got anything to do with forgiveness you can just forget it 'cause I'm not interested," she said and then gulped more wine. I noticed it wasn't quite as large a gulp as earlier.

"No, I'm thinking revenge."

"Now you're talking. You have my permission to shoot both of them and leave them face down in the mud. I'll pay you, just name your damned price."

"Look, Heidi, listen to me, the best way to get even is to get happy."

"Happy? When in the hell did you suddenly become practical? Don't you see what I look like? Happy? God, I look insane is what I look like."

"No, you don't. You look ... umm, beautiful. Settle down and put your big girl pants on, you want revenge? Flout this like you're walking on the red carpet at the Academy Awards and you look like a million bucks, because you do. Has anyone stopped you on the street and told you that you look ridiculous?"

"Well, no, but...."

"Okay, so the entire nation doesn't think you look ridiculous or insane, for that matter. Get out there and flaunt it, start telling people you paid a lot of money for it in New York City or Paris and they'll have a completely different take on it from the one you're giving right now."

"You think?"

"I know. Honest. In the mean time we could eat dinner and maybe just come up with some form of repayment for your buddy, Alphonse."

"I told you, his name is Alexi, but thanks I get what you're trying to do."

We'd barely settled into our meal when my phone rang. Maddie.

"Hello."

"Hi Dev, let me speak to Morton."

"Sure Maddie, hang on, he's right here."

Heidi gave me a surprised look when I climbed off my stool and put the phone up to Morton's ear. He raised his head for a brief moment then returned to his soup bone. After a moment or two he turned slightly to move his ear away from the phone.

Both of us could hear Maddie was using her Morton voice. Heidi sat there mesmerized listening to the one sided conversation coming out of the phone.

"Hi Morton, how's my boy? It's mommy, are you being good, Morton? Morton, say hi to Buster, he's my special friend. Say hi to Morton, Buster?"

There was a pause and then a male voice said, "Hi, Morton."

"Can you say hi, Morton? Say hi to Buster, Morton. Come on, say hello to your new friend."

I panted then barked into the phone, Morton looked at me disdainfully and Heidi had to cover her mouth to stop from laughing.

"Oh, Buster, come on back in the room. You missed Morton saying hi."

I waited a moment then said, "Hi Maddie, hey how are things going for everyone down there?"

"Oh, Dev," she said sounding disappointed. "Mom's making progress. Dad's back at the office. Hey, look I better run, I'll call tomorrow," she said and hung up before I could get another word in.

"What or who, in God's name, was that?" Heidi asked.

"Didn't you hear? That was Morton's mom."

"Look at him, it's like he's already trying to forget about it. He's embarrassed, poor thing," Heidi said.

Morton was lying at her feet, but now his paws were on top of his head like he was trying to hide.

"And what's with that screwball voice, you've heard that before?"

"She calls everyday, sometimes twice a day." I went on to explain the basic situation. I told Heidi about Maddie's tattoo, I skipped anything related to

105

Maddie's convincing argument the other night when she talked me into watching Morton for a couple of days. I explained her mom's bike accident. I mentioned Maddie's Morton voice again, and that she had extended her stay for a few more days and that I thought it was because of this Buster guy and not necessarily her mom.

"So, you're about to join me in the same boat," Heidi said and raised her glass in a toast.

"Hunh?" I said in response.

"I've been dumped and you're about to be. All aboard," she said and we clinked glasses.

Chapter Twenty-Six

Given the wine I suspect both of us probably had a foggy memory of the early morning hours. I know I woke up with a smile, I could hear Heidi down the hall in the shower. Morton was asleep on the floor at the foot of the bed. It was raining just now and had been for most of the night.

Heidi returned from the bathroom maybe twenty minutes later. She already had her makeup on and a towel wrapped around her.

"How's the head?" I asked.

"I'll live," she said getting down on her knees and looking under the bed. "But right now I'm look-ing for my thong, what did you do with it? I want to be in the office and review some files for that inves-tors meet … oh, my, God. Morton, did you do this?" she said and held up the remnants of her thong. Basi-cally, about all that was left was an elastic band to wrap around her waist.

"Damn it, Morton," I said.

"Don't blame him, he probably learned it from you," she said then threw what was left of the thong at me.

"Can you stop and get one on the way?"

"What store is open to sell thongs at seven in the morning?"

"Look at it this way, every guy in your meeting would love to get into…."

"Don't even go there, you perv. Besides, I don't want Morton hearing that kind of talk."

"What?"

"You heard me. I'll just go au-natural to complement this exotic hair."

"Believe me, they'd love it. You should take a selfie and…."

"You are such a sleaze."

"You want me to go out and find some place open, maybe a twenty-four hour drugstore or something?"

"No, thanks, I might stop on the way and pick something up. Hope you enjoyed yourself, Morton."

He suddenly raised his head and his tail began to wag, thumping back and forth on the floor.

"I'd better get going," she said stepping into her dress.

"I'm tempted to make you stay. Just the thought of you without…."

"Stop," she said holding her hand up like a traffic cop. Then she bent down and gave me a kiss. "Thanks for what you said last night it meant a lot to me, Dev."

"And I did mean it, Heidi. You've nothing to be embarrassed about, well, except for maybe all the heads turning to look and wish they were with you."

"That's sweet. Thanks, I'll call you for my luggage, okay. I want to get into the office and be well prepared for these folks."

"Get out of here and give me a call when you can. And thanks for last night."

"Thank you, catch you later," she called from the staircase.

Chapter Twenty-Seven

Lake Phalen is located on the north end of St.
Paul. It was named after a somewhat nefarious early
pioneer, one Edward Phelan, an individual so beloved
that he fled early St. Paul in the 1840's after six
months incarceration and barely beating a murder rap.
He joined a wagon train headed west. Along the way,
his fellow travelers having had enough, murdered the
guy and left him in an unmarked grave somewhere on
the side of the trail.

I pulled into the park around the lake at ten
minutes before ten, just as the rain stopped and the
clouds parted to let the sun through. I parked a few
spaces over from Natasha's camper, then grabbed the
leash and took Morton on a quick walk to wear off
any after effects of Heidi's thong and hopefully calm
him down for a stay in my car. I knocked on the back
door of Natasha's camper at precisely ten o'clock, rat-
tling the glass louvers in the door. The park area was
filled with walkers and the occasional jogger.

"Yes," Natasha's voice groaned out.

"Dev Haskell, Natasha."

"We'll just be a minute," she called.

I waited more like fifteen minutes before the door
opened and a young guy, I guessed about twenty, no
more than twenty-five, called thanks over his shoulder. He looked over at me, winked and smiled then

exited across the parking lot and down the road without saying another word. Natasha and Princess Anastasia made their appearance a few minutes later.

"Good morning, Mr. Haskell, I hope you had a pleasant evening," Natasha said.

"Apparently we both did."

"Oh, umm, my contractor, he'll be working on the house while we're involved in the competition," she said using the Ivy League accent for emphasis.

"A twenty year old contractor, and on foot, who knew?"

She ignored me and walked out onto a large grassy field. There was a guy at the far end of the field throwing what looked like an orange tennis ball to a dog. Natasha took one look, turned to me and said, "Oh, that will never do. Mr. Haskell, would you be so kind as to ask that gentleman to leave. I can't have another dog near Princess Anastasia, especially this close to the competition. We've only a few days left. Would you mind terribly? Perhaps you might suggest some other venue to him."

"I'd be happy to try, but if he says no there's really nothing I can do about it. This is a public park."

She flashed a smile for just a nanosecond that was meant to be anything, but pleasant. Then, in that Ivy League accent said, "But still, please try, we've so much work to do."

With that she began working Princess Anastasia through her paces. I strolled about thirty yards over to talk to the guy, but as I got closer he called to his dog then tossed the ball in the opposite direction and began to walk away. That was probably a good thing because out here in the middle, the field was becoming a lot wetter than it appeared and I was beginning to sink into the ground. I glanced around. Natasha's back was to me, working the princess. I lingered for a moment or two then headed back, prepared to take credit for the pair's departure should she ask.

Over the course of the morning they were watched by various passers by, usually walkers who would stand for a minute or two then continue on their way. Two young mothers pushing strollers stopped for a rest on one of the park benches to sip coffee and watch. They sat there for about fifteen minutes before the kids began fussing and they moved on.

Natasha broke for lunch around one. I hurried over to my car and let Morton out. From what I could tell he hadn't begun to eat the driver's seat. I grabbed a Frisbee off the floor of the back seat and threw it around for some exercise.

I'd fling the Frisbee toward Morton and most times he was able to grab it in midair. Then he'd run back to me and drop it close to my feet. I'd been tossing the thing for a good twenty minutes. When I wasn't throwing the Frisbee, I was watching nice looking women ride past on bikes or push strollers around the lake path. Occasionally one would drive past in a car.

We were just about finished with the Frisbee when a car rolled past, slowing slightly as it neared the camper. It was a flat black Chevy Camaro with heavily tinted windows. I wouldn't have noticed it except as it rounded the curve in the road it appeared to list heavily toward the driver's side, almost like the shocks were broken.

I was pretty sure that wasn't the case. Most likely the shocks were fine, and the vehicle was responding to the dead weight it carried behind the wheel; I guessed a fat guy with thinning ginger colored hair and pork chop side burns. Fat Bastard from the other night. I could only hope he still had the gauze bandage across his forehead along with the black eyes. I wondered if he'd been able to replace his baseball bat.

I watched the car disappear around the bend, traveling deeper into the park. If I hurried I could jump in my car and I'd have half a chance of catching up to him. But then what? And, if I didn't catch up, missed him somehow and he came back this way, Natasha and Princess Anastasia would be alone and there was no telling what he would do.

We settled onto the grass next to the camper and waited for the door to open.

Natasha and Princess Anastasia exited the camper about fifteen minutes later. Morton gave a casual glance as the camper door opened and then was on his feet a half second later when the princess appeared. I barely got hold of him by the collar as he lunged forward in an effort to introduce himself.

"Inappropriate distraction, Mr. Haskell. I would find it preferable if your dog were not present," Natasha said as they strutted past us.

Princess Anastasia pranced by with her nose in the air not paying Morton the slightest attention.

"I'm afraid there may be a slight problem, Ma'am."

"Oh," Natasha stopped and turned. "Can't you simply place him in that car of yours?"

"Yeah, I'll do that, that's not the problem. But, I just recognized someone driving past. It may be nothing, but I had a run in with him the other night."

"Run in?"

112

I gave her a brief history, neglected to mention that it was Morton who left the guy knocked out on the sidewalk. I followed that with the part about the guy with the sandwich who ending up rolling, literally, in the street. Then I told her about getting the ID on the Mercedes, phoning Tommy Allesi and dropping the car off at The Lady Slipper.

"And what? You, for some unknown reason, didn't think this might be important? Didn't think I would be interested? How did you leave things with Mr. Allesi?"

"How did we leave things? Well, actually, Morton pissed on one of his bushes by the front door."

"What?" She smiled and laughed. "Oh, my, God. That is simply splendid."

"Yeah, I suppose. I don't know, I would guess our fat friend out there must have driven a lot of miles before he found us here. Unless, you might have some idea?"

"Me? You're suggesting that what? That somehow I informed Mr. Allesi or one of his henchmen as to our whereabouts this afternoon? Hardly, I can assure you. No, I'm afraid nothing quite so sinister. Unfortunately, this is a spot we used and enjoyed all last summer and fall and in my naïveté it hadn't occurred to me that Mr. Allesi would have seized on the possibility. My fault I'm afraid. So now, what exactly do you purpose?"

"I think you might as well get to work and we'll see what happens. Hopefully nothing will. I'll keep an eye out and then when you do leave I'll be here to make sure no one follows. Maybe choose a spot for tomorrow that's not a regular. Okay?"

Natasha nodded and then started putting the princess through her paces. They worked the remainder of
the afternoon. When I wasn't keeping my eyes peeled
in all directions I occasionally walked a few feet over
to my car to check on Morton. He seemed just fine.

Chapter Twenty-Eight

It was approaching dinner time and the park traffic had thinned out considerably. Hardly anyone was walking on the paths and only the occasional car passed by. Natasha seemed to be bringing things to a conclusion and had worked the princess through a series of drills that caused the two of them to circle further and further away from the camper and toward the center of the large green space we occupied.

I saw the car a moment after I heard it screeching around a curve. It suddenly shot up the handicap access ramp at the corner, across the sidewalk and then accelerated into the field headed toward Natasha and the princess.

The two of them turned to look in the direction of the engine roar as the flat black Camaro sped across the field swerving left and right and tossing clumps of wet sod out from the rear wheels.

"Natasha, Natasha, the car, run, he's coming for you," I called and started toward them.

Natasha gave some sort of hand command with a clap and took off running back toward the camper. Princess Anastasia pranced alongside of her, oblivious to the car closing behind them. I ran toward them, pulling my Sig Sauer out from the holster in the small of my back as they crossed the field. The Camaro cut sharply to the right in an effort to head them off.

Natasha watched as the Camaro fishtailed then skidded in a broad turn, tossing mud and debris behind it before righting itself and picking up speed. Mud and chunks of sod flew from the rear of the vehicle as it cut deep ruts across the sodden grass and plowed ahead, gaining on them.

Natasha cut at a ninety degree angle and the princess followed right alongside her.

The Camaro slid left and then right in an effort to adjust direction then suddenly ground to a halt in the middle of the field with the wheels buried up to the axels in mud. It shifted into reverse and spun the wheels which only served to mire the vehicle deeper into the muddy field.

Natasha glanced over her shoulder then made a bee line for the camper with Princess Anastasia beside her. I jogged a little further then walked the rest of the distance toward the Camaro, circling wide so that I came at it directly from behind.

I couldn't see anything through the dark tinted windows while the driver shifted into drive then back into reverse and continued to spin his wheels. I was maybe fifty feet away and had no desire to get any closer. The tinted windows remained rolled up.

I took careful aim with the Sig Sauer and fired a round at the rear tire, but couldn't tell if I hit the thing. The engine began to roar and the wheels spun in an effort to get out of there, but only succeeded in digging a little deeper hole. I fired twice more, after the third round I heard a definite hiss coming from the rear tire.

I walked a straight line back from the rear of the Camaro and out to the street, watching for any sign of a door opening or one of the windows lowering. By

116

the time I got back to Morton and my car, the camper
with Natasha and Princess Anastasia was gone. I
drove away and parked in a lot overlooking Lake Phelan. I put Morton on a leash, grabbed the Frisbee and
a knife out of the glove compartment then walked
back a quarter mile and sat on a park bench where I
watched the Camaro at a safe distance.

Eventually the driver's door was shouldered open
and none other than Fat Bastard cautiously looked
around before oozing out the door and into the mud.
Even from this distance I could see the black eyes and
the gauze across his forehead. He gave a quick waddle
around the vehicle, stared at the back tire I'd shot then
kicked the Camaro in the rear quarter panel, growled
something foul before he retraced his rutted, muddy
trail out of the field and toddled out of the park leaving a trail of muddy footprints.

I waited a good while before I headed over to the
Camaro. I tossed the Frisbee to Morton a number of
times along the way so we just looked like casual in-
vestigators. When we came alongside the car I
crouched down and pretended to inspect the car from
all sides, slitting the other three tires in the process.

I suppose I could have phoned 911, but that
might have led to some uncomfortable questions
about discharging a firearm in a city park. Besides, I
figured by now the car had quite possibly been reported as stolen, so what would be the point?

Chapter Twenty-Nine

I tossed the Frisbee back in the direction of my car and in twenty minutes we were headed home. On the way home Morton and I swung past the scene of the crime, Alexi's hair salon located on Grand Ave, a trendy retail street in town. The place was one of a series of single-story storefronts with two large windows on either side of the entrance. The name 'Head Case' in bright red letters was painted across the front of the building in a strange sort of script that looked like a five-year old might have written it. It seemed fitting that this was the place where Heidi's hair became multi colored and a portion of her head shaved.

I pulled into a parking place a couple of doors down and walked back to the salon. Looking through the windows it appeared there were three chairs, but only two were occupied.

A blonde woman was working on a customer in the middle chair, busily wrapping a handful of hair in tin foil. The woman in the chair had at least a dozen foil horns arranged around her skull.

"Can I help you?" A bubbly teenager asked from behind a counter as I walked in. The counter was actually a display case with pink lighting and black shelves. A variety of hair care products, presumably for sale, were arranged inside the display case.

The kid looked to be about sixteen and had close to a pound of various metal items imbedded around each ear. Her left eyebrow had three rings running through it. My first thought was "*What a strange place for a cigarette holder.*" A large blue bead hung from her bottom lip and matched the two smaller blue beads hanging from her nose ring. As she talked a silver ball running through her tongue clicked against her teeth and made it sound like she was tapping her toe in cadence to her speech.

I was tempted to ask if she had trouble going through airport security, instead I said, "I was wondering if I could get a haircut?"

"I suppose you can, and there's no one waiting if you want to just take this chair, I'll let Alexi know you're here," she said, indicating the open chair with her hand.

I glanced over at a guy reading the newspaper who hadn't bothered to look up at me. He didn't look like a good fit to the woman with the tin foil horns and I didn't think he was Alexi.

"Oh, don't worry, I guess he's just reading. It's actually my first day," the metal encrusted teen said.

Once I sat down she stepped through a door in the rear of the salon. The guy behind the newspaper continued to read. The woman with the tinfoil horns didn't look all that happy to have me sitting in the chair next to her. I settled into the chair, smiled and waited.

The chair closest to the window was filled to overflowing with a woman who was focused on a magazine with some sort of drying apparatus covering her head and loudly blowing air. I had the distinct feeling that all conversation had stopped once I came in the door.

Alexi stepped out of the rear area about five minutes later. He was about my size, sporting a neatly trimmed four-day beard with his blonde hair parted on both sides and then combed toward the center of his head. He looked familiar, but I couldn't place him. He had a small, red scar, sort of 'S' shaped just at the edge of his left eye,

"How can I help you?"

"I wanted a haircut?"

"A haircut," he said studying me. I felt like a Volkswagen Beetle getting the once over from a sports car enthusiast.

"Just a haircut?"

"Yeah, just a haircut."

"Well, you see we don't really do that sort of thing here. If you wanted to adjust your color, maybe become a little more current with your style, we could help. But just a haircut, no sorry, like I said we don't do that sort of thing here."

"You got a card. I might want to come back and have the color changed."

"Sure," he said and stepped over to the counter.

By the time I climbed out of the chair and followed he was holding his card out with a smile, I read the name on his card, Alexi Tarasenko. It rang a distant bell, I knew there was something, but still couldn't quite place him.

"Thanks for your time, I'll maybe be back if I need a color change."

"Sure thing, you might try the barber shop up about four blocks, they do a nice job and it won't cost you so much."

"Okay," I said and stuffed his card into my pocket.

As I walked back to my car I was more positive than ever that I knew Alexi from somewhere in the

120

distant past. I picked up some tacos for dinner, missed the call from Maddie and was waiting for Natasha to return the phone calls I'd made to her.

Chapter Thirty

We were in the den watching the <u>Big Lebowski</u>. Morton and I, eating Bar-B-Que potato chips and sharing a beer. The movie was right at the part where the Dude was being hustled into the back of Mr. Lebowski's limousine, "Hey, careful man, there's a beverage here." When my phone rang.

"Haskell Invest…."

"Did you get him?"

"Hi, Natasha. Are you all right?" I tossed a couple more chips down to Morton on the floor. He caught one in midair and lapped up the other on the first bounce before looking up at me expectantly.

"Just tell me you executed that malcontent."

"Um, actually no, sorry to disappoint."

"Why in heaven's name not?"

"Murder charges for one. I seem to have an aversion to them. He did have to leave his car out there in the middle of that field stuck in the mud. Most likely the police have impounded it by now. Where are you by the way?"

"We're at the airport."

"The airport, you're leaving town?"

"No, we're just spending the night in the parking ramp, up on the top level. There are regular patrols through here and I have to believe this is the absolute last place anyone would think of looking for us."

"Do you want me to come out there?"

There was a long pause before she said, "No, we'll be fine, but thank you."

"I would suggest that if you're going to work Princess Anastasia tomorrow you…."

"I most certainly am, I intend to win at Blessington and nothing, not even that homicidal maniac this afternoon will deter me in my quest."

"Okay, I get that, but maybe pick someplace they won't think of looking. My sense would be somewhere you've never been. For that matter we could report this to the police, file a complaint. If nothing else it might make things a little more difficult for the owner of that Camaro."

"Don't you worry, I fully intend to deal with him."

"Deal with him? You know who the hell it is?"

"Yes, that fool Denis Malloy, that's Denis, D-E-N-I-S, spelled like penis only with a 'D' and lacking all of the more intriguing characteristics."

"You know this guy?"

"It's a long story. I'll phone you with our whereabouts tomorrow."

"Wait Natasha, Natasha," I said, but she'd already hung up.

I tried to phone her back a couple of times, but she didn't answer.

Heidi phoned about five minutes after I got off the phone with Natasha.

"Did you get the image I sent you?"

"Image? Are you back to taking selfies again?"

"You wish. No, from my investors meeting today, after it was over I had my picture taken with some of the bigger investors."

"So, it went well, the meeting?"

"Better than I could have hoped for, but I really appreciated the advice about taking a more positive attitude, it made all the difference in my meeting. In fact, I got a number of compliments. And, from people who usually aren't in the business of giving compliments."

"I'm glad to be of service."

"One guy, very successful, in fact he was my biggest worry because he can be so temperamental and difficult to deal with even at the best of times, he sort of took center stage and convinced a number of the others that the investment we were looking at, the one that had under performed was really under valued which presented an even better opportunity. Then he ponied up on the spot for another five thousand shares. Just like that, and he talked a couple of others into doing the same thing. I ended up having a very successful day. So thanks, I intend to make it up to you."

"Maybe you should leave your thong at home more often."

"That wasn't it, you sleaze ball. It was the investment potential I presented to them."

"How does it sound if I come over tonight? I could bring your makeup case and the other stuff and you could explain some of your investment potential."

"Yeah, sure, that's what you'd be coming over for, investment potential."

"In a manner of speaking."

"I'm making sure my doors are locked right now. Anyway, thanks for being there and sorry if I was crabby."

"You weren't crabby," I said, but she had already hung up.

124

I checked my cell, sure enough there was a text message from Heidi. I don't like texting, I'm not a fan of text messages. I clicked on the message anyway, there were just two words, sort of, "*Gr8 mtg*" and an image.

I clicked on the image then waited while it slowly came up on my cell. Heidi, in what looked like a large conference room with maybe a dozen guys. My first thought was none of them had the slightest idea she wasn't wearing a thong. She looked gorgeous despite the bizarre hair colors. I quickly glanced at their faces then paused on the one guy who looked familiar.

His dark hair was slicked back, he had a goatee, wore an opened collar shirt with an expensive looking jacket. I could see a gold chain just peeking out from beneath the right cuff on his shirt. I phoned Heidi back.

"Did I not make myself clear? I don't want you coming over tonight," she answered.

"Hey, just checking your photo out. Everyone looks happy. Let me ask you a question. The guy on the far end of the group, with the goatee, is that Tommy Allesi?"

"How do *you* know him?"

"Chance meeting. You ever hear of a guy named Denis Malloy?"

"No, I don't think so?"

"So tell me about Tommy."

"He's the investor I mentioned who purchased another five-thousand shares and got some others to do the same. To tell you the truth he saved the day. Wow, who knew, small world, isn't it?"

"Very small. Actually, it's more like I know *of* him, I've only met him once or twice, but I've never really been formally introduced."

"I might be able to arrange that."

"What, an introduction?"

"Mmm-hum, he gave me a couple of tickets to some sort of private recital he's giving, day after tomorrow. I guess he's really into classical music and he plays the piano. Interested?"

"Very, I'm your date and then we could discuss your payment plan on that debt you owe."

"We could," she said and hung up.

Chapter Thirty-One

Natasha phoned just a little after nine the following morning.

"Mr. Haskell, we're just about to head out to Hidden Falls Regional Park, do you know where that is?"

"I do. And you're sure your friend Denis won't be looking for you there?"

"I've no idea if he'll be looking for us there. I do know it would not make the least bit of sense if he did. I haven't set foot in that area for at least twenty-five years. I think the last time I was there was to protest the Gulf War and Princess Anastasia has never been there."

"Okay, sounds good. How was sleeping at the airport?"

"Sleeping was fair, at least up until about five-fifteen this morning when it seemed a plane was either landing or taking off every three-and-a-half minutes. Every time they flew over it sounded for all the world as if they were no more than six inches overhead. At that point it began to grow rather tiresome."

"I can only imagine. Listen, I'll head over to Hidden Falls and meet you there. Would you mind remaining in the camper until I arrive and look things over, just to be on the safe side? Shouldn't take more than a minute or two, I'll knock on your door as soon as I'm finished."

"We'll await your arrival, but please arrive in a timely manner. We've a good deal of work to accomplish today."

"I'm heading out the door as we speak," I said.

Natasha hung up and I wandered upstairs to find my jeans. I pulled a sweatshirt on, stuffed the Sig Sauer in the small of my back and grabbed my jacket off the hook in the hallway.

The moment Morton saw me reaching for my jacket he began prancing at the kitchen door. "Calm down, pal, we're going. Come on, let's get in the car."

We were only about a fifteen minute drive away, that was if we hit all the stop lights. We made it through all but two of them. Natasha's camper was waiting for us in the parking lot by the time we arrived.

Hidden Falls Regional Park features a small water fall a few hundred yards from the banks of the Mississippi river. The park has a paved parking lot and paths, cut grass, permanent picnic tables, fire pits, and two large, open areas with roofs overhead to protect from the rain or sun. You have to drive through a gated entrance and down along the side of a bluff to enter the parking lot.

Natasha's camper and my car were the only two vehicles in the park this morning. I made a quick sweep of the area then pulled alongside the camper and knocked on the door.

"Coming, Mr. Haskell," Natasha called in response and then opened the camper door a moment later. I noticed her exit seemed to be just a little slower this morning and as if in response she said, "Oh, I'm getting to old to be sleeping in this camper for a week."

128

She proceeded to go through a stretching routine where I occasionally could hear her knees, hips, spine and shoulders snap and pop. I knew the feeling. Princess Anastasia sat off to the side looking straight ahead.

When she appeared to have completed her stretching I said, "Your friend, Denis Malloy what can you tell me about him?"

"Tell you, about Denis? There really isn't all that much to him actually, other than his girth, well and constant disappointment. Poor man has to be a heart attack just waiting to happen, don't you think?" she said, but didn't wait for an answer.

"I've known him since my early school days I daresay he was a few years behind me. His Father and Grandfather did rather well. I think one of his grandfathers was a district judge of some sort. I'm afraid the poor devil never quite seemed to cop on, as they say. Unfortunately, I think the way in which the world works has always remained a bit of a mystery to Denis."

"You'd never guess to look at the man today, I mean, well he's simply dreadful, appalling. But, there was a time when he was quite the man about town. Of course he took up with one of the Mieze girls, which never served anyone well. I believe her name was Chastity, talk about a misnomer. Poor Denis never really seemed to recover once she ran off with some sort of rock and roll character."

"What does he do?"

"Do? I don't think Denis does anything, now that you mention it I don't believe he ever has."

"How does he pay bills? He apparently has enough money for a nice car."

"I think the family found their initial success in the dry goods business, from there on to only God knows what. They've always been connected so the term "business" can cover a multitude of sins. And, well I suppose we saw the result of that yesterday. Frightening, actually."

She began doing jumping jacks at this point, counting out a sort of cadence half to herself. When she stopped she stretched her arms out and began to rotate them first clockwise and then counter clock-wise. Then she bent down at the hip extending her arms toward the toes of her shoes, bending up and down, each time extending down maybe an inch further toward the ground.

"You should try this, Mr. Haskell, an excellent way to start ones day."

"I have my own routine that I work on."

"Yes, I'm sure you do," she said looking like she was biting her tongue on the remainder of her comment.

"Well, there we have it. As to your questions about Denis, I wouldn't concern yourself. Success, in whatever the undertaking, has always seemed to elude Denis. I would simply add yesterday's episode to a long list of failures. No use crying over spilt milk, as they say. Let's just be thankful we were dealing with an individual who is that inept. Come on Princess," she said, then clapped her hand and Princess Anastasia dutifully rose and followed without looking left or right.

I glanced over and caught sight of Morton pacing back and forth across the back seat of my car.

Chapter Thirty-Two

It was late afternoon when Maddie called.

"Let me talk to Morton, Dev," she said not wasting time on a greeting or asking how things were going.

Morton was in the back of my car. I'd just checked on him about fifteen minutes earlier and he was asleep, comfortably curled up in a patch of sunlight and I wasn't about to disturb him.

"Hold on, he's right here," I said then proceeded to pant into my cellphone.

Maddie kicked into her Morton voice. "How's my baby, Morton? It's mommy. Are you being a good boy? Do you miss me? I miss you. I've been so busy, Buster took me out for dinner last night and this morning he made me a special omelet for breakfast. It was in the shape of a heart and we shared it and then we had champagne and I'm just having the most wonderful time."

She went on like that for a few more minutes. I wasn't sure if I should interrupt her and tell her Morton was throwing up or would it just be better to disconnect. I split the difference.

"Hi, Maddie, Dev. Hey, Morton just took off after the Frisbee, it's a gorgeous day and we're out getting some exercise. How's your mom doing?"

"She's doing pretty well, I might have to stay a couple more days, just to make sure she's got her therapy routine down."

131

I wasn't all that sure her mother's therapy routine was Maddie's top priority.

"A couple more days?"

"Yeah, hope it's not a problem. Morton's doing alright, isn't he? He sounded good on the phone. Is he eating properly?"

First of all, that was me on the phone, and second, he just finished a pulled pork sandwich for lunch. He probably hasn't eaten this well, ever.

"Yeah, he loves that healthy dog food. Not to worry, we're getting on famously and we're the two dullest guys in town."

"Perfect, well I'd better ring off, lots to do," she said and hung up.

The remainder of the afternoon was even less eventful. Natasha continued to work Princess Anastasia and just like on past days they drew the occasional passersby who momentarily stopped to watch. No one interrupted their routine.

Natasha clapped her hands a little after six and they headed back toward the camper.

Morton barked as they approached and I could see him pacing in the back seat.

"Oh, good lord, where does the time go?"

"Where to tonight?" I asked as Natasha opened the door to the camper for the princess and watched her hop inside.

"Tonight? I haven't given it much thought other than stopping at home to reload the suitcase and toss our laundry down the chute. I've got someone who comes in to help."

No doubt. "But you're not going to stay at home are you?"

"Perhaps just for a bite to eat, but nothing more than that."

"Maybe I should follow you and make sure no one is hanging around."

"I can assure you that sort of babysitting will not be necessary. I'm perfectly capable of monitoring the situation."

"You sure? It's no trouble to follow…."

"I really think I'm more than capable of dealing with whatever sort of situation might present itself, Mr. Haskell." Then she shot a brief smile in my direction that was meant to be anything, but pleasant.

"All right, maybe I'll just follow you home and…."

"Please don't. Private school for the first twelve years, not to mention the Sorbonne, four years at Radcliffe, two Masters degrees. I must have learned something, somewhere," she said now comfortably settling into her Ivy League accent.

"Okay, just want to make sure everything goes well. You're just a couple days away from the show."

"Competition," she corrected. "Believe me, no one is more aware of the timeframe than myself. On the one hand it seems to be taking forever to arrive and on the other, well just where in God's name did the time go?"

"Alright, you'll call me with your location for tomorrow."

"Just as soon as I know, I'll phone. Au revoir," she said, then stepped into her camper and locked the door.

I noticed next to the bumper sticker that read "Uppity" someone had penned in the word "bitch" using a black marker. I thought for a moment about

133

knocking on the door to point it out to her, but then decided I would just follow orders and drive home.

Chapter Thirty-Three

Over a beer and a couple of Bratwurst I got on the computer and looked up Alexi Tarasenko. I was bumbling my way through a program called Intelius. I bought a pirated copy from a pal down in Kansas City last year. It took a while, but I finally had a mug shot of Alexi up on the screen.

He looked different, but then again the mug shot was twenty years old. The little 'S' shaped scar near the left eye was apparent, he was definitely the guy I'd spoken with yesterday afternoon at the Head Case salon.

The mug shot was from the late '90's. Alexi had initially faced a number of Breaking and Entering charges along with an aggravated assault charge, but he ended up only serving eighteen months in Lino Lakes. My guess was there had been some sort of plea bargain arrangement. From what I could determine looking online, he'd taken the time served to heart and been straight ever since. Other than the crime he committed with Heidi's hair he appeared to be a solid citizen.

I turned the computer off and settled in on the couch, Morton was stretched out on the floor. We were watching another worthless movie, sharing a beer, and more Bar-B-Que potato chips. After Maddie's phone call this afternoon I was half tempted to go out and get Morton a bag of Big Mac's just to show her. But, that would have been unfair to Morton and the guy was growing on me.

My cellphone rang just as the Cougar mom in the lousy movie we were watching returned to college and entered the wrong locker room. I was about five minutes from falling asleep.

"Haskell…."

"Mr. Haskell, I can hear someone prowling around outside."

"Natasha?"

"They were at the camper a few minutes ago, then the back door. I heard them fiddling with a window just a moment ago."

"Where are you?"

"At my home, I didn't want to waste this shiraz I'd opened."

"I'm on my way, hang up and call the cops."

"I'm afraid that's not an option at this juncture."

"What?"

"Please hurry, Mr. Haskell I think I hear them again at that window."

"Take the princess and get upstairs, I'm just a few minutes away."

I sped over to Natasha's house in less than four minutes and pulled to a quick stop in front of her driveway, blocking it. I kept a hand on the Sig Sauer tucked into my waistband and let Morton out of the back seat.

"Come on boy, let's check it out."

Off his leash and at Princess Anastasia's house, Morton bounded out of the car, ignored my direction and made a dash for the front door. He barked at the door as he landed on the front porch, sounding like a canine version of "*A Streetcar Named Desire.*"

136

"Morton, come this way, Morton, come on," I called as I headed up the driveway. The camper was parked haphazardly with two of the wheels a good foot off the concrete driveway and resting on the lawn. The grass was in desperate need of cutting, but you could still see a substantial indentation where Natasha had driven onto the grass. As I walked around the camper I noticed all four tires had been slit. The rear door was still locked.

I walked past the camper, up the driveway and into the backyard. The back of the house had a jungle of leafy vines climbing up the exterior of the house for two and a half stories. The leaves were so thick that you couldn't see any of the buff colored stone and over the past years the vines had grown over a number of the windows. I wondered how anyone could even find a window let alone *fiddle* with it. The branches on the vines were thick enough that you could almost climb them, although that would be a foolhardy enterprise and no one would be that stupid.

The backyard was enclosed on all sides by a stone wall and a double garage. The wall and the garage were constructed from the same stone as the house although from this perspective you couldn't see the stone on the house with all the vines having taken over. The roof of the garage was covered with the same red glazed tiles as the house. It looked like there were gardens along the walls and against the garage, or at least there had been at one time. Now, they were little more than patches of weeds with the occasional dead rose bush and an abandoned trellis or two scattered throughout.

A wooden deck that looked at least twenty years old ran the length of the back of the house. The wood

137

on the deck appeared weathered, cracked and splintered. The deck itself was littered with two grills, a picnic table missing a leg, a variety of aluminum lawn chairs in various states of disrepair, the frame of an old bicycle, a large plastic trash bin, snow shovels, a half dozen paint cans and what was left of a child's inflatable wading pool. The lawn mower that had been discarded in front of the back door entering onto the deck suggested no one had walked out from inside the house in at least five years. More paint cans were stacked beneath the deck.

I walked to the far side of the yard and looked for anything out of place. Frankly, it was hard to tell with all the junk laying around. I walked around a glass top table, minus the glass, and back toward the driveway when I heard a loud snap overhead. I crouched and pulled the Sig Sauer from my waist.

I heard a couple of grunts, another loud snap and then a voice shouted "No, no, don't. Oh, shit," just as large body from up around the second story dropped out of the vines covering the back wall. The body let loose with a high pitched scream on its brief descent until it struck the picnic table. The table collapsed under the impact at the same time I heard a loud "uff." One of the grills seemed to explode in a cloud of ash and a stack of aluminum lawn chairs fell over onto the remnants of the picnic table. The body just laid there, face down and very still.

I hurried up four creaky steps to the deck with my Sig Sauer aimed at the body that had just fallen out of the vines overhead. Even in the dark it looked vaguely familiar and the moment I saw the mutton chops and the thinning ginger hair I remembered, *Denis, like penis only spelled with a D.*

138

Denis Malloy was lying very still. I kicked him with my foot and got no reaction so I pulled out my cell and called 911.

Chapter Thirty-Four

"And you have no idea what he was doing up there?" the officer asked, not for the first time. As he asked the question he absently scanned the upper most portion of back of the vine covered house

"Like I told your partner," my friend called and said she thought she heard someone trying to break into her camper."

"That thing out front?"

"Yeah, right, the camper."

"So, I ran over, checked it out and noticed all the tires had been slit. I know she'd driven it earlier this evening so someone had to have slit them in the past couple of hours. I didn't see anyone out front, the camper was locked so I wandered back here to look around and then that guy just sort of fell out of the vines up there on the house. He was up near the second floor, over by that window." I pointed to the approximate area Denis had fallen from.

The cop shook his head and followed my hand with his eyes across the second story of the back of the house to where a bare patch of buff colored stone shown through the tangle of vines and leaves. I guessed Denis must have made a futile, last minute grab in an attempt to stay up there and tore the vines off on his way down.

"We just might win this week's pool for the dumbest criminal," the cop said.

Four paramedics were in the process of hoisting Denis up on a stretcher. A gurney was waiting at the base of the steps leading off of the deck, but they were afraid they wouldn't be able to get the gurney back down the stairs with the likes of Denis strapped in. They groaned as they lifted the stretcher and one of them growled out, "Oh my God."

They grunted and groaned their way across the deck, stepping over paint cans, lawn chairs, paper bags filled with bottles and cans and last, but not least the formerly inflatable wading pool. The stairs creaked loudly as they cautiously stepped down, taking one step at a time. Another paramedic wheeled the gurney alongside and they set the stretcher down on the gurney.

"Jesus Christ," one of the paramedics exclaimed and shook his wrists to get some of the feeling back in his hands. Someone was cinching belts across Denis lying on the gurney just as another cop slapped a handcuff around Denis's wrist then secured the other end to the rail of the gurney.

"Good to go?" a paramedic asked.

"Get him out of here," another responded.

"And you don't reside here?" the cop I was talking to asked.

"No, like I said she just called and I came over. Natasha Kominski. I think she's inside, giving a statement to either your partner or some other officer."

He nodded then said, "Given everything piled up back here I'm guessing we'll have to have the city inspectors over to check things out. I'm afraid we don't have a choice, its routine. Amazing how folks can get behind so quickly," he said scanning all the junk piled up around the yard.

Just giving a quick glance in the dark I had the feeling all the junk had been accumulating for quite a while.

"Looks like it was a pretty fancy place at one time, what's it like inside?" he asked.

"Never been in there. I've only seen the interior of one room and that was from the front porch. It looked pretty nice, but, well who knows."

"Come on, what do you say we go check it out?"

With all the excitement I had completely forgotten about Morton. Fortunately he was still on the front porch gazing longingly through the window of the front door.

"That her dog?" the cop asked as we climbed the steps to the porch.

"No, actually he's with me. Come here, Morton. Thanks for waiting for me," I said and scratched him behind the ears.

The officer held the door open for me, and Morton quickly walked inside as if he belonged.

"I think everyone is back in the kitchen," the cop said as Morton wandered off in another direction.

"I should probably grab him," I said and started to follow Morton.

"This'll just take a minute, come on," he smiled, but it was one of those things cops say that's more like an order instead of a suggestion. I watched for a brief moment as Morton disappeared around a corner. The cop eyed me, waiting. I smiled and then followed him into the kitchen. I glanced over my shoulder one final time for Morton, but he was no where to be seen.

Natasha was talking at the kitchen table while one cop took notes and another one pushed a recording device toward the center of the table. She was using her Ivy League accent again and had a look on her face like she couldn't believe she had to deal with the lower classes here, in the very sanctity of her inherited home.

"It's been going on for the better part of a week. The most recent incident was yesterday, at Lake Phalen. That maniac attempted to run down Princess Anastasia and myself while we were going through our obedience drills. Did I mention we're competing in less than three days in The Blessington?"

"Yes, I've got that in my notes," one of the cops said.

"And you've known this individual for how long?"

"Denis? Oh since we were children. Well, here's my friend, Mr. Haskell, I didn't know who else to call so I phoned him and he graciously came right over, thank God. It's been weeks since I've seen you, sorry to drag you into this mess," Natasha said then sort of flared her eyes in the hopes I got the message."

We chatted on for another twenty minutes or so before the cops left. Natasha stood out on the front porch waving goodbye. I was standing behind her in the entryway.

"Oh my, a rather busy night. I don't know about you, but I could use a glass of wine. Pardon me for just a moment while I run to the loo," she said then headed toward a door on the far side of the darkened dining room.

Once she closed the bathroom door behind her I immediately set off in search of Morton. He wasn't in the kitchen, the living room, the dining room, a library or the front parlor. I headed up the elaborate staircase calling his name softly. I checked what looked like an office, a TV room, a couple of bedrooms and a bathroom before I found him.

He was in a small bedroom, sort of standing just below an open window. "Morton, what the hell have you been do…." I suddenly saw her beneath him, Princess Anastasia. They were locked in romantic embrace, or coitus as Natasha had referred to it the other day.

"Morton, stop it, no bad dog, bad dog," I whispered, Morton looked like he had a different thought. Princess Anastasia let out a long low groan. I heard a creak on the staircase as Natasha began to make her way upstairs,

"Mr. Haskell, Mr. Haskell, where did you run off to? Are you up here?" Natasha called.

"Morton, come on, man, stop it, the two of you, stop it, now."

"Mr. Haskell, are you up here, answer me." I heard her reach the top of the staircase, mumble some sort of invective as she headed down the darkened hallway in the direction of the three of us.

I made a move toward Morton just as he climbed off the princess and she let off another deep, throaty, satisfied growl.

"Oh, well I see you found them," Natasha said from the doorway behind me.

"I'm sure I can explain. I didn't think that…."

"No need to explain, I won't deny it," she said walking past me toward the small single bed pushed up against the wall.

"I watched you arrive, and then, as you walked up the driveway I heard a noise from the back of the house. I followed it with my eyes as it seemed to rise

144

up the wall. That damned fool, Denis attempting to climb those vines and get in via this window I'd neglected to close."

She reached onto the bed and held up a pair of garden clippers. "My intention wasn't to have him fall. It's just that once we took your advice and came upstairs I was afraid that bastard might come in through a window. I merely intended to cut the branch and deny him access. I'd no idea that he'd fall," she said looking like she didn't believe her own words.

"Did you tell this to the police?"

"Not in so many words, they never really asked."

"So when I heard him plead "*No, no, don't,*" he was talking to you?"

"Quite possibly."

"Well, it seems to have worked in your favor. I would guess Denis won't be around between now and The Blessington to bother you. Look, it's late and we should probably get going, come on Morton," I said and we left Natasha in the bedroom holding the pair of clippers with a very satisfied looking Princess Anastasia.

Chapter Thirty-Five

On the way home I lectured Morton about proper guest behavior, not screwing the hostess and the importance of just saying 'no'. It didn't seem to make an impression. We resumed our positions on the couch, or the floor in Morton's case and promptly fell asleep.

Heidi's phone call woke me at nine the following morning.

"Are we still on for tonight?"

"Tonight?" I groaned and sat up on the couch trying to remember what we had planned.

"Figures, you said you wanted to go with me to my investor's concert. Tommy Allesi. I told you he sent me tickets and you said you wanted me to introduce you to him."

"Oh, yeah. Umm, I'd still like to tag along if you're going."

"Okay, I'll pick you up at six-thirty, don't be late. And please, wear something presentable, I don't want you embarrassing me."

"Embarrassing you?"

"Dev, this is business for me, important business. I don't want you screwing anything up. Tommy Allesi is an important client, one of, if not *the* most important client at the moment. Okay?"

"I get it, not to worry."

"Thank you. Just wear something nice, all right?"

"Don't I always?"

"Don't even go there," she said and hung up.

I phoned Natasha about a half hour later and ended up leaving a message. I phoned her again a little after ten and when I was dumped into her message center I put Morton in the car and we headed back over to her home.

There was a van from a local service station parked in her driveway and a guy was busy replacing the tires on her camper. It looked like he was just starting on the third tire. I left Morton in the car and climbed the steps to the front porch. What looked like breakfast dishes and a tea pot where scattered around the wicker coffee table at the end of the porch. I rang her doorbell.

"Yes, Mr. Haskell," she said a minute later after she opened the door.

"Sorry to bother you. It's just that I hadn't heard anything and wanted to be sure you were okay."

She flashed a seductive smile and said "We're fine, thank you."

"Were you planning to work with Princess Anastasia today?"

"Yes, of course, actually we're in the middle of our warm-up. But, as you can see we're unable to travel anywhere until that gentleman has completed his tasks. Four slit tires, nothing that a thousand dollars won't cure," she said nodding in the direction of her camper.

"To be quite honest, Princess Anastasia seems, I'm not quite sure, distracted, or perhaps ambivalent? I'm afraid the events of last night may have caused her to lose her focus."

Morton, you idiot, I thought.

"We're working up in the ballroom on the third floor. I think for the time being I'd like as little interruption as possible and hopefully we'll be able to regain her focus in time for The Blessington."

"How about I just stay here, outside, keep an eye on things and once your camper is ready to go I'll ring the doorbell."

"That would be perfect. The gentleman from the service station has my credit card information so he needn't interrupt. If you'd be so kind as to run interference I'll return to getting Princess Anastasia refocused." With that she flashed another seductive smile then closed the door, locked it and headed for the staircase.

Chapter Thirty-Six

I sat on the front porch for another forty-five minutes watching walkers, joggers, bikers and the traffic pass by. The service station guy had rolled the slit tires to the back of his van and was loading them up when I walked over to him.

"I guess you got everything you need?" I said.

"Yeah, good to go," he said without looking up then tossed another tire into the back of his van.

"I'll let her know you're finished."

He tossed the final tire in the back then closed the double doors, took a rag out of his back pocket and proceeded to wipe his hands.

"You maybe take a little advice?" he said.

"What's that?"

"I don't know how much dope you got stored in that thing," he glanced over at the camper. "But I could smell it just changing these tires. I know they lightened the law a bit, but from what I could smell I'd say you got a hell of a lot more than a couple of ounces. You get nailed with what I suspect you got in there, you're probably looking at maybe twenty years, close to a quarter million in fines and that don't even start to cover your legal costs. You might want to think about that."

"Dope?"

"Look, whatever. I sure as hell ain't gonna narc on ya, but a word to the wise. Right now you're playing with fire. Wouldn't take much for someone to catch on is all I'm saying. You have a nice day, tell the lady thanks and ah, you be careful."

With that he climbed into his van and drove off.

I walked around the camper sniffing the air. Now that he mentioned it, yeah I could smell dope.

I let Morton out of the car and tossed the Frisbee to him for about twenty minutes then put him back in the car. I went up to the door and rang the door bell.

Natasha opened the door a few minutes later. I was sitting in the wicker couch gazing out at the street watching the foot traffic. The breakfast dishes were still scattered over the wicker coffee table, but I'd moved the tea pot so I could put my feet up.

"Mr. Haskell, I see your man is finished. I'm thinking about returning to Hidden Falls, how does that strike you?"

"Sounds fine. Say, could we talk for just a moment?"

"That's about all the time I have, a moment. What is it?"

"The guy who changed the tires on your camper, he added a note of caution."

"Oh good heavens, don't tell me, it's the brakes, isn't it?"

"Actually no, it's the dope."

"I beg your pardon."

"The dope you've got stashed in there. I didn't pick up on it until he mentioned it, but you can smell it just standing next to the camper. He thought it could lead to some potential problems. Actually, I think his quote was something like, *"twenty years and a quarter of a million in fines."*

Natasha put a hand on her cocked hip, clenched her lower jaw and turned on the Ivy League accent.

150

"This nation's stance on cannabis has been ridiculous to the point of…."

"Please, Natasha, I didn't mention this to get into a discussion about the nations drug policy. I do know you have to have a pretty fair amount stored in there to be able to pick a scent up outside. I was able to do that, so was that service station guy. It's not a huge leap to see the wrong sort of individual getting wind of it, pardon the pun."

"What do you intend to do?"

"Do? Nothing, I'm just warning you, I picked up on it and if I can, so will someone else. Maybe that's what Tommy Allesi or vine climbing Denis was concerned about. I don't know. I'm just telling you the way you have it hidden isn't very safe, for you or Princess Anastasia. That's all on that subject. I do have one more question."

"I think we agreed you would be paid upon completion."

"Yeah, that's fine, but it wasn't my question. I wanted to know why you suggested to the cops last night we hadn't seen one another for the past few weeks? They didn't ask me and so I didn't offer, but if they do ask I would have to tell them the truth, that we have a contract and that we've worked together everyday for almost the past week."

"I just didn't want them to get the wrong impression."

"Wrong impression?"

"If they knew I had hired you, a private investigator, that could possibly lead to questions, far beyond the Blessington Show," she said and glanced over at the camper. "I appreciate your concern and as it happens I'll be making the appropriate adjustment within the next twenty-four hours. Satisfied?"

"I guess for now."

"Splendid, let's get to work then. Why don't you go and secure the Hidden Falls site, Princess Anastasia and I will follow along shortly."

Chapter Thirty-Seven

The rest of the afternoon was uneventful. I did notice the princess giving the occasional glance toward Morton pacing in the back seat of my car, much to Natasha's dismay. I approached her toward the end of the afternoon.

"Natasha, I've got a meeting I have to attend this evening and I'm going to have to leave a little early."

"How early?"

"Now, actually."

"But I haven't finished and we've barely a day left."

"This concerns your situation, you and Princess Anastasia, I don't want to go into too much just now, but I should have a tighter handle on things later this evening."

"If it's something that concerns the two of us I think we certainly have a right to be made aware of what, exactly is happening."

"Nothing's happening. I'm just meeting with some people and want to get a little broader picture is all."

"You're not making any sense. Is this related to our earlier discussion?"

"No."

She looked like she didn't believe me. I didn't want to tell her I was just going to Tommy Allesi's piano concert.

"Well, then, apparently we're finished for the day. Come along Princess Anastasia," she said then clapped her hand twice and the two of them marched off toward the camper. The princess gave a lengthy glance toward Morton, he stared back longingly at her from the back seat of my car.

Chapter Thirty-Eight

I was standing out on the curb when Heidi
picked me up. As I climbed into the car she said,
"That's what you're wearing?" by way of a greeting. I
had on black slacks, a black shirt and a light colored
sport coat.

"Having seen your client twice, he was sort of
dressed like this both times. What? Do you think I
look too formal?"

She pulled away from the curb shaking her head.

"Where is this thing anyway, that country club of
his, The Lady Slipper?"

"No, it's actually at Central High School," she
said pushing the car to a Heidi speed, a good ten miles
above the posted limit.

"Central?"

"Yeah, I don't know, maybe it's about the acous-
tics or something. I know they have a music auditorium, but the reception afterward is at the Lady Slipper. Maybe he invited a lot of people and he has a big
crowd coming."

We pulled into the high school parking lot, then
pulled out a couple of minutes later and parked on the
street because the lot was already full.

"I guess you were right, looks like he invited a lot
of people."

"And families, look at all the little kids," Heidi
said.

"There must be some other event going on here tonight, a kindergarten open house or something."

"They don't have kindergarten in high school, Dev," she said as we climbed the stairs to the front door. Once in, a large sign that read "Music Recital" with an arrow directed us and we followed the flow of the crowd drifting down the hallway. There was the occasional individual dressed in a suit coat or business attire, but I had the distinct impression they were just coming from work and they usually had some child holding their hand.

"Kind of a young crowd for Mozart," I said to Heidi.

"Maybe he invited all his neighbors or his grand children and their friends. Hey, better turn your phone off so we don't interrupt his concert," she said and opened her purse.

I pulled the phone out of my pocket and put it on airplane mode.

The auditorium was full and we had to settle into seats about three rows from the stage. Kids were running up and down the aisle, parents were attempting to direct and the noise level was up there around the danger level. I would have killed for a pair of ear plugs. Heidi didn't say anything, but I could sense the wheels turning in her head wondering "*What the hell?*"

At precisely 6:40, ten minutes after the advertised start the lights in the auditorium dimmed and the noise level gradually subsided. A moment later a conservatively dressed woman stepped out from behind the curtain and stood in front of the microphone. A child cried from somewhere off to the right.

156

"Thank you all for attending our spring concert. We will begin with our first graders and there will be a brief ten-minute intermission following grade four. Our first piece, The Flower Song, will be played by Cynthia Clarken." Then she picked up the microphone and walked off stage as the curtain opened. A very little girl sat behind a rather large piano and began to play after getting some sort of cue from offstage.

"Is it his kids or grand kids playing?" I whispered.

Heidi shook her head then signaled me to be quiet. It took a good hour listening to about thirty-five kids before we got through the fourth grade and made it to the intermission. Finally the curtains closed and everyone applauded.

"I'm gonna go find the bar, you want something?" I said.

"Dev, this is a grade school concert, they aren't going to have a bar?"

"What?" I half shrieked.

"Lower your voice, I think you'll live."

"No bar?"

Some woman carrying a three year old asleep on her shoulder gave me a disapproving stare as she walked past.

"Are you sure we're in the right place?"

Heidi's look suggested the conversation was over. After fifteen minutes the ten minute intermission was finished, the lights dimmed and gradually the noise level subsided. At least the music was beginning to improve from the starter tunes the younger kids had been playing although they were all better than anything I could do. We sat through another forty-five minutes of various kids grinding through their music and then the same woman walked back on stage with the microphone. Close to two hours of kids pounding on the piano seemed to do nothing to improve her attitude.

"Ladies and gentleman, we'd like you to remain seated for one more performance tonight. Our benefactor and level five student, Mr. Thomas Allesi."

Heidi nudged me in the ribs and we started clapping along with everyone else as Tommy strolled onto the stage. He was dressed in a black tux with tails, a starched white collar with a black bow tie and he carried sheet music. As he placed the sheet music on the piano I caught the glint from the gold chain around his wrist.

He settled onto the piano bench and focused on the sheet music for a moment. The auditorium was still with the exception of a little voice from behind us starting to say something and immediately getting cut off with a "Shhh-hhh".

Tommy held his hands up about shoulder height for a couple of seconds before he attacked the keyboard. He was playing some jazz thing that I'd forgotten the name of. It took a few notes, but I definitely recognized the piece, not because it was something played over and over in movies. I recognized the tune because I'd heard it before, at least three different times tonight, the fifth grade level had played it, without sheet music. And, truth be told those kids had done a better job of it.

As he fought his way through the piece, I thought I heard someone off to the left sort of groan. There was a muffled chuckle from a few rows behind us and then Tommy swept his hands across the keyboard, swayed back and forth on the piano bench, glanced out into the crowd, suddenly focused on me for a brief moment and hit the wrong chord.

It took just a second, but the error was glaring and the gasp from the audience didn't help. To his credit Tommy regained his composure and moved on to finish. He stood for the polite applause, bowed, then focused on me with a look that suggested "*What the hell are you doing here?*" His cold stare was just long enough to register, and if it wasn't directed at you I'm not sure anyone else would even notice, but it had been aimed at me and I noticed.

"God, he doesn't look too happy," Heidi said as she clapped.

"Probably still upset with that bad note. I bet he practiced that perfectly a hundred times and the hundred and first time he was out in front of a full house and that's when he made the mistake."

"Now I could use a drink," Heidi said and stood. We shuffled out of the place behind parents herding children and beaming grand parents. One guy was patting a boy on the back telling him he played better than the guy in the tux. His wife admonished him with a stern, "Frank."

__Chapter Thirty-Nine__

"You want another round?" I asked hopefully.

"No, I think we better get over to that reception at
the Lady Slipper. I'm sure he saw us sitting in the
front and I don't want him thinking we skipped the reception because he blew his song."

We'd stopped at the Groveland Tap for a beer
and a glass of wine, giving Tommy a few minutes to
settle into his reception. At this point I wasn't really
looking forward to going to the thing and was afraid
he might blame me for those wrong notes.

"You know it's funny," Heidi said. "I just presumed he was an accomplished piano player, and here
he is taking lessons with a bunch of fifth and sixth
graders."

"I think it's impressive, maybe it's something
he's wanted to do all his life and he finally just bit the
bullet and said to himself *"fish or cut bait."*"

"I suppose, I just wasn't expecting it. Anyway,
come on, we better get going," Heidi said standing up.
I noticed even with the hair, or maybe because of it,
she turned a number of heads on her way out the door.
She, of course, remained oblivious.

I think we took the last open spot in the Lady
Slipper parking lot. As we made our way in through
the front door I noticed the potted plant Morton had
lifted his leg on the other day didn't look to be doing
all that well.

Tommy's reception was in a private banquet room next to the barroom where I'd last met him. The room had it's own bar setup, not quite as grand as the barroom, and it was crowded.

A number of tables had bouquets of flowers lying on them for Tommy. There was a basket by the door that looked like it could have been stolen from a church collection filled with cards addressed to Tommy. A quartet was off to the side playing soft, contemporary music while out on the dance floor a receiving line of folks slowly worked its way toward Tommy to offer personal congratulations.

"Come on, I'll introduce you," Heidi said stepping to the back of the line.

"I'll go get us some drinks."

"No don't, by the time you make your way to the bar I'll be in front of him. You told me you wanted to meet him."

"Yeah, I suppose you're right," I said and reluctantly stepped into line next to her.

It took about five minutes to work our way up the line. Tommy spotted me about a half dozen people back and a cloud seemed to pass over his face. When we finally stepped in front of him he gave Heidi a big hug and she gushed about how much she liked the recital and his performance in particular. Then she half turned to me and said, "I'd like to introduce an acquaintance of mine, Dev Haskell."

I stuck my hand out and said, "We've met once or twice before, nice to be formally introduced."

"Yeah, Haskell, how could I ever forget," he said shaking my hand and then he didn't say anything else. I waited for a very long pause while we stared at one another.

Heidi looked at me, smiled and pinched my butt.

"I wanted to just say how impressive I think it is that you're taking lessons. I'm guessing it's something you always wanted to do and you finally just decided to do it."

His look visibly softened and he said, "That's it exactly, my mom couldn't afford it when I was a kid and I've always been too busy and all of a sudden it sort of dawned on me that I was running out of time, so sort of like you said, shit or get off the pot."

Heidi seemed to breathe a sigh of relief.

"Quite the smart finance woman you have on your arm tonight, Haskell." Then he leaned in and said to Heidi, "You should set your sights higher." He chuckled, but he wasn't joking. "Look, you two go help yourself to something at the bar and thanks again for coming. Charlie," he called out and reached over my shoulder, bringing the next couple in as he hustled us out of the way.

"Oh God," Heidi said as we made our way to the bar.

I turned to ask her what she meant by that just as the bartender stepped in front of me. "I'll just have a pale ale, Summit if you got it."

"Double vodka martini," Heidi said which more or less served as all the explanation I needed.

After her fourth Heidi was in no condition so I decided to drive us back to my place. We stepped inside the front door and Morton bounded out of the kitchen and immediately shoved his nose up beneath Heidi's short skirt.

"God, he is so like you," she said then attempted to pull her heels off. She ended up sitting on the hallway floor and lifting her leg up toward me, "Maybe

162

give a lady a hand and things just might go your way."

I knew which way things were going to go as we headed upstairs and it wasn't in my direction. I guided her up the stairs, helped her into the bathroom, pulled the covers back on the bed, escorted her from the bathroom to the bedroom. I helped her get out of her dress, helped her climb into bed.

"I'll catch you in the morning, honey," she said just as she drifted off.

I got the bottle of aspirin out, placed it alongside the glass of water on the end table next to her. I shooed Morton away from licking her face then waited thirty seconds for her double vodka martini snore.

Chapter Forty

I was at the kitchen counter when Heidi made her appearance the following morning. Her rainbow colored hair hung every which way making her look certifiable. She was wearing the same gorgeous, delightfully slinky little dress from the night before, but somehow it seemed to have lost its magic. Maybe it was the mascara ringing her eyes, the pale skin, or the lack of lipstick that conveyed an inherent sense of depression.

Morton shoved his nose between her legs, but other than giving him a brief pat she didn't seem to notice.

"How's the head?" I asked and poured her a cup of coffee

"My head? It must still be there because I can feel it pounding. Hey, thanks, but no coffee for me. Where'd you hide my car keys? I just need to go home, get cleaned up and then wait for Tommy Allesi to call and tell me he's pulling all his money out of the fund."

"I don't think he'll do that, Heidi."

"Wanna bet?"

"Look, sorry he had that reaction. Maybe he was just pissed off because he did a horseshit job playing the piano."

"He did the horseshit job because he saw you in the audience. Need I remind you I'm the idiot that brought you there? You just seem to have that effect on people, Dev. I'm so screwed," she said and just sort of stared at the floor.

I slid her car keys across the kitchen counter. "I'm sorry," I said.

"You know, Dev, for once I honestly don't think it's your fault. I mean whatever you did he's probably right to be pissed off. God only knows I've been there enough times. But, I know you, given all the dumb things you do, you honestly don't remember what in the hell it was. I get that. I made the decision, on my own, that it would be a good idea to introduce you to my biggest client. What in the hell was I thinking? Look, I gotta go. Oh, hey, last night when we got back here, did we?"

"You got some action from Morton, he licked your face, but you more or less passed out."

"Morton, figures, see you later," she said shaking her head in disgust as she walked dejectedly toward the front door.

I hurried after her trying to come up with some sort of encouraging word, but I couldn't think of any. She let herself out the front door, leaving it halfway open as she walked onto the front porch. She gave a slight groan as she stepped into the morning sunshine then climbed into her car parked out on the street and drove away without looking back.

My phone rang just as Heidi's car disappeared from view.

"Mr. Haskell," Natasha said. "We'll be conducting our final workout at Hidden Falls. If you would head over and survey the area prior to our arrival, I plan to be there within the next forty-five minutes."

"See you there," I said and hung up. Once we arrived it took us, Morton and I, about sixty seconds to survey the park, we were the only ones there. I got the Frisbee out and exercised Morton until Natasha and Princess Anastasia showed up in the camper. Then I returned Morton to the back seat of my car. Natasha parked a good dozen spaces away from me.

I noticed that the back door to the camper was dented. The two glass louvers with duct tape and two more above them were missing. The right side of the rear bumper, from the trailer hitch over appeared dented and hung at an odd angle.

Natasha climbed out from behind the wheel and clapped her hands. Princess Anastasia jumped out of the open door and immediately sat at attention at her feet. Natasha was wearing makeup this morning, I guessed in an effort to cover up the slight discoloration around her right eye. It wasn't working.

"Looks like you had a bit of an accident, someone hit the rear of your camper?"

"Something like that," she said, but didn't go into any further detail. "We haven't a moment to lose so if you'll excuse us," she said. With that she clapped her hands and the two of them headed off to the grassy area and began to work through their routines.

I walked around to the rear of the camper and inspected the damage. It was minor in the scheme of things. Enough to get your attention if you were behind the wheel, maybe jolt you forward a foot or two, but it certainly wasn't totaled by any stretch of the imagination. There was one other thing I noticed, the scent of dope was missing.

Natasha's was busy with the princess, putting her through her paces. Her back was to me and I tried the door on the rear of the camper, but it was locked. I wondered about that black eye.

166

I occasionally walked over to my car and peeked in on Morton, he was stretched out in the sunlight shining in the back seat, sound asleep. Natasha and the princess finished their routines around one and came back to the camper to break for lunch.

"You two are looking very good out there," I said.

"Yes, she seems to have regained her focus from the other day, still not sure what that was about," Natasha said as she unlocked the back door to the camper.

"You alright after the accident?" I asked and nodded toward the dent in the door and the bumper.

"Nothing to concern yourself with."

"That how you got the black eye?"

"As I said, nothing to concern yourself with."

"I get that, Natasha, I really do. But, if there is someone or some incident out there that may cause a future problem I'd like to know so I can be prepared and offer you and Princess Anastasia the best possible protection."

"I'm sure it's over and done with."

"Tommy Allesi or Denis Malloy?"

"Hardly."

"It appears you moved all that dope."

She shot me a look as she opened the door and the princess hopped in. "We'll be ready to resume our workout in forty-five minutes, Mr. Haskell," she said then stepped into the camper and locked the door. I wondered if she removed the dope or had it been taken from her?

Chapter Forty-One

Natasha resumed their workout schedule exactly forty-five minutes later and they worked through the afternoon. A little after five three cars rumbled down the entrance road, pulled into the parking lot and cruised over toward the camper. They parked in a half circle around the camper effectively blocking any attempt Natasha might make at backing up. I had just peeked into my back seat to check on Morton and I don't think they saw me.

Five guys climbed out of the cars. Once the driver climbed out of the third car it leaned decidedly to the right and I spotted the unattractive Fat Bastard face of Denis Malloy through the window. The gauze across his forehead was gone, but now he sported an awful lot of white tape and gauze wrapped around his chin. His eyes appeared dark and swollen. He seemed to move rather stiffly in the seat as he angled his entire upper body in Natasha's direction. His right arm was hanging in a sling.

Denis either hadn't seen me or he wasn't paying attention. The five guys headed across the grass toward Natasha, her back was to them and she was focused on Princess Anastasia. A big blonde guy with a crewcut said something and they suddenly fanned out in a line and continued walking toward her.

I quietly opened my trunk, moved the softball bat I'd relieved Denis of the other night and pulled back a wool blanket. My AR-15 was lying beneath it along with a couple of magazines, each holding thirty rounds. I slapped a magazine in the AR-15 and closed the trunk. The five guys were maybe halfway across the field and appeared in no hurry, Natasha remained oblivious.

I walked along the passenger side of a car, opened the door where Denis sat focused on the group moving toward Natasha and gently pushed the barrel up against the side of his head.

"I think you should get out of the car, Denis, very quietly."

"Hold on, now you just hold on, man I'm a seriously injured person, here."

"That's nothing compared to what I'll do to you if you don't get out, now move."

"Okay, okay, just settle down and take it easy, I'm getting out, okay, I'm getting out." Then he groaned as he slowly turned in his seat. He placed his right foot out onto the pavement and slowly, cautiously swung the walking cast on his left leg out of the car and onto the pavement. He carefully began to stand using his left arm as leverage on the open door. The car rocked back and forth as he gingerly stood and the effort left him gasping for air.

"You armed?" I asked.

"No, no I don't have anything, honest, man," he said.

I quickly patted him down anyway and found a jack knife, not too large.

"I, I thought you meant did I have a gun, honestly. I wasn't trying to screw with you or anything. I just thought you meant a gun is all."

"I opened the knife and handed it back to him, I want you to go around and slit a tire on each one of these three cars. Got it?"

"Now wait just a minute, hold on, you can't just...."

"Actually, not only can I, but I am. Now, why don't you just be a nice guy like I asked and start on those tires? I better start hearing a hiss in about fifteen seconds or you're not gonna like what I have planned. It's just about time to get your friends attention."

With that I heard Natasha's name called out and she turned to see the line of men walking toward her. She made some sort of hand signal and Princess Anastasia quickly moved along side her, as she turned to run into the woods I fired off a burst of three rounds from into the air. Everyone stopped, turned and looked in my direction.

"You got about ten seconds, Denis and if I don't hear...." A heavy hiss suddenly cut off the rest of my statement. "I think that's just about far enough, gentlemen. Why don't you all turn around and very slowly walk back this way. Natasha, you and Anastasia get over here."

A guy with a ponytail seemed to say something to the crewcut standing next to him.

"Don't. Please, just start moving this way and no one gets hurt. Hands on top of your heads, now," I said then shouldered the AR and swept it back and forth along their line. Everyone's hands went up on top of their heads and they slowly moved toward me. Natasha moved behind them with the princess following and directly in my line of fire, oblivious.

I heard another hiss as Denis stabbed the front tire on the second car then gingerly made his way toward the third vehicle groaning with every other step. When the line was about twenty feet away I said, "That's far enough, Natasha get over here."

She walked around them and came alongside of me.

"You got anything you need in that camper?"

"Anything I need?"

"Yeah, we're leaving it here. You got a purse or anything in there?"

"Well yes, but I...."

"Get it, then get behind the wheel of my car, you're driving."

"I don't think that's...."

"Get your purse and get into my car. These guys were almost on top of you and you never even saw them coming. You might be good at training the princess, but your head is up your ass when it comes to taking precautions. Now move."

Surprisingly, she did. I had her pull my car out of the parking lot and over to the entrance road. Once she was out of the immediate area I said, "Why don't you boys turn round and start walking toward the river." No one moved for a moment and I shouted, "Come on, move."

"They're not going to like that," Denis said offhandedly. He was standing in front of me and off to the side by maybe ten feet.

"You can join them, too, Denis."

He looked at me like I was crazy. "Oh, come on I'm in no condition to walk anywhere."

"Get moving," I said and waved him forward with the AR-15.

171

As they slowly walked toward the river I quickly moved toward Natasha waiting for me in my car. I gave a final look back as I climbed into my car. They had stopped walking, but they didn't seem to be in any hurry to head back to their cars. A couple of them still had their hands on top of their heads.

"Let's get out of here," I said. Natasha didn't seem to need any additional encouragement and she raced up the hill.

I glanced into the back seat. Princess Anastasia was seated and looking very happy as Morton tried to sniff various parts of her body.

Chapter Forty-Two

"You know Natasha, I have the distinct feeling you haven't been completely honest with me and I'm thinking it just might be time we have a little heart to heart," I said.

She slowed the car for no more than half a second, gave a quick glance to the right then floored it onto the River Boulevard. I swayed back and forth in the seat as she attempted to straighten out then I glanced back out the rear window just to make sure those guys weren't somehow following up the hill. With her foot on the gas we were quickly up to about seventy sailing along for three or four blocks before she eased off and dropped it down to a steady fifty miles per hour on the city street.

"I've told you on numerous occasions, I positively *deplore* violence," she said in that clenched jaw Ivy League accent then shot a momentary glare at the weapon resting between my knees.

"Me too, that's why I stopped those guys from getting any closer to you. I'm not sure what their plan was, but at the very least they would have taken the princess. And, I'm guessing there's a pretty good chance they would have enjoyed kicking the shit out of you, or worse. Pardon me for being curious, but exactly what sort of logical discussion do you think would have changed their minds back there?"

"They somehow seem to be laboring under the misconception that they are entitled to the cannabis I recovered. And apparently, they seem quite willing to underscore that claim with the threat of violence."

"Underscore that claim? Are you nuts? Threat? They weren't going to threaten; they were going to kick the living hell out of you, Natasha. Stop with the high handed explanation, you're dealing with thugs here, and by the way, your close personal friend, Denis was with them."

"His actions are of no concern to me."

"I would suggest you start making them a concern," I said then stared out the window for a mile or two until I realized she was heading toward her home. "I think you better pack up at home and we'll go to my place, you're spending the night there, you and the princess. It's the only place you'll be even halfway safe."

Thankfully she just gave me a look, but didn't argue. She drove past the Head Case. The lights were on inside and the place was occupied by the same guy I saw in there the other day reading the paper. Tonight he was in a chair talking on the phone. I wondered if he was maybe an owner.

She quickly packed a couple of bags at her house then we hurried over to my place. I pulled into the driveway and parked in front of the garage. I wrapped the AR-15 in the camouflage blanket and carried it into the house. Morton followed, prancing about an inch behind Princess Anastasia and Natasha.

"Charming," Natasha said, meaning anything but, as she stepped inside the front door. I had a couple of T-shirts hanging over the stair banister, some of Moron's toys were scattered around the front entry. There were a few newspapers sort of stacked on the coffee table in front of the couch, a couple of empty beer bottles rested on top of some skin mags.

"I really wasn't expecting company," I said.

Natasha had just run a finger across an end table. You could see the path her finger had made in the dust and she sort of frowned as she rubbed her finger tip and thumb together.

I laid the AR-15 on the couch and headed toward the kitchen. "Come on back here," I said. Once in the kitchen I got a bowl out of the cupboard for the princess, filled the bowl and Morton's dish with dog food then filled the water dish.

Morton glanced at the dog food in his bowl then gave me a look that suggested, *"You gotta be kidding."*

Natasha looked at the dog food bag and said, "Frankly, I'm more than a little surprised, sensible, healthy and here I had you figured as the sort that would feed him table scraps and anything deep fat fried."

"I'd never do that," I said then left the bag of Bar-B-Que potato chips in the cupboard, grabbed a couple of apples out of the refrigerator and sliced them into a bowl. "Would you care for a glass of wine?"

"What do you have?" she said reaching for an apple slice.

"Chilled."

That seemed to bring an uncustomary smile to her face. "Why not?"

We'd eaten two more apples, and were almost finished with the second bottle of wine. I was thinking of ordering out for a pizza.

"Did I mention I was formally introduced to Tommy Allesi last night?"

"Formally introduced?"

"Yeah, actually it was after a piano concert, a big recital for kids taking lessons. He hosted a reception at the Lady Slipper. I guess he funds the concert they had. Anyway, I was introduced to him, formally this time."

"And how was he?"

"I have to say not too thrilled to see me. In fact, he suggested to the woman I was with that she set her sights higher."

"That sounds like Tommy. He's quite intelligent, but once he arrives at a conclusion it's rather difficult to change his mind. His first impression obviously wasn't the best."

"That sort of goes both ways."

"Perhaps, but don't you see, the difference is he's Tommy Allesi and you're, well you're just you."

"So, what was the deal with you and those guys this afternoon?"

She drained her glass and said, "I don't suppose you have any more, do you?"

"I just might," I said stepping over to the refrigerator. "We were talking about this afternoon, your visitors."

"Where to begin? Over the past few years I've been active on a number of fronts, lobbying for the legalization of cannabis for strictly medicinal purposes. I've played a role, somewhat minor, in Washington, California and Colorado. I was one of the Colorado seven, perhaps you heard of us?"

I shook my head.

She sort of gave a look as if to say "*it figures.*"
"Recently I've begun to refocus my efforts here, in Minnesota."

"I don't think you're going to be able to legalize dope here?"

"I'll let you in on a little secret. Once the various state legislatures see the tax revenue generated in places like Colorado and Washington, with the possible exception of Mississippi cannabis will be legal everywhere within the decade."

"That still doesn't explain those guys this afternoon."

"Experience has taught that one of the first things we have to do is minimize the illegal distribution efforts of certain parties."

"What?"

"Your street vendors, pushers as you might call them."

"Or maybe just call them what they are, plain old gangsters and thugs. And you plan to do this *minimizing* exactly how? By reasoning with them?"

"By confiscating their product. If they've nothing to sell, no one can purchase. It's a rather simple business plan."

"Yeah, except for the fact you're talking a lot of money and some not so nice individuals might take exception to the fact that you're *'confiscating'* their property."

"Illegal property, at least under the tenants of current law."

"You stole dope from some pretty bad guys, Natasha. That's what was stored in your camper. Right? Those guys want it back, and they aren't going to stop until they get it."

177

"I don't think they realize just how determined I can be."

I just shook my head. "Natasha, they'll kill Princess Anastasia, just for fun they'll make you watch and then kill you. It's the way they operate. It may not seem logical to you, but that's what they do."

"Well, I'm not about to tell them where I hid it and they'll never find it."

I figured it was probably stacked up out on her back deck with the smashed picnic table and all the other crap. "God, Natasha, I'm guessing your house, right?"

"Wrong, the coal bin in the garage, they'll never find it."

"So, how is Tommy Allesi involved? Is he selling dope?"

"Tommy, oh, heavens no, at least not to my knowledge. No, he simply spouted the same ridiculous nonsense you're saying now, and he wanted to take control of Princess Anastasia until after the Blessington show. I believe I mentioned earlier that he owned a small percentage, one-thirty-second. I believe he wagered heavily on the results of the show. My understanding is a lot of money changes hands, an awful lot."

"So, if Tommy just wants to protect the princess why not let him, why come to me?"

"Quite simply, I'm not sure he'd let her go once the show was over."

"But if the guys we met this afternoon are after the dope you stole…."

"Confiscated."

"….And Denis Malloy is with them, doesn't Denis work for Tommy?"

"Denis is a rather confused individual. He was instrumental in assisting me in the original confiscation, but he immediately wanted to take possession. I suspect he planned to sell the product himself, thereby negating my intentions, and reaping a considerable profit which would afford him the opportunity to payback the rather sizeable debt he's rumored to owe Mr. Allesi."

"Debt?"

"Denis has always been rather adept at attempting to play both sides of the street and then getting run down in the middle. More wine?" she said filling her glass and extending the bottle toward me.

"I'm confused," I said.

"And about to be over served," she smiled and refilled my glass almost to the rim.

Chapter Forty-Three

I woke the following morning with a throbbing head and a very dry throat. My body seemed to ache all over and I felt like I'd been doing sit ups and pushups for hours. I sensed I was resting on the very edge of my bed with a warm body up against me and I thought, "*Damn it, Morton,*" as I slowly opened my eyes.

Unfortunately, I immediately focused on Morton, lying on the floor, snoring. What was left of a chewed up thong was on the floor next to him. Heidi? I rolled over still half asleep. A wave of shock, panic, or maybe just both washed over me as I stared into Natasha's face. She snuggled in, draped an arm around my waist, fluttered her eyes open and pulled me toward her. I prayed I was just having a bad dream.

"Hey there, Tiger, you just don't know when to quit, do you?" she cooed and then threw a leg over my hip.

"I don't think I can do this," I whined.

"Heh, heh, heh," she snickered and began to run a hand down my stomach. "That's what you said the last few times." Then she pushed me back on the pillow and climbed aboard. Princess Anastasia cast a wayward glance from the far side of the bed and then went back to sleep.

I had the coffee going and an embarrassed look on my face when Natasha came drifting into the kitchen. The princess and Morton were eyeing one another over their empty food bowls. I was finding it difficult to face Natasha so I busied myself around the kitchen sink. There were four empty wine bottles scattered across the kitchen counter and another one, more empty than not, that I'd just returned to the refrigerator. I placed the empties in recycling and poured her a cup of coffee.

"Milk, sugar?"

"No, thank you," she said and took a sip. "Umm, we're due to report to the Blessington at eleven this morning. I wonder if it wouldn't make sense to return to the scene of yesterday's crime and retrieve the camper. Then, if you would be so kind as to follow me home and give us a ride down to the Blessington we'll check in."

"What time do you finish up?"

"Finish? Oh, no, it's not like that, we'll be on site for the next four days."

"On site?"

"Exactly, either competing in some facet or getting ready to compete," she said, then squinted, made a face at me and growled. "Grrrr-rrr-rrr, God I needed last night. Too bad you can't stay with us, you know just to relieve my stress levels, but unfortunately, rules are rules."

"Come on, we better get moving and check out that park to see if there's anything left of your camper."

Amazingly, the camper was where she left it in the lot, and perhaps not so amazingly, the three other cars were gone. The camper appeared to be untouched. But, I opened the hood before Natasha started the engine, just to be sure there wasn't some sort of surprise wired up, mercifully there wasn't. After a brief general inspection I deemed the vehicle safe to start and she fired it up, then I followed Natasha and the princess back to her place. She pulled the camper in back and parked next to the garage.

In short order her bags were in my trunk. Morton paced back and forth in the back seat while Natasha held the princess on her lap as we drove downtown.

"The majority of today will consist of registration and grooming," Natasha said, petting the princess. "As far as I'm concerned you've performed all the *service* I'll need from you, at least for the time being." Then she turned toward me, gave a wry smile and a throaty growl.

I gripped the wheel and kept my eyes focused on the road. As we pulled in front of the Xcel Center I said, "I'll grab your suitcase. Maybe I should go in with you? I don't want you running into that gang from yesterday."

"Didn't get enough, did you? Hmmm-mmm-mmm. Thank you, but no, this is probably the safest place to be. Security is extremely tight and will remain so until the end of the show, at which point I intend to take Princess Anastasia, along with our Best of Show trophy out to a breeders for the first of a number of successful litters. The fact that she's never been bred raises the value of her line. She's a virgin and has no idea of the surprises that await, do you darling?" she said and then scratched the princess behind her ears.

I noticed Morton had suddenly slunked down in the backseat and seemed to be doing his best to become invisible.

I pulled up to the curb in front of the Xcel. Before I was out of the car some bellboy in a red cap pushed a four wheeled cart alongside the car. "I'll take your luggage and equipment. Only registered entrants beyond this point," he said.

Three uniformed police officers stood next to the entrance doors and added enough emphasis for my taste.

"Natasha," I said as she and the princess climbed out of the front seat. "I wish you all success."

They both ignored me and regally strode toward the door to the Xcel Center with the bellboy in tow. The police officer at the door checked their credentials and waved them inside. Once the door closed behind them he looked at me and said, "Would you mind moving your vehicle, sir. We have a lot of people coming through. Thank you."

Chapter Forty-Four

I parked in the driveway and let Morton out of the back seat. Despite my being over served and taken advantage of last night I felt like a huge burden had been lifted from my shoulders. Win, lose or draw Natasha and Princess Anastasia were safe and sound, under lock and key down at the Blessington Kennel Club and I had my life back. As we wandered toward the front door my phone rang.

"Hey, let me talk to Morton," Maddie said avoiding the perfect opportunity to tell me when she was returning.

"Hang on," I said then panted into the phone.

"Hi Morton, how's my boy? It's Mommy, Morton." She went on for another minute, or two. I kept thinking as soon as this nonsense was finished there was some cold pizza in the fridge that would make a pretty good lunch and then we could head down to the office.

"We're just about to go out on our walk," I said interrupting the current round of squeals Maddie was making. "When are you planning to come back to town?"

"I'm going to book a flight in the near future, I'll email the details once I do," she said then made some sort of lame excuse and quickly hung up.

Buster, I thought. She's been swept off her feet.

"Come on, Morton old buddy, you like double cheese and sausage pizza?" I asked as I opened the front door.

My first thought was, *"Hey, those are mine,"* when I saw the four guys drinking beer and paging through the skin magazines in my living room. Then I saw the open pizza box with just one piece remaining. I recognized my uninvited guests from yesterday's bunch of thugs although Denis Malloy didn't seem to be anywhere around.

"You're out of beer," the blonde guy with a crew-cut said and then gave the nod to a figure who stepped out from behind the door and cold cocked me on the side of the head. I dropped my phone as I went down.

I woke up on the floor to Morton licking my face. The left side of my head throbbed and Morton's breath smelled of cheese and sausage pizza.

The guy who hit me was casually leaning against the wall. Crewcut was sitting backwards on one of my dining room chairs, resting his arms on the back of the chair. As he leaned down to look at me I noticed he was rather large, a fact accentuated by the body builder arms about the size of my thighs with black tribal tattoos wrapped around massive biceps.

"Like I said, you're out of beer."

"Not a problem, I'll just go get some more, you guys can wait here," I said slowly sitting up.

"You aren't going anywhere, dumbass. I suppose you think you're pretty cute, telling that fat fuck Denis to slit our tires."

"Actually, that was his idea, I told him not to, but he.…"

"Just shut up and listen. Your hippie girlfriend took it upon herself to harvest a growing operation of ours. We want it back, and then we want her."

"I got no idea what you're talking…."

"Ramon," he said and gave a nod to the guy who hit me a moment before.

Ramon seemed to effortlessly pick me up off the floor and bounce me off the wall like a basketball. I felt the sheetrock crack as I slammed into the wall. The painting of a naked lady sitting in a giant martini glass fell off the wall and the frame broke when it hit the floor. I slid down the wall and landed on the floor next to the painting. Pizza breath Morton bounded over and started to lick me again.

"Maybe you're having trouble understanding me. We want that shit back, now, right now."

"This is bullshit," one of the guys sitting on my couch said. He had a ponytail and he tossed the skin mag he'd been looking at into a corner, stood up and headed toward me. He took three steps, then a quick hop and kicked me on the side of the head. I vaguely remember my head bouncing off the wall before I blacked out.

"….can't very well tell us anything if he's lying there unconscious, now, can he?" a voice seemed to echo from somewhere inside my head.

"This is just so much bullshit. I say we kill this bastard now then go and grab that bitch and her damn dog."

"Great idea, she's down at that stupid dog show hiding behind half the cops in town. Your brilliant idea is to kick the shit out of the only idiot who might be able to help us. Maybe just sit down and let's find out what this piece of crap knows. If he can't help then you can do whatever you want to him."

I kept my eyes closed and my face on the floor until someone sat me up and leaned me back against the wall. My head nestled into the indentation in the wall from when I was kicked.

"Haskell, Haskell wake up here, you piece of shit, wake up," Crewcut said then slapped my face back and forth a few times. He didn't slap very hard, but my head felt like it would explode and I attempted to brush his hand away.

"Sorry about that, maybe you can sense the frustration we're all feeling here. Now, I'm thinking you can help us out, as well as yourself, by taking us to our dope that hippie girlfriend of yours stole. You do that and we just might forget we ever met, how's that sound?"

"Sounds like bullshit, I say we go get the bitch," the guy with the ponytail said. He was back on the couch, looking at a new skin mag. The other three guys had yet to look up from their magazines. I figured they must not have a love life.

Crewcut gave a brief glance over his shoulder, but didn't say anything before turning his attention back to me. "Haskell, you coming around here? Listen up, dumb shit, if you can't help us I'm just gonna have to turn you back over to my friends there. Now, not exactly what I want to do, but, well you're not really leaving me with much of a choice. So tell me where the hell that dope is?"

I watched the guy with the ponytail as he reached behind his back. He casually pulled out a pistol and checked the clip and the safety, unaware I'd seen him.

I couldn't tell what caliber it was, but at this stage it really didn't matter.

"She said something about unloading it from her camper, I guess she had it stored in there."

"Her camper? You mean that piece of shit brown and white thing?" Crewcut asked.

I nodded and my head began to spin again.

"Where'd she unload this?"

"I think her house, I could probably show you. Why don't I just follow you guys over there?"

"Yeah, right. I got a better idea. Billy," he said to a guy with his face buried in one of my skin magazines.

"Give the tits a rest and bring my car around, back it in and meet us by the garage. Let's go see what we got. I hope for your sake, Haskell you're not trying to bullshit me." With that he threw a set of keys over to Billy then yanked me to my feet.

A couple of minutes later Billy was backing some sort of navy-blue sporty thing with mag wheels up my driveway almost to the garage. Crewcut clutched me by the back of my collar. The jerk with the ponytail was leaning against the side of my house with a pistol stuffed into the front of his waistband. He didn't bother to conceal it.

Billy climbed out from behind the wheel and tossed the keys over the roof of the car to Crewcut. He caught the keys like a pro and pushed a button to unlock the doors.

I gingerly took a step toward the back seat.

"Don't even think about it, Haskell you can ride back here," he said and gave a little laugh as he lifted the trunk open. "Gonna be a little cramped I'm afraid,

188

see some asshole slit my tire yesterday afternoon."
Then he started to shove me into the trunk.

As I climbed in Billy opened the rear door while Ramon glared for a moment then climbed into the passenger seat.

Crewcut chuckled and said, "Watch your head, dipshit," just a half second before he slammed the trunk closed.

Chapter Forty-Five

The ride over was bumpy, dark, and cramped. It felt like we were driving way too fast. I was attempting to find some degree of comfort wedged around the slit tire and failing, all the while wondering what in the hell I was going to tell them once we got to Natasha's. If I told them the dope was hidden in the garage they would have no further use for me. If I could just somehow get away, maybe hide in a neighbor's yard or God forbid, have someone call the cops. I shifted my weight and pushed the flat tire a few inches further back so I could adjust my position slightly.

That just caused something else to poke me in the side and I tried to shift and find some degree of comfort, but it wasn't working. It was pitch black in the trunk and I sort of turned over and half knelt in an attempt to move whatever was in the way. Suddenly, I wrapped my hand around what felt like a tire iron. I pushed the slit tire an inch or two further back, but couldn't get it to move any further. I tugged and pulled on the tire iron until it began to slide out from beneath the tire, barely a half inch at a time. Slowly but surely I began to work the iron free.

I sensed the car slowing almost to a stop before backing up and making a turn up a slight rise I took to be Natasha's driveway. We seemed to coast a fairly short distance and then the engine turned off and I could hear the doors open.

"Haul his ass out of there and let's get this over with," a voice I took to be Crewcut said.

I heard a slight beep as the locks clicked, a moment later the trunk was opened and two large figures stood blocking a good portion of the sunlight. Ramon reached in and yanked me out of the trunk.

I sort of groaned and the guy with the ponytail pulled his pistol out from behind his back. "God damn it, just shut the hell up and show us where the damn weed is or so help me, God," he shouted then clubbed me across the back of my head with his pistol.

I brought the tire iron up fast and hard, catching him on the chin. I just caught his eyes rolling into the back of his head as he dropped where he stood. Ramon began to spin me around and I clubbed him on the top of his head. He automatically let go and I hit him again across the side of his skull. He dropped to the ground just as Billy came around the side of the car. I was vaguely aware of Crewcut yelling something as I back handed Billy with the tire iron slamming it across his temple. He staggered two steps, fell onto the concrete and began to convulse on the ground.

Someone screamed "Fuck".

A couple of shots rang out from the direction of the street. The windshield suddenly had two, dinner-plate sized webs where the rounds struck. I ducked down behind the open trunk, rolled Ramon over and pulled the pistol from his waist band. I crawled a couple of feet over and grabbed Ponytail's pistol lying on the driveway.

"Haskell, Haskell, come on now, you're taking this all wrong. We can work out a split or something, make this worth your while," Crewcut called from the front of the house.

"You already fired a couple of shots. That's gonna have the cops here in about two minutes, if I were you guys I'd maybe think about leaving."

That didn't get a response and I turned to watch the back corner of the house near the deck, in case someone came around on that side. I didn't have to wait long. I suddenly saw two pairs of feet beneath the deck, one behind the other, cautiously creeping along. The first pair wore bright red shoes. I took careful aim at the red shoes and squeezed off two rounds. After the second shot the shoes jumped, I heard a scream and suddenly I could see them kicking around on the ground. A moment later I watched as they were dragged back by his pal.

Ponytail suddenly started moving and groaning as he slowly began to regain consciousness. I took careful aim and from a distance of about six feet shot him in the foot he'd kicked me with. Blood, flesh, bits of bone and shoe splattered across the driveway.

"You probably got about a minute left before the cops are here. Don't worry, when they pull up, if any of you guys run this way, I'll just shoot you. Clocks ticking," I called and waited for a reply.

Nothing happened. I didn't see or hear anything. I waited for what seemed like an hour, but no one else came down the driveway or around the back of the house.

Ponytail was holding his foot, rolling from side to side and gasping as he tried to swallow his scream. He glared at me with wild eyes and suddenly shouted, "You crazy bastard, you shot me in the foot, you fuck, you shot me."

192

"Yeah, and I used your gun to do it, dumb shit."

Ramon was still out cold, or worse. Billy was face down on the concrete, he continued to convulse slightly and sort of looked like he might be foaming at the mouth. I kept an eye on the driveway. After a few moments I scooted across the backyard to the far corner of the deck, close to where I'd shot the red shoes and peeked around the corner. No one was there.

I hurried up the side of the house toward the front yard and the street. Crewcut was just pushing a pair of bloody legs with red shoes into the backseat of a car. He hopped into the front passenger seat and the car quickly pulled away from the curb before he'd had a chance to even close the door.

I quickly looked around, but couldn't see anyone who looked like they may be watching. Out on the street, traffic seemed to be passing by without the slightest idea what had just transpired. I stuffed Ponytail's pistol into my front waistband, Ramon's pistol into the small of my back, then pulled my T-shirt out to hide them and started walking back to my house.

Chapter Forty-Six

I got a couple of uncomfortable stares from a few shop keepers along Selby as I headed toward my house. Two women crossed the street in the middle of the block so they wouldn't have to walk past me, but no one stopped and questioned me. I think everyone I passed was just glad I kept moving out of their immediate area. When I finally reached my house the front door wasn't just unlocked, it stood halfway open.

I stepped in, pulled the pistol from my waistband and closed the door behind me. I carefully went through the entire house, but the only thing I found was the empty pizza delivery box Morton had torn up, the half dozen beer bottles he'd knocked over to lick up the contents and my phone on the floor next to the front door. After an ice pack and some aspirin, I put Morton in the car and we headed down to the office.

"You look even worse than usual," Louie said by way of a greeting. He was working on the laptop at his picnic table desk. A number of food wrappers lay crumpled and scattered around his paperwork. Two untouched soft-shell tacos sat on top of a stack of files.

"Don't even ask," I said then sunk into my desk chair, grabbed the binoculars and scanned the apartment across the street.

"I already checked, they're not home," Louie said.

"What a day," I groaned, then rested my head on the back of my chair and closed my eyes.

"Someone pissed off you're late on a payment?"

"Hardly. No, it's my stupid gig babysitting this French poodle that Morton has the hots for and her hippie owner."

"Oh, so it's Morton's fault."

"Part of it is, or will be if he knocked up that French poodle."

"He must be a fast learner, he's barely been with you a week."

I opened my eyes and just stared at Louie.

"Sorry, little courthouse humor." Louie said.

"Get this, the woman is into medical dope," I said and went on to explain the last seventy-two hours. I told him about Denis Malloy being cut from the vines, Natasha's camper stuffed with *confiscated* dope, her involvement in medical marijuana in Colorado, California and Washington state, Tommy Allesi's concert and then the visit from Crewcut and his bunch of thugs and the shootout. I neglected to mention waking up to Natasha taking advantage of me in my own bed.

"This was supposed to be the cakewalk gig of the century, and yet you've somehow managed to screw it up," Louie said shaking his head.

"No good deed goes unpunished."

Louie pushed a button on his laptop and a moment later I could hear the thing shutting down. "In light of your morning activities it might be a good idea to conduct yourself like nothing's happened. Besides, I think we could all use a break. Might I suggest we adjourn to somewhere a bit more relaxing?"

We were sitting on our usual stools, Louie was drinking bourbon and waxing eloquent about his latest

DUI case, I was nursing a beer and Morton had a chili bowl filled with water, occasionally I tossed a pork rind his way.

"Don't even think about it," I said as Morton gave a sideways glance at my beer. As if on cue my phone rang, I checked, it was Maddie. I pushed a button that automatically dropped her call into the message center.

Louie gave me a questionable look.

"Just Morton's mom," I said with a shrug then took a long sip of beer. "I guess I forgot to mention while she's been down in Atlanta helping her mother recover from a broken hip. Maddie seems to have managed to sneak in just enough time to shack up with an old high school boyfriend."

"Whoops, sorry about that," Louie said.

I just shook my head. "Don't worry about it."

"Another round, here," Louie called to Jimmy bartending. "You know," he said. "Based on the way your luck is running this may not be the best time to buy a lottery ticket."

"Let me ask you something? The name Alexi Tarasenko mean anything to you?"

"What is it with you and drug dealers all of a sudden?"

"What are you talking about?"

"Tarasenko, he is or at least was, a major player some years back. Did some time, something like thirty-six months, possession with intent to distribute. I don't know if he got religion or what."

"We talking about the same guy? A hairdresser, Head Case is the name of his salon."

"Yup, it's making sense now, that's one of the trades they offer in the Lino Lakes facility, hair dressing."

"God, the guy did Heidi's hair."

"How does it look?"

"His joint is called Head Case, what do you think?"

"Well, she's always been sort of out there when it comes to her hair. How's he fit in to all this?"

"He doesn't, yet. Hey, I better finish this beer and head out, I got a lot of things to catch up on after the last few days."

"What's the rush?" Louie said and took a healthy sip.

"I just got shit to do."

"Probably the most honest thing you've said all week."

As soon as I finished my beer, Morton and I left Louie in The Spot and drove over to the Head Case. It was late in the afternoon and the same guy I'd seen sitting in there twice before was reading the paper in one of the chairs against the wall. Alexi Tarasenko was sitting in one of the salon chairs. There weren't any customers in the place. A bell jingled overhead as I walked in the door.

Alexi sized me up as I walked in the door then said, "So, you decided to get a new hair color, Mr. Haskell."

The guy reading the paper folded it in half, set it on the empty chair next to him, and then gave me an annoyed look.

"I kind of like the color I have, thanks all the same. I wanted to ask you a question, hoping you might be able to help."

"We'll see once you ask," Alexi said then shot me a wide smile.

"I have a friend who comes here, you did some styling for her."

"That's my business, I do a lot of women's hair."

"Heidi Bauer, she's not too happy with her hair right now."

He gave a long sigh, "I was afraid of that. I understand you know her rather well. Yes?"

"Yes, but that's not exactly the reason for my visit."

"Did she happen to tell you that the design was more or less her idea? Did she mention that she came in here with a picture she'd pulled out of an Italian fashion magazine and insisted I do the same to her hair?"

"No, she failed to be that specific? But it doesn't surprise me."

Alexi shrugged.

"Where did you learn your trade?"

"I don't see how that should have any bearing on her particular choice of style. I should have the article she brought in with the photo somewhere on my desk, if you'd just give me a moment I'll get it."

"Actually, that won't be necessary. I might have a sort of business proposition for you."

"My business is hairdressing," he said then opened his arms, glanced around to indicate his salon and smiled.

The other guy in the chair casually took his folded newspaper and laid it on his lap. I guess he had a pistol in his waistband and in the next moment or two he would slip a hand beneath the paper just in case.

"Yeah, I get that. Let me just explain and start off by saying I mean no offense."

The smile vanished from Alexi's face and he said, "If you mean no offense maybe you shouldn't say whatever it is in the first place."

"Let me start by telling you I'm a private investigator."

"I already know that, we checked you out. Let me remind you, in case you weren't listening, I'm a hairdresser."

"I have a client who did something stupid. You may know the type, she is one of those people who is smart, very smart, book smart. But, she is perhaps naïve when it comes to dealing with people, with individuals and business."

"I'm not sure what this has to do with me. Does she want her hair done the same way as your Heidi?"

"Actually, no. What she needs is to get something off her hands, something that doesn't belong to her, that she should not have gotten involved with in the first place."

"Why doesn't she just return it?"

"There are some unpleasant people involved."

"I still don't see how this would involve me, like I said I'm just a hairdresser."

"This woman doesn't live too far from here," I reached into my pocket.

The guy in the chair moved his arm slightly, I knew he had a weapon drawn under the newspaper. The message being; even if I shot Alexi, it was going to cost me, big time.

"I just wrote down her address, thought you might want to drive by, see the house. It's a nice house. She's not going to be home for the next three days, and actually if you looked in the garage, in the coal bin, she stored the items she shouldn't have in there. It's probably worth maybe a quarter of a million, maybe more. I was thinking if you just gave it a look, maybe you could think of some way to eliminate this problem for her."

"And why would I care about this? I've told you before I'm just a hairdresser."

"Yeah, I know, I just thought, you know, incase someone ever asked you, well then you could tell them this story."

"And what do expect from me?"

"Expect? Nothing, I'm like you, not involved. Well, that is except that I would consider it a favor if you were to call my friend Heidi and tell her you'd love to do something special with her hair, um, at no charge."

"Now that is the dangerous part of this business."

Chapter Forty-Seven

Morton and I watched the ten o'clock news that night while dining on smoked ribs from Fat Daddy's. The news led with an off season change to the Vikings coaching staff, then went to the latest budget shortfall at the school district, from there to a ninety-two year old veteran getting a purple heart he was never awarded in World War Two and then just before the weather a forty-five second story about an altercation in the seven hundred block of Summit Ave.

The news footage showed the front of Natasha's house with three separate ambulances and an awful lot of cops. No names were given, but I recognized Ramon and Ponytail as they were being loaded into the back of two ambulances. A third ambulance was parked in the driveway with the back doors open. There was a gurney just sitting by the open doors with a black body bag strapped to it. I guessed it was Billy in the body bag.

Some sort of public affairs officer on site gave the standard message to the news reporters. How they'd like "*anyone with any information to please come forward.*" I debated about calling and finally decided I had to tidy up a couple of things before I contacted the police.

The following morning I placed a call to my pal in homicide, Lieutenant Aaron LaZelle. My luck still seemed to be holding, in other words not changing, as in, remaining bad, very bad. I knew things weren't going to go my way as soon as I heard the no nonsense voice on the line.

"This is Detective Norris Manning."

"Actually, I was calling for Lieutenant Aaron LaZelle, I'll try back a little later and…."

"Haskell? Is that you?" Manning's voice seemed to suggest he couldn't believe how fortunate he was to make my life miserable this early in the morning.

"Right, as always, detective."

"Ready to confess to that murder over on Summit Ave yesterday," he joked.

"Actually, that's sort of why I'm calling. I saw something on the news about it this morning and I happened to be working with the owner of that home this past week."

"The Kominski woman? We've been trying to locate her."

"I think I know where she is, I …"

"We'd probably like to discuss this in person, Haskell. Certainly you should be familiar with our procedures at this point. You at home?"

"Well, yeah I am, but I was just about to…."

"This takes priority, I'll send a car around to pick you up. They'll be there in the next ten minutes," he said and hung up.

About an hour later two patrolmen knocked on the door.

"Hi guys," I said as I opened the door.

I noticed they were both wearing leather gloves and the taller of the two had sort of assumed a position that would allow him to pounce. The other guy had his hand hanging close to his Taser, almost in a quick draw mode.

"Devlin Haskell?"

"Yeah, Detective Manning said you'd be stopping by almost an hour ago, let's get going. I got things to do today."

The two officers looked at one another. Then one of them said, "Actually, Manning's the one who told us to expect trouble."

"Trouble? I called down there to talk to Lieutenant LaZelle. Manning got on the line and said I had to be there in person. Sorry you guys have to take time to drive me, but Manning insisted."

They gave one another a look that spoke volumes, then the tall guy said, "Come on, let's go."

We chatted on the way down. "You familiar with Detective Manning?" one of them asked.

"Yeah, unfortunately. Something goes wrong in this town and he knows if he can just push hard enough he'll find out that somehow I'm connected."

"You're a private investigator?" the tall guy asked, he was driving.

"Yeah."

"Manning isn't gonna like you just on general principles. He thinks you guys are a big part of the problem."

"Well, he's really got an in for me."

"Don't limit it to just you. One thing you have to say is that he's broken a number of tough cases. He's good at what he does."

"Yeah, unfortunately what he does is give me a hard time."

Chapter Forty-Eight

I waited for Manning in a small lobby area just outside the door marked "Homicide." I felt like I had been waiting for at least an hour. I was wrong, it was only fifty-five minutes. I was sitting on a chrome and fake green leather chair that had a torn seat with not so much as a "Watchtower" to read. He finally popped his shiny bald head out the door.

"Oh, Haskell. Sorry about the delay," he said not sounding sorry at all. "But, I expected you sooner."

"You said ten minutes, your guys showed up an hour later. Someone told me you'd be out in just a minute, fifty-five minutes ago. Apparently I'm on city time. I don't suppose Lieutenant LaZelle would happen be available?"

"Unfortunately for both of us, no. Shall we get started?" he said and opened the door so I could step in. We walked past a conference room, two smaller sort of chat rooms, an office, a number of cubicles and then down a hallway to one of the "interview" rooms.

Interview room sounds so nice. But the place seems unnaturally cold and the moment you step into the room you can smell the sweat and fear from past occupants that has now permanently seeped into the cinder block walls.

I'd been one of those sweating past occupants more than once and I knew what the place looked like before Manning even opened the door. There was a metal topped table at the far end of the room. An uncomfortable chair, bolted to the floor so that when you sat in it your back was to the wall. The chair was positioned just far enough from the table so you couldn't quite lean forward and rest against the table comfortably.

To your left, as you sat facing a couple of unsmiling interviewing officers was a wall with two-way mirrors. People could come and go in the room behind the mirrors and you'd never know who was observing you. There was a steel sort of cabinet on wheels with three shelves parked in a far corner. It held a series of recording devices, a flat screen, all sorts of cords coiled up and usually a coffee mug sometimes with lipstick around the edge. A waste basket filled with paper cups from the vending machine that dispensed lousy coffee sat next to the cabinet.

Manning held the door for me. "Grab a seat," he said casually, like we had just strolled into his kitchen or a nice coffee shop somewhere.

"Am I gonna need a lawyer here, Manning? I just wanted to tell you guys that I worked for…."

"Please, we'll get to all that in just a moment, but first take a seat," he said directing me by waving a hand holding a manila folder. He smiled as if to suggest sitting in a chair bolted to the floor would be a pleasant experience.

It was a couple of years ago, but I'd been handcuffed to that very chair and interrogated for about forty hours by Manning, at no surprise. Just the unpleasant memory made me shudder.

"Something the matter?"

"No, no nothing."

"Then please, Haskell take a seat." He smiled, but there was a cautionary tone in his voice now. I'd been on the other side of the table from him enough times to recognize it when I heard it. In case I had any doubt his bald, pink head seemed to take on a slight crimson shade and the ice blue eyes sharpened ever so slightly.

I sat down and Manning's eyes seemed to relax and smile in acknowledgment of his modest victory.

"I'd like you to sign this," he said as he opened his manila folder and slid a sheet of paper across the metal table top to me. "Today's date is the twenty-first."

I read a brief paragraph that basically stated I was there locked in a room with Manning in an uncomfortable chair bolted to the floor of my own free will.

"I'll need a pen."

He gave a soft sigh, then reached inside his sport coat and pulled out a pen. It was dark blue and read SPPD on the side in silver letters, St. Paul Police Department. My tax dollars at work. I signed the form and slid it back across the table. He examined my signature for a moment, apparently checking my spelling.

"I'm just going to record this, if that's alright with you, Haskell," he said then inserted a tape cassette and pushed a button on an ancient recording device without waiting for my answer. He basically read out loud the paragraph I'd just signed then stated the date and asked me if I was in agreement with what he'd just read.

I felt like taking a swing at him across the table, but smiled and said, "Yeah, sure."

"So you called this morning and said you wanted to make a statement."

"No, I called this morning and said I wanted to speak with Lieutenant LaZelle. You told me he was unavailable and that I would have to come down here."

"What did you wish to confess to Lieutenant LaZelle?"

"I didn't want to confess anything. I simply wanted to tell him that I had been employed by Natasha Kominski for the past week. I saw a news report last night on TV about some sort of altercation at her home. I had provided security for her. I dropped her off yesterday morning at the Xcel Center where she is competing in the Blessington Kennel Club show. It's my understanding that she will be in that facility, competing for the next three or four days. I might add, I'm no longer in her employ."

That last statement seemed to excite him. "No longer in her employ? Was there a problem? Why did she terminate your employment?" He sounded hopeful.

"No, there was no problem. Our original arrangement was that my employment would be finished when she went to the Blessington show. I was not terminated, I merely fulfilled my original work agreement."

"The show concludes on Sunday, I believe," Manning said sounding perfectly reasonable.

"That's my understanding."

"How does she intend to get home?"

"I don't know, walk maybe. The term of my employment ended when she registered for the Blessington, yesterday. She didn't mention going home and anyway, I've finished my gig."

"Are you familiar with her residence on Summit Ave?"

"I've been there a few times. I was in the house once, no twice actually."

"When was the last time you were there?"

"The day before yesterday, she packed some items, clothing for herself, some grooming items for her dog along with a leash, a couple of chew toys, a ball, that sort of stuff."

"And then what?"

"And then we went to my house, she and her dog, Princess Anastasia spent the night and I drove them to the Xcel Center the following morning, that would have been yesterday morning."

"Now why would she want to spend the night at your place?"

"I just felt it was more secure and it would make the following morning that much easier, I wasn't sure what the procedure would be to actually register at the show."

"And you left her at the Xcel Center?"

"Yeah, security was tight, they had police officers at the door, some bellboy sort of guy with a red hat loaded up her luggage and wheeled it inside. They, one of the officers at the door, seemed to check her name off a list and then he told me that I couldn't get in and to please move my car."

"Did she tell you she forgot anything at home?"

"No."

"She didn't ask you to get anything from her home and bring it down to the Xcel Center?"

"No."

"Are you saying you did not return to her Summit Ave residence at any time yesterday?"

208

I knew where he was going, Ramon and that guy with the ponytail who kicked me probably fingered me for beating them with the tire iron. That meant they fingered me as the guy who killed Billy, too. I had a choice, plead self defense or insist I was never even there.

"That's correct, I was not at her home yesterday. The last time I was there was the night before. She packed her suitcases and then came to my house."

Manning made a note in the file, I figured he would be checking with Natasha the moment he was finished with me. Then he looked up and smiled at me for a long moment. He took off his glasses and rubbed his face like he'd been up for hours and was exhausted.

"You know Haskell, it never ceases to amaze me that almost every time there is some sort of unpleasant activity in this town you never seem to be too far away. Does that strike you as odd?"

"What, that you're amazed?"

He looked at me for a long moment, then put his glasses back on. His ice blue eyes, magnified by the lenses, had suddenly morphed into lasers boring a hole right in the middle of my forehead. He shook his head slowly from side to side. "It's really only a matter of time, Haskell. Very well, you're free to go, for now, but I'm sure we'll be in touch."

"I look forward to it. Can you have someone give me a ride home?"

Chapter Forty-Nine

True to his word, Manning had someone give me a ride home. I had to wait another hour before he got anyone to drive me, but I eventually got there. The first thing I did once I got home was gather up the pistols from Ramon and ponytail, put Morton in the backseat and we took a drive down to the river. I got the Frisbee out of the car and tossed it around for Morton to fetch along the shore. I checked around for a good ten minutes, but we seemed to be alone and I quickly tossed the pistols as far as I could out into the Mississippi.

By the middle of the afternoon we were back home for a late lunch. Morton was gnawing on a steak bone when the doorbell rang.

"I've got a warrant here to search these premises," Manning said. Then he slapped a search warrant against my chest and pushed me to the side as he led four other guys into the house.

"What the hell is this about?" I asked.

"It's all there in the warrant, please step out onto your porch. You can read it out there so you won't be interfering with our work in here."

"What in the hell are you looking for? What do you expect to find?"

Morton was moving his head from side to side, his tongue was hanging out and he obviously thought it was a great idea that all these guys had come over to play. One of the cops scratched him behind the ears and that got his tail going.

"Take the dog with you," Manning said.

We were out on the front porch, Morton and I. Morton was barking hello to everyone who passed while I talked to Louie on my cellphone. "No, I told you I don't have any idea what they're looking for."

"Okay, look I've got a court appearance in about a half hour, shouldn't take more than a couple of minutes, and then I'll be over, not that I can really do anything about this. The warrant looks in order?"

"Yeah, it's that prick, Manning he does everything by the book."

"Shit. Okay, don't say anything to them and do not, let me repeat, do not make another phone call. To anyone, got it?"

"Yeah, yeah. I get it. Look, we'll be sitting on the front porch."

"What do you mean, we?"

"We, me and Morton."

"Okay, I'll see you just as soon as I can."

We were still sitting on the front porch when Louie arrived. I'd been watching traffic for the past two hours and Morton had been sleeping in the sun.

"So how's it going?" Louie asked climbing onto the front porch.

"How do you think? I haven't seen or heard anything. As far as I know they could be in there drinking all my beer, well, except that I don't have any."

"Let me see that warrant," he said then scanned the thing while I went back to watching the traffic drive past.

"Looks in order. No idea what they're looking for?"

211

"Not really. Maybe they got wind of the dope those guys were looking for, but I never touched the stuff, never even saw it actually." Which suddenly made me wonder if I should call the Head Case salon and give Alexi a warning?

"And you contacted the police?"

"Yeah, I thought it would be best to get my involvement out there. I figured they would hear about it from Natasha sooner or later and that it would just be better if the word came from me. You think I shouldn't have called?"

"No, it was definitely the right thing to do. Are they gonna find anything here?"

"Nothing I can think of."

With that the front door opened and four guys walked out of the house two of them were carrying boxes, a third had what looked like a trash bag full of clothing. Manning followed with two plastic evidence envelopes.

"Alright Mr. Haskell, we'd like to thank you for your cooperation. We'll be in touch, we've taken a few things. Nice," he said and held up the two plastic envelopes. Each envelope contained the remnants of a chewed up thong, one belonged to Heidi and the other to Natasha.

Louie looked over at me, but didn't say anything.

"We've left a detailed list of these items on your dining room table. Any questions?" Manning said in a way that strongly suggested we shouldn't ask any questions.

"We're just glad to be of assistance, Detective," Louie said and smiled.

"Oh yeah, and one more little detail, I'm going to need your cellphone, Mr. Haskell."

212

"My cell?"

"Yes."

"What am I supposed to do without it, how am I supposed to make calls, conduct business?"

"Business? I suppose you might try a pay phone if you can find one. Not really my problem. We'll have it back to you just as soon as we possibly can," Manning said and smiled.

I handed him my cellphone and we watched as they placed the boxes and plastic bags into the trunk of Manning's car. Then they climbed into three separate vehicles and drove off.

"These chicks you date, they get off on you eating their underwear?" Louie asked.

"Give me a break that was Morton. What the hell am I supposed to do without a phone?"

"Least of our problems right now. Let's see what else they took," Louie said.

We read through the list they'd left on the dining room table.

"God my laptop? Really?"

"Probably just wanted to watch the porn you downloaded. Bed sheets, pillows, bath towels, computer, cellphone, wine glasses, some silverware, oh, remnants of two thongs, one red and one black," he said then glanced over at me.

"I told you, that was Morton."

"Yeah, sure," he said and handed me the list. "Now level with me, what, exactly do we have to worry about?"

"Nothing, really. Like I said those thongs, one was Heidi's and the other one, um might have been Natasha's."

"Natasha," Louie said and shook his head.

"I'm guessing they'll get DNA off the bed sheets to correspond with that," I said.

"You didn't change the sheets?"

"She took advantage of me, Natasha, I had no idea, honest."

"Sounds like payback to me. What about your laptop?"

"Nothing on there, some work stuff, a few invoices, that sort of thing, but nothing relating to Natasha or the Blessington Show other than I looked the thing up online just to learn a little about it. Oh, I did some research on Tommy Allesi and, well now come to think of it, Natasha, too."

"That's not incriminating. Anything related to that incident with your visitors?"

"You mean that bunch of thugs? No, I'd taken a couple of pistols off two of those scumbags, but I disposed of them."

"Disposed of them?"

"In the river, actually. Let me check that list, again," I said then ran down the list once Louie handed it to me. "I was just thinking those guys drank all my beer and ate the last of a pizza, I don't see any beer bottles mentioned here."

"Get them out of here all the same. I don't mean put them in the trash. Take them to a recycling center, or somewhere, but get them out of here. Otherwise, I think you're good to go, but you know that damn Manning would like nothing better than to nail you, so let's not provide him with that opportunity. Did you have that phone with you when they put you in the car trunk?"

"No, I left it here, on the floor right by the front door."

"That's one of the things they'll check. See if they can pick up your signal path. So you didn't have it with you when you were at Natasha's, you're sure?"

"Positive."

"Okay. Then I don't see a problem," Louie said.

Chapter Fifty

The problem was Manning knocked on my door the following morning. By the time I got out of bed and downstairs to answer he was pounding on the door, pounding so hard he was shaking the pane of glass. Morton was barking up a storm. There were two rather large uniformed officers standing directly behind Manning out on the front porch.

"Oh, Haskell, did we wake you?"

"It's barely after seven. No, you didn't wake me I've been entertaining a pair of twins, upstairs."

"Well, fortunately for them we'd like you to accompany us downtown. Just a few more questions."

"You could have called."

"Not really, you gave us your phone."

"Actually you took it. This can't wait?"

"No, it can't."

"Let me get dressed, I'll be down in a bit."

"I'll have one of the officers accompany you, Jacobs," he said then indicated with a nod of his bald head. The larger of the two stepped inside and smiled, Manning and the other officer followed.

"Gee, come on in."

"The sooner you're ready, the sooner we can get started and then the sooner we can finish and get on with the rest of our day."

"Let me get dressed, come on Jacobs I know you want to watch."

It was a quiet ride down to the station. Jacobs and his partner, a cop named Medina were in the front seat. I was seated in the back, behind the protective screen. There were no door handles in the back. At least they didn't handcuff me, but I figured that was because it was so early there was really no one around to embarrass me as they placed me in the backseat of the squad car. Manning was driving himself in another vehicle.

"You guys work with him a lot, Manning?"

Medina was driving and looked at me in the rear-view mirror. "Maybe you should just check out the scenery."

I suppose if I had to work with Manning on a regular basis I'd have that kind of lousy attitude, too. Jacobs and Medina brought me up to the homicide unit and deposited me in interview room one. It was the same room I'd had the pleasure of talking to Manning in yesterday. I sat there alone for the better part of an hour before Manning breezed in, I think I had actually dozed off a little.

"Haskell, thank you for your patience, let's get started," he said then sipped from a Starbuck's cup.

"Sounds good to me. The first thing I'd like to do is call my attorney, Louie Laufen and get him down here before we begin."

"I can do that, if you really want to. On the other hand I just have some general questions that shouldn't take too much of your time."

"You pounded on my door a little after seven this morning. You've left me sitting in this interview room for over an hour while you apparently went to Starbucks and now you're in a rush to get things moving? Like I said I want to call my lawyer."

"Suit yourself, this is liable to slow things down, but it's certainly within your rights to do so," Manning said. He didn't look too happy.

"Nothing's happened so far and I'm going on two hours, let me just get him down here. Now, if you don't mind I'll have to use your phone."

Manning looked unhappy, but nodded then brought me out to an empty cubicle. "Just press one-four and you'll get an outside line."

I did as instructed, after two rings I was dumped into Louie's message center, "You have reached Louie Laufen, I'm unable…."

I left a message telling Louie to contact Manning and hung up. I looked at Manning lingering just a few feet away. "Now what?"

"I guess we wait, I'll be working at my desk." The unspoken part was I would apparently be cooling my heels in the interview room.

"You got a magazine or a coloring book or something I could read?"

"No." Manning said and that was that.

Chapter Fifty-One

I thought it was close to four in the afternoon before Manning popped his pink head in the door. "Just heard from your attorney, he's on his way. You need to use the bathroom or anything?"

"No, thanks for asking. I'll be right here."

"Yes, you will," he said and closed the door.

Louie waltzed in about a half hour later. "Sorry, I was in court first thing this morning, had to get a continuance for next week. My client got food poisoning at the workhouse last night. He couldn't sit in the courtroom for more than about five minutes." Louie chuckled at the thought of the City Prosecutor objecting to his client getting sick in the courtroom.

"What the hell time is it, must be going on about five."

""No, it's just a little after eleven," Louie said glancing at his watch. Then he asked, "What are we up against?"

"I got no idea, Manning was pounding at my door about seven this morning with two pretty big guys in tow. They locked me in this room and I've been sitting here ever since."

Louie sort of made a face, but didn't say anything.

"What are you thinking?" I asked.

"I think something must be up, I just have no idea what."

"Join the club," I said.

With that Manning opened the door. "All right to get started?"

Louie glanced in my direction, I gave him a nod and he said, "Please, the sooner I can return my client to the outside world the better."

Manning strolled in with a rather thick file and minus the Starbucks cup this time. "Yes, Mr. Haskell, in our conversation with Natasha Kominski yesterday she mentioned an altercation with yourself and five other individuals. I believe this took place at the Hidden Falls Park. I'd like to hear your version of those events."

"Really not that much to tell, Detective. This bunch of guys showed up, there were actually six of them, it looked like they were going to harm Ms Kominski. Fortunately, I was able to convince them that wasn't the best idea. Pretty much end of story."

"And how did you *convince* them?"

"A rational discussion, I suggested we might all be better served if Miss Kominski and I were allowed to simply leave the area."

"Did this rational discussion have anything to do with discharging an automatic weapon within the city limits, as a matter of fact in a public park?"

"I felt at the time it was the best way to get their attention."

"What was the result of your rational discussion?"

"Like I said, we left the park."

"You didn't damage any of their vehicles in the process?"

"No, I did not."

"So, you didn't slit the tires on three vehicles?"

"No, that was a friend of theirs, a gentleman by the name of Denis Malloy."

"Now why would a friend do that, slit the tires on a pal's vehicle?"

"Beats me," I shrugged.

"Did you happen to threaten this individual, Mr. Malloy?"

"Not in so many words. I just suggested he might help out, so they wouldn't be able to follow us and then we left, Natasha Kominski, her dog, myself and my dog. I figured the sooner we got out of there the better it would be for everyone."

"Did you threaten Mr. Malloy with a weapon?"

"I don't recall."

"I believe Mr. Malloy might seem to think that was the case. Two other individuals who were present at the time suggest he was forced by you, at gunpoint, to slit the tires on three separate vehicles."

"I'm not quite sure what you're referring to."

"I'm referring to your threatening a half-dozen innocent individuals by waving around an automatic weapon. I'm referring to your discharging that weapon. I'm referring to you forcing one of these individuals, Mr. Malloy, a man in the process of recovering from his injuries...."

"Detective," Louie interrupted. "If I might ask a question here. You've named Mr. Denis Malloy, I believe he is most likely out on bail following his arrest after a failed attempt to unlawfully enter Ms Kominski's home. If memory serves, doesn't Mr. Malloy have a bit of a history with your department?"

"That has no relevance to this investigation."

"The other individuals, you've not given us their names, but it sounds like they were in that park for the

221

express purpose of, at the very least, intimidating Mr. Haskell's client. It's not a huge leap to suggest that in fact intimidation was just the beginning of what they had planned. I might point out that Mr. Haskell and his client, a vulnerable, single woman, alone in an isolated park along the river felt more than a little at risk and threatened."

"Your client pulled an automatic weapon on these gentlemen."

"Apparently, with very good reason. Gentlemen? Honestly, Detective, Mr. Haskell was confronted by five, no, make that six known criminals. Within little more than twelve hours two of these individuals were hospitalized and one was dead after being involved in some sort of altercation at Ms Kominski's residence. With all due respect I think you, and your department, should be thanking Mr. Haskell for preventing nothing less than a murder in that park. I'm sure our news organizations and the local paper would find your particular line of inquiry interesting to say the least."

"Once again, your client, Mr. Haskell remains a person of interest in an ongoing investigation."

"And, if you're doing your job you know that my client had nothing what-so-ever to do with the violent episode these gangsters were involved in. You have his cell phone, I imagine you can trace his movements. Have you stopped to ask the individuals who were hospitalized what, in fact, they were doing on private property? I believe you have reports of shots being fired. Have you investigated that little tidbit? Or, are you once again consumed with attempting to link my client to a horrific event that he had nothing to do with?"

"We have a man who was murdered."

"Yes, no doubt a known criminal and no stranger to this department, along with two of his partners in crime who have undoubtedly corroborated their stories in an effort to point the finger at the only bright spot in this entire sordid affair, Devlin Haskell."

"We're examining all aspects of the incident."

"Maybe check with Denis Malloy, the very individual who was transported to the hospital a few nights before after being injured during an attempted break-in at the same address. Have you executed a search warrant on his home? Have you interviewed him? Have you confiscated his laptop and cell phone?"

"We're in the process of locating Mr. Malloy."

"So, in the meantime it's no big deal to just hassle my innocent client and make his life more difficult. The same individual who contacted this office in the first place."

"Save it for a jury," Manning said and stood up. "Okay, you're free to go, get out of here, both of you."

"Always a pleasure," Louie said and headed out the door.

I followed as fast as I could before Manning changed his mind.

Chapter Fifty-Two

"Tidbit? Sordid affair? Bright spot? You sounded like you'd gone through some sort of religious conversion." I said.

"God, that guy can be such a sanctimonious jerk."

"He does have a way of getting under your skin, doesn't he?"

"Tell me about it," Louie said.

We were eating a late lunch at Fat Daddy's Bar-B-Que. Fortunately, Louie, me and Morton were the only ones in the place. Fat Daddy had let us bring Morton in. He was lying at my feet, Morton not Fat Daddy, and gnawing on a giant shoulder bone.

Like always, Fat Daddy was seated behind the cash register, all five hundred pounds of him, just staring out the window and sipping from a plastic glass filled with bourbon and lots of crushed ice.

"You pick up on what he said about Denis Malloy?" I asked.

"You mean that they were looking for him? Yeah, I did."

"So, what do you think?"

"So? I don't know, Dev anything you want to tell me?"

"Tell you? I don't know a thing, well other than the guy seems to be a perpetual loser. It's not too big a leap to think he might have just left town, at least until things cool down a bit."

At this point Louie had dripped Bar-B-Que sauce on the lapel of his wrinkled grey suit coat, his tie and his wrinkled white shirt. He dropped his hand along his side and snapped his fingers to get Morton's attention then let Morton lick the sauce and grease off his fingers tips before he reached for another rib and took a big bite.

"Umm, here's the thing. There's seems to be enough incentive to keep these idiots circling around your client, Natasha…."

"Former client."

"Whatever, and I'm guessing they aren't going to stop until they get what they want. That's point number one. Point number two is, at this stage they may be seeing you as a major obstacle and worth their effort to eliminate you."

"Meaning?"

"Watch your back."

I figured there was no better place to do that than at the Blessington Kennel Club show.

Chapter Fifty-Three

I'd gone to rock concerts that cost less. Close to a hundred bucks for a ticket and not an over served woman in sight. I stood in the 'Standing Room Only' section along the outer rim of the first floor. There's a wooden rail you can lean against and sit and watch whatever event you were attending, for me that usually meant a hockey game. The Blessington was my first dog show.

I'd had to wade through a group of PETA protesters waving signs about purebreds and dogs dying in shelters. Two weeks ago I would have ignored them, now after having had Morton living with me I at least took one of their handouts and intended to read it later.

Various dogs were being worked through a course of jumps, tunnels, poles and more in the agility competition. They all appeared well trained, but I had no idea about the finer points of judging the event. I did know that Morton would have had a hell of a time. I'd brought my binoculars from the office and scanned the crowd from time to time.

After about an hour of leering at a number of higher class women I spotted Tommy Allesi across the way and down in a front row seat. I couldn't spot any thugs sitting around him and made my way around the arena so I was positioned in the back of his section. He remained watching and apparently making the occasional note for another two-and-a-half hours before he finally left his seat. I moved toward the stairs as he headed up toward the mezzanine.

He was dressed in casual grey slacks and a navy blue sport coat that probably cost more than my car. Today he wore a pink golf shirt, embroidered with the Lady Slipper logo, and he had some sort of VIP ID hanging around his neck.

"Mr. Allesi," I said and held out my hand at about the same time as he recognized me and a scowl swept across his face.

"Never figured you for the culture type, Haskell," he said ignoring my extended hand and not breaking stride.

"How's Princess Anastasia doing?" I said falling in alongside him.

"Thus far, she's winning, but it's still very early in the show. I'm sure at some level even someone like you can appreciate the competition at this event. From here on, it's all up to chance, but then that's been my business for the past three or four decades," he said and flashed a quick, but unfriendly smile.

"Your friend Denis Malloy watching?"

"Denis? Hardly a friend. More like a very troubled individual, I should think he'd be more along your lines than mine. As I've stated before, my dealings with him are strictly on a business level."

"You realize he attempted to confront Natasha and the princess with a gang of five other thugs?"

"What?" he said and did a sort of double-take, based on his reaction I think he was genuinely surprised. He stopped in mid-stride and pulled my arm so I had to turn and face him. The crowd heading to various food and beverage counters automatically flowed around us as if we were just two stones in a large stream.

"You don't know about this? The other evening down along the river, at Hidden Falls?"

He shook his head. I still didn't know whether to believe him or not. I proceeded to tell him about the five thugs and Denis going after Natasha and the princess. How I'd grabbed the AR-15 out of my trunk. I told him about Denis slitting the tires on the cars, but didn't mention my encouragement. I had the real sense this was news to him and he was hearing it all for the first time.

"Son-of-a-bitch," he said and I could sense the wheels turning. "What in the hell does she think she's doing?"

"The truth?"

"No, please lie to me. Yes, I want the truth, damn it. What do you know?"

"I'm pretty sure Natasha *confiscated* a rather large amount of dope and…."

"Oh, Christ, don't tell me, the medical marijuana thing, again. She actually believes she's going to convert the world. I think the authorities in Colorado suggested it would be a good idea if she left the state. I'm almost sure that's what they told her in Seattle. She just doesn't get it, she's, I don't know…."

"Book smart, but rather naïve?" I suggested.

He had a disgusted look on his face and shook his head. "Damn it, why aren't you still providing Natasha and Princess Anastasia with security?"

"That ended about forty-eight hours ago. She told me once she was here, at the Blessington that they'd be safe."

"Maybe from obnoxious fans and cellphone cameras, but not from the likes of the morons you described. This is exactly the point I was attempting to make that evening on her front porch."

"And when Denis followed me home?"

"That jackass. No that wasn't me. Yes, I mentioned the incident to him, no to answer your question, I did not suggest that he follow you in the hopes of committing an assault. Denis has a habit of grabbing onto a kernel of an idea and running with it, usually in the wrong direction. He and I may just have to have another chat."

"If you can find him."

"Are you available, can you use some work?"

"To tell you the truth I don't really need another headache. I've got someone down at the police department working overtime trying to tie me to everything from the Kennedy assassination to 9/11."

"I have a large bit of change wagered on this event, The Blessington. There's only three days left, what's your rate?"

I thought for a moment and said, tell you what, six hundred a day, that's eighteen hundred total and expenses, plus one more thing."

"Which is?"

"I want you to include my eighteen hundred in whatever you're betting on, you win, I win. Fair?"

A smile crossed his face and Tommy Allesi extended his hand, "I may have misjudged you, Haskell. I'll have to get some credentials for you so you have freedom of movement, they like to think they have things fairly locked down around here."

"And for my dog."

"That Golden Retriever? The one who licks everyone? A little high class for him, isn't it?"

"He needs to rub shoulders with a higher class crowd."

"Alright, let me see what I can work out, meet me back here in two hours," Tommy said.

Chapter Fifty-Four

That gave me just enough time to wander down the street and buy a pay-as-you-go cellphone, a "Burner" as they're referred to, then I grabbed a couple of bratwurst with sauerkraut and a beer for lunch once I was back at the Xcel Center. I was standing on the mezzanine swimming in a current of caramelized onions and deep fried fat when I spotted Tommy coming out of a door marked "*Security*." He half waved and actually looked almost pleased to see me.

"Here, take this," he said handing me a plastic VIP card hanging from what looked like a giant red shoe lace. "Put this on and it'll give you access to just about everywhere, and here's one for your dog, too. You go through that door marked "*security*" and down the stairs, that'll put you in the boarding area. There's an office down there, just ask and they'll direct you to Princess Anastasia and Natasha."

"Now, I just have to convince Natasha," I said.

"I already spoke to her, she seemed to, oh, I don't know, be rather pleased with the idea. Something about relieving her stress level," he said and sort of raised his eyebrows.

"I had better get down there then," I said and headed toward the door.

A guy in a blue windbreaker with yellow letters that read "*Security*" was just on the other side of the door, he just gave me a nod and waved me past once he spotted the VIP credentials.

Down two flights of stairs and I was in a large auditorium sort of room I never even knew existed. At the far end of the room were a dozen large overhead doors that looked like they led to loading docks. The auditorium itself had been sectioned off into hundreds of small bays equipped with kennels, cots and all sorts of equipment. There was a constant conversational hum, a buzz of noise, lots of barking and the up-to-the-minute play-by-play from large monitors covering the competition going on two floors above. The office was just off to the right.

"May I help you," an efficient looking woman asked. She was standing behind a receptionist sort of counter, next to a large plastic salad bowl filled with red and white peppermints. She looked to be in her mid-forties. I guessed she might have three or four kids and therefore not a lot of time to waste. Behind her sat three guys monitoring a bank of security cameras, none of whom bothered to turn around and check me out.

"I'm looking for Natasha Kominski," I said.

"Oh, yeah, Princess Anastasia," the woman replied and quickly leafed through a clip board on the counter. "Here we go, aisle J, unit eighteen. Just take a right out this door, each aisle is numbered on the floor, number eighteen will be about a quarter of the way down on your right hand side."

"Thanks," I said, grabbed a peppermint and went on my way.

Unit eighteen was exactly where I had been directed; down an aisle with individual areas about ten feet wide cordoned off on either side. Each unit was designated by a number hanging from the top of an eight foot high metal frame, curtains hung from all of the frames affording some modest degree of privacy. Number eighteen was draped with heavy, red velvet curtains trimmed in gold that reached to the floor. A sign about five feet long with twelve inch letters in a fancy gold script and black shadows hung from the eight foot frame and read; "*La Princesse Anastasia.*"

"Natasha?" I called.

"Oui. Oh s'il vous plait, ne venez en," a voice answered from behind the curtains.

I had no idea what she said so I pushed the velvet curtain aside and stepped onto a thick, blue and red, oriental rug. Princess Anastasia sat at attention in a large kennel off to the side. Natasha sat at a makeup table on the opposite side wearing a short red-silk robe. A sleeping cot was positioned in the middle of the area. Her back was to me and she talked as she continued to apply her eye-makeup.

"How very nice to see you again, Devlin Mr. Allesi stopped by earlier and suggested you might be just the thing for a stress release. I couldn't agree more, however we are pressed for time at the moment. We'll be performing in just twenty-five minutes," she said briefly turning to look at me. "Princess Anastasia and I, not you and me," she said then turned back to her mirror. She made eye contact with me via her makeup mirror, flashed a quick smile my way then went back to work with her eyebrow pencil.

I was going to tell her there was some mistake, but decided to keep my mouth shut for the moment. I noticed the cot was barely large enough for only one individual to sleep in, thank God. Next to the cot was a small glass fronted refrigerator, filled with red, green and gold foil covering the corks on about a dozen different wine bottles. An expensive looking mahogany end table with turned legs held her silver tray with the handles and four long stemmed crystal glasses.

"Actually, we, Allesi and I, thought it might be a good idea to just keep an eye on things based on the incidents over the past few days. It would be a shame for you to make it this far only to have something unfortunate happen," I said hoping to refocus on my actual purpose.

"I'll have another cot moved in here for later tonight."

"Oh, not to worry, that won't be necessary."

"Neither one of us will get any sleep if we're both in that," she said with her back to me, pointing at the cot with her left hand. She continued to deftly work the eyebrow pencil with her right hand. Eventually, she put the pencil down on the makeup table. She turned to face me for a moment not bothering to close the red silk robe and said, "Then again, who knows? Just about anything could happen."

Chapter Fifty-Five

"I suppose I'd better get dressed, we're due in the on-deck area in twelve minutes," Natasha said.

"I'll just wait outside."

"Oh, not to worry, you're just the incentive we need for a show stealing performance."

"That's okay, I'll be right outside," I said then quickly slipped out through the red velvet curtains and waited on the far side of the aisle in front of unit fifteen hoping she wouldn't call me.

She didn't call, for a good five minutes. Then I heard, "Mr. Haskell, Devlin, would you mind giving me a hand, please."

At least she wasn't speaking French. I stepped across the narrow aisle, and slipped back in between the velvet curtains. Natasha stood with her back to me, wearing a silky beige blouse, a black thong, flesh colored stockings with a dark seam up the back and a black garter belt. As I stepped inside and pulled the curtains closed she bent over, shot a lingering glance at me over her shoulder then slowly began to pull a tweed skirt up from the floor, revealing a pair of sensible brown walking shoes. She took her time as she slowly hiked the skirt up her legs and over her thighs, moving her hips from side to side as she did so. I had to admit, she looked awfully damn good.

"I wonder if you'd do the honors and just zip me up in back," she said still with her back to me.

I stepped over and reached for the zipper.

"Oh, say, be a dear and tuck that blouse in back there, I can't seem to reach it."

I lightly tucked in her blouse and she gave a slight sigh, "Make sure it's all the way down and not bunched up. Oh, and if you don't mind around the hips, too as long as you're there. Mmm-mmm, nice, yes very nice thank you. Alright, I'm afraid you might as well zip me up."

I pulled the zipper up quickly then immediately retreated back to the curtain. She seemed to chuckle to herself, then picked up a matching tweed jacket from an upholstered chair and handed it to me. I held the jacket open as she slipped her arms into the sleeves then wiggled back and forth as I raised it over her shoulders. The woman who just a moment ago was standing in front of me in a thong and garter belt had suddenly been transformed into a schoolmarm in a conservative tweed suit. She reached over and gave me an innocent pat on the cheek then smiled, slipped on a pair of brown framed glasses and said, "It's show time." She clipped a leash onto Princess Anastasia's collar and we headed up to the competition area.

We took an elevator up to the main floor of the Xcel Center, walked down a very short corridor and stepped into the competition area, not quite the size of a hockey rink. I could see the seats around the entire arena were filled. Natasha and the princess walked over to the side and waited patiently in the On-Deck circle while I was instructed by two security guards to remain outside the competition area.

When the team in front of her, a short, grey-haired guy with a beagle, had finished Natasha waited a few minutes before she was waved forward by one of about a half dozen judges. A voice filled the arena announcing Natasha and Princess Anastasia. As she walked into the competition area she was greeted with a round of polite applause which immediately stopped the moment she gave a signal they were about to begin their routine.

Maybe two minutes into Natasha's routine a young woman walked past me with what looked like a chocolate lab on a leash and headed for the On-Deck circle. A handful of claps and a whistle or two greeted them and one got the immediate sense that something in the atmosphere had suddenly changed. A disdainful glare at the crowd from two of the judges brought the smattering of acknowledgement to a halt.

A ten minutes later Natasha and Princess Anastasia completed their routine. With Natasha's hand signal they both gave a bow to the judges, then to the crowd and left the competition area to polite applause. Just as we headed out of the competition area and back into the short corridor that brought us to the elevator the arena filled with whistles, shrieks and heavy applause.

The announcer's voice was all but lost in the ovation. "Ladies and gentlemen, please welcome Miss Melinda Kissler and Hershey, her three year old Chocolate Lab."

Natasha pressed the button for the elevator then glared at me. "We'll just see how things work out for that bitch over the next two days."

"Hershey is a female?" I asked as we stepped into the elevator.

"What?"

"Hershey, I don't know, that just seems like kind of a strange name for a female."

"He's not a female," she smiled.

"Okay," I said as the doors opened and we headed back to her unit.

Natasha was finished for the day and wasted no time in having me open a bottle of chilled, white wine. Once she was settled into her chair and I'd filled her glass I said, "Hey, would you mind? I was going to bring Morton down here, give him a look around, you know let him hang with high class dogs for a change, see if any of it rubs off."

"I'd prefer that you keep him away from Princess Anastasia. I'd like her to remain focused on the competition. If we make the cut, and I've absolutely no doubt we will, the last thing we need is a distraction, tomorrow's competition will be rather crucial."

"Not a problem." I pulled out my business card and a pen. "I'm getting an upgrade on my phone, here's a number to reach me at if you need anything while I'm gone."

"You are coming back, aren't you? I'd feel a lot more comfortable with you nearby tonight," she said then raised her eyebrows as she sipped.

"Yes, we'll be back," I said, then gave her a little wave and got out of there as fast as possible. I could only hope Morton would prove to be a successful deterrent to whatever Natasha had planned.

Chapter Fifty-Six

On the way home to pick up Morton I phoned Louie. "Hey you anywhere near a computer?"

"Hello to you, too. Yeah, as a matter of fact, I am. What do you need?"

"See if you can look up the betting odds on Best of Show for the Blessington Kennel Club."

I heard some keys clicking in the background and then a long pause.

"What'd you find out?" I finally asked.

"Actually, I'm still checking this might take a while. When did you get your phone back? I thought Manning was going to call me when they released it."

"I didn't get it back, I went out and picked up a pay-as-you-go. I'm working a new gig."

"Really? Well, at least you're not working for that nut case with the dog."

"Not in so many words."

"What?"

"Tommy Allesi, he hired me to provide Natasha Kominski, the nut case, and her dog, Princess Anastasia with security. That's why I wanted to check the odds on a winner for the Best of Show. Tommy said he's got a lot of money running on Princess Anastasia, but there's another dog here named Hershey that at least seems to be a favorite with crowd. Tommy doesn't strike me as the kind of guy who'd let something like sentimentality get in the way of a winning bet."

"It's going take a bit of digging to get the odds, give me the number I can reach you at."

I gave Louie the number just as I pulled up in front of my place. Before I got out of the car Morton was standing on the living room couch, looking out the window and barking.

I got Morton fed, then took him on a mile long walk in an attempt to calm him down. I called the Head Case salon while I was walking Morton, double tasking to my way of thinking. A bubbly voice answered, I pictured the young girl I'd seen in there the other day with all the metal piercings and wondered if they caused any interference with the phone.

"You have reached the Head Case," she answered.

"Alexi, please."

"He's busy with a client just now. Can I take a message and have him call you back when he's free?"

I gave her my name and new number, then piled Morton into the back seat of my car and we headed down to the Blessington Kennel Club show.

Chapter Fifty-Seven

Morton just lounged in the back seat while we drove down and I parked the car. He could not have cared less when I clipped the VIP ID onto his collar. He was relatively calm as we approached the front door. Once inside, he immediately sensed something was up and began to strain at the leash, I had to use two hands to pull him back.

"Morton, settle down, man or you're going to get both of us kicked out of here."

He seemed to dial back, but I walked him over to a corner and just to be sure I said, "Princess Anastasia."

He looked at me as if to suggest, "Doesn't translate."

I said her name a couple more times just to see if I could get a reaction from him. "Princess Anastasia, Princess Anastasia, princess, princess, princess," I said and he gave me a look that suggested I was wasting both our time.

"Okay, good to go, buddy," and we headed through the security door. We had both our passes checked on the other side, Morton remained calm. I almost wondered what sort of chemical he was suddenly on, but figured a heart worm pill wouldn't have this sort of effect. His tail started wagging once we were downstairs. It really took off as we headed up the "J" aisle. By the time we were approaching number eighteen I was holding Morton back with both hands as he strained at his leash.

I pulled his head close to my knee and called through the curtain, "Natasha?"

There was a giggle and then a slurred, "Oui, oui, oui, it's about time, better get that little tushie in here, the party has already started without you."

As we stepped inside, Princess Anastasia, who had been lying alongside Natasha's chair immediately sat up in her best pose, then ignored Morton and looked the other way.

Morton's tail wagged back and forth, beating like a drum against the heavy red velvet curtain.

Natasha sat in her upholstered chair with her feet stretched out across a royal blue suitcase, using the thing as a foot stool. She was wearing her red silk robe, and the black garter belt. A bucket of ice sat on her makeup table and held an open bottle of wine. An empty bottle stood on the floor next to her chair and another empty lay on its side, rolled up against a black suitcase a few feet away. Her sleeping cot had been replaced by a larger affair with what looked like a double sized, yellow air-mattress sitting on top.

"Here's to an interesting night," Natasha slurred then raised her glass in a toast and proceeded to slosh wine over the rim and across her silk robe. She either didn't notice or didn't care.

"Have you had anything to eat?"

"I fed Anastasia at exactly six, right on schedule," she said and took a large sip.

"What about you? Have you had anything to eat?" I asked although at this point I didn't think it was going to make much difference.

242

"Guess I'm just on the liquid diet tonight. Is that Melvin?" she said looking at Morton.

"Close, this is Morton. Morton, you remember Natasha and Princess Anastasia," I said hoping he wouldn't do something stupid.

The Princess casually looked over at Morton. She was sitting very still, but I noticed her tail seemed to race at about ninety miles an hour.

Morton strained at his leash, it took some doing, like about ten minutes worth, but I finally got him to sit and stay relatively calm.

"I better have another and you should pour yourself a glass, maybe see if that will get you in the mood, Morton," Natasha said looking at me,

I figured she was way past the point of correcting. I refilled her glass, poured one for me, but left my glass resting on the silver tray. I'd been here countless times before, on both sides of the table. She took a couple of sips, fought to keep her eyes open, took one or two more sips then let the glass slowly lean to the side. I took the glass from her hand and set it back on the tray, then opened the kennel door and got Princess Anastasia inside.

The lights had been dimmed substantially although not completely off, but things had definitely quieted down. Natasha remained curled in the chair and began to snore. I covered her with the light blanket resting on the double sized air mattress. I laid down on the air mattress then wrapped Morton's leash around my wrist and we gradually went to sleep. Morton slowly edged his way toward the kennel until he could look at the princess and the two of them seemed to fall asleep staring at one another.

Chapter Fifty-Eight

I had no idea what time it was, late, that was for sure. The overhead lights had been turned down even further until there was just the dimmest ring of light along the outer edge of the auditorium. I had been sound asleep until a slight "*click*" noise woke me. At first I thought it might be Natasha pouring herself another glass of wine, but I could hear her snoring in the chair somewhere off to the side.

I opened my eyes and saw a crouched figure slowly opening the kennel door and reaching inside. The princess gave a frightened little whine just before I heard a growl and the figure screamed and jumped to his feet. Morton rose up with him, hanging firmly onto the guy's rear end by his teeth and giving off a vicious growl.

Another silhouette quickly disappeared out through the velvet curtains, he looked large and I think he had a crewcut, but he had vanished too quickly for anything to register.

Meanwhile, screaming and anguished cursing came from behind me as the figure spun round twirling a growling Morton hanging on by his jaws. I swung as I jumped up and caught the guy on the chin, then knocked him down with a left to his temple and a right to the bridge of his nose. As he went down his head bounced off the edge of a foot locker and then he remained very still on the floor.

I pulled Morton off just as the velvet curtain was pulled back and a large shadow stepped in and said, "Security, what the hell is going on."

Morton growled and barked and the guy quickly reached out with some sort of aerosol can.

"No, please don't, don't. We woke up and this guy was in here trying to take the princess," I said, hanging onto Morton's collar and at the same time looking into the kennel to check on Princess Anastasia. She seemed to be untouched, although she was cowering in the far back corner of the kennel.

"You know him?" the guy asked as he shined a flashlight onto the bloodied face lying on the floor. Another security shirt stepped in behind him.

I shook my head and said, "I've never seen him before," Although I thought he could have been one of the five guys from the other day at Hidden Falls and quite possibly one of the guys sitting in my living room drinking up all my beer yesterday morning.

Natasha suddenly snorted a few times then half rolled over onto her side. Her silk robe more or less covered her hip, but her garter belt and the stockings with the seam up the back were clearly on display.

"Just relieving some stress tonight, maybe a little glass or two, too many," I said by way of explanation.

The two security guards gave a knowing glance to one another.

"Whatever," the guy with the flashlight said, then shined his light back on the figure lying on the floor. He was slowly moving his bloodied head back and forth and then raised one of his knees halfway up.

"Looks like you broke his nose."

"Yeah, and my partner here took a chunk out of his ass. He's probably gonna need some stitches."

245

"We'll let the cops determine that. Come on, let's get him out of here. We'll need you to make a statement, sir. You can follow us to the office." Then the two of them roughly helped the guy to his feet and sort of half walked and half dragged him out into the aisle.

Morton got a good rub behind the ears and a hug from me. I double checked the latch on Princess Anastasia's kennel before we made our way to the security office.

Chapter Fifty-Nine

The police were in the office before we even got settled. They radioed in that they'd be taking the guy to Regions Hospital for stitches. "He got bit in the ass," one of the cops chuckled over the radio just before they led the guy away in handcuffs.

Morton had ripped the right half of the guy's jeans open and they now hung as a blood covered flap exposing the guys chewed up butt cheek and what was left of his shredded boxer shorts.

One of the security guys had tossed Morton a dog biscuit, taken his picture and was now busy rubbing his ears and telling him he was "Very good and very brave."

"Stop it, that'll just go to his head and he'll be impossible in the morning."

"That jerk was either going to take that competing dog or worse, if your Morton here hadn't been there, there's no telling what could have happened, I'm not kidding."

I filled out an incident report, gave them my personal information. They gave me a copy of the report, made a copy of my VIP ID along with Morton's and stapled them to the report before we were finally allowed to go back to Natasha and Princess Anastasia.

"Come on, I'll give you guys a light on the way back," the guard named Gary said. He flicked on his flashlight and we followed him back to number eighteen. He held the curtain for us as we entered and said, "Good luck later today," and then left.

Morton strained at the leash in an effort to get next to Princess Anastasia in the kennel. I glanced over at snoring Natasha praying she would stay asleep.

Morton whined then barked.

"Morton, knock it off, damn it, quiet down," I hissed.

He barked again and Natasha snorted a couple of times as I peered into the empty kennel where Princess Anastasia was supposed to be and suddenly realized we had a very big problem.

I pulled Morton back through the curtains then called, "Gary, hey Gary."

He popped his head back around the corner of the aisle and began walking toward us, he seemed to pick up his pace the closer he came, obviously sensing something wasn't right.

"Gary, she's gone. Princess Anastasia, she's not there."

"You sure?"

"Yeah, Morton was the first to notice, I looked, she's not in her kennel."

"Ms Kominski?"

"She's in there, still asleep. I doubt she even moved while we were gone."

"Could she have gotten out, Princess Anastasia?" he asked already reaching for the radio on his belt.

"No, I double checked the kennel myself before we left for your office. Someone must have come in and grabbed her. I'll bet it was that guy with the crewcut, damn it, I shouldn't have left."

248

"Crewcut? All units, possible kidnapping. Princess Anastasia, a white, full size French Poodle. Missing for no more than forty minutes." He put the radio down for a moment. "Any idea what the guy looked like?"

I quickly told him the little bit of information I had.

"Suspect believed to be male, Caucasian, large with a crewcut, blonde hair, tribal tattoos on his arms." He gave me a look suggesting "*Does that sound right?*"

I nodded then looked around in all directions trying to figure out where that guy could possibly have gone to.

"We've got people stationed at every exit. Believe me, they aren't going to just let somebody walk out of here in the middle of the night, especially with a dog. We'll get her back, come on lets check the monitors. That will be the most efficient thing we can be doing right now."

Morton and I followed Gary as he hurried back into the office. We stepped behind the counter and over to the bank of monitors to check the images. The other guy who had helped Gary turn our intruder over to the police was already reversing through images of aisle "J' on one of the monitors.

"Nothing so far," he said without looking up.

With the lights turned down in the auditorium the images were even more dim and hazy than normal. A digital clock on the screen reversed slowly as the guy scanned through the images, one at a time. About ten minutes into the effort he paused, the digital readout on the screen read '3:11AM'. The image was of a fairly large guy, with close cropped hair, maybe a crewcut. He looked like he was carrying a very large bundle of cotton. He was just stepping off of aisle "J" at the far end of the auditorium away from the security office.

"There he is, there's your man," he said.

Gary was on his radio, giving the time and the sighting position to everyone. The guy working the monitor was picking up the phone and calling 911. All Morton and I could do was sit there and wait.

Chapter Sixty

"I'm Allen by the way," the guy at the monitor turned and said. "I think it might be beneficial to check the exterior camera's, Gary. Let's make sure he hasn't left the building yet. There's not that many places he can hide if he's still here."

"Unless he's teamed up with someone in the competition," Gary said.

"Just get on one of those monitors and start scanning we don't have to go back more than an hour. You could get on one too, Mr. Haskell, it'll save time," Allen said.

Gary set me in front of a monitor and I started scanning a series of images from the past hour. I went through them one by one. One image shot every four seconds factored out to be fifteen images per minute, or nine hundred images over the course of an hour. Until you've done it you've no idea how easy it is to become numb just looking at nine hundred images of the same empty sidewalk in the middle of the night.

"Okay I'm finished, I didn't see a thing," I said about fifteen minutes later.

"Good, let me get another camera on your monitor and you can check those out," Gary said just as the same two cops who'd taken the guy to Regions Hospital stepped back into the office.

"Did your dog bite someone else?" one of them joked then immediately shut it down once he saw the look on our faces.

"We got a problem," Allen said then showed them the grainy, dim black and white of the guy carrying Princess Anastasia around the corner.

"Any idea where he might have gone?"

"We're checking that now," Allen said as I started clicking through another nine hundred images and fought to keep my eyes from crossing.

One of the cops took a couple of steps away from us and got on the radio attached to his shoulder. I could hear him talking, but couldn't make out what he was saying. I refocused on the monitor screen bringing up a different length of dim, unchanging, empty sidewalk outside.

"We're going to get some other folks down here," the cop said once he got off the radio. "Have you caught any other images of this guy? Seen him anywhere else?"

"We've been focused on the exterior, making sure he hasn't left the building. I don't think he's been outside, so far," Allen looked over at Gary.

"I haven't seen anything," Gary said.

"Not a thing," I added.

"At least he doesn't appear to be armed, still," he said staring at the screen with the image on it. "I told the team coming over to check in here. In the meantime, why don't you stay on those monitors. If you can direct us to where he was last caught on camera we'll hopefully find this idiot."

Allen walked them out of the office, pointed to the far end of the auditorium and then appeared to give them a brief idea of the layout by pointing in a couple of different directions.

I stared at the monitor with the grainy image of the guy with both massive arms wrapped around Princess Anastasia. He looked like the guy with the crew-cut from the other day, kind of, sort of, I think, maybe.

I worked my way through another nine hundred different images of the same sidewalk only from a different angle and didn't see anyone. Gary loaded another nine hundred up on the monitor for me and I started back at square one, again. I was looking at the east side of the building, Allen told me there were five cameras on that side and I wondered, *"Could it get any worse?"* Then I did some quick calculation in my head and figured that once we were done with this exercise we'd probably have to start back at the first tape we'd looked at to cover the past thirty minutes. It reminded me of one of those math equations from ninth grade, the kind that helped steer me away from any more math courses than absolutely necessary.

Four more police officers arrived and Allen brought them outside of the office and seemed to give them the same directions he'd given the first two cops then came back in to run through more outside images.

"Hey, check this out," Gary said a few minutes later. He indicated the screen on one of the live monitors. A channel eleven news crew had pulled up out on the sidewalk. It was just about five in the morning, and the doors to the Xcel Center weren't due to open until eleven.

"Maybe they just want to make sure they have a good position," I said.

Both Gary and Allen gave me a quick glance.

"I wish," Allen said sounding more than a little worried. The office phone rang a moment later. "Shit," Allen said and reached for the phone.

Chapter Sixty-One

"Security," he answered and then a dark cloud seemed to pass over his face. "No, I have no comment. Thank you, we appreciate your concern, but we have no comment. Thank you, good bye," he said and hung up.

"Not good?" Gary asked.

"Somehow the words out."

"How the hell could that have happened? Who even knows except us, well and the police?" Gary asked.

"This is going to really complicate things. You guys keep scrolling through those images I'm going to have to make some phone calls," Allen said then got up and headed toward a desk in the far corner of the office.

I returned to the images on the screen in front of me. It was kind of like looking for life on a portion of the moon. Nothing changed.

A few minutes later Gary groaned. "Oh, oh, check it out, not good," he said and indicated the live screen with the channel eleven news crew. Another van had pulled up behind it, the camera angle was such that I couldn't read the station it represented, but the antenna's and satellite dishes mounted on top left no question as to what it was for.

"You think they know? Maybe it's been a slow news day and they just want to interview folks waiting in line or something."

"First of all," Gary said. "No one is waiting in line. Second of all, Allen's still on the phone. Not good, not good at all, look for things to heat up in the next sixty minutes."

About twenty minutes later a couple more security folks drifted in, including another computer monitor guy whose name I forgot as soon as he told me. Four more cops showed up shortly after that. Allen pulled himself away from the phone and seemed to give them the same directions as the others just outside the office. Two more guys showed up a few minutes after that and spoke with Allen. I heard the word "hostage" mentioned and then Allen directed them to a couple of desks in the back of the office.

Allen looked like he'd been dragged through a knot hole and I noticed Gary was suddenly clicking through the images on his screen a lot faster than I was. I picked up my pace until it was like staring at a live film of an empty sidewalk. All I needed was some sort of dull, downer poetry recited in the background to make the experience completely depressing.

There was movement and sound emanating from outside the office. People were beginning to move around, some heading toward the restrooms, but quite a few others standing in the aisles, huddled in small groups. Occasionally someone would look or point to the office, someone else would shake their head.

Two women walked into the office a few minutes later. The older of the two, she could have been the mother they looked that similar, said, "We demand to know what is happening." Things quickly went downhill from there.

"Gary, I'm going to have to check in and see if my client has woken up. I'll have to fill her in. I'll be back to help just as soon as I can."

"Good luck," he said not taking his eyes off the unchanging images on his screen. Morton and I wove our way around various groups of people. Occasionally I picked up a phrase here and there; "Murder" and "Suicide" seemed to be two of the more common terms. No one mentioned the word; "Kidnapping".

All too soon we arrived at unit eighteen and I stood out in the aisle for a long moment debating what my chances for survival were. I heard a groan followed up with a hacking cough coming from the other side of the red velvet curtains, so I took a deep breath and entered.

Chapter Sixty-Two

Natasha was in the process of just waking up, stretching and groaning with her eyes closed. She was still wearing the garter belt and stockings as well as her little silk robe although it really wasn't covering much.

"Mmm-mmm, we must have had a good time, God, I can't seem to remember a thing," she said then stretched some more and rolled her head back and forth.

"Actually, there seems to be a slight problem," I said.

Her face clouded and she suddenly sat up straight. "Slight problem? Whatever do you mean?"

There seemed to be something in her response, but I couldn't quite put my finger on it. "Well, it seems Princess Anastasia isn't exactly here … at the moment."

"What?" she screeched and flew off the chair. In one fell movement she was on her knees in front of the kennel. She unlatched the kennel door, tore it open and half crawled inside apparently thinking Princess Anastasia might suddenly appear.

"Where is she? What have you done with her?" she yelled. She was down now on all fours and half-way inside the kennel.

"I haven't done anything. As a matter of fact, Morton and I fought off some guy who snuck in here last night. You were passed out in the chair, or at least asleep and didn't wake up. We had security in here. I've spoken with the police, they arrested the guy and hauled him away. They're here now, the cops, looking for the princess. As far as we can tell she hasn't left the building."

"Hasn't left the building," she screeched rocketing off her knees and up into my face. All sense of Ivy League propriety had vanished in an instant. "You don't know where she is? Oh my God, you worthless, worthless excuse for a man. We're scheduled to compete this noon. I've got to get the authorities involved," she said then pushed me out of the way as she stormed through the velvet curtains.

By the time Morton and I stepped out into the aisle she was running in the direction of the security office with the short silk robe flowing behind her like some sort of super hero cape. All heads turned as she rushed past. We quickly followed in her wake.

Natasha was screaming, "Security, police, security," as she ran. By the time Morton and I entered the office a crowd had followed and was gathering just outside. They stared in through the office windows, wide eyed.

Allen had Natasha by the arm and was escorting her to the rear of the office where two officers in civilian clothes were sitting. Morton and I made our way thru the gathering crowd and into the office.

"Well then, exactly what *do* you intend to do?" Natasha was screeching at the cops by the time we made our way through the crowd and entered the office.

Both cops had a deadpan look on their face, like they were waiting for her to just get all the emotion out before they could get down to business. Based on the invectives and abuse being hurled at them by Natasha right now they were going to have a long wait.

It never failed to amaze me when people responded this way toward the very individuals whose help they so desperately needed.

"Apparently, neither one of you is listening. Let me repeat myself, I want to know what, exactly, you intend to do."

"Please Ma'am if you would just calm down for a moment, we need your name and then we can start…."

"My name? Listen here you young fascist, this has nothing to do with my name. I'll tell you what I need. I want the name of your superior, right this instant. How could you let something like this happen? My name? What difference does that make ? I…."

"Natasha Kominski," I said walking up from behind. "My name is Dev Haskell. I was in here after we caught the one guy earlier. It looks like that's when this other slime bag snuck back in and grabbed the dog, Princess Anastasia."

"The poodle?" one of the cops asked.

"No, a standard sized poodle, you might wish to write that down as long as you're just sitting there wasting valuable time," Natasha said, she'd found her Ivy League accent at this point.

Neither of the cops wrote anything down. One of them was running his eyes up and down her figure taking note of the black garter belt extending a few inches beneath the silk robe. He seemed to be making a general assessment that I figured began with something like, "*Maybe I could get your private phone number…*"

"Natasha, everyone is here to help, right now, both you and your attitude are getting in the way and slowing things down. I think these gentlemen might have a few questions to ask you and if we could maybe just give them as much information as possible then they could do their job."

"Oh, thank you, isn't that nice. If you'd been doing the job I'd assigned to you in the first place we wouldn't even be here right now."

"And if you hadn't passed out from the three bottles of wine you drank last night maybe you could have watched Princess Anastasia while I had to deal with the intruder we stopped and had arrested. Really not the point right now, is it? So, let's get down to business, as you so gracefully suggested, and stop wasting valuable time. Please," I said and indicated an office chair for her to sit down.

She sat down with a flourish, crossed her legs and folded her arms tightly across her chest where she remained red faced and smoldering. Her posture suggested this was going to be anything but productive.

"Can you describe the individual we're looking for?" asked the cop she'd called a young fascist just a moment ago.

"No, it was dark," Natasha replied.

"And, you were passed out and snoring," I added. "He's white, tall, six three or four, blonde hair, a crewcut, no facial hair. Big guy, body builder type, I guess he'd come in at about two hundred and twenty pounds. It looked like he was in a dark colored T-Shirt, didn't notice any writing on it, but that doesn't mean there wasn't something. I think he was wearing blue jeans. Oh yeah, and tribal sort of tattoos over his biceps."

"I've got Gary printing off the image we have from one of the security cameras. It's not the best, but it's better than nothing," Allen said.

Natasha frowned and let out an exasperated sigh, "Oh, for God's sake."

"Did he have the dog on a leash?" the fascist asked.

Natasha didn't have a clue, of course and looked over at me.

I waited and gave her a look suggesting, "*Go ahead, you seem to know everything.*"

"He was carrying her, at least in the image we have." Allen said.

"Natasha, would you go back to your area and see if the leash is still there, he might have brought his own, but at least we'd know he didn't take yours."

She glanced around quickly then got up and left without making a comment. Allen and the two cops watched her hurry out of the office.

"Sorry about that guys, she's pretty upset."

"Understandable under the circumstances so don't worry, it comes with the territory. At least she's easy on the eyes," one of them said, then watched as Natasha hurried out of sight.

Chapter Sixty-Three

Natasha returned about ten minutes later. She was wearing a T-shirt, jeans and a much better attitude. "I wish to apologize for my behavior earlier. I hope you can understand, this is quite disconcerting for me."

"No need to apologize, Ms Kominski," the young fascist said.

"Don't worry about it," the other cop said. "Is there anything you'd like to add?"

"All three of the leashes are right where I left them. Beyond that, nothing else seems to be missing. I realize this is sketchy information at best, but it's all we have to offer at the moment," she said then looked over at me.

"If its okay, I'll get back to looking at exterior shots just to make sure this guy is still somewhere in the building," I said.

"And we'll get these images out to our people as well as your security folks," the cops said.

"Thank you," Natasha added and quickly made her exit.

"I'm really sorry guys, this is her worst nightmare and unfortunately you guys caught the flak," I said once Natasha was out of the office. As I spoke we all watched her through the windows making her way past the crowd and heading back to her booth. She wore a look that suggested she didn't know where to turn.

"Like I said, it comes with the job, we better get moving," the other cop said and they were suddenly up and out the door.

I joined Gary back at the monitors, there were two other guys with him now reviewing images.

"Anything?" I asked.

"The good news is no, we haven't seen him outside. If you've got time we could have you start going through the interior shots, couple of cameras covering the areas where he was last spotted. We're just about current with the exterior images and he hasn't shown up."

"Yeah, I'll do that. It just occurred to me, wouldn't it make sense for him to try and leave here once the doors open? You know when it's crowded, much more difficult to spot him at that point," I said.

"Doors open at eleven, usually there's a crowd waiting to get in. If he could find a place to hold up for a few more hours that would maybe make sense," Gary said.

"Offices, storage rooms, maybe even rest rooms," I said.

"I'll get people on it right now. We've called in everyone we can think of for added security around here," Gary said.

I started going through the first of thousands of interior shots Gary had just sent to the computer in front of me. Morton took a brief look at the computer screen before he laid down, rested his head on his paws and closed his eyes.

It was more of the same for me, only these mind numbing shots were of the interior. Gradually, as I worked my way through the files individuals began to appear in some of the images. That was fine initially

264

and brought a welcome change to the numbing sameness, but in short order it slowed down any real progress I'd been making. A second or two longer to study the individuals in every image multiplied by literally thousands of images brought any sense of progress to an almost dead crawl.

And then another hour or so later of looking at images and there he was; crewcut, jeans, what looked like a plain black T-shirt. He was standing in the middle of an aisle, looking completely relaxed and sipping from a coffee mug. He looked like your average early morning riser. In the image three people were just walking past him and appeared not to give him a second glance. The princess was nowhere in sight.

"I got him," I said and looked at the digital readout, the image had been taken almost two hours ago.

Gary rolled his desk chair over next to mine, repeated the catalog number of the image a couple of times to himself then rolled back to his keyboard. He brought the image up next to the first one of the guy carrying Princess Anastasia down aisle "J".

"Definitely the same person. Looks like he might still be here," Gary shouted and a couple more guys crowded round his monitor. He input the catalog number and brought up another dozen images that had the guy gradually moving down the aisle and out of camera range.

Gary brought the images up from the next camera on the aisle, there the guy was again, casually walking down the aisle sipping from a coffee mug. Gary tracked him through two more cameras, and then he disappeared.

There were a number of us gathered around his screen watching as the guy seemed to suddenly disappear from view. "Where in the hell did he go?" I asked.

"He's gotta be in one of those booths right around there, he must have just ducked into one."

"Oh no," Allen groaned and we all turned to focus on the flat screen mounted in the upper corner of the back of the office.

Chapter Sixty-Four

The morning news show was just in the process of breaking to a live report. A headline ran across the bottom of the screen, black letters on a yellow background. "***Breaking News - Kidnapping at the Blessington Kennel Club - Breaking News - Kidnapping at the Blessington Kennel Club – Breaking News – Kidnapping at the Blessington Kennel Club***...."

"Where are they getting this?" someone asked. "*We* barely know what in the hell is going on."

Allen changed the station only to find the same story was being covered live albeit by a different reporter. This would only serve to make the task of finding Princess Anastasia more difficult.

"Who recognizes this aisle, anyone?" Gary asked drawing our attention away from the news reports and back to the specific issue at hand, finding Princess Anastasia.

"I think it's toward the back of the auditorium, close to the restrooms," a guy said.

There was a distinctive set of leopard skin drapes hanging across one of the booths. I saw no point in waiting. I just grabbed Morton's leash, a grainy printout of the guy's image, and we headed out the door toward the back of the auditorium. We made our way to the restrooms then started heading up and down aisles looking for the leopard skin drapes. We found them in the third aisle.

I reminded myself that the leopard skin drapes meant nothing more than Crewcut had been here, or near here. I forgot to tell Morton, however. As we approached the drapes he suddenly charged through and barked before I could get hold of him and pull him back.

As I pulled him back into the aisle he was followed by a very tall, very lean guy with knobby knees and elbows stepping out from behind the drapes. His yellow teeth appeared much too large for his thin lipped mouth. The hair from the nostrils of his large, hooked nose seemed to flow directly into his handle bar mustache.

"Sorry about that," I said and tried to dismiss Morton's entrance with a laugh.

"Really, I'm not sure what you were thinking, perhaps you weren't, thinking that is. Given the unfortunate circumstances of this morning, not to mention the ongoing competition, one would hope this sort of intrusion wouldn't occur. May I ask what, exactly, *you* are doing here? Are you even allowed in this area?" He looked down disdainfully at Morton and then appeared to be even more disappointed when he finally settled his gaze on me.

"Really sorry, we're looking for a friend and thought he might have been here? I wonder if you wouldn't mind taking a look at this image and…"

"Hardly sufficient reason for the intrusion," he said then appeared to examine our VIP badges, shook his head and scoffed, "Oh for God's sake, will it ever end?" Then he slipped back behind his leopard skin drapes and yanked them closed.

We walked to the next booth, knocked on one of the aluminum posts and I called, "Excuse me."

A moment later the curtain was pulled back and a woman stepped out into the aisle. I immediately recognized her as the owner of the chocolate lab named Hershey. The one that had received such a rousing round of applause once Princess Anastasia had left the competition circle yesterday and at the moment the odds on favorite to win the best of show.

"Yes?" she said giving me the distinct feeling I was interrupting something.

"Sorry to bother you, I'm wondering if you may have seen this individual," I said and handed her a copy of the grainy black and white image we'd printed off.

She seemed to study the image for a long moment before handing it back to me. "No, afraid not. I've no idea who that might be, was there anything else?"

"No, sorry to bother you." I said as she quickly slipped back behind her curtains and pulled them closed.

We stepped across the aisle and knocked on another aluminum post. No answer. We knocked on the booth next to that a moment later. A short, stout woman pulled the drapes aside and peeked out.

"Hi," she said. Then immediately bent down and asked, "Now who is this?" She gave Morton a good rub behind his ears, which set his tail wagging.

"I'm sorry to bother you, I'm looking for this individual," I said handing her the image of Crewcut. He was right in this vicinity maybe an hour or two ago. Any idea where I might find him?"

She took a quick look at the image and said, "Why that looks an awful lot like, Cecil."

"Cecil?"

"Yeah, the Kissler's. Hershey, Melinda and … well there he is now. Say Cecil, Cecil, just what have you been up to? Look, this guy's got a picture of you here," she laughed and waved the image up over her head.

I turned round and there was Crewcut, just stepping into the aisle directly across from us with a shocked look on his face, icy blue eyes widened in surprise and his mouth opened as if he were about to say something. Instead, he suddenly shoved a passer by into me and took off running in the opposite direction.

"Cecil, say Cecil?" the woman called as he sped away.

Morton and I took off after him.

Chapter Sixty-Five

The aisles were crowded with an awful lot of people who apparently had time on their hands and seemed to be wandering aimlessly. There were a number of photographer's taking pictures and dogs. Lots of dogs. In between pushing people out of his way, Crewcut stepped over a Cocker Spaniel and then a Basset Hound, hurtled over a Great Pyrenees clipped an Irish Setter and stayed well clear of a German Shepard. We were in hot pursuit as he headed for a stairwell.

"Call security, call security," I kept yelling. Morton seemed to pick up on what we were doing and increased his pace. He looked up at me as if to say *"You're really slowing me down."*

I let go of his leash and yelled, "Go Morton, go, Princess Anastasia. Get him Morton, get him," I called after him as he took off. In a matter of seconds he was on Crewcut.

Crewcut heard Morton give a vicious bark and growl and did a quick glance over his shoulder just as a maintenance guy wheeled a large plastic trash bin around the corner. He was just in the process of turning back around when he ran into the trash bin at full speed. Bottles, cans and papers flew in all directions as he stumbled and Morton leaped onto his shoulders. He tore Morton off and threw him against the brick wall. Morton gave a loud yelp as he bounced off the wall then rolled across the floor and seemed to shudder.

Now it was my turn and I slammed into Crewcut just as he was getting back on his feet. I wrapped my arms around his shoulders and pulled him back down. He rolled with the tackle giving me an elbow across the side of my head in the process that had me seeing stars as my head bounced off the concrete floor. He seemed to twist away effortlessly and was climbing back to his feet when I grabbed his ankles and he went down again. He gave me a knee on the chin then kicked his heel into my nose before he snatched up a beer bottle from the trash scattered across the floor. He bounced the bottle off my forehead and I curled up into a fetal position with my hands trying to protect myself as he smashed me over the head with the bottle. He scrambled to his feet then stepped back to kick me in the face and I knew I was finished.

Thank God Morton wasn't, he suddenly sailed out of nowhere with a deep throaty growl and his teeth bared. He clamped onto Crewcut's thigh taking him down and then hung on, Crewcut dropped the beer bottle as he fell. He rolled over, wrapped his massive hands around Morton's neck and began to squeeze just as I wound up and slammed my fist right between his eyes.

I remembered a combat instructor in the army telling us to think past the target. Don't think about hitting someone in the face, visualize punching all the way thru to the back of the head. I wound up and swung punching thru to the back of Crewcut's head, connecting with everything I had just as he half turned and focused on my fist heading toward him. I don't think I've ever hit anyone harder in my life.

272

It knocked him back, and he released his grip on Morton just before his skull bounced off the concrete floor and his eyes rolled up into his forehead. I blacked out and learned later that I had kept on hitting him. I guess it took two of the security guys and a cop to pull me off him.

They transported Crewcut to the hospital in the back of a squad car. Morton and I had the luxury of the paramedics and an ambulance ride. Morton had a fractured rib, a sprained hind leg and a cut that required six stitches. When next I saw him he wore one of those cones around his neck to keep him from 'attending' to his wounds.

I got two black eyes, a fat lip, a powder-blue nose splint and a temporary cast on my wrist after hitting Crewcut as hard as I did.

Apparently Princess Anastasia was found safe and sound, locked in the same kennel with her arch rival Hershey the Chocolate Lab. It turned out that Cecil "Crewcut" Kissler was estranged from his wife, Melinda and the initial thought had been that he'd kidnapped the princess and placed her in Hershey's kennel to embarrass her. At least that was Melinda's version.

Natasha and Princess Anastasia missed their one o'clock competition for the semi finals. I guess that meant they were out of the running which was really too bad, but there wasn't a damn thing I could do about it.

For my part, I was just glad to be finished with the entire, sordid affair.

Chapter Sixty-Six

It was close to dinner time, Morton and I were finally home, splitting a beer along with a large bag of Bar-B-Que potato chips and just taking it easy. We were watching <u>Topless in Tropicana</u>, sort of an artistic DVD. The dialog was a little weak and I had been thinking, "*If I never went to another Blessington Kennel Club show it would be alright with me,*" when the phone rang.

"Haskell, Tommy Allesi."

"If you'll just give me a moment I can explain everything, I think. See, Natasha drank three or four bottles of…."

"That's not why I'm calling."

"Oh?"

"Where are you now, you out of that hospital yet?"

"Yeah, we're both at home here, resting."

"We?"

"Morton and I."

"Morton? Oh yeah, that dog, even better. I'll have a driver pick you up in ten minutes."

"To tell you the truth, Tommy neither one of us is in any condition to work. I've got a cast on my wrist, a nose splint, a ringing in my ears, a goose egg on my forehead and I can't walk without limping. Morton's been stitched up, has a fractured rib, a hind leg in a splint and one of those protective cones on his head."

"Sounds perfect," Tommy said.

"What?"

"You haven't been watching the news? Natasha and Princess Anastasia got some sort of special dispensation or something. They're competing in the semifinals, tonight at six. It's been all over cable news and the internet, the story's gone viral."

"I was just checking out some international news," I said and picked up the remote to turn down the sound. Six girls in Tropicana were giggling, about to step into a pool of jell-o and wrestle wearing only blindfolds.

"Look, my car is on the way, Natasha could really use your support down there, plus well, it will give you a better shot at winning."

"Winning?"

"Yeah, you told me you wanted the eighteen hundred I'm paying you, placed on the princess, remember?"

"What are the odds?"

"They were about a hundred to one when she was kidnapped and I placed the bets. Now that you found her they're back to about fifteen to one and getting tighter by the minute."

I figured I could do the math while waiting for Tommy's car. "We'll be waiting out front," I said then picked up the remote again and turned off the tube just as the first innocent stepped into the pool of jello.

"Car's on the way," he said and hung up.

Morton and I had been waiting outside for no more than a minute or two when a shiny G class Mercedes, dark blue not black, with shiny chrome wheel rims pulled up at the curb and we hopped in back. Mercifully, this time the driver wasn't Denis Malloy.

"Here are some security passes, for you and your dog, Mr. Haskell," the driver said handing them over the seat as he sped down toward the Xcel Center and the Blessington Kennel Club. "Mr. Allesi sent along a cane for you to use."

"I'm just limping, it'll be okay."

"Actually," he said looking at me in the mirror. "He sort of, you know, would prefer that you use it. Kinda give folks the idea that you were involved in a struggle, like."

"I got a nose splint on and a pair of black eyes that make me look like a raccoon for Christ's sake."

"Sorry, I'm just following orders. They'll have some sort of handicap assistance for you at the door, take you right down to a front row seat. I'll drop you off at a special entrance, Mr. Allesi has it all arranged."

"Yeah, okay whatever." I was starting to understand what Tommy was doing, which led me to a whole lot of other questions.

Chapter Sixty-Seven

The Mercedes cruised to a stop at the handicapped entrance and a cop stepped over to open the
door for us.

"Hey, don't forget the cane here, Tommy wants
you to use it. I'd appreciate it too, it'll be my ass if
you don't, you know."

I nodded, reached over the front seat and took the
cane. I clipped on my ID, then Morton's and we gingerly stepped out of the Mercedes.

"Great job, earlier today, guys," the cop next to
the door said just as the handicapped door to the Xcel
Center opened and another cop made a sweeping gesture with his hand and said, "Your welcome awaits."

There was one of those motorized carts with a
driver, just like at the airport, waiting to take us to our
seats. Only this cart had a sign on either side that read
"Morton" in large black letters and then beneath that,
my name sort of as an after thought, in much smaller
letters. Red, white and blue banners were draped on
either side and the back of the cart.

The crowd parted like the Red Sea as we drove
along the mezzanine. All sorts of cell phone's were
flashing and taking our pictures, people were pointing
at us, clapping. A buxom blonde bounced toward the
cart, but just as I thought I might get lucky she
squealed, grabbed Morton's nose and rubbed it in her
cleavage. Eventually we were dropped off at some
sort of press entrance. We hobbled through a door and

down a short ramp toward the front row on the ground level.

Tommy Allesi was there waiting for us at the end of the ramp just before we entered the seating section. A gorgeous redhead in a form fitting ushers coat, very short black leather skirt with slits up the side and sheer black stockings stood leaning against Tommy with her arm linked in his.

Morton did his usual gorgeous woman greeting and thrust his nose up under her skirt. She didn't so much as blink.

"Great to see you, Haskell. I gotta say that nose splint and your dog's protective cone couldn't be better," Tommy said.

I sort of shrugged.

Tommy nodded at the redhead then said, "Let Pinkie here put a sling on that arm." He nodded toward the temporary cast on my wrist.

"Oh, thanks, but that's really not necessary."

He ignored my comment and moved his head slightly in my direction. Gorgeous Pinkie sprang into action gently running a deft hand along my neck and then across my shoulder during the process of fitting the sling on my shoulder.

I was thinking maybe this wasn't such a bad idea after all. She settled my arm into the sling, gave me a quick peck on the cheek and stepped back, smiling. I became momentarily lost in the faint scent of sensuous perfume.

Tommy's cellphone suddenly beeped and he pulled it out and read a text message. "Okay, they're just about ready to start, Pinkie will lead you out there."

"You're not joining us?"

"No, they don't need to see me, besides this is your moment, Haskell so please don't screw it up. Okay, honey," he said then patted her on the rear and Morton and I followed her through the door.

We stepped into a darkened arena with a number of spot lights sweeping round, back and forth over the crowd. It took a moment for my eyes to adjust, but from what I could tell the place was packed to standing room only.

Chapter Sixty-Eight

Pinkie stood there looking gorgeous, exuding her sensuous perfume and waited. Just as I was about to ask her what was up a smooth voice came over the loud speaker system.

"Ladies and Gentlemen, a special round of applause for our two hero's of the competition. Won't you please welcome three year old golden retriever, Morton." The arena erupted in cheers and then as sort of an after thought he mentioned, "Along with Morton is Mr. Devlin Haskens." The spot lights swept back and forth across the crowd and then suddenly landed on the three of us. The roar of applause, cheers and ear splitting whistles grew even louder.

Pinkie gave a big, happy, sexy wave to the crowd, then turned and shrugged at me. "Doesn't matter what they call you. Come on now, you just stay real nice and close to me, baby." Then she sort of blew me a kiss, winked and stepped off. We followed her to our seats as the applause and whistles continued.

Morton acted like this was just an everyday occurrence as we limped behind Pinkie to a plush viewing box sitting on a raised platform. The seats were upholstered and as Pinkie bent over to prepare the seats and move a foot stool in front of my seat her short leather skirt rose up even further and a fresh wave of whistles and applause erupted.

"Have a fun night, maybe we can link up later," she said, slipped a note with a phone number into my hand, then deftly ran her fingers up the side of my face and strutted off.

The lights came up in the arena and things gradually seemed to settle down. The judges, there were six, walked out one by one into the competition area as their name was announced. Once they were all assembled in the middle of the competition area a hush fell over the entire arena and the lights dimmed. It became eerily quiet for a long moment before the announcers voice boomed out and the spotlights all focused on the entrance to the competition arena.

"Ladies and Gentlemen. For the first time ever, in the ninety-three year history of the Blessington Kennel Club a *very special*, scored, semi-final competitive trial. Please welcome Princess Anastasia, a three year old standard poodle and Ms Natasha Kominski."

Once again the place erupted into deafening applause. I clapped, but I literally couldn't hear my own hands clapping. Natasha strode out into the spotlight with the princess on a leash, waving and smiling at the crowd. She did a full circle around the competition area acknowledging everyone before she headed over to Morton and me. They both made a graceful bow which only increased the noise level by another ten decibels.

I saw Morton barking at the princess, but I couldn't hear him. I attempted a gracious bow back toward them, Morton's tail was wagging a mile a minute. And then things finally settled down and Natasha began to run the princess through their routine.

When they'd finished their routine, fifteen minutes later, the scores from the judges flashed up on screens throughout the arena. The eighteen thousand plus crowd went wild as each score came up on the screens. Four perfect and two near perfect scores flashed out over the crowd on the giant monitors.

Forty-five minutes later Morton and I were being driven home in the back of Tommy Allesi's Mercedes. Morton seemed about as tired as I felt and to tell the truth, I was looking forward to a cold beer or two and the rest of the night on my couch.

"We'll pick you up tomorrow right around the noon hour," Tommy said turning around in the passenger seat to talk to me.

"Tomorrow?"

"Yeah, what, you forgot? It's the damn finals."

"Do we really have to?"

"You gotta be kidding me, Haskell? Were you paying attention out there or just focusing on Pinkie's rear end? You and your dog there were worth at least twenty points on the score sheets, the emotional impact was tremendous. I knew it would work, but I never figured it for this much. If I had any sense I'd probably have Simon here rough you up a little so we could grab even more sympathy at the finals tomorrow."

Simon looked over and chuckled.

"We're going to hang onto the cane and that sling, they worked wonders. You could maybe use something to darken that bruising around your eyes. Maybe fatten that lip up with a hammer or something."

"I don't think so."

"Yeah, you're probably right, no sense in overkill. Tell you what might help, just a slight, occasional grimace as you're sitting or standing. You know, just to keep the crowd hooked."

"I think you might have the wrong guy for that sort of bullshit, Tommy."

"Well, let me just remind the *wrong guy* that his eighteen hundred bucks is riding on that Princess Anastasia winning. That doesn't happen, I'll be more than a little unhappy, not to mention, you got your ass handed to you by Cecil Kissler for nothing."

I could suddenly see the logic. "I think that sling and cane might just do the trick. I'll pet Morton out there on our viewing platform. What do you know about the other dogs in tomorrow's competition?"

"There's only one, the former favorite, Hershey. But I never…."

"Hershey? The owner is Melinda Kissler? Her husband's Cecil? The guy who kidnapped the princess in the first place? How the hell are they even competing?"

"Some extenuated circumstances, sort of an estranged marriage, maybe. Lot's of questions, anyway, she's the competition. Look, we couldn't have asked for anything better. Talk about good versus evil and like I said, just having you and Fido there will be worth a solid twenty points with the judges."

"His name is Morton."

"Yeah, whatever. Anyway, Princess Anastasia needs to win by fifteen points for you to get paid. You be there tomorrow with a limp and a grimace and that alone will be worth twenty points. I don't like doing anything halfway, I want to make sure they win." With that Simon pulled to the curb in front of my place and Morton and I carefully climbed out.

283

"Tomorrow," Tommy said then closed the door and they sped off.

Chapter Sixty-Nine

Morton and I were waiting on the sidewalk for Tommy Allesi a few minutes before noon. Tommy's Mercedes pulled up promptly at twelve and we climbed in.

"Good job, Haskell, fantastic, you look even worse than yesterday," Tommy said.

"Gee thanks, same drill today? The grand entry and all that nonsense."

"You can't tell me it didn't work. By the way," he said and tossed the sling over his shoulder into the back seat. "Slip this thing on and don't forget to use the cane. Remember, I'll want you doing the occasional grimace out there as well. The dog is still limping, right?"

"Yeah, Morton's still limping, not to worry."

"Good. We'll all meet afterward down in that flop house area where they've been sleeping. Get some PR photos taken, that sort of nonsense. Then, you want out, Simon will be happy to take you wherever you want to go," Tommy said and glanced over at Simon.

"Sure, sure thing," Simon said.

They dropped us off at the handicapped entrance and I grabbed the cane before hobbling out of the car. Just like before there was a courtesy cart with signs on either side and red, white and blue banners waiting to deliver us to the door marked "Press". The crowd parted to make way for us, people applauded and so many cellphone cameras flashed I was afraid my PTSD would kick in.

Once through the "Press" door Morton and I waited alone for a good twenty minutes before Pinkie strolled down the ramp. I could hear her stiletto heels clicking before I saw her. She looked even more sexy than last night, if that was possible.

"Hi, Pinkie, great to see you," I said.

Morton gave her his version of a greeting again beneath her short skirt.

"Mmm-mmm, very good boy," she said rubbing Morton behind the ears before she shot a sexy smile in my direction and blew me a kiss.

A few minutes later we heard the announcer come across and introduce the judges again, one by one, to polite applause. I looked over at Pinkie and she gave me another sexy little smile and shrugged just as the announcer said, "And now, the heroes of the show, the team that made it all possible, Morton." The area exploded in applause as we followed Pinkie out the door and then just stood there while the announcer began shouting, "Morton, Morton, Morton," and the crowd picked up the chant.

Search lights swept back and forth across the standing room only crowd before they finally zoomed in on us. Between the whistles, the cheers and the applause the welcome was deafening. It grew even louder than the night before and the announcer finally said, "And Mr. Devlin Haskens." My name couldn't be heard above the din of the "Morton" chants, not that I really cared.

I grimaced, waved and then focused on sexy Pinkie's tight little leather skirt as she led us to our elevated viewing box. It took a good ten minutes for the applause and cheers to die down. We were seated and then I grimaced to my feet a half dozen times and waved at the crowd which got them to begin to quiet down, but then Morton would bark and they started back up again. Finally the crowd settled down and the two semi-finalists were announced.

First came Hershey, with Melinda Kissler. The two of them walked out into the competition area where they were received with a rather chilly reception of tepid claps and more than a few hisses. The announcer's voice seemed almost flat and one of the judges leaned over and said something to the judge next to him. She in turn shook her head and gave a shrug which seemed to translate to something like, "*Serves her right. What do you expect?*"

Both Hershey and Melinda appeared to be more than a little intimidated as they glanced around the arena. Melinda wore a toothy, pasted on smile and eyes that seemed to scan the crowd in terror. Hershey seemed to pick up on the fact that things weren't right and began to act rather skittish.

After a painfully long moment of mostly quiet punctuated by the occasional hiss the announcer said, "And now, without further ado, Princess Anastasia and Ms Natasha Kominski."

The place erupted. Between the applause, the whistles and the cheers I was sure I was going to suffer permanent hearing loss. Natasha and the princess walked what could only be described as a victory lap around the area, waving and smiling before the final round of competition had even begun.

I watched Melinda Kissler and Hershey off to the side and you could see whatever crumb of confidence they might have had coming into the arena had now completely vanished.

As the applause for Princess Anastasia and Natasha finally died down they took their place off to the side and waited for Hershey to be put through his routine.

The judges gave a formal nod and Melinda and Hershey began. He started into the first obstacle, weaving in and out of a length of upright poles placed rather closely together. Halfway through he more or less quit and simply bolted to the far end. At least there weren't any hisses or boos, but the two of them were finished. He did alright jumping over obstacles until the last one which he just avoided and ran around to Melinda's feet with his tail between his legs. The final obstacle was a plastic tunnel Hershey had to crawl through, but instead of crawling he just sort of hid in there.

One of the judges finally stepped over and said something to Melinda. She gave a nod to the judge, a whistle to Hershey who finally came out of the plastic tunnel and they began to walk out of the competition area. Melinda looked like she was ready to cry and Hershey strained at his leash just wanting to be anywhere, but there. Other than a smattering of polite applause the crowd remained silent.

Hershey's disappointing scores flashed across the screens in the arena. Whatever average may have been these had to be way below that. Unless she bit one of the judges the princess appeared to be a shoe-in.

Princess Anastasia got the formal nod from the judges and the arena immediately filled with applause which was then just as quickly hushed up as she began her routine. She sailed through one obstacle after another. Each time she finished a round of applause, stronger than the previous rippled through the arena. By the time she was crawling through the plastic tunnel the crowd had all it could do to not give a standing ovation. When she finally finished the place exploded and all eyes were glued to the screens as her scores flashed across. Each new score brought even louder cheers, applause and whistles with it. My ear drums were ready to burst by the time the announcer was declaring her this year's winner and "Best of Show".

Pinkie was suddenly next to us and escorted Morton and I back through the press door. Once inside she said, "Mr. Allesi would like you both to follow me downstairs for some photos."

We did just that, posing for pictures for the better part of the next hour. Morton and Princess Anastasia were clearly the stars, Natasha and to a much lesser extent myself were the "also-rans." Tommy Allesi was not to be seen, but I had the feeling he was always nearby. I could only hope he was busy collecting my share of the winnings.

The public relations session lasted a couple of hours. I was dragging by the time it was over. I still couldn't hear properly and my ears were ringing after all the noise in the arena.

Simon caught my eye and then took me aside. "I'm supposed to tell you, Tommy's got a little private get together happening at the Lady Slipper later tonight. He'd appreciate it if you were there," he said and flashed a smile.

"Thanks Simon, but I gotta tell you, I'm really dragging, and all I want to do is…."

"I don't think you heard me. Must have been all that clapping and cheering from earlier, got your ears screwed up or something."

"No, I heard you, I…."

"Tommy would like you there, understand," he said and began applying pressure to my hand right at the end of the temporary cast.

"Ouch, what time?" I said.

"I'll pick you up at nine."

"I think I'll drive if it's all the same."

"Okay, just make sure you're there or Tommy's gonna send someone to get you and it won't be pleasant. Oh, and you can leave the pooch at home."

Lucky Morton.

Chapter Seventy

Morton was flaked out on the kitchen floor and seemed more than happy to stay home. I left the flat screen on just to keep him company and tossed some Bar-B-Que chips in his bowl.

The parking lot at the Lady Slipper was crowded, but not completely full and I found a place in the rear, next to the dumpster.

Tommy's soiree was in a private banquet room down the hall from the room where we'd met the last time I was here. There were two rather large guys wearing suits that looked just a little too tight leaning against a wall out in the hallway. Both of them had thick necks, heavy shoulders and close cropped hair.

One of them had the name *Maureen* tattooed on the side of his neck. The other guy had just one long, large eyebrow that looked more like a piece of shag carpeting. He stared and gave me the once over as I limped toward them. When I got close enough to them he said, "You're the dog hero guy, right?" Then they both laughed like they were in on some sort of private joke.

"I was told Tommy wanted me here tonight."

"That's right," the guy with the *Maureen* tattoo said then reached over, turned the knob and opened the door for me. Heads turned as I stepped inside the banquet room and suddenly light applause rippled through the room. I glanced around and smiled, but I didn't recognize anyone. Soft background music came out of a speaker system in the ceiling and plush, royal-blue carpeting with little gold crowns covered the floor. The crowd seemed to sort of magically part and suddenly there was Tommy Allesi, standing in front of a long table with candelabras and platters of hors d'oeuvres. He was holding a champagne flute toward Pinkie who was standing next to him and pouring from a large green bottle.

Pinkie wore a delightfully clingy sort of gown that went all the way to the floor and still left nothing to the imagination. It was cream colored, backless and almost frontless, slit all the way down to the jewel piercing her navel and apparently somehow glued to her breasts.

"Haskell, come on, help yourself to whatever you think you'd like," Tommy said waving me forward.

Pinkie raised her eyebrows and smiled showing just a little of her snow white teeth before slowly running her tongue back and forth across her upper lip as she stared at me.

"Get the man a glass of champagne, Pinkie."

"That's okay," I said.

"Come on, Haskell a '98 Clos des Goisses, celebrate, after all you earned it."

"Tell you the truth, champagne has always been wasted on me. You got a beer, I'd go for that."

Tommy laughed then said, "Okay, okay, better go grab him a beer, Pinkie."

I watched Pinkie make her way to a corner bar not realizing I was staring.

"Nice, isn't it?" Tommy said.

I wasn't playing that game. "Yeah, place must be at least a hundred years old, you're lucky it's in such good shape," I said and glanced around the room.

Tommy smiled and nodded then studied me over the rim of his glass. We made small talk about the Blessington for a moment. Then I said, "So how did you come out?"

"On the wagers?"

I nodded as Pinkie returned and handed me a pint glass with a nicely chilled lager.

"We'll get to that in a moment, but not here," Tommy said.

He proceeded to introduce me to some of the city's upper crust; developers, attorneys, judges, entrepreneurs, the sort of folks who could get away with things, keep a straight face and were smart enough not to brag. These were the real criminals in town, not the sort of folks I ran with.

By half-past-ten things were winding down. I chatted with a handful of folks. Polite sort of conversation, what did I do, who were my folks, where did I go to school, nothing worth the time it took to converse. Pinkie remained at my side, disappearing occasionally, but only to fetch me another beer.

Suddenly I looked around as Tommy closed the door to the banquet room. It was just the three of us, Tommy, Pinkie and me. "Shall we," Tommy said and extended his hand to a door behind the bar area. "Peter," he said to the bartender. "That will be all for tonight, the morning crew will clean up. Thank you."

As Peter nodded and made his way out of the room Tommy gave a nod toward my half empty glass. Pinkie took my pint glass, stepped behind the bar and topped it up, perfectly.

"Thanks, I could get used to this."

"Haskell," Tommy said and held open a door. We stepped into a dimly lit library sort of room with couches on either side of a fireplace. Solid oak shelves filled with leather bound books lined three of the walls. The fourth wall, the one with the fireplace had an oil portrait with a gilded frame hanging above the mantel. It was a portrait of Tommy wearing a suit and tie and standing behind a chair looking very proper with a rolled up sheaf of papers in his hand.

"Is that a dart board?" I asked.

Tommy glanced back at me, but didn't smile and Pinkie sort of studied the polished oak floor swallowing her smile. "In thru here," Tommy said and opened a door next to the fireplace.

We entered an office, not huge but certainly not small. There was a large mahogany desk with a couple of black leather chairs in front of it. Off to one side was a wooden side board with four crystal decanters and some nice bottles of bourbon and whiskey. A bay area held a mahogany coffee table with a brown leather couch that sat in front of the window. Two wing backed chairs were at either end of the coffee table. Natasha Kominski sat in one of the wing backed chairs sipping a glass of wine. A bottle rested on the floor next to her chair.

Cecil Kissler, Crewcut, sat in the corner of the couch, his face was swollen and bruised and looked about as bad as mine except he didn't have a nose splint. His left leg was wrapped from the knee up to his thigh and stretched out on the couch. A metal crutch lay on the floor in front of him.

He and Natasha were in the middle of some sort of joke, laughing hysterically as we entered the room. Natasha sort of wound down her laughter as she focused on me for a brief moment then took a hearty gulp from her wine glass.

294

Cecil nodded and raised his bourbon glass as if to toast me.

I turned and looked at Tommy Allesi.

"Please, Haskell take a seat," Tommy said and indicated the open wing backed chair. "Maybe a bourbon for Mr. Haskell, I'll have the same. Makers Mark," Tommy said to Pinkie.

She filled a couple of crystal glasses with the equivalent of about two shots. Then strolled over and handed a glass to Tommy. She reached down and traded my beer glass for the bourbon, lingered a moment then ran a deft hand across my shoulder as she exited the room and closed the door behind her.

Chapter Seventy-One

"Oh honestly, Mr. Haskell don't looked so surprised, you can't possibly be that naive." Natasha said.

"Just part of doing business," Cecil said in a voice that sounded like his nose was plugged then he took a sip and smiled at me. "Ten stitches by the way," he indicated the bandaged thigh where Morton had clamped onto him.

I couldn't think of anything to say and looked over at Tommy Allesi. He'd set his bourbon down on the desk and picked up three white envelopes. He handed one to Natasha, one to Cecil and then the thinnest envelope to me. "I never like to take anymore chances than absolutely necessary."

"Are you telling me this whole thing was rigged? Fixed?" I looked from face to face.

"Heavens no, nothing like that. I told you, you and your dog were worth twenty points. But at the end of the day Princess Anastasia and Natasha still had to perform, and perform they did."

"But the other dog, Hershey, your wife?" I looked over at Cecil.

"Soon to be ex-wife, she and Hershey gave what had to be the worst competition performance they've done in the past year. Those low scores had nothing to do with the, *"Kidnapping."* He had placed his glass on the coffee table, raised his hands then wiggled his fingers up and down twice to indicate quotation marks when he said the word. He reached for his glass and took another sip. "Those low scores had everything to do with their poor performance."

"Princess Anastasia?"

"performed spectacularly," Natasha said. "Did she feed off the energy generated by the audience, certainly. But it could have gone the other way, she certainly had no idea this had been staged, she never will. I wasn't aware of it until after we'd won and Tommy was gracious enough to…." She held up her thick envelope then tossed it onto the coffee table. "Besides, with this victory, and Princess Anastasia having never been bred, we'll be looking at six figures."

"A hundred grand just for a litter?" I said.

"No, that's per pup," she said and smiled.

I suddenly thought back to the night in her home when Denis Malloy fell out of the vines onto the picnic table and I'd caught Morton mounting the princess. I didn't want to think about the consequences of Morton being first in line.

"Come on Haskell, you've made more than four times your bid. That nose of yours will be healed up in a few days."

"I almost got killed by you guys when you hauled me out of the trunk of that car. Those assholes weren't kidding around."

"They got a little carried away, I'll admit that," Cecil said. "But it worked out, they…."

"Worked out? Two of those guys ended up in the hospital."

"Just overnight and I'm not going to be pressing any charges," Natasha said.

That sounded more like a promise that she wouldn't stir the pot. But then, why would she? She wasn't there. She wasn't dragged out of the car.

"A guy is dead, that young guy, Benny. I, I hit him with a tire iron when he attacked me."

"I think you're referring to Billy," Tommy said. "That's the name of the gentleman you killed, Haskell. It's very unfortunate, I suppose it's not really your fault. Possibly. I'm not sure what the court system would decide if you really wanted to pursue the matter, after all it would be your word against well, all the other individuals who were present."

Cecil nodded. "Sometimes it's best just to count your winnings and shut the hell up."

"I don't believe any contraband of any sort was discovered in anyone's possession, was it?" Tommy asked. "Now, we do have the late involvement of a Mister Alexi Tarasenko and some acquaintances of his regarding a modest amount of contraband. I believe you spoke to him on at least two occasions, correct? And then your *friend*, Miss Heidi Bauer, didn't she just receive some sort of free service from Mr. Tarasenko? Be a shame if something unfortunate happened to Miss Bauer."

I looked at Natasha, but she just stared into the far corner of the room and didn't reply.

"Tell you what, Haskell. I have a contact on the force, very adept, highly regarded in the department. I'd be glad to contact him for you, Detective Norris Manning, maybe you've heard of him? Or, well, I wonder if it wouldn't be wise to just take that rather handsome payment for a short weekends work and consider yourself a winner, as well," Tommy said.

"And I'd like to add to that, Devlin." Natasha said then reached into her envelope, pulled out a handful of bills without counting them and tossed the pile on top of my envelope.

I looked at her and suddenly my first thought was "*Morton still screwed Princess Anastasia.*"

"What are you thinking, Haskell?" Tommy asked.

"I don't know what to think, I, I just don't know what to think."

"Maybe go home and think about your options, if you'd like me to call Detective Manning for you in the morning, I'd be happy to do so. Let me warn you, once he's fixed on a case, he isn't the type to let go."

I picked up my envelope plus the cash Natasha had tossed across the table and stuffed them into my pocket then stood up.

"Pinkie will see you out," Tommy said and held out his hand to shake. "Pleasure doing business," he said.

Cecil raised his almost empty glass in a toast. "No hard feelings, Haskell."

Natasha continued to look the other way and Pinkie suddenly opened the door and stepped into the room.

She linked her arm in mine and half led me out of the room. I heard someone close the door behind us before we'd walked through the library. She stroked my arm as we walked down the hallway toward the Lady Slipper's front door. The lights were dim, it was very quiet and I figured with the exception of Tommy's office the building was empty.

Pinkie gave a quick glance over her shoulder once we got to the front door then she gently stroked the side of my face, took my head in both her hands and kissed me gently on my swollen lips.

"Allow me to give you some advice. Tommy always, always gets what he wants. I'm not sure about all you were involved in, and really, it's not important. Just be very careful. I'm guessing you made a profit, more than you expected to make. Take that and don't think about anything else. He usually mentions a family member or a friend. Consider that a warning. They'll be hurt first, before he sends someone after you. And he will send someone."

"Then what are you doing here? Why do you stay?"

She leaned forward and gave me another kiss. "Because, I'm just like you, I don't really have any other option," she said then turned and walked back toward Tommy's office.

Chapter Seventy-Two

At first I thought it was my head throbbing, but the noise continued, interspersed with the jarring ring of my doorbell. Since Morton was stretched out across my bed and I'd been pushed over to the very edge again it didn't take much for me to just roll off, then pull on a robe and stumble downstairs to the door. Morton lifted his head to give me a quick glance. He had a look on his face that suggested, *"Get that, will you?"* Then he snuggled back into my bed and began snoring again.

Whoever it was pounding this early they were awfully damned determined.

Still half asleep I opened the door and tried to focus.

"It's about time, I've been trying to call you since I landed last night. Do you ever answer your phone?"

"Oh yeah, sorry about that, the police have it, my phone. I had to get a pay-as-you…."

"God, what the hell happened to you, you really look like crap," Maddie said then brushed past me. "So where's my Morton?" she asked glancing around expecting him to be at the door.

"He's still sleeping. What the hell time is it anyway?"

"Still sleeping? It's almost noon, for your information," she said and took off toward the kitchen.

There were a number of beer bottles on the kitchen counter, more on the floor in the den along

301

with an almost empty bag of Bar-B-Que potato chips and a pizza delivery box. I quickly stuffed the bag of chips in the pocket of my robe then closed the door to the den on my way to the kitchen.

"What the hell is this?" she said picking up Morton's water dish and sniffing it.

That lightweight Morton had left some beer in the thing. "I don't know, God did he pee in it?"

"Err-rrr-rrr," she growled, then set the dish on the kitchen counter. Her eyes widened when she saw the pizza crusts left in his food dish.

"I guess he's not really into the crust," I said then quickly rinsed out the water dish and set it back on the counter.

"Morton, Morton, it's Mommy," she called suddenly shifting to that obnoxious little girl Morton voice. If he had any sense given the tone of her voice he wouldn't respond. "Morton, Morton? Morton, baby." It was like nails on a chalk board.

A lazy sounding "Woof" came from my bedroom upstairs just as Maddie opened the door to the den and saw more beer bottles and the pizza box. "Oh. My. God." She gave me a vicious look then pushed me out of the way, this time using both hands. She rushed up the stairs calling. "Mommy's coming, Morton, not to worry, darling. Mommy's coming."

Morton "*Woofed*" a couple more times.

I followed Maddie and was halfway up the stairs when I heard her scream. By the time I made it into the bedroom she had crawled onto the bed and was gently petting Morton. His tail flopped back and forth a little, but nothing like when he was excited by Princess Anastasia.

"My God, what did you do to my poor baby," she cried. Morton lay on my bed with the splint on his hind leg, the protective cone around his head and his side bandaged from the bruised rib and the stitches, milking it for all it was worth.

"Oh, that. He sort of saved the day on a kidnapping Saturday. It was in all the papers, on the news, even made Youtube."

"Kidnapping?"

"Yeah," I proceeded to give Maddie some of the highlights of our week. I left out the part about him mounting Princess Anastasia, drinking beer, eating Bar-B-Que potato chips, cheeseburgers and pizza. I saw no point in mentioning his chewing Natasha and Heidi's thongs. I did mention his tripping Denis Malloy, capturing that guy in the middle of the night at the Blessington and then saving me from Cecil later in the day, although I didn't tell Maddie Cecil's name. I told her about the special seats in the private viewing box we got for the Blessington, the cheers and applause. Once she calmed down we all went into the kitchen and I showed her the newspaper articles with Morton's picture on the front page under the headline *Canine Hero*.

"Oh God, Dev. I don't know whether to kiss you or kill you."

"I've got a better idea," I said and loosened the belt around my bathrobe.

"Oh please, sorry, um, look, there's no easy way to tell you this, so I'm just going to say it. Please do not interrupt me."

"Okay."

"I sort of met someone else. I actually knew him a long time ago, I mean when we were kids, sort of.

303

Anyway, I'm moving back to Atlanta, not 'cause of this guy, but just to help my folks. I got a job at one of my dad's firms. But anyway, Morton and I are driving down to Atlanta, we're leaving day after tomorrow."

Buster.

We sat at the kitchen counter. I put the coffee on, made some breakfast, filled Morton's food dish with dog food and put water in his dish. He gave me a look that suggested he wasn't all that thrilled with his menu.

Maddie went on and on about all the wonderful things Buster did, how great the new job was going to be and how fun Atlanta was. "It's just that, well I feel like I'm really going home, Dev. You know what I mean?"

I nodded like I did, but I really didn't have a clue. We loaded Morton's stuff into her car and I helped him into the back seat. He gave me a look like a kid having to cut spring break short and head back to school early. I reached in and scratched him behind the ears and all of a sudden there was a big lump in my throat and my eyes started to water.

"We better get going," Maddie said, she was checking the side view mirror for traffic and not really watching us.

Morton moved his head and I bent down so he could lick my face. "Thanks for saving me, buddy."

He gave me another big lick and then whined a little.

"Hey, Morton, Princess Anastasia," I whispered and his tail started thumping in overdrive. I reached into my pocket, took out a couple of Bar-B-Que potato chips, held them in my hand for Morton to devour in one quick lick.

"We gotta go," Maddie called.

I closed the door and Maddie gave a quick wave without looking at me. She waited half a moment for a car to pass then slowly pulled away from the curb. Morton wedged his head with the protective cone and his paws up onto the back seat and stared out the rear window at me as they drove off.

"Princess Anastasia, Princess Anastasia, Princess Anastasia," I yelled suddenly running down the sidewalk after them, tears rolling down my cheeks.

Morton continued barking and kept it up until they turned a corner and drove out of sight.

The End

Thanks for taking the time to read <u>Dog Gone</u>. If you enjoyed the read please tell 2-300 of your closest friends. If you have the time, please take a moment to write a favorable review, it really helps. Thanks…

Corridor Man is written by Mike Faricy under the pseudonym Nick James. It's a lot more gritty and vicious than the Dev Haskell tales, so you might just want to leave the hall light on when you go to bed…

Nick James

Corridor Man

Chapter One

The cinder block walls were painted a glossy dark grey to a height of about five feet then painted a lighter grey from there up to the bare concrete ceiling. The only light came from the dusty, flickering fluorescent fixture hanging at an odd angle and about a foot off center on the ceiling. It was a sunny, spring day outside, not that you'd have any idea sitting in the damp, windowless interrogation room.

The uncomfortable chair Bobby Custer was sitting in was bolted to the floor. The thing positioned just far enough away from the steel topped table so that you couldn't quite comfortably rest your elbows on the table top.

Bobby glanced at the two federal agents wearing suits seated across from him, then glanced down at the file they'd placed on the steel topped table before looking back up at the agents.

"Your choice, Bobby. You don't want to take the offer, that's fine, you're more than halfway finished serving your sentence as it is. It's your *life* after all, so I'm maybe guessing you're maybe thinking what's three more years to a sharp guy like you?"

When he emphasized the word *life* his partner smiled, like it was an 'in' joke, just between the two federal agents.

"Come on, I never said I didn't want to take the offer, it's all just coming at me a little fast. The first I've heard of it was when you sat me down in this chair," he said then shifted from side to side in an effort to find a more comfortable position.

"That's right," the grey suited agent said. He'd been doing most of the talking, but Bobby couldn't tell if he was the man in charge or just the messenger.

"Well, so, I mean, you can understand I need a moment or two to collect my thoughts."

"Sure, go ahead and collect them, but just remember we leave this room without an answer and the deal comes off the table with us. Gone. Forever. We'll just give it to someone else who maybe has a little more incentive."

"But, what I don't understand is how you get them to hire me, to take me on? Denton, Allan, Sawyer and Hinz is a heavy duty firm. Last time I checked I was still disbarred. The odds of me getting a license back to practice are just about zero. That is, unless you guys could maybe pull some strings." He sounded hopeful then looked from one blank face to the other and all hopeful thought immediately disappeared.

"That's not gonna happen. Let me make myself clear, again. This would be an entry level position, and it would remain just that, entry level. You are not going to regain your license to practice law. That's not in our offer. Are we on the same page here?"

"Yeah, okay, I get that, sort of, I mean, yeah. But, then why would they hire me? They're going to know all about my past, the disbarment, my conviction and the sentencing sooner or later. Aren't they?"

"Not only will they find out, we intend to tell them sooner rather than later so there is no question at all. I'm going to say it again, you will not be practicing law."

"But then…."

"What you will be doing is anything they tell you to do and anything *we* want you to do. It's that simple. They want you sweeping floors, emptying wastebaskets, making coffee or putting toilet paper in the rest rooms that's what you do. And then you report back to us."

"I don't know, I…."

"That's fine," the pinstriped suit spoke for the first time then pushed his chair back and stood. He had a deep, gravelly voice. "You were just one name on a long list. You've grown fond of your routine here, fair enough. At the end of the day it's your choice after all, so enjoy the next three years, Bobby. By the way, that's one thousand and ninety-five days plus some change. Okay, Stan let's get the hell out of here," he said then stood and pushed his chair in.

The grey suit nodded, closed the manila file that had sat open on the steel topped table for the past forty minutes. He stood, didn't bother to push his

310

chair in and looked down at Bobby. "Nice talking, Custer enjoy your next three years."

"Now wait, hold on, can you just hold on a minute? Please?"

"We're out of time, Bobby. It really just comes down to a simple yes or no from you. No pressure."

"Okay, okay, Jesus yes, I'll, I'll do it. How soon can you get me out of here?"

"We can have you in a halfway house tonight, you'll do sixty days there, just to get you reintroduced to society and make you look legit. Once you're out of the halfway house you'll apply for the job, and they'll hire you. Yes or no?"

"Yes, yes, for God's sake, of course. Yes." Even in the musty, damp room he could feel himself sweating and a long trickle suddenly ran down his spine.

The grey suit tossed the manila file back on the table. "Open it up, sign the top page, initial the three lines at the bottom of the next three pages, then sign the last page with today's date. Not surprisingly, it's Friday the thirteenth," he chuckled.

Chapter Two

The neighborhood was made up of old, three story, Victorian homes from the 1890's with large front porches. Dutch elm disease had wiped out the massive boulevard trees in the late seventies and the replacements, now forty plus years old had begun to add character along with some shade back to the streets. Once designated by the infamous intersection of Selby and Dale the area had rebounded over the past five decades with an influx of 'urban pioneers'. Property taxes increased accordingly and the tonier designation of "Cathedral Hill" had been adopted by developers.

Despite the institutional blinds on the unwashed windows the three story brick structure looked deceivingly elegant from the outside. Today was day sixty. Moving day for Bobby, he was all packed and staring out the front window while he waited for his younger brother to pull up.

All his worldly possessions were stuffed in a worn black suitcase and three brown paper grocery bags with handles. Everything neatly lined up out in the hall near the front door of the halfway house.

He had filled out and submitted his paperwork at the end of last month. He'd said his goodbyes almost six hours ago at seven-thirty this morning, while standing in the dining area with a coffee mug. Now, it was just a matter of his brother driving the get-away vehicle to deliver him from this hell-hole of positive thought and naïve intentions. His brother was four-and-a-half hours late and counting.

Everyone is supposed to learn patience in prison. Bobby learned a number of things. Don't react. Don't take offense. Be nice to the correction officers. But as for patience, well three out of four ain't bad.

He had counted the days. Every day, one-thou-sand-four-hundred-and-ninety-eight of them in the Duluth Federal Prison Camp, FPC for short, just a lit-tle over four years, each day about twenty-eight hours long. Then these last sixty days of "reintroduction." Hell of a price to pay for a minor dalliance with a trust fund. Add to that the heavy fine, loss of all financial support, loss of his license to practice law, his di-vorce, estrangement from just about everyone he ever knew and last, but not least, his disbarment. It was probably a safe bet the Minnesota Bar and that of every other state would be in no rush to talk with him anytime soon.

"Everything okay, Bobby?"

He had been focused on the empty street outside and hadn't heard Baker waddle up behind him. Baker was one of the counselors, not that he was ever much help to anyone, worthless might be a more accurate description. He slurped from a white coffee mug sto-len from a near-by restaurant. The mug seemed to be surgically attached to his right hand. He had at least a half-dozen Oreo cookies crammed in his left hand, with another two or three already stuffed in his mouth. He wore his usual sandals, shorts and the black t-shirt emblazoned with the moniker *'Got Change?'* that served as the staff uniform. He had a gleaming bald head surrounded by a fringe of graying shoulder length hair all pulled back in a thin, wispy, ponytail.

"Think maybe your ride forgot?" Baker actually sounded serious then crammed another Oreo into his mouth.

"No," Bobby said staring out the window.

"Weren't they supposed to be here this morning? Early? It's after lunch," Baker said then swallowed to make room for another Oreo.

"It's my brother, he's got kids, little guys, twins actually so he's always running a bit late."

Andrew didn't have twins. As a matter of fact he didn't have any children. You'd have to have sex with your wife before you could bring children into the relationship. Bobby didn't think Andrew's wife, Fern was interested in sex, it might mess her hair.

"Alright. Course you know our policy," Baker droned then paused to slurp more coffee. "We really can't release unless a vetted, qualified individual integrates…"

Bobby tuned him out. Baker quoting chapter and verse policy in-between tossing more Oreos into his big mouth was not what he needed just now. He checked his watch, Andrew was now four-hours-and-fifty-minutes late, but who was counting?

"Think we should make a phone call, maybe reschedule?"

"No, I'm sure he'll show up in just a couple of minutes."

"Got your key to the new place?"

"Yeah, I got the key." He'd been clenching the damn thing in his pocket for the past three hours.

"Any problems, you know we're always available."

"I don't plan on any problems."

314

"If you say so," Baker shrugged not sounding all that convinced. He tossed the last of the Oreo's into his mouth and absently wiped his hand across his beer belly. "Well good luck, man," he said, spitting bits of Oreo in Bobby's direction then slurped some more coffee before he trundled off to the kitchen. No doubt ravenous after the counseling session he'd just provided.

<u>Chapter Three</u>

Andrew's red Subaru pulled to the curb just as Baker pushed through the steel security door into the kitchen.

"He's here, he's here," Bobby shouted excitedly, sounding like a six-year-old waiting for Santa Claus. He quickly gathered his possessions, pulled the front door open and raced out to the street.

Andrew sat behind the wheel looking more grim faced than usual. He gave the slightest of nods and pushed a button on the dash. There was an audible click as the back hatch unlocked and Andrew gave another nod with his head indicating the rear of the car. Bobby placed everything in the rear then climbed into the back seat directly behind Andrew and as far away as possible from his sister-in-law, Fern.

Her hair looked perfect, her face betrayed no emotion. She wore diamond post earrings about as big around as a nickel and what looked like the latest fashionable top. A fragile silver chain hung around her shapely neck and no doubt some diamond pendant dangled temptingly on her surgically enhanced chest. If he had to guess, Bobby would have said she'd been clenching her jaw for the past week, ever since she learned they were going to serve as his designated driver this morning. Her door was locked and she stared straight ahead, not that you could really tell behind the pair of designer sunglasses.

"Need to sign out or anything? Maybe turn in a key?" Andrew asked. He eyed Bobby cautiously in the rearview mirror.

"No. I'm good to go."

"You're sure? We really don't need you doing something stupid, again. Creating some sort of incident this afternoon," Fern said as she continued to stare straight ahead. "God knows we don't want to have to come back here."

"Thanks for coming to get me. I really appreciate it."

"We really didn't have much choice now, did we?" Fern replied.

Andrew exhaled audibly, then put the car in drive and pulled away from the curb. Bobby buckled up for safety.

No one spoke on the way over to the efficiency apartment as Fern silently stared out the window oozing toxic displeasure.

Bobby felt like telling her he'd been locked up with rapists and murderers for the last four years and if she didn't put a smile on her Botoxed face he was going to get a couple of them after her. She probably wouldn't have been intimidated. Besides, he didn't really know any. The Federal Prison Camp he'd been held in was a minimum security facility, about the worst he'd be able to conjure up would be something like an irate financial adviser with a penchant for spanking.

They sped across town in almost complete silence, the exception being Fern's occasional sigh reminding everyone she was less than happy. Fourteen very long minutes later Andrew rounded a corner and screeched to a stop a good half-dozen car lengths from the front door of the apartment building. Fern glanced over at her husband and Bobby felt the heat from her glare all the way into the back seat.

Andrew pressed a button and unlocked the rear hatch.

Bobby climbed out into the fresh air. Placed his suitcase on the sidewalk, gathered up his grocery bags and closed the hatch. Fern leaned over slightly toward Andrew and said something to him. Her lips curled into a sneer, but Bobby couldn't hear what she was saying. Then Andrew motioned him over with wave of his finger and lowered the window.

"Thanks for signing for me, guys. I appreciate…"

"Bobby, I think it would be best if we didn't hear from you," Andrew said.

"Ever, again," Fern added looking over the top of her sunglasses.

Then Andrew raised his window and they quickly drove off.

Chapter Four

At about the same time and no more than six blocks away a burgundy colored Escalade pulled alongside Sexton's, a neighborhood institution known since the dawn of time for cheeseburgers, homemade fries and free pour drinks. Directly across the street a woman cutting lilacs along her chain link fence gave the vehicle no more than a passing glance.

Later, when interviewed by the police, she could only describe the vehicle as large and guess the color incorrectly, insisting it was black. She was unable to describe any of the individuals or even tell the police how many there had been.

The driver remained behind the wheel, shielding the three small teardrops tattooed on his left check with his hand while he pretended to talk on a cell-phone. His two passengers, brothers Dubuque and Mobile, quickly entered by the side door and casually approached the bar.

Mobile was the taller of the two, ginger haired and neatly dressed in a casual way. He ordered a couple of tap beers, buying time to get the lay of the place while they waited.

Kevin O'Brien, their intended target, sat on his usual stool at the far end of the bar with his back to the door. He was involved in a phone conversation and casually scanned yesterday's newspaper as he talked.

There was the bartender, which was to be expected, and unfortunately a table with two, thirty-something sisters lingering over a late lunch and a second glass of wine.

The brothers couldn't see any wait staff as they glanced around and they completely missed Kate Clarken, passed out in the corner booth next to the front door.

The bartender placed their beers on two round coasters and slid the frosted pints across the bar. "You fellas interested in some lunch menus?" he asked as he pushed his bifocals back up the bridge of his nose.

The brothers looked at one another for a long moment as if weighing their options then nodded in unison and pulled out the Glocks. They looked overly large, the Glocks. Of course the four inch silencers screwed onto the barrels would have that effect.

Dubuque, the brother sporting dark, curly hair and a pug nose calmly raised his weapon. Before the bartender could voice an objection Dubuque placed a round into the bartender's forehead from a distance of no more than two feet. Blood and brain matter sprayed across the bar's selection of twenty-one different whiskeys as he crumpled to the floor.

At the far end of the bar, O'Brien remained involved in his phone conversation, oblivious. He began to casually turn on his stool as his ginger-haired assailant leisurely strolled toward him. Mobile's Glock spit a round through O'Brien's cellphone ending the conversation before exiting out the far side of his head.

Before they had the chance to scream Dubuque had turned from the bartender and shot both women. The bleached blonde was dead before she hit the floor. Her sister sort of jumped backwards in her chair as a slug slammed into her chest so Dubuque fired a second round into her forehead just to be sure.

Both men quickly walked to the rear of the place, leisurely checked the kitchen area and both restrooms, but didn't see a soul. They calmly walked to the bar, clicked their frosted mugs together and took a celebratory sip. Dubuque took a couple of French fries from one of the women's plates, ran them through a puddle of ketchup and tossed them into his mouth before he exited out the same door they'd entered just a few minutes earlier. The brothers climbed into the burgundy Escalade and very leisurely drove off down the street.

The woman across the street was just bringing her lilacs in through the back door, lost in their lovely fragrance.

It would be close to twenty minutes before the police were called and another four or five minutes before they actually arrived. Kate Clarken was still passed out in the front
booth when the cops finally entered the gruesome scene.

Chapter Five

It was probably a good thing his brother Andrew and Fern didn't come up to the third floor efficiency. There wouldn't have been enough room for the three of them. Fortunately, Bobby didn't own any furniture so there was a little space to move around in.

The third floor efficiency apartment was basically one room, about three times as large as the cell he'd been confined in for four plus years. Through a grimy, cracked glass window the efficiency offered a nice view of the dumpster and the three recycling containers. There was a bathroom and a closet in one corner of the room and a kitchen area with a stove, an antique refrigerator and a sink in the opposite corner.

The kitchen counter was a sort of dingy-white Formica with a gray spot worn through on either side of the stainless steel kitchen sink. A protective coating of crumbs that looked like very old, burnt bread or maybe chocolate cake was scattered across the counter. Bobby didn't plan on doing a taste-test to find out what the crumbs were.

The kitchen faucet had a drip pattern that dinged audibly as it hit the aluminum sink. The former tenants were kind enough to leave half a tomato and some milk in the refrigerator for him. At least he thought it was a tomato, the light didn't work in the fridge so he wasn't quite sure.

Whoever the last person in the bathroom was, they'd forgotten to flush, maybe because the door didn't close completely and they were just embarrassed. They'd left an open tube of eyeliner and some lip gloss on the bathroom sink, neither one in his color palate.

The linoleum on the bathroom floor was in a paving brick pattern. It almost looked real except where it had curled up and away from the tub. The shower head dripped in time to the kitchen sink and had left a rust colored stain on the tub that directed ones eye to the drain. Home sweet home.

Still, it was bound to be better than three-times-a-day counseling sessions at the halfway house. He wasn't going to miss lights out at ten and living with a dozen other men with a recidivism rate hovering right around ninety-percent.

It took him just a moment to unpack. He placed the three paper bags side-by-side then unzipped his suitcase, pushed it against the wall next to the bags and he was finished. All settled in.

He learned later that night that the large front burner on the gas stove didn't work, so he grilled his dinner over one of the smaller burners. He snapped a branch off a dead bush back by the dumpster and used it to impale two hot dogs. He slid the gourmet treats onto the buns sitting on the counter, squirted a line of nuclear yellow mustard along the length of the dogs and *voila!* Dinner was served.

He sat quietly on the floor opposite his suitcase and paper bags. His back was against the wall as he slowly ate the hot dogs and tried to tune out the steady drip coming from the kitchen sink. He didn't have to listen to fantasies about women, talk about basketball, hear complaints about the system or comments about the man. There was no reminder of a group session starting in ten minutes. It all seemed like heaven.

As the sun began to set, he realized he'd forgotten to buy light bulbs. Shortly after that he was sitting in the dark, alone in his thoughts. No one whistled, made cat calls, sang off key or shouted *'shut-the-fuck-up'*. He was enjoying the peace and quiet.

He woke before sunrise, wide awake on the worn carpet. He felt his way to the bathroom, showered in the dark then dripped dry looking out the window at the dumpster before he got dressed.

After a breakfast of another grilled hot dog, he walked two-and-a-half miles to the Ramsey County Courthouse. Built in the midst of the great depression it served not only as the St. Paul Courthouse, but City Hall as well. Although his purpose was to simply apply for a driver's license he was worried about who he might possibly run into. His apprehension grew as he approached. By the time he could see the twenty story building he was seriously considering turning around.

Chapter Six

Meyer's was a dingy, working class bar known for strong drinks and agreeable women. It served a daily private breakfast to the very limited clientele of one customer and one customer only.

"So let me get this straight," Morris Montcreff threw the newspaper back down on the table and glanced up at the barroom ceiling in an attempt to collect his thoughts. He ran his tongue over his teeth extracting the last of the blueberries and a hint of maple syrup.

"You take out the intended target, O'Brien along with three other individuals and you miss some broad sitting all by herself in a booth next to the front door?"

The brothers, Dubuque and Mobile, glanced quickly at one another, each one silently blaming the other for the error.

"Well?"

"We checked the place out, Mister Montcreff, honest," Mobile said.

"Checked behind the bar, the kitchen, men's room, women's can. We didn't see shit," Dubuque added.

"Isn't that just wonderful. Great job, except you two jackasses just happened to miss this bitch sitting by the front door, no doubt watching everything happen."

More worried looks between the brothers.

"Listen here you two morons. You find out who she is and where she is and you take care of her. Jesus Christ, a simple job and you screw the thing up. Headlines the past two days, now this," he pointed at the front page of the Pioneer Press. "She was sitting in there apparently watching the whole thing go down and you two just couldn't be bothered. Honest to God, what the hell am I paying you for?"

"You ain't got to pay us none, Mr. Montcreff, least wise till we make this right by you," Mobile said.

Dubuque shot a quick glance at his brother, but didn't say anything.

"You're right about that. Let me make you two a little promise. You get this situation taken care of, quickly and need I remind you, quietly, or I'll have someone else tie up all the loose ends. And I mean *all* the loose ends. Do I make myself clear?"

The brothers nodded in unison.

"Get the hell out of my sight. I don't want to see or hear from either one of you until this is taken care of, now go, damn it."

"Yes sir," the brothers said in unison and sort of just stood there and stared at their feet.

"Go on, get the hell out of here and make this right while I'm still in a forgiving frame of mind," Montcreff shouted and glared, providing some additional incentive, not that any had been needed.

Chapter Seven

Bobby took the driver's license test on a computer and in less than twenty minutes was informed he'd managed to fail. Do you park five, ten or fifteen feet from a fire hydrant? Who cares? He knew enough not to park in front of one. Apparently the Minnesota Licensing Bureau cared a little more than Bobby did.

The clerk flashed a quick civil service smile from behind the counter then handed back his exam.

"Apparently *we* have some work to do. Here is your exam booklet, you might want to study this. There's an online site listed on page three of your booklet. This will allow you to take a practice exam, maybe a couple of them," she added as an afterthought. "You can sit for your next exam five days from now, that would be on the, let's see, yes the seventh. Questions?"

He felt like asking why the questions on the exam were so stupid, but instead said, "No, see you in five days, thank you." Then he folded the exam in a half hearted attempt to disguise his failure and headed for the door.

The main lobby of the courthouse had floors of polished white marble. Black marble piers rose up three stories to a gold leaf ceiling. Bobby had spent a good part of his previous life in here groveling and working various angles and schemes on behalf of clients.

Back then, he'd known all the nooks and crannies, which restrooms were empty and when. He had developed internal radar that apprised him of when and where court was in session. He knew which deputies were friendly and which ones to stay clear of. He knew who liked bourbon, who like beer and who was a teetotaler. He knew a lot of the secrets and made up some of the lies. But now, he was an outsider, just another tourist, or even worst, well, best not to go there.

He was staring up toward the ceiling, lost in distant vague memories, the hustle, the drama, the pressure, the….

"Bobby? Bobby, is that you?" As he inspected Bobby his flushed face moved up and down, audibly scraping his chins against the heavily starched collar.

"Well hello, Ben, yeah it's me."

Bennett Hinz esquire. A prick if there ever was one. He'd been a year ahead of Bobby in law school, light years ahead of him in the scheme of life. On one side a family fortune he had nothing to do with other than inherit, on the other a bottomless trust fund. The sun seemed to rise and set on Bennett which probably accounted for the tan face contrasting with his white shirt and the mane of silver hair combed back like some retired rock star. Bennett was the Hinz in Denton, Allan, Sawyer and Hinz the law firm who was going to hire Bobby with the help of some *federal persuasion*. The firm was known as *DASH* in hallway parlance.

"When did you get back? It was seven years wasn't it? God, has it really gone by that quickly?"

"I made it out in a little more than four," Bobby said almost in a whisper.

"That-a-boy, can do. Fresh start, eh, Bobby," Ben said, giving a 'go-for-it' sort of nod. It was one of the many negatives with Benny. Always sounding like Mr. Positive although Bobby was pretty certain Benny never, ever had had to deal with any real adversity.

"Yeah, that's what I'm doing, Ben starting fresh."

Benny nodded as if he had some vague notion of what Bobby was talking about. Then he gave the proverbial, "Great chatting, Bobby. I'd better get a move on, things to do, places to be, you probably remember what its like."

"Nice seeing you again, Ben."

Bobby watched as he waddled a few steps, and was about to give Ben the finger when he turned and in a booming voice bellowed, "Say, Bobby, momentito. You're not actually thinking of reapplying after your disbarment, are you?"

Bobby thought, *'Thanks for broadcasting that little fact, Ben.'*

"To the bar? No Ben, I don't think that would be a wise career move, at least not at this time."

"Career move," Ben half laughed then nodded knowingly, he glanced left and right, stepped a little closer and in a conspiratorial tone said, "Just wondering, my friend. Have you given any thought to what you're going to do? You know, employment, finances, how to get the old jingo?" He rubbed his thumb and forefinger together, and raised his bushy eyebrows.

Bobby thought about hitting him in his fat, perfectly tanned face then pushing him over the brass railing and watching him drop down a couple of floors to bounce off the marble floor of the lobby.

"Working on it, but haven't come up with any-thing definite yet, Ben. I'm exploring a number of op-portunities." He didn't feel the need to mention that the feds had arranged a one o'clock appointment with Noah Denton at Ben's firm.

"Reason I ask is my firm just may have a need for someone like you."

"Gee thanks, Ben."

"Now, Bobby, I wasn't about to suggest you practice. Good Lord, we're not crazy. They're hardly about to reinstate you." He must have seen the humor before Bobby did because he chuckled again and said, "I mean we're not that stupid."

Bobby nodded ever so slightly and thought, *'We'll see about that'*.

"But, actually we might be able to use someone of your, oh ahhh talents, shall we say." Ben chuckled again.

Bobby wasn't sure what the joke was.

"What, exactly, do you have lined up, Bobby?"

"Lined up?"

"For employment."

"Actually that's my next stop, start looking. I've got a number of people who want me to contact them. I was just planning to sort of catch my breath for a day or two, before I jumped in."

Ben nodded and looked like he didn't believe a word. "I see, I see, well look, when that falls through please consider us, might not hurt to stop by and just chat," he said then produced a business card out of thin air and handed it over.

Chapter Eight

Bennett Hinz was famous for grabbing lunch and a sauna over at the Capitol City Club from noon until about three on most days. Bobby was standing tall in front of the Denton, Allan, Sawyer and Hinz receptionist counter just before one and hoping Ben Hinz wouldn't be returning in the next hour.

"I'm here to see Noah Denton. I have a one o'clock appointment," he said. He could have been wearing an orange jumpsuit labeled Ramsey County and he didn't think the receptionist would have blinked.

"May I tell him who's calling?"

"My name is Bobby Custer," he said then waited for alarm bells to start blaring throughout the offices.

"Let me check for you," she said not looking at him. She had salt and pepper hair in a sort of bouffant hair style that looked like it wouldn't move in a hurricane force wind. She wore a headset with a thin, white microphone that ran along the right side of her jaw. She quickly clicked a number of keys on her key board and then scanned the screen. "I see he's got a motion hearing at three this afternoon. But, I can't seem to find your name, anywhere. Are you sure your appointment was for today, this afternoon?"

"Yes, one o'clock," Bobby said then felt his face flush and the sweat beginning to form on his brow.

"Let's see what we can do," she said then clicked a few more keys and stared off in the distance.

"Yes sir, Mr. Denton, sorry to bother you, this is Marci at the front desk. I have a Mr. Custer out here," she said as she looked up at Bobby and nodded. "He said he had a one o'clock appointment with you, sir, but I don't seem to have him on your schedule." Whatever the response was she remained stoic. "Mmm-hmmm let me check, sir." She looked up, "You said Bobby?"

"Yes, Custer," he nodded.

"Yes, that's correct. All right sir, very good," she said then disconnected. "Would you be able to wait a few minutes, Mr. Custer?"

He glanced at his watch pretending he had somewhere else to be that afternoon. "I think I can wait a few minutes." All he had for the rest of the afternoon was the hour long walk back to his empty apartment.

Two Sports Illustrated later he heard a beep from the front desk and then the receptionist said, "Yes sir, I'll send him right back."

He stopped gazing out the window at the river traffic and looked over at her hopefully.

"Mr. Denton can see you now, sir, if you'll just follow this hall all the way back he's the large corner office on your right, his name is on the door."

"Thank you," Bobby said and headed back to the corner office.

Noah Denton was waiting, posed with an open file on his neatly arranged, massive mahogany desk, the very picture of professional dedication. Beneath his dyed brown hair he wore a navy blue suit with just the hint of a pin stripe and a flash of bright red silk lining on the coat. He casually looked up then jumped to his feet as if Bobby's appearance in the doorway was some sort of unexpected surprise.

"Robert, come in, come in. Sorry for the delay, I didn't want to alert our receptionist or anyone else for that matter about our meeting," he said, charging around his desk with an outstretched hand. He clamped Bobby's hand in one of those death defying grips then proceeded to yank Bobby's arm off at the elbow, shaking, while all the while muttering, "Robert, yes Robert. Have a seat," he commanded with a sweeping gesture then quickly closed the office door and sat down placing his imperial desk between the two of them.

"Robert, Robert, Robert."

"Nice to meet you, Noah. Please, call me Bobby." Bobby said then waited for a very long moment. "I ran into Ben Hinz at the courthouse this morning."

It suddenly dawned on Bobby that Ben Hinz was probably just cutting through the courthouse on the way to some social destination, a bookstore, a steamroom or maybe a bar.

Noah Denton nodded, and pretended that seeing Ben at the courthouse made sense. "Oh, so you really did see him? Here I thought you were just, well you know under the circumstances, maybe playing a little coy. You seem to have some rather influential acquaintances," Denton said then glared.

"Well, we're still in the early stages of our relationship," Bobby sort of half laughed.

"Just so we understand one another. Their involvement is really the only reason I agreed to talk with you. I find your past conduct nothing short of reprehensible. I've been promised there's not a chance in hell you'll ever be back practicing. I want to be very clear on that point?" he said.

"That's my understanding, at least at this time."

Denton ignored that last part and forged ahead. "Let me be completely honest here. I have to say I fought tooth and nail not to have you associated with this firm in any way, shape, or form. You sitting there in that chair, in *my* office, is not at all what I wanted. I've offered my protests and they have apparently fallen on deaf ears. I must say the authorities offered an unfortunately compelling argument or two that forced us into this situation" he said, but didn't elaborate.

"I appreciate the opportunity."

"Opportunity? For God's sake you make it sound like we were given an option. Well, I've told you where I stand, the board, in its wisdom voted my suggestions down. What, exactly do you think you might accomplish here?" The implication being since you're disbarred, can't practice and are wasting my time, what the hell are you going to do?

"Ben Hinz mentioned something about having a need for my talents."

"Your talents?" Denton said sounding incredulous.

Bobby nodded.

"I'm not sure what, in God's name, he would have meant by that, exactly. Of course you're no stranger to Bennett Hinz and you know how he operates. I have to say, I'm still inclined to do the right thing and simply send you packing. I have to tell you, Custer I don't care how long you were in Federal custody. To my mind it wasn't long enough. You're a stain on our profession and I, for one, am not the least bit happy with the idea of *you* having anything to do with this firm."

Bobby slowly rose to his feet. He was broke, disbarred and sleeping on the floor of an unfurnished efficiency apartment, but the feds and by extension Bobby seemed, for some reason, to have Noah Denton by the short hairs. "If I can be of any help to you please keep me in mind, sir." He extended his hand, looked Denton in the eye and braced himself for his death squeeze.

Denton remained seated behind his desk and didn't bother to extend his hand. He fumed for a long moment and waited until Bobby was almost out the door before he said, "You know, there is one thing, possibly."

Bobby paused at the door.

"We're involved in the defense of a class action lawsuit. Our client is being sued on some trumped up charges. Anyway, there will be a series of subpoenaed testimonies we're taking over the next few weeks, not the best class of individuals, some undesirables. Which just might make you the right man for the job, make sure they get here on time, sober, able to respond to questions." Noah Denton swallowed hard then spat out the word. "Interested?"

"I just might be."

"Good, why don't you give me your phone number, if and when this develops we just might call."

"How about I check in with you instead? I'm having a bit of difficulty with my service provider." Actually, Bobby didn't have one, but then again he didn't have a phone, either.

Noah nodded like he wasn't fooled and continued on. "You'd have to drive, pick them up, and bring them back to wherever they came from, once they've been deposed."

"I don't see a problem."

"You can check with Marci, out at the front desk. She'll have the information. Of course under these circumstances you'll only be a contract hire, I want to be clear on that. We wouldn't want you on the firm's payroll, for obvious reasons. And, it will look more credible if you don't start immediately."

"Marci," Bobby nodded, "I'll check with her."

"Please do. In fact, I'd prefer if I didn't have to see or hear from you, ever. Do I make myself clear?"

"I'll check with Marci," Bobby said and closed the door on his way out.

Chapter Nine

"They'll begin in two days. I've a list of six individuals along with their addresses and phone numbers. It all seems pretty straight forward," Marci said over the phone. Bobby had been checking in with her every day for the past week, twice a day. He wedged the receiver on the payphone between his ear and shoulder then wrote '*2 days*' on the back of the envelope.

"All you have to do is pick them up. Once they've been deposed, here, you bring them back home. Really not much more to it than that. Each deposition shouldn't last more than an hour or two. We're hoping to have everything completed by the end of the day, Friday."

There was the little matter of no driver's license and no car, but he didn't want to cloud the issue of his employment with petty details.

"We'll need you to fill out our contractor form. Just the standard sort of thing, you know social security, valid insurance, driver's license, shouldn't take more than a few minutes."

"Not a problem," he said, wondering how he was going to pull that off?

"I could email this list to you?" she suggested.

"That's okay, Marci. I'll get it from you when I fill out that contractor form. I'm tied up for the rest of the day, I could be down there tomorrow morning if that works."

"Yes, it will, Mr. Custer, tomorrow then," her tone suggested she didn't quite believe him.

"Tomorrow," he said and hung up the pay phone. He'd have to get moving if he wanted to walk down to the licensing bureau before they closed.

He was posing for his driver's license photo an hour later. He had passed the test by two points, which some might consider too close for comfort, but at this stage didn't matter to him in the least.

"Okay, and look this way, sir. That's it, look into the red light. There, I'll have an image for you in just a moment so you can make sure it's okay."

She was an attractive thing, he guessed maybe thirty-five and probably Hispanic from the dark eyes and hair, well and the nametag that read *L. Montez*.

"Would you please just look at the screen here, sir and let me know if this image is acceptable."

It looked like someone much older staring back at him on the monitor, thinner, maybe a bit dubious looking, but in the end still Bobby. "Yeah, that's me, but can you make me look about ten years younger?" he joked.

"So it's okay?" she asked not finding any humor in his comment.

"Yes, it is."

"All right, sir, you'll see your license in the mail in two to three weeks time. This temporary license is good for thirty days. Have it in your possession at all times when you're driving," she instructed, then handed him a yellow carbon copy of his license application.

"Thank you."

338

Chapter Ten

He still needed a set of wheels. He made three phone calls from the pay phone in the lower level of the downtown public library. He was calling former acquaintances, hoping they might help. He left messages on all three calls which was stupid because they couldn't call him back. This wasn't working.

He walked a mile and a half up West Seventh Street to a used car lot, of sorts. There were nine cars in the lot under a hand painted sign advertising "FAST EDDIE'S AUTO L". The tale end of the sign had been broken off, just after the word letter 'L'. Suggesting maybe there had been another word there at one time like, 'Lot' or 'Land'.

Eight of the vehicles were priced north of fourteen-hundred-dollars and out of his price range. There was a faded blue, Geo Metro in the back corner with a sign on the dash that said 'Runs Good' along with a lot of bird droppings on the windshield.

He crossed the street to a McDonalds and called the number on the 'Runs Good' sign from a pay phone. Fast Eddie answered on the third ring.

"Yeah."

"I'm calling about a car I saw at 'Fast Eddies'.

"You looking to buy?"

"Yeah." Bobby said wondering why else he would be calling?

"You there now?" Fast Eddie sounded hopeful.

"Actually, I'm just across the street, grabbing a bite at McDonalds."

"I'll be at the lot in just a couple of minutes."

Fast Eddie looked a little larger than a couple of the cars on his lot. He came in at about three-hundred-and-fifty-pounds and probably rarely got off the couch. Sizing him up, Bobby had a tough time believing he had ever been *fast*.

Eddie eyed Bobby the moment he stepped out of the McDonald's and watched while he crossed the street.

"You the guy that called?" Fast Eddie asked as Bobby stepped onto the curb. There was no one else in sight of the car lot.

"Yes, I am."

"Looking at that Ford Ranger? I hate to let it go for that, but I've got to move it, make room for a delivery I've got coming in. I'm gonna be losing money on it for sure."

Bobby thought maybe the only delivery Eddie had coming in was from Domino's. "Actually, I'm interested in that Geo Metro you've got tucked away in the back corner there."

"You're kidding?" Fast Eddie said and appeared crest fallen.

"You've got nine-hundred on it. I can give you seven-fifty."

"No can do. She's got fairly recent tires and I had my team go over her, gave it a tune up, pretty new wiper blades. The radio works." Then he added, "Sometimes," just under his breath.

"Those tires look like the tread isn't much more than a memory. I can give you seven-fifty, cash."

340

Fast Eddie gave him the once over and said, "Eight hundred, no questions asked."

"Seven-fifty and you can ask all the questions you want. I got nothing to hide."

He seemed to think about that, shrugged like he didn't believe Bobby and said, "What the hell?"

Bobby paid him and then spent fifteen minutes filling out the rudimentary paper work. After some gentle coaxing the thing started and he drove off the lot. Then he drove back to the public library and jumped on one of their computers to fabricate his car insurance information.

Chapter Eleven

"Thank you, Mr. Custer," Marci said. He had just handed a clipboard back to her with the 'contractor form' filled out and a copy of the insurance card he'd dummied up on the library computer.

"Please, call me Bobby."

Marci smiled in a way that suggested she wouldn't dream of it.

"Is Noah Denton available, I'd like to touch base with him if he has a couple of minutes."

He sat in the lobby for another twenty minutes rereading the Sports Illustrated before she called him.

"Mr. Custer, Mr. Denton will see you now. I believe you know the way?" Marci said then smiled as if to suggest she couldn't wait to get him out of her lobby.

He walked into Denton's office and greeted him with, "Hi Noah, thanks for putting me on. I appreciate the opportunity."

Denton looked up from a file and motioned him forward with a wave of his finger. He laid his pen down, took off his glasses, collected his thoughts and waited for a long moment before he spoke.

"Please, don't bother to sit down. Let's get something straight, from here on in, I'm Mr. Denton. Not that you have to really remember that, because I can't foresee the occasion where we would need to interact. You are a contract employee which means you are employed for a very finite amount of time. You'll fulfill the terms of your specific contract and then vacate our premises. While under contract you'll receive your marching orders from Marci, at the front desk. I have difficulty envisioning the need for you to venture anywhere beyond Marci's desk. Should you need a restroom there is one down in the first floor lobby."

"I just wanted to thank you for the opportunity, Noah. That's all."

"So noted, and its Mr. Denton."

Bobby nodded.

"Anything else?"

"No, you've made it pretty clear."

Noah motioned toward the door with his chin dismissing Bobby.

Chapter Twelve

The following morning Bobby was shuttling individuals to and from the firm's office for depositions. Two geriatric men were his morning passengers. One of them had a cane he kept pounding on the floor of the back seat just as he reached the punch line in a long list of non-stop jokes.

Bobby was allowed forty-five minutes for lunch so he high-tailed it back to the McDonald's across from Fast Eddies. The oil light came on just as he was leaving the drive through and he ended up eating his cheeseburger while he watched two quarts of oil pour into the engine.

He picked up a woman named Maxine at one-fifteen. She looked twenty years older than he suspected she actually was. Her skin seemed weathered, maybe too much time laying in the sun or working outdoors. Her hair had been dyed a sort of dishwater blonde sometime back and now she sported a good inch of substantially darker roots. Her clothing, a pants suit even Bobby realized was out of style, was tight, but not in an attractive way. He guessed she had possibly grown a size or two larger since she'd purchased the outfit.

She didn't ask to smoke. She just lit up and then fired up another four successive cigarettes from the butt of the previous one as he made his way down to the law office. Along the way she barked a phlegmy smoker's hack about every three blocks.

He pulled in front of the building, turned and peered at her through the cloud of smoke.

"Just inside, take any elevator up to the twelfth floor. I'll be waiting for you in the lobby when you're finished."

"You ain't taking me up there? I have to find my own damn way?" she said then sucked about a half inch off her current cigarette.

"You can see the elevators right there, through the lobby window. Just get on one and press twelve. The elevator opens right into the office. I've got to park this and then walk all the way back here."

The idea of a walk seemed to halt any further discussion. "I suppose," she groaned then slowly slid across the back seat and climbed out onto the curb.

He found himself wishing he'd dropped her off at the wrong building. She fired up another cigarette on the curb, rubbed the old butt out against the side of his car and headed toward the building. He could only hope she'd be in with Noah Denton.

"Oh dear," Marci said as he cooled his heels up in the twelfth floor lobby. "I'm afraid our last deposition of the day, this Kate Clarken may have forgotten. I'm not getting an answer when I call. I had a feeling she might be a problem from day one," she said under her breath and more to herself than anyone else.

Maxine suddenly came into view. Actually the phlegmy cough announced her approach before she came around the corner. She moved like a two ton truck toward Marci seated behind the receptionist counter. You could hear her thighs swishing against one another with each step.

"When do I get paid?" she half shouted, then wheezed and coughed.

"We'll be issuing checks on Tuesday, you should see your payment forty-eight hours after that," Marci said leaning back as far as possible while still remaining in her chair.

"You're shitting me, that'll make it next Thursday before I can cash the check," Maxine groaned then reached in her purse and fired up a cigarette.

"That was the original agreement, ma'am. And, I'm sorry ma'am, this is a no smoking area, actually the entire building is smoke free." Marci smiled and looked happy like this might be good news to Maxine.

"Not now, it ain't," Maxine growled back and barked her cough a couple of times. "That damn check better not be any later than Thursday or I'm gonna come back here and kick your uptight ass, bitch. You," she pointed her cigarette in Bobby's direction. "Get me the hell out of here."

She walked to the bank of elevators and pushed the down button. Just before the door opened she sucked a good inch off her cigarette, exhaled a massive blue cloud back into the office lobby then stepped onto the elevator barking her cough.

Bobby followed politely behind.

Chapter Thirteen

He parked across the street from the address on his list. Kate Clarken's residence was in the four hundred block of Thomas Ave. in the middle of Frog Town. It had never been the best area in the city, but debatably was no longer the worst. That didn't suggest things had begun to improve in Frog Town, it merely meant another part of town had fallen on even harder times.

Frog Town was an area Bobby had never had a reason to be in until now. Kate Clarken's residence seemed to symbolize many of the reasons why. The structure was a peeling white clapboard building that had been unattractive since the day it was built over a century ago. It had originally been erected as a single family home although for the past fifty years it had sported a half dozen cheap mail boxes haphazardly hung to the right of the front door.

Leaded glass panels on either side of the front door had long ago been replaced by sections of plywood clumsily nailed in place. The address was 411, although the middle 'one' was missing so it read 4 1. A large, unwashed picture window was centered on either side of the front of the house with the front door in the middle, between the two windows. The stain glass that would normally rest above the picture windows had been removed or stolen outright at some point in the distant past.

A chain link fence surrounded the front yard and served to collect a fair amount of the shopping circulars and plastic bags blowing up and down the street. The pounded dirt area enclosed by the fence theoretically once supported a lawn. The front gate hung askew, wedged against the edge of the sidewalk and looking like it hadn't been closed in years.

Bobby climbed the three wooden steps onto the porch that ran across the front of the house. The broken bits of turned porch railing seemed reminiscent of the toothless grin on a Halloween pumpkin. A stuffed couch sat beneath one of the picture windows and from a distance of ten feet he could smell the damp mold on the fabric and stuffing. Empty beer cans and an empty half-pint of vodka were scattered around the couch. There was a hole in the trim around the front door where the doorbell used to be with two cloth covered copper wires hanging out. The front door was unlocked so he turned the knob and stepped inside.

Kate resided in unit 5, up three flights of stairs into what was originally an attic. Bobby had to stoop slightly due to the roof line ceiling as he knocked on her door.

He knocked a second time and waited. A quick examination suggested the door had been kicked in more than once. The trim around the door had been broken and half heartedly repositioned. There were a couple of large footprints on the door just next to the wobbly knob. Each footprint sported a different tread mark. Bobby unconsciously wiped his hands clean on his trousers.

A low voice from behind the door growled, "What you want?"

"I'm here for Kate Clarken."

"She ain't here."

"I was supposed to pick her up."

"What did she do now?"

"She has an appointment, that she'll get paid for, she's not in any trouble."

What sounded like two locks unsnapped and the door opened part way until the chain on the far side stretched taut. A flushed face peeked out, though Bobby couldn't determine if the individual was male or female. Hard to say how old, but if he had to guess he would have pegged it at maybe fifty.

The face was bleary eyed with a red nose heading toward purple. The hair was short, unkempt and looked like it was trimmed by someone wearing a blindfold. Sporadic facial hair coated the upper lip and chins.

"She'll get paid?" the voice growled still partially hiding behind the door. The individual was barefoot and wore faded jeans without a belt, a too small grey T-shirt that partially covered a beer belly with stretch marks. The T-shirt was soiled with the remnants of various meals, although it was difficult to tell if they'd been on the way in or out.

"Yes. I'm supposed to pick her up and then give her a ride back. Do you know where I can find her?"

"What are they gonna pay her for?"

"I don't know, exactly it's for some legal stuff. Look, I need to get her downtown so she can be interviewed. If I can't find her she won't get paid. Simple as that."

"She's either drunk at Moonies, drunk at Foxies or drunk at Sextons, except Sexton's is still closed on account of that trouble a while back."

"So Moonies or Foxies?"

"Maybe."

"I'll check there. I don't find her I'll come back here, if she shows up have her stay put."

"Yeah, sure, that'll work," the creature gave a raspy laugh then apparently couldn't be bothered any more and closed the door.

Chapter Fourteen

Bobby knew of both places though he'd never been in either one. Moonies sat on a corner, it was probably a typical neighborhood local sixty years ago although he wasn't sure what you'd call it now. Rough and shitty were two words that sprang to mind, parking was on the street.

The place was dark. It was a sunny mid-afternoon outside, but you'd never know it from inside Moonies. It took Bobby a moment or two before his eyes adjusted and he could make his way to the bar. He appeared to be one of three guys in the place including the bartender. The two guys on the paying side of the bar sat a-half-dozen stools apart staring at empty shot glasses and half finished beers. Neither one bothered to look as Bobby approached the bar.

The bartender walked down the length of the bar and gave him a look like Bobby was interrupting something important. He didn't say anything and didn't look too excited about new business.

"I'm looking for a woman, Kate Clarken. I was told she might be here."

"You see her?" the bartender snorted.

Bobby held his gaze for a moment. He looked around the place, the four booths on the far wall were empty, no one sat at the tables, unless she was passed out on the floor she wasn't here.

"Has she been in?"

"What's she done now?" he asked.

"Nothing, I'm just giving her a lift downtown."

He shook his head like he didn't believe him then walked back down the length of the bar bringing an end to the conversation.

He headed three blocks west to Foxies. At least it had a parking lot, although he still parked on the street and went in the front door. It was a step up from Moonies, but not much of one. A little more crowded, maybe a half dozen guys none of whom were talking to one another, but then the business at Foxies was drinking and they were all attending to business. He approached the bar.

"What'll it be?" The bartender barked. She was a heavy set woman, maybe late sixties. A sort of swirled hair style left over from the Kennedy administration and pink frame glasses with little rhinestones in the upper ends where the frame came to a point. He could smell the cigarette smoke coming off her from across the bar.

"I'm looking for someone named Kate Clarken."

"Kate? Thank God, would you mind getting her out of here? She's been here for a couple of hours. I got the day shift crowd due in here shortly and I don't need any problems, not tonight anyway."

"Where is she?"

"Her usual booth, back there by the juke box," she directed.

Two more customers had entered, but she didn't pay any attention to them as they settled in on a couple of stools.

"You'll take her out of here, right?" She sounded hopeful as she came around the bar and headed toward the juke box. Bobby followed her to a corner booth.

There in the darkest corner of the darkest booth sat Kate Clarken. Her eyes were half open, but she appeared comatose and looked to be drooling. There were three empty shot glasses on the table and a small glass with beer. The beer looked like it was warm and had gone flat.

"Kate, time to go," the bartender said.

"Miss Clarken, I'm supposed to give you a ride downtown, for a deposition. They're going to pay you." Bobby added thinking that might instill some movement. It didn't. He reached over to shake her shoulder.

"Careful," the bartender cautioned.

"Kate, Miss Clarken?"

She slapped his hand away and attempted to focus on him. "Who the hell are you? I ain't bothering anyone."

"I know. I'm here to give you a ride, downtown."

"You a cop."

"No. You're supposed to give a deposition, they'll pay you, but I have to get you down there pretty soon, we're already late."

This seemed to register.

"And you'll give me a ride?"

"Yeah, and a ride back home."

"Give me a ride back here?"

"No," the bartender said under her breath then retreated to her new customers.

"Anywhere you want, but we have to leave now."

"Let me pee first," she said and began to slowly slide out of the booth. She got to her feet although she seemed a bit unsteady.

Bobby looked around for the rest room and saw the lighted sign that said 'toilets' just above a doorway.

"Come on Kate, let me give you a hand." he said and walked her back to the ladies room. What little conversation there was slowed, and some guy at the bar mumbled, "Jesus." A number of people laughed.

"I'll wait out here for you," he said and pushed the door labeled *'LADIES'* open.

Kate sort of gave a half wave over her shoulder and staggered inside the ladies room. He heard what sounded like a stall door creaking. A while after that the unmistakable sound of someone vomiting. Better here than in my car, he thought.

A few minutes later a guy walked past. He looked to be mid-twenties, dark curly hair. If Bobby had to guess he'd say a construction worker's build, solid, thick and strong. He stepped around Bobby and was about to enter the ladies room.

"Wrong one," Bobby said and pointed to the door labeled *'MEN'*.

He looked like he might argue the point. Some loud laughter drifted in from the barroom and he eventually nodded and said, "Yeah, thanks."

Bobby waited, standing against the wall for a good five minutes. He was about to poke his head in and check when he heard what sounded like a stall door opening. A moment later he heard water running in a sink, then the towel dispenser being pulled. A minute or two after that the door finally opened and a pale-faced Kate Clarken shuffled out.

He took her by the arm and led her into the barroom headed for the front door. All conversation stopped. A couple of guys snickered.

354

"Thanks," the bouffant bartender called.

"Lots a luck, don't forget to wear protection," some guy yelled and everyone laughed.

Chapter Fifteen

Once they were outside, Kate took two steps and threw up on the sidewalk. She wiped her mouth with the back of her hand like it was an everyday occurrence, which maybe it was. Bobby directed her into the back seat and rolled down the window in case she got sick again. He walked around to the driver's side and rolled down the back window just to play it safe. Kate had already stretched out on the back seat with her eyes closed.

He climbed behind the wheel then cautiously backed up to within an inch of the burgundy Escalade parked behind him. Two guys stepped out of Foxies and looked frantically up and down the street. He recognized one as the curly haired guy who almost went into the ladies room. He waited for a couple of cars to shoot past before he pulled the Geo into traffic.

They were headed downtown. Bobby was aware his passenger was in no condition to give a deposition. In her current state he'd be lucky if he could get her into the building let alone past polite Marci at the front desk. As if to confirm his thoughts she suddenly bolted upright in the back seat and thrust her head out the window, gasping. She made all the right sounds, but nothing came up. After a long minute and some very surprised glances from other motorists she sat back and wiped her hand across her mouth.

"Where the hell are we going?" she asked and looked out either side of the Geo in an effort to try and get her bearings.

"You were scheduled to give a deposition this afternoon at Denton, Allan, Sawyer and Hinz," he said then glanced at her in the rearview mirror. His answer didn't seem to register with her.

"Do you remember? They had you scheduled for four this afternoon." It was almost four-twenty at this point and obviously a stupid question.

"Whatever."

A moment later she thrust her head back out the window. Her hair blew across her face. She gathered up a fistful and yanked it behind her head just as she lurched forward, mouth open, eyes bulging. Not what you'd call attractive. Nothing came up. She lurched forward a few more times then settled back in against the seat and closed her eyes.

"Can we stop and get something to eat? I need to calm my stomach."

"I'm really sorry, Kate. You mind if I call you Kate? We're going to be close to a half-hour late by the time we get down there. To tell you the truth I don't think they're going to allow you to give a deposition today. It's fairly obvious you've been drinking. If you can hang on I'll stop on the way back and you can get something. That sound okay?"

As he spoke he glanced in the side mirror, there were three cars passing him. There was a space he could pull into after the third car and hopefully speed up and cut a couple of minutes off their arrival time.

"Come on, come on, pass damn it," he said, waiting for the third car, a black Prius. The woman seemed to hold a position just off his rear wheel, like she was keeping pace. He took his foot off the accelerator and waited for her to pass. Once she drifted past him she did the same thing with the car in front of him, keeping pace just off the rear wheel and blocking Bobby.

He honked a couple of times, then put his blinker on hoping she'd pick up on the fact he wanted to get in her lane. It seemed to make her grip the wheel even tighter. She remained focused straight ahead not looking left or right.

"Damn it," he said then saw his opportunity completely evaporate as a burgundy SUV raced up behind the Prius eliminating any chance to change lanes.

He glanced over at the SUV just as the tinted window was lowered. There was something about it. It probably registered in a nanosecond although it seemed like it took a long time. Everything in slow motion. He recognized the young face, the curly haired guy from Foxies. Then he recognized the burgundy Escalade from in front of Foxies. And then there was that large pistol suddenly pointing out the window.

Chapter Sixteen

Bobby couldn't tell if the curly haired guy looked deadly serious or had he just gathered that from the fact a very large pistol was pointed at him. He jumped the curb and slammed on the brakes just as the guy with the gun leaned out the window. The windshield on the Geo's passenger side suddenly sported two spider web patterns. Bobby swerved around a boulevard tree and onto the sidewalk, taking out a portion of a white picket fence in the process.

"Shit," Kate screamed as she slammed into the back of the front seat then dropped to the floor when he hit the brakes. He heard her gasp and maybe vomit down there, but he had more pressing issues to deal with at the moment.

The escalade fish-tailed back and forth, then hit the brakes and was immediately slammed in the rear by a white delivery van that pushed it into the oncoming traffic lane. There was another screech, then a loud bang and the Escalade spun around facing the opposite direction just two lanes over. The hood was buckled and steam rose from the engine. Tires screeched in all directions. Bobby continued down the sidewalk took a sharp right into an alley and floored it.

He heard Kate coughing down on the floor.

"Jesus Christ. You all right?" he asked, picking up speed as he rocketed down the narrow alley, slamming into two ill-placed plastic trash bins along the way.

She coughed a couple of times then screamed, "What the hell is wrong with you? Are you crazy? Let me get my ass out of here."

"Just stay back there, damn it and shut up," he screamed back.

"Oh, Jesus, look at this I'm a mess. I've got puke all over me. You dumb shit. Just let me out, please." She placed her hands on the back of his seat and pulled herself up. She was right, she was a mess.

"I don't know who those guys were. They were at Foxies, did you know them?"

"What guys?"

"The ones shooting at us."

"Huh."

"The guys, in the Escalade, they were shooting at us. Didn't you see?"

"What the hell are you talking about? God, I could sure use a drink."

"Look at my damn windshield. They tried to kill me."

"When did that happen?"

"Just," he let the rest of it go. "Do you have a phone, a cell?" he asked.

"Why?"

"I was thinking of calling the police. You know since there was a maniac on the road shooting at people. I thought it might be…do you have a cell?"

"Quite yelling, for Christ sake. Oh, God, look at this, you made me puke all over my cigarettes," she said then held up the dripping package of cigarettes to prove her point.

He felt his stomach begin to lurch, but swallowed it back down. He wasn't going downtown and as he thought about it, maybe a little more than a week out of the halfway house wasn't the best time to call the police about a shooting. He sure as hell wasn't going back anywhere near Foxies.

"I'll take you to my place. You can get cleaned up there."

Chapter Seventeen

"Hey, you got a towel?" She called through the bathroom door.

Bobby had been dividing his time between standing guard at the bathroom door and running to the window to see if there was a burgundy Escalade parked out by the dumpster.

"I just moved in and they're all still packed away. Hang on, just a minute," he said then ran and grabbed two T-shirts from one of his paper bags. He knocked on the bathroom door then pushed it partially open and stuck his hand in with the T-shirts. "Here, I'm afraid you'll have to use these. You can dry off with one and slip the other on until your clothes come out of the laundry downstairs."

He caught her reflection in the bathroom mirror as she took the T-shirts from his hand. She was shaking her head like she couldn't believe what he'd just told her. Her hair was wet and hung down over her shoulders. A series of black and blue bruises ran up and down her side, more from falls than any beating he guessed.

There was a sense that she may have been attractive at one time in the distant past, even just out of the shower and still looking like a mess. But, it would have been a very long time ago. He guessed she was somewhere in her fifties. Her figure had fallen prey to the life-style. It had been over four years since he had seen a woman naked, let alone been this close. It would be a while longer before he touched one and it certainly wasn't going to be this woman. He pulled the door closed until it wedged against the door frame and wouldn't close any further.

"I'll go check on your clothes," he said.

He had the drier cranked on high and he put another buck-and-a-half worth of quarters in the slot, he pushed the coins in and hoped the drier wouldn't stop. He wanted her dressed as soon as possible.

He heard her rummaging in the kitchen area when he stepped back into the efficiency apartment. She was standing on her tip-toes peering into the small cabinet about the stove. The rest of the cabinet doors were half open. The T-shirt had risen over her rear and exposed a new set of black-and-blue bruises. Red blotches appeared on the back of her thighs.

"This place is empty and you don't have shit to drink around here. I really need a drink."

"My name's Bobby. I guess we weren't exactly introduced."

She ignored the hand he extended and bent down in a very unlady like pose to look under the kitchen sink. "Where the hell do you keep it? I told you, I need a drink."

"Hey look, Kate, like I said I just moved in. Everything is still packed away, in the delivery van. I don't have any alcohol here."

She looked up at him from the empty cabinet. "Any blow? Crank? Come on, you gotta have something?"

"No, nothing, honest."

She stood up and faced him. The T-shirt barely reached her hip bones leaving her exposed. She either didn't notice or didn't care. "I really need a drink, Mr.

Bobby, I'll make it worth your while, let you do anything you want. Anything. I just need a little drink is all."

"I don't have anything to drink here, Kate."

"Well then go fucking get something," she shrieked. "Jesus Christ. You're making it sound like it's such a big deal. Just go get me something. Now."

"We just had some asshole shooting at us, Kate. I don't know why, I think it might have something to do with you. But, I honestly don't know. I've been out of town for more than four years so I'm pretty sure it's not me. Maybe now just isn't the best time to go traipsing over to some liquor store."

"Well he missed, didn't he? So we should be celebrating. Now either go get me something to drink or get me my clothes so I can get the hell out of here."

"Let's just calm…"

"I want my clothes," she yelled. Then she suddenly began to shake and slowly slid down on the floor, sobbing. "Please just get me a drink and I'll do anything you want, anything. Please, please."

If this wasn't her rock bottom she had to be within sight of it. There was a liquor store about four blocks up. If he left now he could be there and back in twenty minutes.

"If I go get you something, a bottle. You'll be here when I get back?"

She smeared the tears to either side of her blotchy face, sniffled and looked up at him. "I promise. I will, I'll be here for you, really."

"Okay, I'm going to walk. It'll take me about twenty minutes. You'll stay here, promise?"

She nodded from the floor then hugged his leg. "Thank you. I promise I'll be here, just hurry."

364

As he passed the dumpster in the parking lot he glanced up at his window. He could see her standing there watching him through the grimy glass. She gave him a half hearted wave or was she just egging him on to move faster?

Chapter Eighteen

The two guys ahead of him at the liquor store were buying wine. The first guy dropped fifty-six-bucks on two bottles of Chateauneuf du Pape. The second guy bought a bottle of Pinot Noir for sixteen-bucks. Bobby had a plastic fifth of Cosmonaut Vodka that went for eight dollars.

The kid behind the register looked at him for a moment, but didn't say anything.

"I know, it's a joke," Bobby said by way of explanation and handed him a ten.

The kid smiled and nodded like it suddenly all made sense.

"Have a nice night," Bobby said, picked up his paper bag and hurried out the door.

He spotted her a half block away. Oblivious to the fact his T-shirt wasn't covering her as she stood in the window with her arms folded across her chest. Waiting. He looked up at the window once he'd passed the dumpster, ready to give her a friendly wave, but she was gone.

She met him in the stairwell on the second floor.

"Come on, Kate, you're not even dressed."

She grabbed the bag out of his hand then marched back up the stairs. She dropped the paper bag near the top of the stairs and tore the bottle cap off in the hall. Just before the door she tilted her head back and put the bottle to her lips.

Bobby picked up the paper bag, squeezed past her then took hold of her arm and guided her in so he could close his apartment door. He heard her gulp and swallow as he watched the bubbles rising in the up-turned bottle.

"Ahhh-hhhh," she finally gasped, coming up for air. She'd knocked close to a good two inches off the contents.

"You want a glass?"

"Forget it I already checked, you ain't got any," she said then took another long swig. Her faced seemed to grow a little crimson and she belched. She held the bottle tightly, leaned against the wall then slid down to the worn carpet.

He folded the paper bag and placed it in the trash under the sink.

"Soon as it gets dark I'll take you back home. I just don't want to risk those guys seeing me, seeing us. You got any idea what that was about?"

She shrugged, took another sip, seemed to relax a little more and ignored his question all together. "I ain't got no reason to go home. Drop my ass at Moonies."

"I can do that. Let me ask you again. Do you have any idea what that was about this afternoon? Those guys shooting at us."

She shook her head and took another healthy sip then closed her eyes. "Maybe you just pissed them off, you got that way about you, acting high and mighty like."

"No, they came into that bar, Foxies. They were looking for you. One of them tried to go into the la-dies room while you were in there. They left the same time we did, they just didn't see us until we pulled away. I didn't put it together until I was walking back here. It all seems to fit. I just don't get why they were willing to do me in just to get to you."

She kept her eyes closed, took another very healthy swig and half snorted. "Me? Shit no one wants anything to do with me."

He couldn't argue that point. "Why were they going to depose you this afternoon?"

"Do what?" she opened her eyes and attempted to focus on him. Her glassy stare had already returned.

"Why were they going to take your deposition, talk to you? They were going to pay you for your time. The lawyers. Downtown."

"Bankers and lawyers, bankers and lawyers. They're just out to screw all of us one way or the other. Just grab your ankles Mr. Bobby, you'll get yours soon enough," she said then took a couple of gulps and smiled.

"But what were they going to ask you about?"

"Well, I guess I don't really know since you never got my ass down there. I 'spose now I ain't gonna get paid."

"I'll call them in the morning, get them to re-schedule you."

She snorted. "Shit. Don't waste your time, I'll probably be gone by then," she laughed, put the bottle to her lips and started swallowing. When she put the bottle back down it was almost half empty.

"Maybe you should back off on some of that, Kate. Give it a rest for a few minutes."

"Maybe you should just shut-the-hell-up," she said then raised the bottle to her lips again to empha-size her point.

"I'll go see if your clothes are dry."

368

Chapter Nineteen

Mercifully her clothes were dry and he tossed them on the carpet next to where she was sitting. Even though they were just out of the drier they still looked dirty. Jeans, socks and a T-shirt. No underwear.

She'd already made it past the halfway point in the plastic bottle. As she looked up at him with glassy eyes she bounced her head off the wall then put a half hearted grin on her face.

"Want to do me?"

"What?"

She spread her legs apart on the carpet. "Come on, just a couple of bucks."

"No thanks."

"Suit yourself, high and mighty. Probably couldn't get it up anyway, besides I can get better than you anytime I want," she said then took another sip.

"Come on, why don't you get dressed and I'll drive you over to Moonies."

"Good idea," she said then sat there with a half smile on her face.

He pulled her jeans on her legs then helped her up. She leaned against the wall and giggled, never letting go of the vodka bottle. She seemed oblivious to his T-shirt so he just left it on her and pulled her's over on top. She slipped into one of her shoes unaided, but couldn't get the other one on so he helped her. He tied both of her shoes, then walked her down to the car and poured her into the back seat.

She curled up with the vodka bottle, closed her eyes and smiled.

He pulled around the corner at Moonies and parked. As he got out he looked cautiously around before he opened the back door to let her out. She'd been asleep or just passed out since she'd laid down in the back seat.

"Kate." He shook her gently.

"Don't touch me," she snapped then snuggled the bottle closer to her.

"We're at Moonies, time to get out."

The mention of Moonies seemed to awaken something. She slowly sat up and looked around although he was convinced she couldn't see six inches past her nose.

"Come on." He tugged on her arm expecting another outburst. But to his surprise she got out of the car, steadied herself and said, "Get your damn hands off me. I can make it just fine from here." She staggered to the side for a step or two then turned and looked at him. "Looking to party? Give you a deal, just ten bucks."

"No thanks, I'm going home."

"Your loss, mister," she said then headed for Moonies front door.

That was all the encouragement Bobby needed. He quickly got back in his car and drove home.

Chapter Twenty

"I really wish you would have called. Your oversight inconvenienced a number of very busy people," Marci said.

Bobby was almost standing at attention in front of the receptionist counter. It was barely eight-thirty the following morning.

"I suppose we'll have to reschedule Ms Clarken," she said oblivious to the fact that the woman would be unfit regardless of the time or the day.

"They wouldn't have been able to depose her," Bobby said not for the first time.

"That's the sort of determination a qualified individual will have to make," she snapped back implying Bobby was anything, but qualified.

"She couldn't stand, she'd thrown up a number of times. It didn't take a qualified individual to determine she couldn't be deposed."

"The flu?" Marci asked still not catching on.

"Bottle flu, maybe. No Marci, she was drunk, so drunk she was throwing up."

"Are you sure? How could that be? It was barely four in the afternoon."

"I think she inhabits a little different world than you, or even me for that matter. My advice is to strike her from your list and…"

"As I said before, that's a decision for a *qualified* individual to make."

"How qualified do you have to be to determine someone is so intoxicated they can't stand and they've thrown up on themselves."

"Never the less."

"Okay, next time I'll bring her down here for a *qualified* individual to judge her condition."

That seemed to please Marci.

"Here are the four individuals you'll be delivering today. Please have them here on time. You've no idea the havoc caused when schedules aren't adhered to."

As he took the list he wondered if Marci was aware of the havoc caused when some idiot tried to ruin your day by shooting at you from a moving vehicle? He determined the wiser decision would be to just shut up.

"Any special needs, here?" he asked, trying to be overly solicitous. "Walkers, oxygen tanks or maybe just an escort? Two of the folks yesterday seemed pretty elderly."

Marci nodded. "And the third downright unpleasant."

"Maxine."

"Exactly."

They were friends again.

"No, I don't believe we'll have any special needs today. Let's just hope everyone arrives on time," she said and stared at him over the top of her glasses.

"I'll do my best."

"Very well," she said and dismissed him.

The day was uneventful. Everyone was ready and waiting at the appropriate time. No one smoked. No one had been drinking, at least that Bobby could tell. Everyone asked about the windshield and accepted his

372

errant softball as an explanation. It was all wonderfully dull.

Chapter Twenty-One

He was driving back to his apartment dialing in the news on the radio and caught just the tale end of the news story.

'Police have identified the victim as thirty-eight year old Katherine Clarken, a St. Paul resident. Anyone with any information is asked to contact authorities. In other news today the St. Paul City Council voted to oppose...'

Since none of the buttons worked on the Geo's radio he attempted to adjust the tuning by hand and couldn't land on a station broadcasting news to save his soul. Every station was playing music the one time he didn't want any.

He parked next to the dumpster, then climbed out of the Geo and looked around cautiously. There was no reason to believe he should be a target, but he wasn't taking any chances. As far as that went there was no reason to believe Kate Clarken had been a target, either. Well, except for the fact that two guys had chased them and attempted to murder them. It seemed more likely she died from alcohol poisoning, or maybe in a drunken stupor she simply staggered into an oncoming car. Still, he walked the four blocks up to the retail corner and purchased a newspaper and some light bulbs. He noticed laundry hanging on a clothesline on the way home.

He sat on the carpet and read the paper. There'd been a shooting outside Moonies the previous evening, just after midnight. At the time the paper had gone to press the victim remained unidentified. The article listed the victim as a Caucasian female and he figured it was a sure bet at that location it had to have been Kate Clarken.

He thought it was a pretty safe assumption it wasn't accidental or even a case of mistaken identity. Which left only one question in my mind, was he safe?

At a little after midnight he cut across the parking lot, past the dumpster and made his way up the street. After two blocks he took a right at the corner and then a left down the alley. About a half-dozen houses in, he spotted the clothes line. Mercifully the laundry was still hanging. Two minutes later he was walking home at a brisk clip. He had six towels and a set of sheets. Now he just needed a bed.

Chapter Twenty-Two

Bobby was driving a woman named Ardis Dempsey downtown for her deposition. Based on the fumes wafting from the backseat making his eyes water she must have cornered the market on cheap perfume. She apparently rolled her face in a tin of pancake makeup, then applied a slightly off-center layer of fire engine red lipstick just before he picked her up.

"… so Donny, that's Carol's third, is in the Navy. He's on an aircraft carrier in the gulf. God, the worry. I say a rosary for that boy every night."

"We never stop worrying," Bobby said trying to give her a chance to take a breath.

"Isn't it the truth. My oldest, James, fortunately he missed all that nonsense in Viet Nam. He was with the Marines in Korea, brought home a lovely girl. Now they've got two daughters, one just finishing med school, the other teaching. That little Kim, she's the mother, she runs a very tight ship. Course with Jim she might just have to. You know, I can't seem to remember if I locked that darn back door. Honest to God, there are some days I'm not sure I could remember my own name. Fortunately it's on my driver's license," she said and laughed.

"Here we are Mrs. Dempsey. I can escort you in if you'd like or you can just walk through those doors, onto the elevators and press twelve. The doors will open right into the lobby of the law firm. Marci is the name of the receptionist."

"I'm quite capable of making my own way, thank you."

376

"That's what I thought, I'll just let you out and watch you to make sure. Then I'll park this car and be waiting for you in the lobby when you're finished. Most of the other depositions seem to be taking right around ninety minutes."

"Drive carefully. I don't know how you can even see out of that windshield," she warned as she got out, then walked, cane in hand into the lobby.

He sped off, figuring if he hurried and made all three lights he could be on her back steps in about ten minutes.

He made it in eight minutes and she was right, she had left the back door unlocked.

"Hello," he called as he entered, called again from her dining room and once again at the base of the staircase. He didn't get a response and hurried back into the kitchen. He doubled up a couple of trash bags, then placed four plates, four sets of silverware, four glasses and two coffee mugs inside.

He doubled up two more trash bags, stuffed some wash cloths, a pillow and a blanket in there along with some cans of soup and a bag of Doritos, then made his way out the door. He was sitting in the lobby waiting for Ardis when she finished her deposition.

"Aren't you just the prompt person," she said coming around the corner.

He glanced toward battle ax Marci and smiled, but didn't respond.

Chapter Twenty-Three

He walked up to the grocery store a few nights later. He still looked around suspiciously whenever he came out of his building, or any building for that matter, but he never saw anything suggesting he was being watched or followed. Still he'd waited until dark, which meant he had to hurry since the grocery store closed at nine.

He was literally the only person in the checkout lane and he thought he was probably the last customer in the store. As he grabbed his bag and made his way toward the door the checkout girl was already busy closing down her register, probably hurrying to make a hot date. All he knew was she didn't have time to pay attention to him. He stole a newspaper off the rack. Big deal, they'd be sent back first thing in the morning with tomorrow's deliveries anyway, so it wasn't like the grocery store was really losing anything.

He was sitting on the floor, nibbling on some of the Doritos he'd taken from Ardis Dempsey a few days back while he read his stolen copy of the paper. He'd made his way through the news, such as it was, and began working his way through the obituaries.

There it was, "Katherine 'Kate' Clarken. Died unexpectedly. Visitation between six and eight. Thursday evening. Private internment."

That was tomorrow night. It struck him that the visitation service was short, just two hours, with no funeral service or survivors mentioned. Given the few hours of Kate's life he'd been exposed to, Bobby didn't find it surprising there wasn't a throng of people lined up to bid a tearful good-bye. Still, in a way he felt sorry for her.

* * *

He parked on the street about half-past seven hoping to avoid any crowd. He needn't have worried. The Geo Metro was the only car parked on the street for a block in either direction.

The Capitol City funeral home had been in business for close to a century. When Capitol City first started out, this section of town must have been some kind of neighborhood. Bobby guessed the area had fallen on hard times during the Great Depression and then life just sort of skidded downhill from there. Now, the place was a jumble of nondescript two-story brick warehouses, the odd little ugly frame house, a few small salvage yards and a sleazy bar named Harold's that advertized Happy Hour All Day Long directly across the street.

He grabbed his four-dollar bouquet of grocery store flowers from the passenger seat and headed inside the Capitol City funeral home. The lobby was small and nondescript. Off to the right was a small office illuminated by the glare coming off an old television sitting on a desk.

"Can I help you?" a man asked from about a foot behind the television and flicked on a light. He was dressed in an out-of-date dark suit, a white shirt yellowed around the collar with age and a dark tie. He didn't bother to get up. For that matter he didn't really bother to look at Bobby. He just quickly glanced in the general direction and then returned to the television.

"Katherine Clarken," Bobby said.

That seemed to get the attendant's attention. He studied Bobby for a long moment, glanced at the bouquet of flowers in his hand. "Straight ahead, second door on the left." Sounding like he couldn't quite believe someone had even asked for her.

"Thanks."

The hallway wasn't all that long and sported trim and ceiling molding that looked like it came out of a 1940's movie. The ceiling had grayed over time and both the walls and trim were painted the same sort of icy pale green color. There was a definite grime pattern on either side of the hallway from seven or eight decades worth of hands running along the walls. The carpeting looked to have once been a burgundy sort of affair with a floral motif but was now in desperate need of a good cleaning or maybe it should just be hauled outside and burned.

The second door on the left led into a small, claustrophobic room in need of ventilation. The room was poorly lit with a dreadful dirge droning in the background over a crackling speaker. There was a grey vinyl partition hung from the ceiling that had been pulled across the rear of the room to accommodate smaller affairs. At the front of the small room a dozen brownish metal folding chairs were lined up in three rows of four, two chairs on either side forming a sort of pretend center aisle. At the very front of the room, past the folding chairs a small card table stood draped with a white table cloth. Placed in the middle of the card table was a very plain wooden urn. In case there were any doubts, a 4 x 5 card lay in front of the urn with the handwritten name in black marker, *Katherine Clarken*. The stuffy room was empty except for one young guy sitting off to the right in the rear row of folding chairs.

Bobby walked up to the front of the room, past the chairs and stood in front of the card table. He didn't know what to do, but felt it would be rude to just turn and leave. So he stood there and pretended to say a prayer. Then he placed the flowers on the card table next to the urn, careful to lay the $3.99 price tag face down. He bowed his head then as he turned to leave he nodded at the young man in the chair.

The young man gave a curt nod in response, then his eyes narrowed and he growled in a deep voice, "Who the hell are you?"

"My name's Bobby," he said and extended his hand.

The young man brought a massive paw over and wrapped it around Bobby's hand. He squeezed gently, but left him with the sense it would have been no problem to simply crush Bobby's hand. He was solidly built, with a weightlifters chest and a very thick neck. He wore a black short sleeved shirt, just three buttons, all undone. The sleeves were stretched around large biceps tattooed in some blue Celtic-looking pattern. His hair was clipped short, almost but not quite shaven, and his eyes looked red and puffy. He'd been crying.

"Thanks for coming. You're the only one. She would have liked those." He lifted his square chin in the direction of Bobby's grocery store bouquet.

Bobby smiled and nodded. "I only met Katherine, Kate, a few days ago, really just a simple business arrangement. I was supposed to pick her up and, well..."

"Pick her up? Business arrangement?" There was suddenly an edge in his voice.

"I was hired by a firm, a law firm downtown to drive people so they could give depositions. Katherine, Kate was one of the people I drove."

"You brought her downtown?"

"Actually no, see, we ran into some difficulty and we weren't able to get there in time, get to the attorney's office. I ended up driving her back. She wanted me to drop her off at Moonies that night and well..." He thought it best not to go on from there and stared at the floor. He was beginning to feel very uncomfortable.

"So you're the one who brought her to Moonies?"

"Only because that's where she told me she wanted to go. I picked her up at Foxies, that's where they followed us from," Bobby said.

"Followed you?"

"I really don't want to get into it. She couldn't tell who they were, she didn't know. At the end, she just told me to drop her at Moonies so that's what I did. Then I heard about this awful..." He stopped there, ready to give another nod and leave.

"Sit down," the young man said. Not so much an invitation as a command.

Chapter Twenty-Four

Bobby ended up telling him the story. He told him the entire story, almost. About going to Kate's apartment, Moonies, Foxies, those idiots shooting at them and how he took off down the alley to get away. That was the point where the young man told him he was Kate's son and Bobby made the decision to leave out the part about buying her the cheapest bottle of vodka he could find, dressing her and dumping her in front of Moonies in a quasi-comatose state so he could flee the scene.

"So Bobby, what you're telling me is you saved her life." The young man's eyes watered up as he gazed at the wooden urn.

"Anyone would have done the same thing."

The young man scoffed, "Don't bet on it."

"I just wish I could have prevented what happened later. We talked about her going there, I suggested she go home or I was even willing to get her a hotel room. She just wanted to go to Moonies and begged me not to call the police. She was fairly insistent so in the end I went along and did what she wanted. I wish I could change all that now," Bobby said and sort of let that hang out there for a moment hoping the opportunity would present itself so he could get up and leave.

"You did your best, man," he said, then sort of came back to reality and focused on Bobby. "You need a ride or anything?"

"Me? No, thanks, I'm parked right out front. Kind of you to offer, but its not necessary."

"Come on, we'll walk out together, the three of us," the young man said, then went over to the card table, picked up the urn and tucked it under his arm. "Let's get the hell out of here."

They walked down the dimly lit hallway together, past the small office and out the front door.

"Thank you, gentlemen." A voice called from the office, but never left the glare from the TV to see them out.

They stood out on the street, Bobby's car sat at the curb, wheezing.

"That yours?" the young man asked.

"Yeah, that's me. Look I…"

"What happened to it?"

"I told you, someone pulled along side of us, a burgundy Escalade. They lowered the window, stuck a cannon out, I slammed into the side of the Escalade a couple of times, but they still got two rounds off before I pushed them into some oncoming traffic. I just wanted to make sure Kate, I mean your mom was safe so I hit the brakes and drove onto the sidewalk then took off down an alley. I was pretty sure they wouldn't follow."

"You really did save her, man," he said looking at Bobby's windshield.

Bobby nodded.

"They were aiming for her, weren't they? She was sitting right there in your passenger seat. You didn't have those quick reactions they would have shot her, right then."

There seemed to be no advantage to telling him Kate was passed out in the back seat having just finished throwing up.

"Yeah, they stuck that pistol out the window I knew they were aiming for her so I slammed into them, figured it would be the one thing they wouldn't be expecting."

"And that's your car?"

"Yep, one of a kind. I get some money saved up, I'm gonna get that windshield replaced."

"Better do it sooner rather than later, cops take a dim view of that sort of thing."

"Yeah, things are just a little tight right now. But it's first on the list."

"Say Bobby, I wonder if I can ask a small favor of you." He said it in a way that eliminated the response "No" right off the bat.

"Possibly, what is it you need?"

"I've actually got an appointment in a bit. I wonder if you wouldn't mind taking my Mom home with you, just for tonight, keep her safe. I'll come by later and pick her up. That sound okay with you?" Again with that tome of voice that said "No" was not an option.

"It would be my pleasure, be happy to help."

He handed Bobby the urn, then pulled his phone out, swiped his finger across the face, pushed the screen twice and asked, "What's your number?"

"To tell you the truth, I'm just switching cell-phone carriers so I'm sort of between numbers," Bobby lied.

"You got an address?"

Bobby told him.

"Great, got it. I'll be in touch, Bobby," he said, then shut the phone off, nodded and crossed the street.

Bobby placed Kate's ashes on the floor of the passenger seat, then watched in his side mirror as her son stepped inside Harold's, "Home of the all day happy hour". Bobby climbed behind the wheel and drove Kate back to his place.

He set her urn on the kitchen counter and put a pizza in the oven. He was a little curious and opened the lid on the urn, it looked like it had been filled with cat litter. Maybe it had and Capitol City just dumped folks in a large hole somewhere. He decided it might be better to just focus on the pizza.

Chapter Twenty-Five

He'd been moved up a notch in the pecking order of Marci's roster. Violet Oxley had been subpoenaed to testify in a court case. He was to drive her down to the Courthouse. Then sit with her in the hallway outside courtroom '2' cooling his heels until she was called to testify. His guess was, at three-thirty-five in the afternoon that it had grown too late in the day for Violet to be called. Unless, of course, there happened to be a real jerk on the bench presiding, which there was as a matter of fact, her honor, Judge Susan Eckersbe, a decidedly unhappy individual. Back when he had been practicing he'd had the distinct displeasure of finding himself in her courtroom on a couple of occasions. Those appearances had never seemed to go his way.

"Goodness, I almost hope they don't call me, now," Violet said at three-forty.

"I'm pretty sure they won't, this time of day they usually like to wind up around four. Gives the attorneys time to file motions, get things lined up for tomorrow. The judge will be able to beat the traffic home." He raised his eyebrows to emphasize the joke which seemed to bring a smile to Violet's face.

"I hope you're right."

"Trust me, I've been around this particular block more than a few times"

At four-ten the bailiff stuck her head out the door and called, "Violet Oxley?"

"Dreadful," Violet said an hour and a half later and not for the first time. "Just positively dreadful.

387

Where do I send my complaint? Because believe me I'm going to write one. That woman could do with a good thumping," she said, then stared out the window of Bobby's back seat.

It was almost six and they were still inching along in rush hour traffic. They weren't being helped by the construction lane closures that had this section of Snelling Ave. going from three lanes down to one. There wasn't a construction crew within sight to save Bobby's soul.

"Yeah, that's Judge Eckersbe. Not a very happy person."

"I should say not. She practically shouted at me while I sat in that chair out in front of everyone trying to gather my thoughts."

"The witness stand."

"It was worse than being on stage. For pity's sake, I thought it just might be important to give correct information. She apparently couldn't be bothered to grant me the second or two I needed to gather my thoughts before I began. Dreadful, absolutely dreadful."

"No argument from me, Ms Oxley," Bobby said then turned off Snelling and headed West on Larpenteur. He turned right two blocks down and then pulled into a toney cul-de-sac a few moments later.

"Just pull up in front if you would. I don't want you dripping oil on my driveway."

"Yes ma'am," he said and pulled up next to her mailbox.

"Thank you, Bobby. You'll be here at eight-thirty tomorrow morning?"

"I will," he said and climbed out to open the rear door for her.

388

"Try not to be late. I'll be waiting," she said, then stepped out and walked up the driveway to her front door. She unlocked the door and stepped inside without looking back.

He gave her the finger from behind the passenger door and drove off.

Bobby was just tidying up the kitchen area after dinner when someone knocked on his door. Since he didn't have a peep hole to look through he had to ask, "Who is it?"

"Kate's son. Here to get my mom."

He glanced over at the kitchen counter. Fortunately, he had just removed the plate he'd washed and leaned against the urn to dry along with the fork he'd set on top of it. He opened the door.

"How's it going, Bobby?" The young man smiled and walked in. He was dressed in a nondescript T-Shirt and jeans, the T-shirt stretched taught over his muscular chest. The fabric around his large biceps looked like it was about to rip. A black guy about the same age and size followed in behind him. The guy had a toothpick hanging out of the corner of his mouth. Neither one bothered with any form of introduction.

"I set the urn right over here, on the kitchen counter," Bobby said making a beeline for the urn. He kept talking as he grabbed a dish towel and wiped a few drops of water from the fork he'd left on top. "Lovely little bit of wood, I'm sure she would be pleased," he smiled and pretended to polish the top and sides.

"Not sure she'd even know," her son said looking around the sparse surroundings before he asked, "Exactly how long you been living here?"

"Me?"

The two visitors both looked at Bobby like he was nuts.

"Just a couple, well maybe four weeks. I'm sort of getting resettled."

Kate's son nodded and smiled. "You just got out, didn't you?"

Bobby nodded.

His visitors grinned.

"I knew it. Picked up on it the other night, you had that sense about you. A fella can tell, just a certain way about you." He flashed a quick smile, then got serious, very serious. "So maybe those two you mentioned, driving the Escalade, maybe they were looking for you all along."

"The shooters? Not likely."

"You locked up with some bad asses, you give 'em some of that privileged boy attitude? A lot of folks don't like that shit."

"I wasn't locked up with real criminals, I was with bankers, lawyers, and accountants."

"Not real criminals? Shit, now that's funny. You think that's funny Arundel?" he said to his sidekick.

"Shit."

"Listen, they weren't after me. Just for starters they were looking for your mom at Foxies. I'd never even been there before, Foxies. I told you one of them tried to go in the ladies room after her and I had to stop him. Told him to get the hell out of there, he backed off, went away, once he realized he'd have to deal with the likes of me. Then they were out on the street looking for her. Hey, they would have got her right then and there if I hadn't pulled into traffic the way I did. I tried to lose 'em in traffic, but the bastards found us, somehow. They would have had her for sure if I hadn't reacted when they shoved that pistol out the window, it looked like a .45 or maybe a .357, big damn thing. Most guys would have frozen under fire. I didn't have that luxury. I slammed into them a couple of times, then jumped the curb, raced down the sidewalk and blasted down that alley so I could get her the hell out of danger. I lost count of how many rounds they got off. Of course, I was more than a little preoccupied at the time."

"You knew they were following you?"

"Following me? You think if they were trying to kill me I would have shown up at the funeral home? Hell, I'd be halfway across the country by now. Instead I brought her ashes home and ..."

"Okay, I get it. You can't take a little joke, Bobby, sorry. I didn't think you'd get that upset."

"I'm not upset," Bobby half yelled.

"Good, glad to hear it. So, like, what are you going to do about furniture? I mean, this is more than a little pathetic." He glanced over at the stolen blanket and pillow lying on the floor next to the suitcase and the three brown paper grocery bags holding clothes.

"I like to live simple," Bobby said.

They both nodded, but didn't say anything.

Chapter Twenty-Six

"And you were what, a banker?" Arundel asked and glared.

"Actually a lawyer, with an accounting background, a CPA."

"But not a criminal," Arundel said. He smiled coldly and moved the toothpick with his tongue from the left to the right side of his mouth.

"I never shot anyone, never meant to harm anyone."

"Right, leave that to us folks without them fancy college degrees," Arundel said. "You just left them penniless. Left 'em to fend for themselves in a world where your kind make all the rules. 'Course, if they needed any help it would just be cash up front. Kinda like them insurance types. You know, you pay year after year, then when you finally file a claim they don't pay it and then they raise your rates just cause you tried to get what was owed you in the first place."

"It wasn't like that."

"Oh really, then just what the hell was it like, Mr. Lawyer, accountant?" Arundel moved a half step toward Bobby.

"All right now, Bobby you'll just have to excuse Arundel, here. He holds some points of view ain't all that popular with certain folks. But he don't mean no harm, now. Do you Arundel?"

"Just making a point," Arundel said and gave Bobby a hard look.

"Tell me again about these two looking to go after my mom."

"In the Escalade?"

Her son nodded.

"Well, like I said, they were driving a burgundy Escalade. I think it got pretty smashed up, maybe even totaled, but I wasn't going to keep your mom there while I checked it out."

"What'd they look like?"

"Can't tell you too much. Both white. Younger, maybe mid-twenties, the one I stopped from going after her in the ladies room at Foxies, he was the same one put the window down when they drove alongside and then shot at us. He had dark curly hair, sort of a pug nose. They were both big, maybe not the size of you two, but not little. I'd say they were in pretty good shape."

"And the other one?"

"The other one, the driver. I only caught him for a few seconds. Not dark hair, but not blond either, brown maybe heading toward red. Some might call it ginger colored."

Arundel gave a quick glance, just a flash of his eyes, but Bobby couldn't determine what, if anything had been communicated.

Arundel asked, "The one in the ladies room…"

"He never got in there, I stopped him and wouldn't let him in."

"…he have an accent?"

"Not that I recall, he might have said just two or three words. I don't remember an accent, but like I said, I can't be sure."

Arundel nodded and rolled his toothpick over to the other side.

"You guys think you know who it is?"

They both shook their heads no, but in a rather unconvincing manner.

"Why would someone want to hurt your mom?"

"That shooting a while back," Kate's son said to Arundel.

"Sexton's," Arundel replied, then nodded like it all made sense.

"Thanks for keeping an eye on my Mom."

"Not a problem, you want to put her in a paper bag, I think I've got a spare around here," Bobby said opening the cabinet below the sink.

"No, you hang onto her. I'll grab her a little later on. We're out of here, take care of yourself, Bobby."

"You're not taking the urn?"

"I just told you, I'll get it a little later," he said and they walked out the door.

From where he stood Bobby watched them head down the stairs then he walked over, closed his apartment door once they were out of sight and made sure it was locked.

Chapter Twenty-Seven

He wasn't due to pick up Violet Oxley for an hour. After which, he could look forward to an entire day of sitting and cooling his feet in the hallway outside Courtroom 2 while Violet gave her testimony. There was a newspaper delivered every morning at the front of his building by the mail boxes. If he hurried down there he could steal the thing for a half hour and return it on his way out the door without anyone being the wiser.

He opened the apartment door and two wooden chairs fell onto the floor. Two more were stacked out in the hallway along with a card table, a chest of drawers, a box spring, mattress and a bed frame. They all carried a tell-tale smoker's smell.

The hallway was unoccupied and Bobby couldn't hear anyone on the staircase. Beggars can't be choosers. He hauled everything in as fast as possible and locked the door. He pulled the drawers out and stood them on end in front of the open window to air them. He looked at his watch and decided he would have to deal with all this at the end of the day. Right now it made more sense to arrive early and pick up Violet Oxley.

* * *

"Well, Bobby. I hadn't figured you for the early sort. Let me just set the alarm," she said. A moment later he held the screen door open as she closed and locked her front door. He followed her down the driveway and opened the rear door to the Geo Metro.

"You really must do something about that windshield, Bobby. Is it even legal?"

"My insurance company is sorting it out as we speak."

"Good luck with that. Say, Bobby, are you a smoker?" She gave an audible sniff to the air.

"No ma'am, fortunately a vice I've never had."

"God, I think I can, well now I can't really tell if I can smell cigarette smoke or not."

"If you would prefer I could lower a window?"

"No, I'll be fine, thank you. Let's just hope things move a bit faster today," she said and settled back for the drive.

They didn't. Move faster that is, at least not for Bobby. It was almost two when Violet stepped back out of the courtroom and into the hallway. He laid the copy of yesterday's paper on the marble bench where he'd found it and stood as she approached.

"All finished?"

"Yes, and not a moment too soon. Do you happen to know where the restrooms are located?"

"I do, come on I'll show you and then we'll get you home."

The drive back to Violet's home was completely uneventful and made even more boring by her diatribe of family history beginning with the 1870 immigration from Germany to Canada.

"Oh wow, fascinating, I'd love to hear more, but we're already at your home," he said and pulled in front of her driveway. He jumped out of the car and ran around to the passenger side unable to wait another moment to be free of the history lesson.

"Thank you Bobby, now here, your lucky day, I don't have any change so I'm giving you this," she said and handed him a dollar.

"Oh, that's really not necessary, Ms Oxley," he said taking the dollar.

She'd already started up the driveway toward her front door. "Nonsense, now I insist. You should do some research, the town of New Berlin, Ontario they changed the name to Kitchener at the outbreak of the First World War. Now my grandfather…"

He was already behind the wheel trying to figure out where the closest drugstore was located. He felt in desperate need of some aspirin.

Chapter Twenty-Eight

So much for airing out the new furniture. As soon as he opened the door to the apartment it smelled like some three-pack-a-day guy had been living in there with all the windows closed for the better part of a year. He went to the kitchen sink, took two aspirin for his Violet Oxley headache, then headed out on foot to the grocery store.

He spotted it on the way back, parked on the street across from his building. He didn't know a lot about cars, but this was big and black. An SUV with forty inch chrome wheel rims and windows tinted so dark they had to be in violation of some sort of state law.

He immediately thought the shooters. He was armed with a grocery bag full of air freshener, a package of chocolate chip cookies and wondering which way to run when he heard his name called.

"Bobby. Hey, Bobby, get your ass up here."

Kate Clarken's son was standing in his apartment, yelling out the window waving from behind a pair of dark sunglasses. Bobby still wasn't sure, but he couldn't think of any other option so he went inside. He knew he'd locked the door before he left, but it was half open as he climbed the final flight of stairs to the third floor.

Kate's son smiled as Bobby stepped inside. He was sipping what Bobby presumed was one of the two cans of coke he'd had in the refrigerator. What looked like the other can rested on the window sill, half crushed and apparently empty.

"Been looking for you, Bobby."

"Just walked to the grocery store to get some air freshener and cleaning supplies. I had the windows open to air all this stuff out, it smelled like cigarette smoke and I was hoping to get rid of the smell. I think all it did was stink up the entire apartment. You wouldn't happen to have any idea where this stuff came from, would you?"

He smiled and held out the palms of his hands in mock surrender. "Just a friendly little way of saying thanks and helping you out at the same time, man."

"Thanks? For what?"

"For trying to help my mom, dumb shit. Not like she had a lot of friends. Tell you the truth she didn't have any, unless you were buying. I mean she was my mom and all, but I'd be the first to tell you she could be awfully mean and she was pretty much totally worthless, and those were her good points," he joked.

"Where did you get all this?"

"Like it," again with the smile.

Bobby dodged the direct answer. "Well, it's certainly better than the stuff I didn't have. But you must have brought it up here in the middle of the night. I mean, it was all piled up against the door first thing this morning."

"Arundel and me, it all belonged to my mom. Pretty obvious, she's got no use for this shit now," he laughed.

"Did you get it from her apartment? That little third floor place over in Frog Town?"

He pulled off the sunglasses and eyed Bobby suspiciously. "You been there?"

"Never inside. I just knocked on the door once. Whoever answered told me to look for Kate, your mom, at Moonies or Foxies. That's how I knew to go to those places. Otherwise I never would have found her. To tell you the truth, I couldn't determine if it was a man or a woman who answered that door."

He nodded. "That would have been Cookie."

"Cookie?"

"Yeah, hard to believe, but I guess she was something in her day, used to dance all over the state."

"Dance?"

He nodded. "You know, among other things. Used to be able to name her price from what I hear."

Bobby shook his head. "You're right, it is hard to believe."

"She crashes there sometimes. I guess she wasn't there when we grabbed this stuff, at least I didn't see here. Suppose she could have been passed out in a closet or out in the hallway." He said it absently as if it was a logical possibility. "But this stuff is gonna work out for you, right? Like you said, better than what you didn't have."

"No, I mean, yeah, I appreciate it. I'm sorry things are kind of tight on my end. I really can't pay you for all this right now."

"What the hell you talking about? You don't have to pay me, man. I owed you. Course, now we're even," he said and fixed Bobby with a quick stare. "I hope you don't mind, but I put the bed together for you. God the stories that thing could tell." He took two steps over to the bed, placed his hand on the headboard and rocked it back and forth causing the frame to squeak. "Yeah, that brings back memories."

"God, I wish I had something else to offer you. I got a half eaten bag of Doritos?"

"No thanks."

400

Bobby sort of half laughed and thought, since we're pals now it might be nice to know your name. "One thing, I don't think you ever told me your name?"

"You're right, I didn't," he said.

Chapter Twenty-Nine

Despite the tales the bed could tell it was a lot better than sleeping on the floor and Bobby slept wonderfully. An uneventful day followed, most of which was spent in the hallway on the fifth floor of the courthouse, waiting while individuals gave their testimony. The case was some sort of class action suit brought against a company theoretically providing flood insurance.

Like so many cases the devil was in the details. He was delivering people to and from the courthouse who lived along sections of the Mississippi river. Judging from the homes, all very nice, he would guess the places used to flood or were in danger of flooding maybe once every fifty years. Beginning in 2008 they'd flooded six out of the last eight years and the term "flood of the century" had been relegated to the dust bin. This past spring's flooding had been particularly bad.

It was a no-win deal for everyone involved, home owners, municipalities, even the insurance companies who Bobby usually had no patience with. He was glad to get home and spray another heavy dose of air freshener and rub furniture polish on his recent acquisitions.

He parked the Geo in the back of the building and then, as had become his routine, he walked the four blocks up to the retail corner and did some shopping. He had written a grocery list, consisting of six basic items on the back of a Courthouse tourist brochure.

He was almost home, squeezing between his Geo and the dumpster when he caught sight of an SUV with forty-inch chrome wheel rims and dark tinted windows parked across the street and down maybe half a block. He was not in the mood for company tonight.

Resigned to his fate he climbed the stairs, unlocked the apartment door and walked in. No one was there to welcome him. Thank God. It's not like there were a lot of places to hide, but just to be sure he checked the bathroom, the closet and looked under the bed. Nothing. Kate's ashes still sat on a corner of the kitchen counter.

It took him no more than half a minute to put the groceries away. He put the TV dinner in the oven and glanced out the window. Everything looked okay. He ate his dinner, read the grocery circular he'd found in the bag and then sat in the dark looking out the window and waiting for the expected visitor that never showed up.

He went to bed about eleven, sleeping fitfully and waking a half dozen times to get up and look out the window. The SUV remained parked across the street with not so much as an inkling of activity. He heard someone walking down the outside hallway a little after four in the morning, but the footsteps were followed by a lock snapping open and an apartment door slamming closed. Most likely one of the neighbors he'd never met coming home after a late night.

He stared out the window onto an empty street while he ate a bowl of oatmeal. Then he dressed and got ready for another day of watching the second hand on the clock take its own sweet time while he cooled his heels in the courthouse hallway.

He was back home by four that afternoon and couldn't quite put his finger on it, but he had the sense someone had been in his apartment. Not that there was anything worth stealing unless you counted one of the four beers on the bottom shelf of his refrigerator.

He made his evening pilgrimage up to the retail area where he purchased a roll of scotch tape and for some unknown reason decided to pocket a Milky Way candy bar. He kept his eyes peeled but didn't spot the black SUV anywhere on the street. He sat with the lights off in the apartment and ate a chicken sandwich looking out the window as night fell then finally turned in a little before midnight.

He was up at two to use the bathroom. He left the lights off and walked to the window. There it was, the SUV, parked across the street, almost where it had been the night before. He was tempted to go out there and ask Kate Clarken's son what he thought he was up to. Upon brief reflection he decided that wouldn't be the best idea and went back to bed. When he checked an hour later the SUV still hadn't moved.

It dawned on Bobby that maybe the vehicle was just parked there and the occupant was either in one of the apartments in the building or one of the homes up the street. Between the tinted windows and the dark of night he couldn't tell if the thing was occupied.

He left to make his first pick-up at eight forty-five the following morning. Once he locked the door he attached a length of scotch tape to the frame and then to the door itself, just opposite the lower hinge. If someone opened the door in his absence they'd pull the tape off and he'd know he had been visited.

Chapter Thirty

It was the fourth day twiddling his thumbs in the same hallway of the courthouse. The retired school teacher he'd brought in for testimony in a reckless driving case was fascinated with the whole legal process and had reentered the courtroom, pen in hand, to observe and record.

He was left to his own devices out in the hallway, slogging through the historical romance novel he'd pocketed in the basement coffee shop. *Love's Dark Fury* had the same woman involved in an affair with Confederate and Union commanders on the eve of the Battle at Gettysburg. Just in case the previous days weren't long enough this tale made the clock come to a complete stop. He made a mental note to get a library card and a decent book as he turned to the next page.

"Mr. Custer, Bobby, is that really you?"

He looked up and although it had been almost five years since the one time they'd met he recognized Everett Zeller. Of course it hadn't been everyday he'd been arrested and hauled out of his office in handcuffs so, given the circumstances it had been difficult for Bobby to forget.

"Sergeant Everett Zeller," Bobby said, drawing out each word. For a moment he debated pushing the man over the railing, but there were too many potential witnesses to get away with it.

"What are you doing here, Bobby? It's gone that fast, six, or was it seven years?" Zeller seemed to be taking great joy in suggesting to anyone within earshot that Bobby should still be behind bars. Thankfully, they were the only two out in the hallway waiting for the world to pass them by.

"Sorry to disappoint, Sergeant, but I was out in just four plus. Good behavior."

"Amazing," Zeller said shaking his head like he really couldn't believe it.

Bobby wasn't sure if the amazing part was just the four plus years of his life that had apparently passed so quickly for Zeller, or the idea that Bobby would have been released early due to good behavior.

"Still keeping the world safe?" Bobby asked.

"We try. Of course there's always someone who thinks they're a lot more clever than we are." He nodded ever so slightly indicating Bobby. Then shook his head some more. "Humpf, amazing, just four years. Simply amazing."

Bobby smiled.

"You're not thinking of practicing again, are you?"

"Just helping out these days, Sergeant. Like you, I'm just doing my best to see that justice is served and trying to be a responsible citizen."

Zeller nodded and began to leave, then turned and said, "You know, I wonder if I did hear something. Your name wouldn't have come up in connection with some gangland slaying, now would it?"

"My name?" Bobby gave him a look suggesting he had lost his mind. "Sorry to disappoint, but not very likely."

"Hmmm-mmm, just wondering is all. You know the, how shall we say, *liaisons* one might make behind bars."

"Based on the sort of individuals I was with, I think about the only information I'd have would be a list of beaches in the Caribbean."

Zeller looked at Bobby like he wasn't following.

"Off-shore accounts, Sergeant." Bobby said, then watched the light flash across Zeller's face.

"Ev, you ready? Let's go." A voice called from behind. A lean guy with coke-bottle glasses, a dark suit and matching briefcase walked up from the direction of the rest rooms. He slowed but didn't stop as he gave Bobby a nod and continued making his way toward the elevator.

"I'm sure we'll be in touch. Enjoy that romance book," Zeller chuckled and began to follow.

"Thanks for the warning, Sergeant," Bobby replied, then watched the two of them as they disappeared around the corner toward the elevators. Mercifully the retired school teacher emerged ten minutes later ready to go home.

Chapter Thirty-One

The ride back to her building was quiet. She sat in the back seat oblivious to everything around her while she studied her notes from the day's proceedings.

"Here we are, back in the same day," Bobby said and quickly pulled to the curb in front of the old Commodore Hotel. The place had been converted to exclusive condominiums a good thirty plus years ago, but the conversion construction still seemed to be on going.

"What, here already?" she asked looking up.

"Goes quickly, doesn't it?" Bobby said, wishing she would make it that much faster by just getting out of his car.

"Do you think I could go back down there tomorrow?"

He half turned to face her in the backseat. "Tomorrow? Didn't you finish your testimony today? I didn't think they were planning to call you back on the stand tomorrow."

"Oh, no I've finished with my testimony. But, I was just so fascinated I thought it would be fun to go down and watch. Well, maybe not just tomorrow, but the entire process until it's conclusion for that matter. Who knows where all this could lead," she said, then waved her notebook in the air.

"It's open. I mean anyone can go in there and watch. Unfortunately, much as I would like, I wouldn't be able to give you a ride downtown."

"Oh, I wasn't expecting you to," she said, then seemed to give an involuntary shudder as she quickly glanced around the interior of the car. "I'll just drive myself."

"Well, if you do that make sure you park in one of the ramps. They'll ticket you on the street if you run a minute over and I think there's a maximum two hour limit on parking with those new meters." He waited a long moment for some sort of response, but didn't get one.

"Thank you, enjoy your evening," she said eventually, then quickly got out and walked briskly toward the door.

He drove back downtown to the main public library and got a library card. He took out a couple of books and left *Love's Dark Fury* on a table in one of the reading rooms as a civic contribution before he drove home.

He climbed the stairs to his apartment and had the key in the lock when he remembered the scotch tape. He glanced down and sure enough the tape had been pulled loose from the door. Someone had gone inside.

He unlocked the door and stepped into his unit. It seemed quiet. He walked through the place checking the bathroom and the small closet. That took all of about fifteen seconds. No one was there and after a cursory glance nothing seemed to be out of place. Kate Clarken remained untouched on the kitchen counter.

About an hour after nightfall he glanced out of the window and there was the SUV, parked out on the street. He was tempted to go knock on the window, but then what? He sat in the dark and stared at the SUV until close to midnight, then went to bed.

He read his borrowed newspaper the following morning. On the way out he attached another piece of scotch tape to the door, then returned the newspaper to the front entry. The SUV was nowhere to be seen.

His day was spent delivering almost a dozen subpoenas around town. He had to have a signed receipt on each one so in four instances he delivered the things to people at their work place. Fortunately none of it came as a surprise and there were no incidents. Two of the subpoenas went undelivered because the individuals weren't home. He returned them to Marci at the end of the day. She looked up at him as he handed the undelivered notices to her across the receptionist counter.

"On these two no one was home," he said.

"Did you even go back and try a second time?"

"Actually, I went back twice for a total of three times," he lied. She'd have no way of verifying.

"And they didn't answer the door?"

"There didn't seem to be anyone home. I even went around to the backyard, you know in case they were gardening. That was at the Mendel place, the other one, who is it, Johnson?"

"Johansson." She read off the envelope.

"That's a security building, so all I could do was call them on the security phone from downstairs. No one ever answered. They could have just been out shopping or on a week-long jaunt out to Las Vegas." He shrugged.

"Unimpressive," she mumbled.

"Tomorrow?"

"Well, I suppose we'll have to attempt to deliver these again. I'll have someone reach these individuals by phone first. Plan on calling in first thing tomorrow instead of just showing up, no sense racking up your hours if it's unnecessary." She squinted and flashed a toothy grin that struck him as more like baring her teeth than a smile.

"I'll talk to you tomorrow, Marci."

She didn't bother to look up, which meant he'd apparently been dismissed.

Chapter Thirty-Two

The piece of tape had been pulled from the door, again. He'd placed it in a slightly different spot this morning just in case there was something on the door that had caused it to release. He was convinced someone was going through his apartment every day but he couldn't figure out why. There was nothing to see or find for that matter and once through the place you wouldn't think of returning a second time. Was it whoever had murdered Kate? Kate's son? The feds? It didn't seem to make any sense.

He walked up to the retail area and noticed on the way that he hadn't seen anything hanging from that particular clothesline since the night he'd stolen the bath towels. He bought a four-pack of skinless chicken breasts listed as a manager's special. On the way home he searched up and down the street and on the side streets. If the SUV was lurking somewhere he was unable to see it.

He applied another coat of furniture polish and sprayed more air freshener while the chicken baked. He glanced out the window halfway through his chicken sandwich and saw the SUV parked up the block. It was dark outside and with the tinted windows it was impossible to tell if the thing was occupied. Once again he decided against walking up to the vehicle and knocking on the window. He kept the apartment light off, grabbed his book and read in the bathroom behind the closed door.

He got ready for bed a little after midnight, the procedure amounted to draping his clothes over the back of a chair and climbing into the creaking bed. The SUV was still out on the street although he could swear it had moved about thirty feet. Then again, maybe he was just remembering where it had been parked last night or the night before. He thought about the SUV until he eventually dozed off.

It was the flashing lights bouncing off the ceiling and walls that woke him. He couldn't recall hearing any sirens although when he looked out the window three squad cars were out on the street with their roof lights flashing. What looked like two more cars, unmarked, sat in the parking lot just below his window with lights flashing on their dashboards.

There was a paramedic unit out on the street with flashing red and white lights that seemed to bounce left to right. The rear doors were pulled open on the paramedic unit and a number of people were standing around an empty gurney, all looking pretty official. Bobby stood in the dark and looked down on all of it for the better part of two hours and learned absolutely nothing. The SUV was nowhere to be seen.

The following morning the activity from the middle of the night had ceased. There were still two squad cars out there, but they appeared to be empty and were parked along the curb with their lights off.

Bobby was reading his stolen copy of the newspaper and sipping from his second cup of coffee when there was a knock on the door. It wasn't quite seven-thirty.

"Who is it?"

"Police officers, we've just a couple of questions."

Perhaps he should have asked for some sort of identification, a badge number or even exactly what they wanted. Instead, he just opened the door. There were two of them, in uniform, a man and woman.

"Good morning, sir, sorry to bother you so early," the male officer said.

"We're wondering if you were aware of any sort of disturbance around your building last night?" the woman asked.

"Disturbance? No, did something happen?" He tried not to sound insincere.

"You weren't aware of anything happening last night, say around two-thirty, maybe three o'clock?" she asked.

"No, nothing. I'm a pretty sound sleeper to tell you the truth. I've got some coffee on, would you like to come in for a cup?" That seemed to smooth over any potential problem.

"No, thank you, we have a number of doors to knock on. If something does jog your memory or if you hear or maybe notice something, anything, please give us a call. No matter how insignificant it might seem," she said and handed him a card.

"Thank you, I'll be sure to do that," he said looking briefly at the card. "What happened anyway?"

"That's what we're trying to determine. Sorry to interrupt your morning, sir," the male officer said. They gave him a curt nod in unison and walked down to knock on the next door. He watched them for a moment until the *'We're on business here, please move along'* sort of look drove Bobby back into his apartment.

They had worked their way down to the first floor by the time he dropped the newspaper back at the front entry and went out the door. He put ten bucks worth of gas in the Geo at Super America and called

414

Marci from the pay phone mounted on the side of the store to see if she wanted him to attempt to redeliver her subpoenas.

"We contacted both parties, they insisted they were home yesterday, all day," she said, raising her voice at the end and then letting the silence just hang out there, suggesting he had maybe been trying to pull a fast one, and clever Marci had caught him.

"Then why didn't they answer? I rang the door-bell and knocked at the one place, called on the lobby phone at the other. Are they elderly?"

Marci ignored the question. "They'll both be home this morning. The sooner you come in and de-liver these, the better."

"I'll be there shortly," he said, then listened as Marci hung up.

Chapter Thirty-Three

"Once you have these properly signed I won't have need of your services for the rest of the day. Maybe just phone in tomorrow and I'll see if there's anything we need." Marci flashed another one of those teeth-baring grins and squinted her eyes for a second or two then returned to her blank face.

Bobby saw no point in trying to explain he'd done his utmost to deliver the things yesterday. Instead he half-whispered a meek, "Thank you," and departed.

Twenty minutes later he stood on the front stoop and rang the doorbell three times before the door finally opened an inch.

"What is it?" a woman's voice creaked out from behind the door.

"Hi, just making a delivery, I'm afraid I need a signature."

There was a pause before the door swung open and a woman stood there, not elderly, but maybe mid-sixties. She had a metal crutch tucked against her right arm with a metal brace around her forearm.

"You were here yesterday. They phoned me earlier this morning." She spoke in an unpleasant tone like she was accusing him of spray painting the front of her house.

"Yes, ma'am, I stopped by a couple of times yesterday, but…"

"Probably these darn meds I'm on. The fools have me sleeping almost sixteen hours a day, don't

416

hear a damn thing. Give me that," she said and snatched the envelope from Bobby's hand.

"If I can just get you to sign here," he said and held out the clipboard with the attached pen.

"An awful lot of bother if you ask me," she replied, then half balanced on the crutch as she dashed off a scrawl three lines high.

"Yes ma'am," he said and smiled.

"There. Satisfied?" She thrust the clipboard at him in an almost stabbing motion.

"Thank you," he said and quickly fled her front door.

He was outside the lobby of a senior high-rise waiting for the phone to ring on the other end. He was getting the once-over from two women with matching walkers who had stopped and were staring.

"Hello?" a voice answered just after the second ring.

"Mrs. Johansson, I've a notification for you down here in the lobby. I'm afraid I need a signature."

"Not a problem, they called earlier and said you'd be by. I'll buzz you in. I'm in seven-twenty, come on up."

He hung up. The two women followed him over their shoulders as he went through the security door and onto the elevator. Seven-twenty was halfway down the hall on the left-hand side. The door opened as he approached.

"Wonderful, thank you for being so prompt," the woman said. She smiled a nice smile, signed his clipboard, handed it back to him, took the envelope and closed her door. The entire exchange took less than ten seconds.

He stopped for coffee on the way back, lingered over a second cup and assessed the people around him. The coffee shop seemed to be full of an awful lot of people with very little to do on a workday morning in the middle of the week.

He was standing tall in front of Marci's receptionist counter before eleven.

"Any problems?" she asked looking halfway surprised.

"No, everything went just fine. The one woman was on a crutch and mentioned her medications so I figure she must have been asleep and unable to hear me yesterday. The other woman, Johansson, couldn't get rid of me fast enough."

That last bit seemed to make perfect sense to Marci. "Very well, tomorrow I want you to call first. We'll see if we have need of your services." Fortunately she didn't flash her grin, instead she simply stared at Bobby as if to ask, "Anything else."

"I'll be sure to check in tomorrow," he said and walked onto the elevator just as a couple of suits walked off.

He returned home in the early afternoon. The squad cars were gone and the scotch tape on the apartment door was still attached. He spent the afternoon reading and occasionally looking out the window. He never saw the SUV. He made dinner, finished the book later in the evening and went to bed around eleven. He was up once in the middle of the night but still was unable to spot a trace of the SUV.

Chapter Thirty-Four

Bobby phoned Marci the following morning to see about working.

"Hi Marci, how are you this morning?"

"Fine, thank you." He could feel the chill coming from the other end of the phone.

"This is Bobby, calling to see if you have anything for me today."

"Yes, I recognized your voice. No, everything is quite in order. We certainly won't be needing your services today. Perhaps try again tomorrow. Anything else?"

"No, I guess not."

"Thank you," she said attempting to sound cheerful before she abruptly hung up.

He wasn't all that disappointed.

He received the same response from Marci the following morning and was only too glad to get off the line. The newspaper had a sketchy, vague article about an "incident" at his address but not much else in the way of information.

Wild and crazy guy that he was, he went to the library and picked up another book. He logged onto the library computer to see if he could learn anything else about the incident, but all he found online was a copy of the newspaper article. On the way home he stopped at the grocery store and picked up a few items. The SUV was parked on the street when he turned into his parking lot.

He parked in his usual spot next to the dumpster and quickly entered the building. He noticed the tape detached from the door before he took the key out of his pocket. He cautiously turned the knob and the door swung open.

"Bobby, 'bout time. What'd you bring us for dinner?"

Kate's son smiled as he sat in the chair he had pulled away from the window. The chair was angled in such a way that he could keep an eye on the street without really being seen. He watched as Bobby closed the door, then glanced back out onto the street.

"How'd you get in here?"

"What? Didn't you miss me?"

"I haven't seen you around the last couple of days, ever since that excitement the other night."

"What excitement?" he asked, then stared back out the window. Bobby noticed the bulge against his back and assumed he was carrying a gun of some sort.

"Yeah right. Who was it?" Bobby asked.

"Why would you think I know anything about that?"

"The act is getting pretty old. Either you're a bad liar or you're too dumb to know. I don't happen to think you're too dumb."

"Arundel." He answered nonchalantly, like he was listing off which day of the week it was or what he'd eaten for breakfast. He returned to staring out the window.

"Is he going to be okay?"

He turned slowly and looked in Bobby's direction, but he wasn't focused, at least not on Bobby. The cockiness left him for a brief moment and he shook his head ever so slightly. "He's dead."

"Dead?"

"I think that's what I just said. The man's dead. Someone took him out, killed him."

"Who? I mean, why was he…"

"You think I'd be sitting on my ass in this dump if I knew the answer to any of that shit?"

"What was he doing here? In this building?"

"He wasn't *in* your building, Bobby."

"But he was here, in the middle of the night. Right?"

He nodded and went back to looking out the window.

"So what was he doing here? Does he know someone here? Have a girlfriend? What?"

"You."

"Me?"

"That's what I just said."

"What did I do? I've been gone for four-plus years. Except for my ex-wife, who would probably still like to kill me, I'm off everyone's radar."

"'Cept those two fucks that murdered my mom."

"Kate?" Bobby nodded toward the urn on his kitchen counter. "This doesn't make any sense. I can't identify anyone. I don't know who killed her. No one knows for sure if it was even the same two guys who chased us. I never talked to the police, never told anyone about any of that."

"Well, they came here looking for you," he said almost in a whisper.

"The killers? But, how would they even know who I was? How would they know anything about me, let alone where to find me? Like I said, I'm not on anyone's radar."

"We might have put the word out, sort of, maybe."

"You what?"

"Well, yeah. See we knew who it was soon as you described them, one's got reddish hair, the other's is dark and curly with that pig nose."

"Pug," Bobby corrected.

"Whatever. We let the word out, Arundel and me. Figured they might come looking for you. Guessed they wouldn't expect to find us, well except they did. They caught Arundel out back in the parking lot. Spotted him standing by that piece of shit you're driving. Just sort of came outta nowhere, like."

"But the cops, they knocked on my door the other morning. I told them I didn't hear anything, no shots, nothing."

"They slit his throat, then left him by the back door. Make it look like he was maybe trying to get in here. 'Course it don't really make no difference now, does it?"

"Did you tell the police? I got a number here you should call. They'll want to talk to you. In fact, they'll need to talk to you and find out what the hell you know. I'm sure they've got an ongoing investigation…."

"Shut the hell up, will you? Not you, not me, no one is gonna be calling the cops, Bobby. That ain't happening. Understand?"

"This isn't some game you're playing, here. This is the real deal. Now a man's lost his life. A man has been murdered and he was your friend. You've got information that…."

"Shut up, damn it. Jesus Christ, I gotta tell you? For someone who's supposed to have pulled four years you sure as hell didn't learn much in there."

"Didn't learn much? Listen here you swaggering little street thug. Let me tell you what I learned. I don't know what exactly happened to your mother over there on my kitchen counter, but the bottom line is she was murdered. Based on what you just told me I'm guessing the same two guys who took her life murdered your pal Arundel the other night. They murdered him out there in the parking lot because you two dipshits were using me as bait. Weren't you?"

His look gave him away and suddenly Bobby knew all he needed to know.

"Yeah, perfect. You two were going to surprise them, right? Extract your own warped little version of vengeance, like this is some sort of B-grade movie. Of course you happened to be parked out on the street in that one of a kind pimped-out ride of yours that can be spotted from a hundred yards off."

He stared back out the window and didn't say anything.

"Perfect, how very professional. I suppose the two of you planned to settle this in your own little tough guy hoodlum way. Sneak up behind them and shoot them a half-dozen times in the back. Let me take a wild guess, the dome light goes on inside the car when you open the door. Right? So you can announce to everyone when you're going to begin sneaking around. God, other than shooting them and then doing your celebration dance, did you even *have* a plan? And thanks, by the way for using me as bait. You know maybe if you'd kept me informed, told me your name or some of the other secret shit that seems to not be going your way, maybe things could have worked out differently. At least they may have worked out differently for your hapless dead pal, Arundel."

"Precious."

"What?"

"Precious. My name, you're standing there bitching that you wanted to know, so I'm telling you. It's Precious."

"Precious?"

"You got a problem with that?"

"No, no problem. That's what everyone calls you? Precious?"

He looked back out the window. "They call me Prez."

"Precious, Prez?"

"It's what they call me, man."

"Okay, I'm cool with that, I get it. So, what do you plan to do, *Prez*? I'm guessing what happened to Arundel just made whoever slit his throat that much bolder. And you think it might be the two guys who killed Kate?"

"There's no *think* about it."

"Well no offense, but I'd like to have a little stronger confirmation than your hunch that the same…."

"Dubuque and Mobile," he said staring out the window.

"What?"

"Dubuque and Mobile, that's their names. They're brothers. The ones that killed Kate and then they killed Arundel the other night."

"It sounds like something off a rightwing propaganda sheet. Dubuque and Mobile, like the towns? And you know this how?"

"I know it. You described them. We knew who they were right away. They killed some guy a few weeks back, name of O'Brien. Contract sort of thing. Arundel was going to wait for them inside, except they jumped…"

"You saw this happen, didn't you? You actually saw them murder Arundel. Have you told any of this to the cops? Oh, God, why do I even bother to ask? Of course you haven't. Because you have some master plan, right? A master plan which so far seems to be that first Kate and now Arundel get murdered by these two assholes."

Prez gave a small shrug and continued to stare out the window.

"So, I'm guessing you're between a rock and a hard place here. You know who did this, but if you go to the police that opens the door to all sorts of other *activity*, correct?"

He gave the slightest of shrugs in response.

"And they're going to be out there, somewhere, looking for me because you put the word out that I know who they are. Didn't you?"

He nodded slightly, but kept staring out the window.

"Jesus Christ. Okay, look, you're staying for dinner. I hope you like chicken thighs and roasted potatoes. You want some Doritos?"

Chapter Thirty-Five

"I still don't get why you won't go to the police," Bobby said. He'd left the lights off in the apartment and they had finished their dinner in the dark.

Bobby was leaning against the kitchen counter while Prez sat looking out the window. Although night had fallen outside he could still make his figure out in the chair silhouetted against the window.

"What part aren't you picking up? Having the cops come in just opens me up to all sorts of problems. They'll do a search of my place. Next, they'll want to know everything from who I'm sleeping with to where do I get my money. I really don't need any of their bullshit investigation coming down on top of me. Okay? God, they've already been through Arundel's place, carried out bags of evidence including close to thirty grand in cash, thirty grand that by rights belongs to me."

"You two were keeping that much on hand, just lying around, thirty grand? Planning to invest it somewhere?"

"Lying around? No, not really. How dumb do I look? We had it hidden. Arundel kept it in a shoe box in a space under the floor."

"Gee, amazing they found it?"

"You're being a wise ass, right?"

"I'm going to guess it was in his bedroom. Just for the record, most people hide their valuables in the bedroom. So a shoe box under the bedroom floor isn't really rocket science."

"So where would you hide it?"

"I wouldn't, at least not in a shoe box under the floor."

"What?"

"You start to lose money the moment you decide to hide it like that. You need to launder that stuff, get it invested and producing a revenue stream for you. It's what you guys never understand. Cash in hand does not make you wealthy."

"Invested, you mean like stocks and that sort of shit? Talk about stealing, Jesus Christ, talk about crime."

"No, not stocks, at least not right now. But there are a lot of opportunities that can present themselves. A small investment in a business, a bar, certain types of real estate. Places where you can write off losses and gradually show a gain, maybe an increase in property value. A taxi business could be a great revenue stream for you or maybe even a bar."

"Taxi. You think I want to drive a taxi around town? Just for starters, it's dangerous," he laughed.

"You don't actually have to drive a taxi. Maybe a limo would be a better option. The key is it's basically a cash business, same with a bar."

"That how you got nailed?"

"Me? No, I got nailed just like everyone else. I was stupid, well, and impatient. I've maybe learned a thing or two since."

Prez nodded, but Bobby couldn't determine if he really understood.

"You stockpile cash, I don't care how much, you're just never really going to get ahead. If you do some research you'll find there are tons of guys who are sitting on a pile of cash one day and the next day they're broke again. Why? Cause they didn't have a plan. Or they had half a plan. They got the cash, but then what? You have to plan carefully and keep a low profile, always."

"That what you're doing? Keeping a low profile by driving that piece of shit out there with the windshield all shot up. That's your plan?"

"No. I'm just starting over, but this time I plan on doing it right."

Chapter Thirty-Six

Bobby went to bed a little after midnight. He presumed Prez slept, but he didn't know for sure. He did know Prez was staring out the window when Bobby fell asleep and he was staring out the same window when he woke up at six the following morning. Bobby had also come to a decision.

"How about some coffee?" he asked coming out of the bathroom.

"Yeah," Prez grunted.

"You see anything last night?"

"Actually, I been doing some thinking, 'bout what you said. Working smart and all."

"Get your money working for you. It takes time, just like anything else, but it can be done. Just think what it would be like to wake up on the first of every month and you know all your bills are paid. That can start to make for a very happy life."

"Yeah, maybe."

"Maybe? Look, without giving me specifics I'm guessing your pal Arundel isn't the first guy you know who checked out of here that way. Right?"

Prez just stared at Bobby.

"I'm also guessing, just by its nature, whatever business you're in, there will always be some guy who is faster, more violent, has more people, better contacts or is just plain luckier. I don't even know exactly what you do. But I can tell you there probably aren't a lot of old guys who have been doing the same thing. Don't you ever get tired of always looking over your shoulder? Looking out the window of a dumpy apartment waiting for a couple of guys to show up who want to kill you."

"They'll be showing up to kill you, not me."

"We're going to deal with that, too. But we're going to do it with a plan in place, not some knee jerk reaction that ends up getting you thrown in jail for the next fifteen years or God forbid, ending up like Arundel. By the way, just to keep you interested, these two guys, what's their name? Dubuque and Moline?"

"Mobile. Dubuque and Mobile, I guess it's a town, Mobile."

Bobby let that go. "Those two idiots most likely have a list. I might be at the top, but you better believe your name is probably number two, right behind me."

"So then what's your great idea?"

"We make some coffee, then pick your brain on those two and we go after them. Get to them before they get to me and then you."

Over a breakfast of oatmeal with bananas and a second pot of coffee they formulated their plan. **To be continued...**

Thanks for taking the time to check out my latest work of genius, **Corridor Man**. Not bad, Bobby Custer has been released for little more than a week and he's already up to his neck in trouble. Dubuque and Mobile can't very well leave Bobby out there able to identify them. Noah Denton seems to have something up his sleeve, God only knows what Morris Montcreff's story is and then, well Bobby Custer doesn't seem to be the most honest guy in town, and what's up with the Feds? Grab a copy on Amazon, **Corridor Man** by Nick James and be sure to tell 2-300 of your closest friends. Many thanks!

Mike Faricy
Scam Man

Chapter One

Her name was really Amanda Jane, but she and everyone else referred to her as AJ. I met her a couple of weeks back at a friends party and we seemed to hit it off pretty well. I asked her out a couple of nights later.

On our first night out we'd gone to dinner at a small, very private little restaurant overlooking the river. Romantic, expensive and both of us had a lovely time. We met at the restaurant. My experience had been there's no "dinner with benefits" on a first date. I get it. She was a classy gal and just getting to know me, so I was prepared. I got a text from her later that night saying, "Thanks."

On date number two we grabbed a movie, some chick flick that she just loved and I worked to stay awake. I kept cautiously checking my watch to see how much longer the torture would last, thinking more than once that the watch had stopped. We grabbed a glass of wine at an up-scale bistro place after the movie. She mentioned the big important meeting she had the following morning after I suggested a drink at my place. So, I kissed her goodnight on her front porch steps and got the distinct impression that a grope was there for the taking, but it was only date number two and her ultimate mission was to prove she wasn't a slut. Against my better judgement I remained a gentleman. Mission accomplished.

Tonight was date number three. Experience suggested since she'd already proven she wasn't a slut, tonight would be the clincher. I'd pulled out all the stops since there was a better than even chance we might end up at my place. I laid in a couple of bottles of her favorite wine, put fresh flowers on the dining room table and in the den. I vacuumed, cleaned the bathroom, placed a scented candle next to the bathroom sink, hung clean towels, changed the sheets and tossed the pile of laundry waiting to be washed into the basement.

I had eggs, bacon, sausage, and a cinnamon coffee cake set to go for breakfast. The coffee pot was programmed to start perking at eight tomorrow morning. Just in case, I'd even picked up a couple of different teas. All my bases were covered.

I made a reservation for 8:30 at Bobby's, a trendy little place just a five-minute drive from my house. I wanted to miss the hurry-up crowd, the folks who had somewhere else to go that night. We sat and laughed over a glass of wine for a good half hour before we even looked at the menu. AJ wore a slinky, low cut black dress that was so tight it looked like it was painted on. A little gold cross dangled intriguingly at the top of her cleavage and I pictured myself at exactly the same spot in just a few hours. I ordered a soy sauce mushroom appetizer to share and we took out time eating.

AJ nibbled a mushroom then said, "Would you mind ordering dinner for me? I kind of, well, you know, sort of like being told what to do." Then she raised her eyebrows in a suggestive way.

I ordered two sixteen ounce steaks, medium rare. I finished with a clean plate, AJ had the remaining two-thirds of her steak placed in a white Styrofoam takeout container. Our plates were cleared just after ten.

"May I interest either one of you in a dessert? Our special tonight is a delicious caramel custard made with free-range eggs and heavy cream from a local Minnesota dairy farm. I strongly recommend it," our waiter said then flashed a charming smile.

"What do you think?" AJ asked. She brushed a sexy blonde lock back over her ear and bit her lower lip.

"If you want, or we could maybe go to my place for a nightcap, you know, if you're feeling up to it." I crossed my fingers and counted to my-self one, two, three, four…

"I better take a pass on dessert. The steak was delicious."

"Sir?"

"I think just the check when you have time."

"Actually, I'd love the dessert, but the night cap might be more…interesting," she said smiling.

I immediately wondered where in the hell the check was.

I got a lingering kiss just inside the restau-rant before I held the door for her.

"Goodbye, thanks so much," she called to our waiter on the way out.

"Have a fun night, folks," he replied.

"I plan to," AJ said and made a beeline for my car parked at the curb.

I held the door for her and she gave me another kiss before she slid into the passenger seat. Once I started the car she said, "Would you mind if I turned the channel on your radio? There's a station that plays real romantic music until midnight on Fridays. Really gets me in the mood."

"Oh, yeah, great idea. I love romantic mu-sic."

She hummed along with the song as we raced to my place. As I drove, she gently rubbed her index finger up and down my neck. I made the five-minute drive in just under three and pulled to the curb.

"I've been dreaming about this all week, I really want to see…your place," she said. Then she undid her seat belt and waited for me to get out and open the door for her.

I hurried around the back of the car, wondering what her favorite perversions might be, all the while reminding myself not to get her too drunk. I opened the passenger door and she brushed up against me as she stepped out. "Come here," she said and gave me a long probing kiss. Then she looked at my front porch and said, "Did you get some packages delivered?"

"What?" I turned and stared at a number of items piled on my front porch just as a head suddenly popped up from behind a grocery bag and barked. "Morton?" I cried and leapt over the front steps, ran up the sidewalk, and took the steps up to the front porch two at a time. "Morton."

He jumped out of the basket placed in front of the door, but his leash had been tied to the door handle and he couldn't go any further. His golden retriever tail was wagging a mile a minute, slamming into the dog food bags and knocking over the grocery bag full of dog toys.

"Morton, Morton, hey boy, what are you doing here?"

"You have a dog?" AJ asked walking up the sidewalk behind me.

"No, this is Morton. He belongs to a…to someone I know, I mean used to know. I watched him for a couple of weeks last spring while she went to take care of her mom and dad, some sort of medical thing. She ended up moving down to Atlanta, got a great job offer, and reconnected with some nitwit she knew in high school. God, she took Morton down there with her. He saved my life actually."

"The dog?"

"Yeah, didn't you, boy? Oh good boy, good boy. It's so good to see you. Did you miss me, Morton? Did you?" I said scratching him behind the ears as he licked my face.

"So, ahhh, you need some help carrying this stuff inside?"

"What? Oh yeah. Come on in. Let me just get him untied here," I said undoing the leash from the door. I took my keys out and unlocked the door. Morton pushed with his shoulder just as I began to open the door. "Grab one of those dog food bags there, AJ. Hey, Morton, you remember the place, don't you? We had some good times, didn't we?" I hurried after him as he barged into the entryway, charged through the house into the kitchen and then ran back out into the living room. He hopped onto the couch, barked a couple of times at a car driving down the street then followed me as I made my way to the kitchen, turning on the lights as I went.

"I bet you're hungry, aren't you fella? Here how about this," I said pulling a food dish out of the grocery bag I'd brought in from the porch. Morton barked, and hopped back and forth as I set the empty bowl on the floor.

AJ walked into the kitchen and set the dog food bag on the floor then set her Styrofoam container with the steak on the kitchen counter and started brushing dog food crumbs off the top of her dress. "Oh God, look, I've got dog food all over the front of this new dress."

I couldn't really tell, and gave a quick glance as she bounced her breasts up and down. "If you need a paper towel, there's some over by the sink," I said, then went back to scratching Morton behind the ear. AJ seemed to hesitate for a long moment before she strutted over to the sink and tore off a paper towel. I took the dog food bag and filled Morton's food dish. He suddenly looked disappointed.

"Do you have any hand cream?" AJ asked a few minutes later. She was bent over looking in the cabinet under the kitchen sink. As I turned to look at her, she glanced at me over her shoulder and smiled with her perfect bum up in the air. Her tight black dress had risen up an inch or so and just barely exposed the hint of a silky black thong.

I gave her a brief glance, then rubbed Morton some more. "Come on, Morton, you must be starving."

"Hand cream?"

I glanced over at AJ again. She was still bent over only now her entire rear was exposed.

438

The thong ran up her backside to where three little sparkling jewels connected with the waistband. I caught just a glimpse of a lacy tattoo running across the small of her back.

"Oh yeah, it's not down there. It's in that white thing with the push top, right along the back of the sink. Come on, Morton. Don't you like the dog food? You've got to eat. Come on. Here, try this piece."

"So, ahh, any chance on getting that night cap?"

"What? Sure thing, sorry about that. You can just help yourself. I got hard liquor out in the dining room, help yourself to whatever's in the cabinet with the crystal decanters. White wines are in the fridge, or if you want red I think there's a bottle in the dining room. It's got a twist off cap."

"Thanks," she said. In retrospect, I don't think she really meant it.

Morton ignored the dog food in his dish. I tried for a couple of minutes to hand feed it to him, coaxing him one nugget at a time; but he wasn't having any of that action. "Okay, okay, you big baby. But, only because it's your first night, sort of a welcome home treat," I said, then opened the Styrofoam container and placed the remainder of the steak in his dish just as AJ walked back into the kitchen with a glass of dark brown liquid.

"Did you make me one?" I asked.

She glared just as the doorbell rang.

Morton barked and headed toward the front door.

"Who the hell is ringing my doorbell this late at night?"

"It's for me, I called a taxi," she said and took a big sip, sort of shuddered, then set the glass down on the kitchen counter and strutted toward the front door.

"Whoa, AJ. Wait up, wait up," I called and hurried after her.

"It's certainly been memorable. Sorry to interrupt your little boys' reunion. Nice to meet you, Morton," she said.

He hopped off the couch, then shoved his nose in between her legs. She half jumped, then grabbed the back of his head and thrust it back under her skirt. "Oh, God, really cold nose. Well, Dev, I can promise you, he's getting a lot more than you will. Enjoy your night, boys," she said then slammed the door behind her.

"Hey, hey wait, AJ, AJ," I called. Morton jumped back and forth in front of me and by the time I got to the door and opened it, the taxi was pulling away from the curb. I watched until the taillights faded up the street then walked back to the kitchen and dumped the bag with Morton's toys onto the floor. A little handwritten note floated onto the floor.

"Hi, hope all is well. This just isn't working out. Turns out Buster has an allergy to dogs. I figured you wouldn't mind, besides he likes you, I think. Maddie"

Chapter Two

I was sitting in my office chair staring through a set of binoculars, alternating between the working girls waiting for the bus down on the corner and two girls getting dressed in the third floor apartment across the street. In between times, I was thinking of Morton and then wondering how I could get back into AJ's good graces.

I suppose she was right to be pissed off, but I'd been so happy to see him. I was wondering if I could somehow give her the impression I was really a caring, sensitive guy and my sensitive side got in the way of taking care of her needs…scratch that. Maybe if I just sort of suggested the caring, sensitive part and…

"Hey, you're in early. I didn't expect to see you until around noon. So how'd the big night go, take any pictures?" Louie asked. He's a pal, my attorney, my officemate and half crazy. He tossed his computer bag on his picnic table desk, then emptied what was left in the coffee pot into his giant three-cup mooch mug. "Don't spare any of the details," he said setting his mug on the edge of my desk then holding his hand out for the binoculars.

"Not much to tell," I said handing the binoculars over to him.

"Come on, it was the third date. Didn't you take her to that restaurant near your place? I thought you said it was a sure thing? She tell you she was married or something?" He said then proceeded to focus the binoculars on the apartment across the street.

"No, a surprise visitor, actually?"

"What the hell time is it? God, they're already dressed," he groaned and handed back the binoculars.

"Yeah, they must have an early meeting or something, I think they're a good half-hour ahead of their normal schedule."

"Let me guess. It's either a boyfriend or she's into other girls, right? Oh wait, the husband called, right?"

"No, wrong, wrong and double wrong. Actually, the dinner went great. So great that we skipped dessert, raced to my place, the kisses were coming hot and heavy. We pull up in front of my place and there he is, on the front porch."

"Who?"

"Morton."

"That dog? The one that knocked up that fancy French poodle show dog?"

"Yeah, Princess Anastasia. He was tied to the front door, along with his bed, a couple of bags of dog food, and his dog toys. Turns out the idiot that Maddie linked up with down in Atlanta has an allergy or something. So she put Morton in the car, drove up here and left him on my front porch along with a thank-you note."

"You're kidding?"

"No, dead serious. Anyway, AJ got all pissed off and well, I don't know, maybe she just doesn't like the idea of me having a dog."

"Wait a minute. Didn't you tell me she has a dog, a candy something?"

"A chocolate lab, actually. Yeah, so I'm not really sure why she went off the deep end. I'm getting Morton settled, and the next thing I know she's heading out the door without so much as a good night kiss. Go figure."

"Doesn't sound like the woman you've described to me. You sure you didn't say something or do…?"

"No, like I said, she just left."

"Strange, so where is Morton?"

"I left him at home, he…"

"Didn't he, you know, chew everything up and trash the place last time you left him there?"

"Yeah, but I'm thinking he might be a little more mature now. Besides I've got him confined in the kitchen.

"Wasn't that the room he trashed?"

"Well, yeah, come to think of it." I glanced out the window, the bus had just pulled back into traffic and was heading down the street carrying its lovely cargo toward downtown. The living room light was off in the third floor apartment across the street so I tossed the binoculars back on the desk.

"I hope you know what you're doing," Louie said.

"I think they went to work."

"I meant your lady friend. Sounds like you screwed up."

"I'll give AJ a call, maybe give her a day or so to calm down first."

"You really want to pursue that? Sounds like it could end up being a lot of work."

"I think maybe Morton's arrival sort of threw her off course or something. It'll work out. If it doesn't I'll give Heidi a call."

"That sounds a little more promising," Louie said.

"Heidi's a good friend, but she seems to only be able to take me in little doses."

"You ever think that might have something to do with your lifestyle?"

Chapter Three

Over the next couple of days, I left no less than three voicemails for AJ and she hadn't responded to a single one. So, I phoned Heidi.

"Hey, Heidi, how are things going?"

"I'm not bailing you out if that's why you're calling."

"Why do you always say that? When was the last time I needed bail money?"

"That's not the point. I'm just not doing it anymore, that's all I'm saying."

"Are we crabby today?"

"Why did you call?"

"Are you okay?"

"Yes."

I'd gone this far, so I figured I might as well continue. "Well, it's been a while since I saw you, since we were together. I just thought it might be nice to grab a bite to eat, you know catch up and…"

"And then you could ply me with wine or margaritas or something and I'd hop into bed with you. Is that it?"

This wasn't going the way I'd planned. "No, I just wanted to see how you were, make sure everything was okay, that's all. Hey, if you don't want to get together, okay, fine. I just thought it might be nice to see you and…"

"We can meet, but let's not make it your place."

"Okay, should I just bring dinner? I could pick up…"

"No, some place public. A restaurant might be nice."

I began an internal debate about hanging up.

"Are you still there?" she asked.

"Yes, just trying to think of a restaurant."

"Geno's, I could maybe use some Italian."

"Tonight works for me if you can make it," I said, then hoped she might be busy.

"Say, seven-thirty?" she said.

"Sure. I'll pick you up and…"

"I'll drive myself if it's all the same."

"I'll see you there around seven-thirty. I'll call for a reservation; I know how you hate to wait."

"That would be nice," she said, then hung up.

I didn't know what, but something was wrong. I'd just lined up a dinner date where I'd have the pleasure of dropping a good chunk of change and spending the evening with a very un-happy individual. I could hardly wait.

* * *

True to my word I made the reservation for seven-thirty, then waited until a little after eight before Heidi finally showed up. I stood as she breezed around the corner. She half-dodged my attempt to give her a kiss, turning her head

446

so I'd plant the kiss on her cheek. Then she pulled away at the last second and sat down while I sort of kissed the air.

"Have you been waiting long?" she said, then stared at the bottle of wine that was now two glasses shy.

"Only since seven-thirty."

"Oh," she said, making it sound like forty minutes wasn't such a bad thing.

"How about some wine?" I said raising the bottle toward her glass.

"No, none for me."

"No wine?"

"I just told you, no."

"Hey, Heidi, I haven't seen you for at least three weeks. I think we know each other well enough that we can level with one another. So what's going on, what's wrong?"

"Why does something have to be wrong? Just because I don't want a glass of wine doesn't mean…"

"This isn't about the wine, I don't care about that because it just means there's more for me. But your attitude… you were barely civil on the phone this morning. You're almost forty-five minutes late, no text, no phone call…"

"And no dinner date," she said, pushed her chair back, stood, and walked out of the restaurant.

I sat there by myself for ten minutes, hoping she'd come back. She didn't. I was beginning to wonder if it was me? First AJ, now Heidi who was usually open to just about anything.

"Would you care for an appetizer?" the waiter asked, sounding like he already knew my response. Fittingly, he was dressed for a funeral in a black button down shirt, black trousers and a long black apron.

"I think just the check, please."

He reached into a deep apron pocket and handed me the black book with my check already prepared. As he walked away, I pulled a couple of twenties out of my wallet, tossed them on the table and left.

Chapter Four

I'd been leering at the girls in the apartment across the street through my binoculars. The blonde was wearing a black thong and bra, the dark haired girl just had a white towel wrapped around her. From what I could tell they both seemed to be talking nonstop while putting on their makeup and sipping coffee at the kitchen counter. Multitasking.

"Haskell Investigations" I answered, then picked up the binoculars again.

"Hi, Dev."

"Heidi, hi, how are you doing?"

"I just wanted to apologize for the other night. I didn't mean to walk out. It's just been kind of stressful lately."

"Everything okay?"

"Yeah, I think so. I'm calling because I want to be honest with you. I should have told you the other night, not really sure why I didn't."

"You okay?"

"I've met someone."

Shit. "Heidi, that's great. I'm really happy for you."

"You're not mad?"

I'd tossed the binoculars on my desk, spun around in my chair and was reaching for a pen. "No, no I'm very happy for you. Tell me a little about him," I said thinking I'd like to go and smash his car windows.

"Well, we met at a business luncheon. He's an attorney, practices here in town. He helps the handicapped, looks out for their needs."

"Helps the handicapped? Like what, he's a crossing guard on a busy street or he holds the door open?"

"Very funny. No, he takes legal action on behalf of people with disabilities. You know, making sure buildings, retail shops and things like that are in compliance with the law."

"Wow, an upstanding guy. Sounds like I probably don't have a chance. What's his name?"

"Austin, Austin Hackett. He's originally from Chicago, but he's been practicing up here for fourteen or fifteen years."

"Interesting," I said writing down the bastard's name on a bar coaster advertising Two Hearted Ale. "What firm is he with?"

"He has a private practice. Say, you're not thinking of poking around and making his life miserable are you? That's not why I called. If you think…"

"Hey, calm down. I'm not going to poke around, as you say. I was just curious, I know a lot of legal beagles in a number of different firms. I thought I may have run into him before, that's all."

"I don't think he spends much time in the sort of places you go, Dev. No offense, but, well, he doesn't mingle with criminals."

"Good for him," I said. "So, how long have you been seeing each other?" The last time I'd spent the night with Heidi had been over a month ago.

"Oh, we've been together for a good three weeks," she said making it sound like it had been three years. If memory served, Heidi's relationships usually tanked right around week four. I reached over for my desk calendar, flipped the pages seven days ahead then penned her name in and added a question mark behind it.

"Heidi, I'm really happy for you. I'd love to meet him sometime," I lied.

"You know, that might not be such a good idea."

"Oh?"

"Well, we wanted to be completely honest with one another and one night we just, you know, told each other about all our past relationships and things."

I couldn't believe Heidi told this guy about all her past relationships, there wasn't enough time in the day. Three weeks? God, she'd still be unloading. She must have skipped an awful lot.

"What about him?"

"Actually, I'm his first. He was always so busy. He took care of his sick parents. Then, once they passed away he became a Navy Seal. He went to law school and when he graduated at the top of his class he decided to dedicate himself to helping others in honor of his parents."

451

Heidi is one of, if not *the* sharpest business woman I know. She's made enough money to never really have to worry about money anymore. That said, if she's got a weak spot, it has to do with romantic interests feeding her a line. The bigger the line the more readily she seems to believe it.

"Wow, he sounds like a really great guy. No wonder you fell in love with him, and he'd be crazy not to go after you." The jerk. "How 'bout we get together, a celebration in honor of you two finding one another?"

"You're not mad?"

"Well, I'd love it if he hadn't found you, but I'm happy for you, Heidi. Really, I am. You pick the place and I'll pay for dinner."

"You're sure? You don't have to, you know."

"Yeah, I know."

"And I'm not going to bed with you, Dev. I just want to have dinner and then we'll go our separate ways at the end, okay?"

"Yeah, I get it, believe me. Just a little celebration. I'm really happy for you, honey, honest."

"Okay, let me think of a place and I'll just send you a text. What night works for you?"

"You name the night and I'll cancel whatever I have going." The only thing I had on my calendar was a note that The Spot bar was doing two for one night on Thursday.

"You're sweet. Thanks for not being all mad and going crazy."

"Heidi, you've just become the one who got away. It's my loss, but I'm really happy for you."

Chapter Five

Louie stepped into the office just as I slammed down the phone.

"Whoa, take it easy. You'll break that thing into a hundred different pieces. Someone coming after you with a paternity suit?"

"No. God the way things are going there's no chance of that happening in the foreseeable future. Hey, you ever hear of a guy practicing named Austin Hackett? I guess he does some sort of disability work."

"That prick? Is he jacking around someone you know?"

"Sort of, but not legally. At least I don't think so."

Louie grabbed his coffee mug and headed toward the pot as he spoke. "Austin Hackett. He's got a private practice, works a scam on small to medium business folks. He has at least a couple of guys that I know of. I think he keeps them on retainer. One's sight impaired, the other's missing a leg. They fake an injury at some small business, you know maybe trip on a step, fall in the bathroom or out on the side walk, stuff like that. Then Hackett sues on behalf of his 'clients' and scams the business into settling out of court."

"At what point does the system wise up? Sounds like it could be grounds for disbarment."

"It probably could, if it ever goes to court. What Hackett does is he comes up with a laundry list of potential problems, entries, exits, elevators, handicap access to the restroom, all sorts of shit. By the time he's finished the bill to fix all that usually starts around six figures and climbs. A lot of little places just can't afford that. So, being the good guy, Austin Hackett offers to settle for, oh five, six maybe ten grand, depending, and the cases never go to court."

"And that's legal?"

"Technically, yeah. I think the state has looked into him a couple of times. Not sure about the bar association, but like I said, it's legal."

"Sounds like a scam."

"Oh, absolutely. Go on the low side, say he settles for just fifty percent. Fifty percent of five grand is twenty-five hundred. Pay your handicapped guy two hundred and basically Hackett is netting something like two grand or more a day, every day. Nice work if you can get it."

"And he's getting away with this?"

"He seems to be, at least thus far. Google him, he's within the letter of the law. He suing someone you know?"

"Not suing. It's Heidi, she's seeing him. From the sound of things, she's fallen head over heels for the bastard. Thinks he's the greatest thing since sliced bread. Navy Seal, took care of his dying parents…"

"Who told you that shit?"

"Heidi. I just got off the phone with her. We're going to have a farewell dinner."

"She's not marrying Hackett, is she?"

"Only because he hasn't asked. According to her, they've been seeing one another for three weeks now."

"Get her away from him, Dev. He'll find a way to take her for every cent she's got, then just cast her aside. Oh, and Navy Seal? I'm pretty sure he couldn't swim from here to the door and back. Navy Seal? Jesus," he said and just shook his head.

Chapter Six

I put the binoculars back in my desk drawer, left the girls in the apartment to their own devices and started looking into Austin Hackett online. There were almost three pages' worth of links, all pretty much the same, just like Louie had described. The newspaper seemed to sort of tout him as a crusader. He'd been sued twice and lost both cases. I made note of the people who filed the complaints. I'd want to talk with them and hopefully their attorneys.

Toward the bottom of page three, two links mentioned a lawsuit filed on behalf of a wounded veteran, one Marcel Barker. If it was the Marcel Barker I knew, he was indeed a wounded veteran, but his 'wound' had occurred at the hands of a disgruntled husband returning home two days early to Portsmouth Naval Shipyard from some sort of test cruise back in the early seventies. Marcel, I knew him as "Woofy", was a guard at the Portsmouth Naval Prison up until the time he was shot in the ass by that returning husband. There were political connections somewhere along the way and Woofy was discharged and placed on disability. To my knowledge the husband never served any time. In fact, I don't think the case ever went to court.

I hadn't seen Woofy in a number of years, but I had a pretty good idea of the half dozen different places I might be able to find him.

"I gotta check out some stuff. Lock up if you leave," I said to Louie.

"I'm in court at eleven, pleading a no contest. You want me to ask around about your pal Hackett?"

"You mind?"

"No, I've never liked the guy. Along with most other practicing attorneys I would love to see him get nailed with something, anything."

"Yeah, see what you can find out. I'd appreciate that," I said, then headed out the door to find Woofy.

I asked about him at Wangs, the Yuk Club, the Poodle, and Ugly's. They'd all seen him recently, but didn't know where he was at the moment. I was running out of options when I found him at the fifth place I checked, the Manhole.

The Manhole isn't that far removed from its name. Not a lot of people go there, for a variety of reasons. But the few who do enter are well looked after because they're there to do business, and the business is drinking.

It's a dark, dismal little place on a crusty side street in a back corner just off the downtown railway yard. The front door had a handle that I think was supposed to be brass, at least at one time, but it was so crusted with grime you couldn't really tell. The door itself had a window, four inches wide and maybe five feet long running from the top to the bottom, and had been boarded over with a sheet of weathered plywood for as long as I could remember. The story I heard was there had been a shooting back in the late 80's. Fortunately the shooter was too drunk to hit anything other than the window.

It was the middle of the afternoon on a pleasant, sunny day when I entered the place. None of the dozen people in there bothered to look up as I stepped inside and let my eyes adjust to the inky darkness. As my vision began to return, I could make out a number of folks sitting alone at the bar. It seemed they'd all made a point of positioning themselves at least two stools apart so they could focus on the task at hand, drinking, and not be interrupted. Two women occupied a back booth and seemed to be the only people engaged in any sort of social interaction.

"What'll I get you?" the bartender said then sort of smeared whatever had spilled on the bar with a rag that looked like it had been used to clean the floor in the men's room.

"I'm looking for someone and I wondered if…"

"They ain't here," he said then sort of tossed the bar rag back on the floor and walked down to the far end of the bar.

"Kenny's a real asshole, ain't he?" the guy sitting a couple of stools away said. He sort of shrugged his shoulders like he was laughing to himself and didn't bother to look at me.

"Yeah, and that's probably his good side. Can I buy you another?"

"Never turned one down," he said then raised his glass to catch the bartender's attention. "Who you looking for?"

"Woofy Barker, you know him?"

"Yeah, everybody knows Woofy. What's he done this time?"

"Surprisingly, nothing. I just wanted to ask him about a guy."

"You a cop?"

"Me? No, I'm trying to find a guy Woofy knew a while back. Thought he might be able to help is all."

The guy nodded, but didn't say anything else. His drink arrived a moment later, "Three seventy-five," Kenny said looking at me and trying to sound friendly. I wondered how he knew I was paying then figured the guy I was chatting with probably came in every afternoon and nursed the same drink for three or four hours.

I handed a five-dollar bill over.

"You want change?" He sounded hopeful.

"Yes."

He tossed the change on the bar a moment later, the quarter rolled off the bar, but I managed to catch it before it hit the floor. He glanced longingly at the dollar bill floating in the beer puddle on the bar then frowned and wandered back down to the far end. Once he left, my guy drained his glass then pulled the fresh drink in a little closer.

"So you're looking for Woofy. You sure he's not in any trouble?"

"Well, from what I know of Woofy, yes, he probably is in trouble, but not with me. I just wanted to ask him some questions is all."

"And you're not a cop?"

"Nope, actually just trying to find something out about another guy."

He seemed to think about that for a sip or two, then said, "You want Woofy, he's catching a little nap back in that corner booth."

I looked across the dark room toward the corner booth. Sure enough a pair of feet were just barely hanging out of the booth, three or four empty glasses littered the table.

"You said the bartender's name was Kenny."

"Yeah, and I also said he was an asshole."

"No disagreement from me." I signaled Kenny with half a wave. He took his time, finished the conversation he was involved in, then slowly made his way back down to me. He glanced at the dollar bill still floating in the puddle, more wet then dry.

"Yeah."

"Just a cup of coffee, keep the change," I said then laid another five on the bar.

Chapter Seven

Kenny poured steaming coffee into a white ceramic mug. The coffee was so hot you'd swear it was going to burn the glaze off the mug. I could smell the stuff from across the bar, burnt coffee. It had probably been on the burner for the past forty-eight hours. Guaranteed to give you heart burn. But then, who drank coffee in this place?

I carried the mug back toward the feet hanging out of the corner booth. I picked up my pace as I headed across the room because the mug seemed to be getting hotter and it was beginning to burn my hand. I set the mug down on the table, then kicked the pair of feet a few times until I started to get a reaction.

"Humph, argh, cough, groan, cough, cough."

The two women sitting a couple of booths away were suddenly quiet for a few seconds before they started up again. "I sure hope that isn't contagious," one of them said.

"Hey, Woofy old pal, good to see you. Come on, wake up. Look, I bought you a drink." That seemed to get things moving and the figure slouched in the booth suddenly began to move and pull himself upright. He squinted across the table at the empty glasses trying to get his bearings.

"What the hell, is that coffee?" he said, then peered up at me with an uncomprehending look.

"Just to get started. Once you're awake we'll see what you need."

That provided some added incentive and he reached out with a shaky hand and slowly pulled the mug toward him. He sniffed and blew on the mug a half dozen times then slurped a little and made a face. "Oh God, that shit's really bad."

I was pretty sure I couldn't argue the point. I waited while he sipped some more then said, "So Woofy, you happen to know a guy named Austin Hackett."

"That asshole?" he said then blew on the mug a few more times before he slurped again. "Argh, this is really bad."

"What can you tell me about Hackett?"

"You some kind a cop?"

"Nope, I'm the guy who's buying you a drink once you finish that coffee. I just want to find out anything you can tell me about Austin Hackett."

"Well, he made me a sweetheart deal, then when it come time to pay up, he didn't. Simple as that."

"What was the deal?"

"Nothing fancy. I went into this doctor's office. I think he was one of them chiropractors. Anyway, I go in there, see about making an appointment. Course I didn't, then on the way out," he glanced toward the bar, I guess checking to see if anyone was listening then lowered his voice. "On the way out I fake a fall, see? He's waiting down on the corner, Hackett is, and he calls 911 for the paramedics. Couple of days later, he threatens to sue this doctor. He's got all sorts of these trumped up charges that'll run 'em over a hundred grand. Then, he offered to settle for I think it was eight grand." He took another slurp then cringed as the coffee burned its way down to his stomach. "God, but this is bad."

"And what did you get out of it?"

"Well, first of all, I'm a disabled veteran," he said and sat up just a little straighter in the booth.

"Yeah, well look, about that, Woofy. I think you were shot in the ass by a disgruntled husband if I recall, but they gave you the disability anyway."

"Oh, so you know about that, do ya?"

I nodded. "I don't really care about any of that. Did this Hackett make it worth your while?"

"Hell no," he half shouted. "Bastard was supposed to split the money with me. Ended up giving me a couple hundred bucks cash, and told me if I complained he'd have someone put me in the hospital for real."

"What did you do?"

Woofy looked at me like I was crazy and said, "Well, I took the money, of course. I didn't like what he done, but then again it was cash."

"Anyone from that doctor's office ever contact you?"

"There was some sort of meeting that was gonna be set up, me being dispossessed."

"You mean deposed?"

"Yeah, that's it. But Hackett told me not to worry, things would never get that far. Next thing I know, he's telling me it's all over and all he could give me was two hundred."

"You do anything else for the guy?"

"No, never heard from him again, which is just fine by me. I been screwed around enough in life. I don't need to go looking for someone to do it."

"What are you drinking?"

"You buying?"

I nodded, then said, "Tell you what, here's twenty bucks, get whatever you want. I appreciate the help."

"Anytime, man, anytime," he said then snatched up the twenty I'd just tossed on the table and slid out of the booth.

Chapter Eight

I was thinking about what Louie had said, reminding me how Morton destroyed the kitchen the last time I left him alone in there. So, after I left the Manhole, I drove to my place. Morton hadn't trashed the kitchen, but only because he'd somehow gotten out of the kitchen and trashed the entire house. He'd carried a feather pillow down from my bedroom upstairs, then apparently ran through the house with the thing leaving a trail of feathers all over the first floor.

He'd gotten hold of the coffee cake I'd planned on serving AJ and devoured that, breaking the plate it was sitting on and knocking over a kitchen stool in the process. He chewed two of the legs on the kitchen stool. He found his way into my pantry cabinet and dragged one of the dog food bags through the first floor scattering dog food in among all the pillow feathers.

It must have taken quite an effort because when I got home he was asleep on the living room couch with feathers hanging from his nose. I just closed my eyes and hoped it would all go away. It didn't.

* * *

Morton barked and ran over to the door when Louie came back in the office.

"I thought you said he was at home, in the kitchen or something," Louie said, then bent down and gave Morton a good rub behind the ears.

"He was. I just got to thinking maybe he shouldn't be there the entire day by himself, so I thought I'd bring him down here for a bit. You okay with that?"

"Not a problem. What the hell is this? A feather?" Louie said then pulled a small white feather from Morton's tail.

"Wow, I wonder where he got that?"

"Yeah," Louie said sounding suspicious, but he didn't go any further.

Fortunately, my phone rang. "Haskell Investigations."

"Hi, Dev, it's AJ, I'm returning your call."

"Calls," I said and waited.

"Well?"

"Look, I'm sorry if I upset you, I..."

"Upset me? Oh no, Dev you didn't upset me. You couldn't be bothered. As a matter of fact, you completely ignored me."

I put on my knee pads and began to grovel. "Look, you're right and I was wrong, very wrong. I was just so caught off guard when I found Morton on the front porch, I didn't know how to handle it. I guess I didn't realize how important he was to me. Did I mention he saved my life?"

"Actually, you did, I think a couple of times."

"Oh, well look, I'm sorry if I upset you, but I just got sort of blindsided. I had a wonderful time with you, and well, I was hoping I could maybe see you again."

"Hmm-mmm."

"Oh yeah, and I'm sorry, too. Really I am." I saw the look in Louie's eye, but I didn't care.

"Thanks, that was sweet, sort of. It's not that I don't like dogs. I do, I told you about Lady Godiva."

"Who?"

"Dev, Lady Godiva, my chocolate lab. She'll be three this fall. I just love her."

"Yeah, you did tell me. I've just been so focused on you, I guess I wasn't paying attention."

Louie rolled his eyes.

"Hmm-mmm, okay, forgiven as long as it doesn't happen again."

"Yeah, you're right. So, I was wondering if maybe you'd consider getting together sometime, if that would be okay. I promise not to get distracted, believe me."

"I'd like that. I tell you what, you know that coffee shop just down the street from you?"

"You mean Nina's?"

"Yeah, why don't you and Morton meet Lady Godiva and me for a cup of coffee tonight, say half-past-seven? They can get to know one another, and well, we can get reacquainted, too."

"Tonight, half-past-seven. I'd like that."

"So would I."

"Okay, we'll see you there."

"Good, and Dev, thanks for the phone messages and for the apology. It means a lot to me."

"Thanks for returning my calls, AJ."

"Bye, bye, bye," she said and hung up.

It felt like a weight I didn't even know was there had suddenly been lifted.

"Sounded like your groveling did the trick," Louie said without looking up from his laptop.

"I make no bones about it, I can grovel with the best of them. The only thing I care about is that it seemed to work. Come on, Morton. Let's head home and get that mess cleaned up. We just might be having sleep over company tonight."

Chapter Nine

Morton and I were at the coffee shop fifteen minutes early. I tied him up to the wrought-
iron railing out front then went inside and
grabbed a coffee. I described AJ and told Jimmy,
the barista I'd pay for her coffee and anything
else she wanted.

I watched AJ approach with Lady Godiva
about twenty minutes later. Godiva was lean,
sleek, and appeared to be very well trained. AJ
was wearing a pair of skin-tight shorts and a top
with spaghetti straps and a plunging neckline.
When they stopped on the corner and waited for
a car to pass, Lady Godiva immediately sat.
Then they stepped off and the dog kept perfect
pace as they crossed the street. A guy driving
past tooted his horn a couple of times, but AJ ignored him.

She greeted Morton outside with a big rub
under his chin, then she attached Lady Godiva's
leash to the wrought-iron railing right next to Morton's and came inside. A couple of heads turned
as she waved at me and signaled she was going
to order a coffee.

"Oh, that was sweet of you," she said, giving me a little peck on the cheek as she sat
down. "You didn't have to buy me coffee." She
placed her mug on the table, some frothy thing,
Jimmy had made a design in the shape of a
heart floating on the top.

"I thought it was the least I could do. Would you like a pastry or anything? They've got a great apple tart."

"I'd love one, but it will go right to my hips so I'll just take a pass. Well," she said and took a sip. "How have you been?"

"I just want to say in person how very sorry I am about the other night, I…"

"Dev, it's okay, we all make mistakes. I'm hoping we can just move on."

"I'd like that."

"So, tell me what you've been up to," she said, then took a sip from her mug and sexily ran her tongue over her upper lip. "Mmm-mmm."

"Well, I just took on a new case, looking into someone trying to work an angle on people with disabilities. I…"

"What? God, some people can be so low. Can you imagine? I hope you get him, jail would be too good. Who in their right mind…" She went on for the next ten minutes about how awful people could be. I might have added to her rant a little by telling her I was doing the case pro bono, that I just wanted to set things right. I didn't mention Austin Hackett by name and only slightly embellished certain aspects. Naturally, I didn't mention Heidi.

"You really are a sweet guy, Dev," she said once she'd finished her rant. Then she slid her chair over, reached beneath the table, ran her hand back and forth along the side of my leg a few times and smiled. "I'm glad we're talking again, I really missed you," she said.

There was laughing from the front of the room and about a half dozen people were standing and staring out the window. One guy started clapping and some woman yelled "Oh my God." I was curious, but didn't want to interrupt the AJ action under the table.

The couple at the table next to us got up and moved to the front window to see what the commotion was all about. AJ gave a subtle look around and then moved her hand onto the top of my thigh, sort of tickling with her fingers, moving a little closer with every rub to where I hoped she'd end up.

She smiled and stared into my eyes. I could tell her breathing was as heavy as mine. "I've wanted you ever since the first time I laid eyes on you," she said then started to rub her nails along the inside of my thigh as her eyes flared. "Do you think you have enough dog food for two dogs at breakfast?"

"If I don't I can always go get some. I'd like to do an up close study of that little tattoo you have."

"I've been counting on it. Shall we continue this at your place?"

Two women shrieked in the crowd up by the front window, now there were at least a dozen people crowded around looking at something and laughing. Virtually everyone in the place, except AJ and I, stood at the window. Jimmy, the barista, was hurrying our way.

The same woman screamed again, "Oh my God!"

"Hey, Dev, we've got a sort of situation out front. Is that your dog, looks like a golden retriever?"

"Morton, yeah, why? What's he doing?" I asked.

AJ said a worried sounding, "Lady Godiva," removed her hand from inside my thigh and hurried toward the door. I was right behind her. A number of heads in the crowd turned as we stepped outside.

One guy called, "Thanks for the show."

Some old bat yelled, "Absolutely disgusting."

AJ gave a short scream and yelled, "Morton, get off her. Dev, do something. Oh my God."

I stepped out to see Morton mounted on Lady Godiva. A city bus was stopped on the corner. The driver had opened the door and just sat there staring and smiling as Morton rode Lady Godiva for all he was worth. For her part, the Lady seemed to be giving as good as she got, letting out deep groans that suggested she just might be enjoying herself. All of the passengers on the bus were looking out the window, pointing and laughing. A couple of cellphone cameras flashed.

"God, Dev do something, do something,"
AJ shouted. Her mood had definitely changed
from just a moment ago.

"Morton, damn it, come on, get off, get
off," I said undoing his leash and gently tugging.

Morton gave me a look that suggested,
"You've got to be kidding."

"Come on, Morton, come on," I said coaxing him off Lady Godiva.

AJ had untied Lady Godiva's leash from
the wrought-iron railing and was encouraging her
in the opposite direction. Gradually we broke
their embrace. Clapping and cheers erupted from
inside the coffee shop and on the bus as folks
slowly returned to their normal activities. Some
guy in the coffee shop took a cellphone picture of
AJ.

"God, what is wrong with you two?" she
said glaring first at Morton, and then at me. Her
face was red and she wasn't looking all that
happy. More like she wanted to kill. Fortunately,
the bus pulled away. We could both hear the
scattered applause as it headed down the street.

"I don't know what to tell you. He's never
done anything like that before. Is your dog in
heat?" I didn't feel the need to tell her about Morton impregnating Princess Anastasia at the dog
show last spring.

"God," she screamed, red-faced, just as a
cellphone camera flashed from inside the coffee
shop again. I glared at the guy and he gave a little wave before returning to his table.

"Come on, let's head over to my place and maybe things will look a little better after…"

"Your place? Are you crazy? After this?" She half screamed, then yanked on Lady Godiva's leash and took off down the street.

"Hey, AJ, AJ," I called, but they kept on moving and didn't look back. Some guy drove past and whistled out the window at the two of them. AJ gave him the finger and shouted something I couldn't quite make out.

Morton gave off a little whine as we watched them depart.

"Don't even start, you."

To be continued…

Well, Dev's done it again. He's going to have to catch a break sooner rather than later if he has any hope of linking up with AJ, no thanks to Morton. And what's the deal with Heidi and that Austin Hackett guy? Dev is gonna need all the help he can get. You better get on Amazon, grab a copy of **Scam Man** and see what happens.

Many thanks, and enjoy the read, Mike Faricy.

Check out my list of titles they're all works of genius!

All the stand alone titles are available on Amazon.

The following titles comprise the Dev Haskell series;

Russian Roulette: Case 1
Mr. Swirlee: Case 2
Bite Me: Case 3
Bombshell: Case 4
Tutti Frutti: Case 5
Last Shot: Case 6
Ting-A-Ling: Case 6
Crickett: Case 7
Bulldog: Case 8
Double Trouble: Case 9
Yellow Ribbon: Case 10
Yellow Ribbon: Case 11
Dog Gone: Case 12
Scam Man: Case 13
Foiled: Case 14
The following titles are Dev Haskell novellas.
Dollhouse
The Dance

All the Dev Haskell titles are available on Amazon

*The following titles comprise the Corridor
Man series
written under the pseudonym Nick James;*

Corridor Man
Corridor Man 2
Corridor Man 3
Corridor Man 4
Corridor Man 5

(Corridor Man novellas)
Corridor Man: Valentine
Corridor Man: Auditor

All the <u>Corridor Man</u> titles are available on Amazon
just click the appropriate link.

Contact Mike;
Email: mikefaricyauthor@gmail.com
Twitter: @Mikefaricybooks
Facebook:
DevHaskell &
MikeFaricyBooks
Website:
http://www.mikefaricybooks.com

Thank You!

15199561R00271

Printed in Poland
by Amazon Fulfillment
Poland Sp. z o.o., Wrocław